P9-CSE-960

WITNESS FOR THE DEAD

FORGE BOOKS BY MICHAEL FREDRICKSON

A Cinderella Affidavit
Witness for the Dead

Witness for the Dead

Michael Fredrickson

A TOM DOHERTY ASSOCIATES BOOK
NEW YORK

For my mother, Evelyn Fredrickson,
who taught me to love reading and to laugh,
no matter what

WITNESS FOR THE DEAD

This book is printed on acid-free paper.

Design by Heidi Eriksen

A Forge Book
Published by Tom Doherty Associates, LLC
175 Fifth Avenue
New York, NY 10010

www.tor.com

Forge® is a registered trademark of Tom Doherty Associates, LLC.

Library of Congress Cataloging-in-Publication Data

Fredrickson, Michael.
Witness for the dead / Michael Fredrickson.—1st ed.
p. cm.
"A Tom Doherty Associates book."
ISBN 0-312-87447-2 (alk. paper)
1. Fugitives from justice—Fiction. 2. Undercover operations—Fiction. 3. Irish Americans—Fiction. 4. Boston (Mass.)—Fiction. I. Title.

PS3556.R3826 W5 2001
813'.54—dc21

2001017141

First Edition: May 2001

Printed in the United States of America

0 9 8 7 6 5 4 3 2 1

CONTENTS

PART THREE

FOREWORD

First off, my wife would like me to make it absolutely clear that none of the sex scenes described in this book have anything to do with her. On further reflection, she doesn't want me to say that after all. Perhaps it is enough to point out that this is a work of fiction. There.

I am grateful to so many people for their assistance. The Hon. Charles B. "Brownie" Swartwood III kindly showed me around his chambers and through the back corridors of the Worcester federal courthouse, while U.S. Marshals Sue Williams and Kevin Wahl gave me a tour of that building's lockup and sally port. I had the good fortune to be led through the intricacies of the federal grand jury system by Janis M. Berry, a fine lawyer who, like Danielle, once hauled grumpy gangsters in to testify. Senator Thomas Birmingham, president of the Massachusetts Senate, granted me a private visit to his magnificent quarters, which are the model for the office of Governor Jackie Crimmins. I got a primer on greyhound racing and rescue from Bob Fast and Billy O'Donnell, received lessons on how to track missing persons from private detectives Paul "Jake" Pekham and Susan "Snow White" McKeon, checked on weaponry with Tellis Lawson, heeded Bill Flanagan's sound advice not to seek a technical resolution to the computer search for my fugitives, and stole jokes from Kandi Kane, Susie Maxie, Steve Gallos, and Nick Ruf. Events described in a crisply rendered newspaper column by Howie Carr were woven into the grave-digging scene depicted in Chapter 25.

I owe a special debt to the Demos Writers' Workshop for its generous support during the writing of this book; in particular, Samuel Shem was astute and appropriately brutal in his comments on the manuscript.

My peripatetic editors, Rusty Russell and Dan Crane, managed to ingest the manuscript one chapter at a time and still live to give me suggestions and encouragement. Ruth and Dvora Tager read the whole thing with eyes as sharp as any copyeditor's. Connie Vecchione, as usual, spotted the main problem with the plotting and pointed the way out of it. All I can say is, it's a good thing I have smart friends.

Thanks again to my editor, Bob Gleason, and to my agent, Sam Pinkus, for their patience and mysterious faith in me and the book.

And, Jolly, I could never have done it without your love and support—and indulgence. You, too, Zeke.

Does it go without saying that there is no such dogtrack in Bradenton, Florida, no restaurant called Aufiero's, no motel called the Peace River Inn, no website called *Houndbytes.com*? I hope so. And I pray no one gets the false impression that I mean to belittle or ridicule those who rescue greyhounds. These people make up, as Mavis says, a "human chain of love" to save harmless creatures from destruction or worse. God love them.

By the way, there really is a software product called Cato, a slick business program designed for caterers by Geotronics Corporation. And Slim's Deep South BBQ sits in the shade of a big water oak in Arcadia, Florida. Try the kumquat pie.

"My soul?" our Faust may have answered. "And what if I had no soul?"

But perhaps it was not for an individual soul that Mephistopheles had inconvenienced himself. "With the gold you will build a city," he was saying to Faust. "It is the entire city's soul that I want in exchange."

"It's a deal."

—Italo Calvino
"The Tale of the Alchemist" from
The Castle of Crossed Destinies

PART ONE

If you would sup with the Devil, you must bring a long spoon.

—English proverb

Never believe anything until it's officially denied.

—Jim Hacker in *Yes, Minister*

CHAPTER ONE

NICE PEOPLE

MONDAY

Larry the Rabbit had a problem. They had hauled Arthur Patch before the grand jury and were trying to make him talk. The lawyer said he could fix it, but Larry wasn't so sure. As far as he could tell, this made Arthur a *mina vagante,* a free-floating mine in a busy sea-lane. Larry was wondering if maybe he shouldn't just clip the guy.

"So, you figure Artie's gonna stand up?" Larry asked the lawyer immediately, right after sitting down. He had a rheumy voice that always left the lawyer waiting for him to clear his throat, but he never did. Larry's dull gray eyes canvassed the face of his lawyer for an answer.

"He won't testify, if that's what you mean," said Sheldon Grutman. He struggled to keep the annoyance out of his voice. "Arthur couldn't have made that any clearer."

"You talked to him?"

"Yes, Larry," said the lawyer. Thinking, *Duh.* "He understands. I'll go with him for the hearing on the contempt motion tomorrow. The judge will allow the government's motion and then give Arthur an opportunity to purge it by agreeing to answer questions before the grand jury. When he tells him he still won't answer, they'll take him into custody."

Larry was silent, his gaze intent on the lawyer.

"There's nothin' to sweat, Larry," said Niccolò Tramontana, his features twisted into a knowing smirk as he looked at Larry. "Last night, when me and Bobby finished talking to him, all he wanted to do was pack his fuckin' bag and go, go, go." He pumped his arm like the drive rod of a locomotive.

Larry and his two companions laughed shortly. The lawyer smiled uneasily. Larry seemed to pick up his lawyer's discomfort, for he asked, "You wanna coffee, Shelley? *Cannoli,* maybe? They're good here. He don't fill 'em till you order."

Grutman looked about the Caffé Roma as if getting his bearings for the first time. Aside from him and his party, the café had no patrons. An espresso bar, flanked by display cases filled with pastries and *gelati,* commanded the left front quarter of the room. The remaining space was littered with black-metal tables and chairs.

"Nothing for me, Larry," answered Grutman, shifting his rear end in search of comfort on the mesh of the seat. He and his client were facing one another across one of the tables. It seemed absurdly tiny for the four men gathered around it. Larry screwed himself around to get the barman's attention, but he was already loping toward them with an air of servile anticipation. The lawyer waited patiently while the client ordered three espressos.

Ilario "Larry the Rabbit" Coniglio was a sharp-featured little man with deep-set gray eyes like nail heads. A maroon polo shirt was stretched out like cheesecloth over his melon of a paunch. To his left sat his oldest son, Pietro, a handsome, dark-haired young man wearing a beige sport coat over a peach T-shirt. He had shoved up the jacket's sleeves to reveal the dark hair on his manly arms. Tramontana, Larry's *capo,* completed the foursome. He was rangy like a matinee cowboy, but with a child's delicate features. All his movements seemed to take place at half speed, and his blink was as slow as a cat's. He sat across from Pietro and showed a languid smile as if at some private amusement.

Larry had led the lawyer on a serpentine trek that afternoon. Greeting him with nothing more than a conspiratorial nod at his social club on Sheafe Street, Larry immediately marched him away, around the corner onto Salem Street, to a left on Prince, and then southwest up Hanover. Eventually he ducked, abruptly and as if on impulse, into the Caffé Roma. The lawyer had had to pull up short not to miss the last turn, which caused the two tailgating goons to bowl into him. *Like the Three Stooges going through a door,* he thought with irritation.

They were very aggravating, these crude security precautions of Larry's. By leading his lawyer to undeclared and always shifting destinations before exchanging a word, Larry figured the odds of successfully planting a bug at the site of their meetings was almost zero. The lawyer couldn't argue with him there; Larry's older brother, Francesco, was serving an eighty-five-year sentence after boasting moronically into the FBI's hidden microphones. But even so, this scurrying along to keep pace as Larry hopped through the claustrophobic alleys of the North End had begun to wear on the lawyer.

"How long can they keep him?" asked Larry the Rabbit.

Grutman shrugged. "It's civil contempt, which means until he complies with the court order. But the order lasts only as long as the life of the grand jury. Then they have to release him."

"How long is that?"

"Eighteen months."

Larry stared through the plate glass at the street, ignoring the pedestrians breasting one another on the sidewalks of Hanover Street. As the noisy main drag of Boston's North End, Hanover was the broadest street in the neighborhood, but the chaotically double-parked vehicles (including, inexplicably, an unattended fire truck) constricted traffic to the pace on its narrowest alleyways. A rival bar—the older, smokier Caffé Vittoria, in which Anthony "Tony Boots" Buscemi had once held court—sat directly across the street. Out the door of Mike's Pastry to the right bounced a beaming young couple, the man dangling a white cardboard box by its string. A plump, unsmiling old woman, with her hips squeezed into a sagging aluminum beach chair, watched after them as they passed her and strode hand in hand in the direction of the Harbor. If anything out there registered with Larry, he gave no sign.

" 'Course, I'll prolly end up eating his marker," Larry said morosely. He swung his head toward his son, on Grutman's right. "Remember this, Peetie," he lectured, ponderously bobbing his finger. "Don't lend money to your friends. They don't pay, you gotta be able to treat 'em like every other asshole. You getting this? No special treatment. And that's hard, with your friends. 'Cause you wanna cut 'em a little slack. That was my mistake with Artie. Once he couldn't make the vig, I shoulda put him in a fuckin' cast. Made him look like one of them Mexican things, fulla candy—whatcha call 'em? Panetta or something."

"Piñata, Pop," his son corrected him. "Panetta was a congressman."

Larry rolled his eyes skyward. "Don't talk to me about no fuckin' politicians! I got enough bullshit with those cocksuckers. Even the ones s'posed to be my friends. And now there's this asshole U.S. Attorney, trying to make his bones on me. Him and that good-looking broad works for him—what's her name?"

"Danielle Gautreau," Grutman replied, wincing inwardly. "She's just doing her job." Giving in to an impulse to defend a colleague.

Larry's jaw muscles twitched like a ferret in a sack. "Doing her *job*! This ain't no fucking 'job' we're talkin' here! And it ain't no fucking lawyer's game, either. This is my ass they want. My *life*, Shelley. She does her 'job' better'n you do yours, you go home. *Me*, I go away. So don't give me no shit about her doin' a 'job.' You understand American?"

"Of course, Larry. But we've got this thing pretty well in hand."

Larry paused and squinted. *Thinking now.* Grutman pictured machinery sagging under an unaccustomed load.

"And you say he'll only pull eighteen months, max? No more?"

"Yes," said Grutman. "That's the normal limit."

"What do you mean, 'normal'?" Larry's voice rose again. "I'm trying to figure my exposure here, for Chrissake."

His exposure, thought Grutman wryly. "Well," he said, "the U.S. Attorney *could* seek to extend the life of the grand jury. But that's very rare. And then there's that wild business with Susan McDougal and Whitewater, down in Little Rock. After the grand jury closed down and she still hadn't testified against Clinton, Ken Starr brought *criminal* contempt proceedings to keep her in jail. That's highly unlikely, but it *is* possible."

Larry cocked his head, eyeing him slyly now. "You tell Artie all this? About Whitewater and shit?"

"Naturally. He wanted to know the extent of *his* exposure," Grutman said. There was an edge to his voice, but it eluded Larry.

"Christ with diarrhea," Larry muttered. His features clouded over again in thought.

Grutman felt a vague chill, as if from a draft somewhere in the room, but before he could place it, Larry shoved his chair back and stood up. His mirthless grin revealed a drunken row of yellowed teeth.

"You're doin' good work, Shelley. Keep it up."

Grutman stood, too, and started to put his jacket on. He had filled only one sleeve when Larry draped an arm around his neck and pulled him toward him. "You take him in tomorrow and tell him we're with him. All the way. Am I right, Nick?" His eyes never left Grutman's.

"We're with him," said Tramontana, nodding gravely. "A hunnert 'n' ten percent."

"And tell him from me not to worry about business," Larry added. "Anybody fucks with Artie's restaurant, they fuck with me." Larry spat a little when voicing the fricatives, but Grutman managed not to flinch. *When he talks, people glisten.*

Still clasping Grutman's neck, Larry leaned toward him and chucked him under the chin. The lawyer tried not to look at the stump where Larry's middle finger should have been. " 'Cause I take care of my friends," Larry whispered hoarsely. "Good care. You be sure to tell him that, Shelley."

Grutman promised to relay the message, then broke away as soon as he could. The man's breath would stagger a buffalo. Taking his leave, Grutman shook hands with the other two men. He then made for the door. The barman, balancing a tray of tinkling coffee cups, scuttled over to open it for him.

Walking down Hanover in the direction of Haymarket Square, Grutman grasped his lapels and squared his jacket. He exchanged his wire-rims for sunglasses and squinted into the sun. He had to pick his way through the heavy foot traffic, past young men talking and smoking together in groups of two or three, around old folks quietly taking the summer sun from doorsteps and folding chairs. His thoughts were back in the café, however, as he tried to dispel the miasma of foreboding that had hovered over the meeting at the end. And to shake off the afterstink of his client's rotting breath. *Maybe I've been doing this too long,* he thought. *Too many cheesy psychopaths with halitosis.*

Then he smiled at his own sudden and unwonted squeamishness.

Laughing at himself, he thought, *Every man's breath diminishes me.*

Tipping his head toward the plate glass, Larry slurped the sweet viscous coffee and watched his lawyer walk up Hanover Street.

"I don't like it, Nick," he said mournfully. "What we got here is we got a fucking mess. I don't like it one fuckin' bit."

"He'll stand up, Larry. I'm sure of it." An unlighted cigarette bobbed up and down from Tramontana's mouth as he spoke.

Larry absently rubbed his mouth and chin with the webbing of his right hand. "I don't know. Thing is, I don't really know the guy."

Tramontana struck a match, then lit the cigarette. He fastidiously laid the spent match on his saucer. "Well, it's your call. Me, I'd trust him." He released a tight stream of smoke toward the ceiling. "He's so fuckin' scared he wouldn't make a peep if his hair was on fire."

Larry shook his head ruefully. "Jesus, he could cook. You ever try those *arancine* he makes over at his place? Fried 'em just right. You bite through the breading and hit that chewy rice and then the *mozzarella* in the middle. Or spinach, if you didn't want the cheese ones. I'm tellin' you, they're to fucking die for. A *great* little trattoria."

Tramontana took in the look of disgust on Pietro's face and smiled to himself.

"I had it all set up," Larry continued dreamily. "A couple more months with him scratchin' to pay the vig, and I'da owned that place—and him with it. But nooo." With a sharp click he set his cup down on the saucer. "Those fucking idiots!" he spat at the ceiling. "After all I told 'em, they gotta shoot their mouths off where the feds can listen in. And about *my* business!" He emphasized the possessive by thumping the pads of his fingers against his chest. "It's bad enough they get busted, but they hafta drag in this business with me and Artie."

Larry paused to bank the fires of his rage. When he turned to face his lieutenant, his expression was softer, almost pleading. "I can't have it, Nick," he said quietly. "Bein' in his power like this. They'll put on all the pressure they got on him." He looked away again, shaking his head. "The jeopardy is a little too much for me. I can't have it."

"I understand, Larry," said Tramontana, his face without expression.

The three men were silent for a short while, as if out of respect for the dead. The only sounds were those of the barman washing cups and Tramontana smoking.

Tramontana was the first to break the silence. "Who you want me to use?" he asked. "Ain't no way he's gonna get in the car with *me*." His sleepy smile was back.

Larry snorted his agreement. "*That*'s a fact. And the help I got right now ain't exactly quality, you know what I mean? You couldn't trust 'em to arrange soup in a bowl, let alone whack a guy. Besides, the feds are all over 'em now anyway. No, you gotta use a sucker."

Tramontana took another drag. "Could take a while to find an indie. I'll need to scope out the right guy."

Larry jerked to attention. "We don't have *time* for that," he hissed. "You gotta do it *tonight*. If he's going in tomorrow, it's gotta be tonight." Then the intensity left him as suddenly as it had come on, and he turned wistful again. "I wish Tommy was around. There's an independent you could count on."

"You're right there," Tramontana agreed. "Tommy is nice people."

"Him and Phil both," said Larry. "*Great* fuckin' team. They was here, I could just tell 'em once, 'Do this guy,' and they'd get it done. No bullshit, no problems. Businesslike, ya know?"

"Fuckin' A," Tramontana nodded. "These are nice people."

"Harry Spunt." The name came from Pietro Coniglio, speaking for the first time since the lawyer's departure. The other two men looked at each other. Cocking his head in appreciation, Larry smiled at Tramontana.

"Yeah," he said, warming to the suggestion. "Harry Spunt. Tough fucker when he's gotta be. He's no genius, but this ain't exactly rocket science here. He's back, right?"

"Got outa Walpole two weeks ago," said Tramontana. "I hear he's staying with his sister in Canton." Tramontana crushed his cigarette in an ashtray and got to his feet.

"Not bad thinking, Peetie," Larry said to his son. "Maybe you're not such a dumb fuck after all."

The two older men laughed, and Pietro smiled, awkwardly hunching his shoulders to hear such scarce praise.

"I'll take care of it," said Tramontana, moving toward the door.

Larry looked up sharply at him. "Tonight, Nick. It's gotta be tonight."

Tramontana smiled his secret smile and nodded.

CHAPTER TWO

THE JUDGE

THURSDAY, THREE DAYS LATER

The knock on the door almost made the judge spill his morning coffee.

It wasn't its sharpness that made him jump. The knock was soft, timid even. What startled him was its source and timing: it came from a heavy walnut door to a corridor not accessible from the public hallways, and—as he confirmed with a glance at the ship's clock on his desk—it was still only 8:10.

At sixty-three, the Honorable Henry Eberle Biddle was a man whose habits coursed through ruts cut deep in the hardpan of his daily life. His detractors claimed he circled his desk like a dog every morning before sitting down, but if he did, there were no eyewitnesses to the ritual. It was his unvarying custom to reach his chambers on the eleventh floor of the Boston federal courthouse before eight on weekday mornings, the better to savor in tranquillity the day's only coffee (an expensive latte from the Seattle chain across the way on Milk Street). This morning, with the prattle of his secretary and law clerks still a good half hour away, he had lapped up a tiny dollop of the foamed milk and was letting it dissolve luxuriously on his tongue when the knock intruded.

He waited a few moments for his irritation to settle. Then he carefully set the paper cup back on his desk, pulled himself to his feet, and made his way across the carpet to the door.

"Yes?" he barked as he turned the knob. His thoughts lingered with the cooling coffee.

It had better not be someone I know.

But it was. She had a tentative smile on her face, a sheaf of typewritten papers in one hand, and the other raised to knock again.

The judge felt a jolt of ancient excitement to behold the handsome Assistant United States Attorney who was poised to enter his chambers. Though almost thirty years her senior, he had never once looked at Danielle Gautreau without feeling swamped by an atavistic male regret that such exquisite creatures should be forever denied him.

"Ms. Gautreau," he said as flatly as he could, masking a tremor of delight. Summoning an air of displeasure, he knotted his eyebrows to demand an explanation.

She held her smile, her bottle-green eyes warm and bright on his. "Good morning, Judge," she said. "I'm sorry to disturb you like this. But I have this motion, you see." Her eyes flicked to the papers in her hand, then back to him. "And it's very important that no one know about it yet. That's why I came so early. I even took one of the S-elevators up here."

She punctuated this last with a peek over her shoulder at the route she had taken. It was a back corridor that allowed judges to slink unseen from chambers to courtroom. After a couple of turns the hallway broadened into a small foyer for the two secure elevators used to transport prisoners up from the marshal's office. She had taken unusual measures indeed.

She turned back to him. "It's about that witness, Judge. Arthur Patch—you remember? He wants to talk to me." She beamed, triumph overcoming her nervousness.

Judge Biddle's frown turned genuine. Of course he remembered Arthur Patch. He had jailed the man only two days ago, after finding him in contempt for refusing to answer Danielle's questions before the grand jury. And Mr. Patch would damn well stay there until he agreed to testify.

Judge Biddle reached out and took her motion papers before she could offer them. Tilting his head back, he peered at the first page through the lower lenses of his bifocals. "What do you mean, a motion nobody's supposed to know about?"

"It's an *ex parte* motion, Judge."

He looked up. *Ex parte* meant the motion would be heard without notice to the other side. Judge Biddle's revulsion at *ex parte* motions was no secret. He viewed them with the same disdain Earl Weaver had once shown the sacrifice bunt. Even on those rare occasions when he did consider a matter without both sides present, he felt it stank of impropriety. Glowering now at Danielle, he gathered about him a cloak of shivering rectitude.

He watched her quail slightly, then rally to brave the storm. "It's all in my affidavit, Judge. Patch had a note delivered to me last night. At home, no less." Still standing in the threshold, she tipped forward so she could flip the pages for him, her gleaming hair falling to cover the side of her face. She pulled away when he had the document she wanted before him. Her fingers grazed his in the process, but the spell of her presence had been broken.

"His note is right there," she explained. "He wants to talk to me. About cooperating. But he says his lawyer can't know anything about it. He's adamant about that. And the rule says I can't talk to somebody who's represented by counsel without the lawyer's permission. Unless . . ." She shot him a sly smile as her voice trailed off. "Unless I get a court order from you saying it's okay. That's my motion."

She stood up straight and waited, observing him closely as he took all this in. The storm had blown over now.

"You mean," he asked, "he's scared of his own lawyer?"

"Bingo." She was grinning now.

Danielle sat in a burgundy button-back chair across the mammoth desk from Judge Biddle. She ran her palms along the smooth old leather tucked under the arms of the chair and watched him work his way through her motion papers. At one point he lifted them off the desk blotter and leaned back in his chair, swiveling to his right while turning over the page. With his change of angle, the morning sun lit up the white swatches of hair that clung to his bald head like alpine tufts on an icy crag. She waited impatiently for the thaw.

He's a stiff one, all right, she thought. Like Henry James or Henry Kissinger, this was one Henry no one ever dreamed of calling Hank.

When he finished reading, he lowered the papers to his lap, his eyes fixed on a point in the middle distance, somewhere off to her left.

"I've seen this before," he said at last, still not looking at her.

She cleared her throat. "I'm glad one of us has."

"Usually," he continued, "you see it in drug cases, where a courier, say, gets arrested. His superiors hire him a lawyer—it's part of the employee benefit package. Then the courier decides he wants to make a deal, but he knows whose interests the lawyer is *really* looking out for. So he wants the lawyer left in the dark. But that's not this case, is it?"

He swiveled about to fix her with a sharp eye.

"Oh, I don't know," she answered. "Is this really that different? I mean, Coniglio is the target of my investigation and his house counsel, Grutman, shows up to represent Arthur Patch as well. If Patch is scared of Coniglio—and who wouldn't be, in his situation?—he must be getting pretty uncomfortable with Grutman, who's got to be telling Coniglio everything that goes on with Patch and the grand jury. Which, by the way, is why Grutman should be disqual—"

As if stopping traffic, Judge Biddle silenced her by raising his right hand. "I'll not get into that," he said crisply. "You will not discuss *that* motion without the other side being present. Just stick with the one you brought me this morning."

"Sorry," she said.

Just last week she and Shelley Grutman had argued her motion to disqualify Grutman from representing both Patch and Coniglio. It was a conflict of interest, she had insisted, for Grutman to represent both the target of the grand jury and a witness whose testimony she hoped would put him away. Grutman countered that there was no conflict because Patch was rock solid in his refusal to testify against Coniglio, and if both clients wanted the same thing—Patch's silence—their interests were identical. Judge Biddle had yet to rule on the motion. But now that fissures were appearing in Arthur's granite resolve . . . ? Well, if Arthur's note didn't convince him to grant her motion now, nothing would.

"And they're *not* the same," the judge continued, apparently still stuck on his drug mule. "There's been no indication that Patch is a participant in Coniglio's alleged criminal enterprise. He has no record whatsoever. From everything you've shown me, this is a legitimate restaurateur you're squeezing for information."

"Who just happens to do his commercial banking with La Cosa Nostra?" Her tone was theatrically incredulous. "I don't think so, Judge. And he *does* have Grutman representing him."

"You're the one who tells me he's scared of him," he rejoined, smiling for the first time. "Did it ever occur to you that Grutman's attentions might have been forced upon him in the first place?"

Smiling back, she dipped her head to concede the point. "Maybe," she said. "But look what I've got, Judge. I got racketeering indictments against most of the hierarchy of the Coniglio family. What's left of it, that is. I have them on tape, almost all of them. But not Larry. Oh no, not Larry. He's too cagey for tapes, after Francesco. But what I *do* have on tape is his men talking about Larry's *personal* involvement in loans he made to Patch. These are very interesting recordings, Judge. And unusual behavior. Even Larry's people can't figure out what he's up to, getting personally involved like that. It goes against type. Plus, they talk about how soft he is on Patch. Any other borrower who didn't pay would have had a very unpleasant visit from a couple of Nick Tramontana's boys by now. How come Patch gets a free pass? What's Larry's soft spot for Arthur Patch, if he's so legit?"

The judge seemed not to hear her questions. "Tell me," he asked as if just musing, "if Mr. Patch is the lowlife you think he is, why does he want to talk to you all of a sudden? The other day he seemed fully prepared to spend many months in jail. Surely, two short nights in our excellent facilities aren't enough to work such magic. What changed his mind?"

Danielle was stupefied for a moment. In the flush of excitement on receiving Patch's note, she hadn't thought to ask this question. But the judge was right. Patch had been unshakable in his refusal to testify. "There are no words that could come out of your mouth," he had told her with a tight smile, "and nothing you could do to me, that could make me testify." She had been sure he wasn't bluffing. This was no braggart. No, her only hope was that a few months in jail would bring him around.

But two *days*? In fact, he had spent only one night before sending her the note. He had caved in much too quickly. Why?

Judge Biddle burst in on her puzzlement. "Your motion is denied," he said shortly. "I'm not going to let you interview Arthur Patch without counsel present."

Danielle was outraged. "But Judge—"

The judge raised his hand again. "The denial is without prejudice. And I didn't say I was going to bring in Grutman. We'll find someone else to represent him in his interview with you. I'm not going to let him go naked."

"Who?" she asked after a brief pause.

The judge paused himself. "Hmm. Good point. The Federal Defenders Office can't do it. They're already representing one of the people you've indicted in this mess. I don't want to sit through any *more* disqualification motions." He smiled briefly at this. "We'll have to get him somebody private."

He hit the intercom button to his right and stared into the speaker. "Harriet? Are you in there yet?"

She was. He told her to call down to Room 707 and get the name of the next lawyer on the Federal Defenders' private appointments list. He turned back to Danielle, then ran his finger down the office diary open on his desk.

"If he's foolish enough to refuse a new lawyer, I'll have him in here . . . say, tomorrow afternoon. To read him his rights. Then, if I'm satisfied he understands them, you can have him. But not until then. Is that clear?"

She nodded agreement. "But what happens if he says yes? A new lawyer will signal to Grutman—and Coniglio—that something is up."

"I didn't say he had to enter a formal appearance right away."

"Or she," she interrupted. A reflex.

"Or she. We'll hold off filing the paperwork. Patch will talk to his new lawyer first, and *then* you. If you guys decide you can't do business, we'll just send Patch back to detention and the new lawyer will disappear. He never existed. If, on the other hand, you all make a deal for his testimony, then the cat's out of the bag anyway and the new guy enters his appearance. At that point it will be your job to protect your witness. Isn't that what you wanted all along?"

It was indeed. As the judge began to scribble a draft of his order on the pad before him, she pictured Arthur Patch as he stood before her that first day. A small, compact man in a Harris tweed jacket and a blue dress shirt open at the neck. Actually kind of cute, in a too-tightly-wrapped sort of way, with his square face, thick dark hair, and those clean blue eyes that bored into hers each time he refused—ever so politely—to answer her questions. A straightforward guy. She had to give him that. Quiet, too. Other than in the grand jury room, they had scarcely spoken except to say good morning. Well, it looked as if they might soon have more to say to one another after all.

A loud metallic buzzing interrupted her thoughts.

"Yes, Harriet." He stared intently at the intercom.

"They just called back, Judge," said the middle-aged voice. "The next lawyer up is James A. Morrissey. Of Boston."

Danielle squeezed her eyes shut and groaned out loud.

CHAPTER THREE

A PREDATORY INTENT

James A. Morrissey would have savored the tasty symmetry in all this. At the very moment Danielle was groaning at the mention of his name, he himself was undergoing something of a spiritual experience. He had just heaved the contents of his empty stomach into the toilet of the men's room behind the Supreme Judicial Court.

It wasn't that he was ill. He was not drunk or hungover. Nor did this betoken the return of pretrial jitters from his early days at the bar; even then, performance anxiety had never made him sick. It was nothing like that.

No, he had thrown up because he was flat-out scared.

This discovery, coming hard upon him with sudden clarity as he leaned over the porcelain bowl, cracked open a shimmering new vista of self-awareness. For he was afraid, he now realized, that he might actually lose his license to practice law. Today. Despite the bleak prognoses of his counsel, Kenneth Twohig, and despite everything else going on around him, it had never fully sunk in, until this moment of peristaltic epiphany, that a debacle of such magnitude might actually await him. He was blind but now he saw and, his vision restored, he found himself preternaturally alert to his surroundings. Objects in the stall—the gleaming rim of the bowl, the chipped black texture of the raised toilet seat, the winking chrome on the flush handle—all these took on crisp definition and snapped into vivid relief. Colors throbbed with intensity. Everything was in its place, in harmonious proportion, with the universe unfold—

He blinked. He gave himself a shake. *Is this some cornball acid flashback or what?*

He straightened up and flushed the toilet. Stumbling to the sink, he washed his hands, then rinsed the bile out of his mouth with tap water, deliberately splashing a little on his face in the process. He avoided the mirror. He was still drying his face on a paper towel when he heard Twohig's knuckles on the other side of the door.

"Jimmy? You finished in there? Come on, fella, we're up. The clerk's gonna send for the judge."

Morrissey took a deep breath, let it out, and pulled the door inward. His lawyer filled the doorway, then stepped back to let him pass.

"I'm ready," Morrissey said. "Let's do it."

Kenneth Twohig looked like a larger version of Morrissey. They were both in their early fifties, round and solid, with florid complexions and curly white hair. But Twohig had nine inches and a good thirty pounds on Morrissey, which made people see the former as a big bruiser and the latter as roly-poly. Twohig stood before him with his thumbs slipped under his suspenders. They dug into his flesh like the twine around a bale of hay.

"You okay?" he asked.

"I'm fine." Morrissey drifted across the room to the bubble cooler near the exit.

The two were in the Lawyers' Conference Room, through which one had to pass to reach the only public men's room on the thirteenth floor of the courthouse annex. Bookcases filled with musty beige volumes of *Massachusetts Reports* lined the walls, and the center of the room was taken up by a long black table and a dozen beat-up chairs. The room was empty now, but the first week of each month, when the SJC was in regular session, a man needing the toilet had to pick his way around small clumps of lawyers as they whispered strategy to one another or read over their notes for oral argument.

Morrissey swallowed the cool water, crushed the emptied paper cone, and dropped it in the wastebasket. Then he followed Twohig out the door and through a little vestibule with a wooden phone booth and a coatrack. Turning hard to the right, they entered the grand courtoom itself.

"But these are details, Your Honor," the bar counsel stressed as she headed into the home stretch of her argument. "When the misconduct is considered as a whole, it is apparent that a suspension of some length is required. Mr. Morrissey took advantage of a solitary, vulnerable old woman who had looked to him for comfort and guidance. He knew she was failing. As her lawyer, he also knew she had valuable assets, including a bank account with more than $85,000 in it and the two-family home she had recently vacated. He knew there was no obvious heir to step forward and challenge him in the probate court. So he drafted a will naming himself as her executor and sole beneficiary, and then he induced her to sign it. Right there in the nursing home. To say her testamentary capacity was questionable is a gross understatement. Two days before Mrs. Nee executed the will, she mistook her night nurse for Dinah Shore."

She paused to let this tell, as Morrissey would have done himself, then moved on.

"He would have gotten away with it, too, if a nephew in North Adams had not gotten wind of his aunt's death. Yet even after objections were filed, Mr. Morrissey vigorously defended the will in court. And to hedge his bets, he made a claim against the estate for fees he said he had earned before her death—including for drafting the very will by which he hoped to inherit."

She turned over the last page of her notes and looked up at the judge. Justice Elizabeth Mallow was leaning way back, sagging down in her chair as usual, so that, short as she was, Morrissey couldn't see her face. *She could be wearing nothing but a bustier up there and nobody would know it,* he thought. He watched the top of her gray head as he waited for the bar counsel to wrap it up.

"Your Honor, Mr. Morrissey abused the trust of Mrs. Nee. He took advantage of a weak and infirm client in a predatory effort to line his own pockets. For the protection of the public as well as the integrity and standing of the bar, we recommend that he be suspended for at least one year."

She was a husky, slope-shouldered woman almost as tall as Twohig, with a massive jaw that belonged on a horse. Her real name was Andrea Vyshinsky, but she was known as Sieglinda to those she tormented—lawyers for whose ethical lapses it was her duty to prosecute. She gathered her notes and started for the counsel table to her left.

"At *least* a year?" asked Justice Mallow, freezing her in midstep.

"I beg your pardon, Your Honor?" Sieglinda said, tiptoeing back to the podium. All three lawyers leaned forward as far as they could in hopes of hearing the judge. Morrissey had often wondered if Lizzie Mallow did this on purpose, mumbling scarcely audible questions, just to keep the lawyers off stride. It was always a close call whether to ask her to repeat the question (which tended to piss her off) or pretend you heard her and just tell her something you wanted her to focus on anyway. Morrissey usually opted for the latter, all the while stifling an urge to scream, WHY CAN'T YOU SPEAK THE FUCK UP!

"Well," she muttered, "your papers say you want a year. Today you're telling me at *least* a year. So which is it? Do you really want more than a year?"

Morrissey definitely did not care for the tenor of this question, but he refrained from looking over at Twohig, seated beside him.

"Your Honor, I meant only to stress that a suspension of one year is the least acceptable sanction under the circumstances. We stand by our recommendation for one year."

Sieglinda waited to see if this was all, which apparently it was, because she then sidled over to her table. Twohig squeezed his client's arm reassuringly with a skillet-sized hand and hauled himself to his feet. He gripped both sides of the podium like the steering wheel on a tractor. *Plowman, dig my earth.*

"Your Honor." Twohig's rich *basso profundo* rooted in the marrow like the lower stops of a church organ. He sounded saddened by Sieglinda's calumnies. "Let's back the truck up here, *please.* Right back to the loading dock. We have no real disagreement over the basic facts. Ms. Vyshinsky and I agree, and Mr. Morrissey now realizes, that he did wrong in drawing a will under which he stood to inherit. But there is no evidence of this *predatory* intent she talks about. He took advantage of no one and he injured no one—except himself and his own professional standing.

"This is what the uncontested facts establish. Maryann Nee was a client and a longtime friend. Estranged as she was from her family, she had no natural object of her bounty. It was Mr. Morrissey here who looked after her affairs. It was he, not her Johnny-come-lately nephew, who arranged for her to reside in an assisted-living facility when it became clear she could no longer care for herself. It was Mr. Morrissey who found the home for her, helped her move in, liquidated and marshaled her assets to pay her nursing home bills. The facility's records show he visited Maryann weekly, when no one from her family bothered. He was the one—"

"Mnnrr isolate manudders?"

Twohig blinked at her and Morrissey could see he was wrestling with the Lizzie dilemma just mentioned. Finally, he shot her a big grin, and said, "Excuse me, Your Honor. I was so wrapped up in my eulogy I didn't make out your question."

She rocked forward, and Morrissey could see the smirk on her face.

"Aren't eulogies spoken over the dead, Mr. Twohig?" she asked, clear as a bell—now. "You seem awfully eager to bury your client."

Twohig's grin turned self-deprecating, a man who enjoys a good one even at his own expense. Sieglinda sniggered into her cupped hand, but there was no response from either the clerk or the court officer—fortunately, the only other people in the courtroom.

"I asked you," Lizzy continued, "if he didn't do all that to isolate her from others. Couldn't one infer that he cut her off from her family so he could talk her into making the bequest?"

Morrissey was pissed, which he tried to convey to Twohig with angry glances at the judge and him, but his lawyer seemed not to notice. *After all I did for that ornery old broad!*

Twohig sounded wounded by such cynicism. "Absolutely not, Your Honor. That puts it backwards, in fact. It was precisely *because* her family had nothing to do with her that Mr. Morrissey was compelled to take the measures he did. He *found* her isolated, and he arranged for her to join a community so she would not be alone. That's one of the reasons she felt so grateful to him."

Nobody ever said Kenny Twohig lacked bat speed, thought Morrissey. *I could never have turned around on that one the way he did.*

"It was natural, when she began to consider how to dispose of her estate, that she turn to the friend who had taken care of her. She wanted to make a gift to him, a bequest to the one—the only one—who stuck by her. So she asked him to draw the will.

"Now, up to this point, Your Honor, there's nothing untoward here. No misconduct. Quite the contrary, in fact. But then Mr. Morrissey made his mistake."

Twohig looked over at his client as if he wanted to join in the reprovals. Morrissey understood; in this business even an argument in the supreme court needed a little bit of theater.

"Mr. Morrissey should have said no. He should not have agreed to draw the will as Maryann requested. He should have advised her that the ethics rules flatly forbid him from drafting an instrument that gives him a gift. And he should have seen to it she got independent counsel to advise her and to draw the will. But he didn't do that.

"Why not? Out of ignorance, Your Honor. *Not* predatory intent. Ignorance. He was unaware of the prohibition. As Your Honor will recall, Massachusetts only adopted this specific rule some five or six years ago. Before then there was no express prohibition against drawing such a will. Now, it's my sad duty to bring you the bad news, Judge. If thirty percent of the bar is aware of the rule, I'd be astonished—and so, I submit, would Ms. Vyshinsky." He smiled wolfishly in Sieglinda's direction, but she just gave him the hard eye. "And Mr. Morrissey is no probate lawyer. He's a trial lawyer, mostly—civil and criminal. He doesn't do wills on a regular basis. He's done maybe a dozen in his whole career. So there was little reason for him to notice the rule when it was adopted.

"Does this excuse what he did? No, of course not. He is a lawyer, an officer of the court. He is charged with the duty to know the law and to execute it. But it does *explain* what happened. And it rebuts any implication that he sought to prey on an old woman. Or that he was out to 'line his own pockets.'

"Jimmy Morrissey has been forthright with bar counsel since she commenced her investigation. He has cooperated fully and testified truthfully in these proceedings. He is a chastened man who deserves—and acknowledges that he deserves—to be disciplined for what he failed to do.

"But to take away a man's *livelihood* for such a mistake? No, Your Honor. That's not right. That's excessive. And to what end? To destroy a man's professional life over a single, ignorant lapse of judgment?

"This is a man with an unblemished record in over twenty-three years at the bar, and for whom the law has been his entire life. He deserves a public reprimand, yes. That's appropriate here. But let it stop there. Don't suspend Jimmy Morrissey."

Twohig paused to hold her eye, then said, "Thank you, Your Honor," and walked back to the table and his client. He rolled his eyes to the ceiling in mock supplication.

"I'll take it under advisement," Lizzie murmured. The lawyers jerked to their feet as she made her exit.

It was not a smooth one. She swatted helplessly in search of an opening in the folds of the huge black curtain behind her, and it was not until a uniformed court officer appeared from behind the curtain that she was able to slip between the folds and disappear. The officer, Morrissey knew, would pay dearly for his tardiness and her embarrassed fumbling. Morrissey hoped she wouldn't take it out on him as well.

Morrissey stared up at the famous portrait of Oliver Wendell Holmes, who seemed to be shooting him a disappointed glance above his foppish handlebar mustache. He wondered if the old Yankee ever swallowed his words like Lizzie Mallow.

He turned toward Twohig and realized his neck was killing him. The whole hearing had taken less than thirty minutes, but he'd been straining so intently to hear every syllable, he must have cranked up the tension on his neck muscles a few extra notches.

It's not so easy being a client.

Sieglinda was gone now, and the two men were standing outside the courtroom near the elevators. Morrissey told his lawyer what a great job he had done, which he meant, and Twohig told him they'd just have to wait and see. Morrissey could smell the sweat on him and realized his lawyer had had a workout of his own.

"You know what you did, lad?" Twohig asked, a loopy grin creasing his face. "You broke the Schneider rule."

"What's that?" Morrissey returned his smile, but he didn't have a clue what he was talking about.

"You remember Charlie Schneider? Had a small shop on his own down in Dedham? He used to throw me a few cases when I was starting out. He'd get half in the bag and tell all us youngsters his rules for a lucrative law practice. Well, you broke one of Charlie's rules." He wagged a mocking finger and intoned, "*Never write yourself into a client's will without including a good-sized bequest to the Archbishop.* That way you'll have Royce & Bell in there defending the will."

They both laughed hard at that one. Royce & Bell was high-priced talent, the biggest law firm in town. It felt good to laugh after the wringer he'd been through.

The smile seeped out of Twohig's face. "I started to worry there at the end," he said. "That Lizzie might ask me why, if this was such a simple legal error, you didn't just cave in when it was brought to your attention. Instead of spending eight months in a will contest before giving up the ghost. I didn't know what I would say."

Morrissey looked him straight in the eye, drilling his disappointment. "You would have told her," he said, "that a man tends to dig in his heels when somebody calls him a fraud and a thief."

Twohig took a couple beats, then nodded. "Yeah. I might have thought of that."

The realization hit Morrissey like a physical blow.

"You're wondering did I *do* it!" he said in astonishment. "You think I might have bamboozled the old broad, don't you?" He was surprised at how much it smarted, but he shouldn't have been: the two of them went way back.

"Aw, come on, Jimmy," Twohig said with a sour look on his face. "You've been a lawyer a lot longer than you've been a client. You know I don't make judgments like that."

"That's just my point." Morrissey felt himself getting madder by the minute. " 'Cause you been my friend longer than you been my lawyer. So I *expect* you to make those judgments—and in my *favor.*"

"I do, Jim, I do," he said, but he didn't sound all that persuasive.

"So what's hangin' you up? Tell me, damn it."

They fell silent. As Twohig ran a hand through his hair, Morrissey stared into his big lumpy kisser, a plum-colored relief map of County Galway. Just then the image of Maryann Nee washed up like a dead fish at his feet, and he was right back on Breed's Hill, sitting in that filthy little sty of hers. With a Virginia Slim in her mouth and her greasy gray ringlets up in curlers, she stank of cigarette smoke, old sweat, and urine. To get around in the place you had to pick your way among heaps of newspapers and magazines, giant balls of soiled string, plastic jugs with curds of spoiled milk, and trampled garbage bags spilling rotted cat food, yellowed paper, unwashed reeking laundry, smeared feces—and, yes, bankbooks and loose cash. After he got her out of there and into Sycamore Crescent, it took him a solid week to find a cleaning service that would tackle her apartment. Most of them never got past the front door.

Christ, she was a nasty old hag! Tight as a rabbit's ass in winter and bigoted into the bargain. She had time for nobody. Tenants in the upstairs unit seldom lasted more than six months. "It's them niggers!" she would shriek into his phone at all hours of the night. As if the black population of Charlestown ever climbed above six and her tenants were anybody other than the timid Irish couples she hounded out of there like one of the Valkyries. Morrissey would end up getting his ass chewed in housing court trying to defend her against charges of code violations, failure to escrow deposits, and breach of the covenant of quiet enjoyment.

Testamentary capacity? *Puh-lease,* he wanted to spit. She could flit in and out of lucidity like a ballerina. Or a fox, was more like it. He could never be sure if she was ready for the state hospital or just playing him for a sucker. Like the time she told him she'd once had a long affair with Jimmy Durante. She carried his picture, she claimed, in a locket around her neck. When, despite his begging her not to, she produced this tarnished keepsake out from between her oily sunken dugs, hauling it up by the chain like a bucket from a well, the man in the photo turned out to be Jack Webb. *Jack Webb!* She gave Jack's puss a big smooch and croaked, "Good night, Mr. Calabash, wherever you are!" Then she screwed up one side of her face and cackled derisively until her emphysema kicked in and cut off her air supply. He still didn't know how much of it was an act. But he was willing to bet she had rehearsed that Dinah Shore business for days, just waiting for the right nurse to spring it on.

In the end, he was convinced she had given him the money less out of gratitude (and, God knows, he had earned it, after all her demeaning little errands) than to spite her own family. Sure, she had talked about a nephew who'd grown up in Malden. Some doubtless imaginary slight on his part had gnawed at her innards for years, and it gave her no end of satisfaction to picture him bewailing his disinheritance. As for Morrissey, he always believed she had signed the will just to keep him on the string. He fully expected she had squirreled another one away somewhere, one that revoked the will he had drawn. But if she had, nobody ever found it, and his was the only one offered for probate. It looked as though he would get the money, too, until the nephew showed up. Morrissey spotted Sieglinda wheeling overhead soon afterward.

He'd told his lawyer all this before, but he went over it for him again, there in front of the elevator bank on the thirteenth floor. And Twohig stuck on the part about the nephew.

"It's the notice?" Morrissey asked him. "Is that what this is about? I didn't try hard enough to find him?"

"If you hope to inherit from your own client," Twohig said, "you gotta expect extra scrutiny. But there won't be any if those likely to squawk don't *know* about your good fortune. You published notice of the probate proceedings only in the *Metro West News* and the Malden paper. Did you really think that was adequate?"

Morrissey was getting exasperated now. "Kenny, all I knew from her was he started out in Malden and went 'out west' somewhere. I thought she meant like California or Montana. How was I supposed to know he only got as far as North Adams?"

"Jimmy, they found his old letters from Berkshire County among her things in the nursing home. *You* ended up with the letters. It should have been a no-brainer to publish in the *Berkshire Eagle.* How could you not notice the letters?"

He had him there. He felt a little niggle of guilt at mention of the nephew's yellowed letters. "You're right," he admitted. "I missed them. They were right there and I didn't see them. But to this day I couldn't tell you if I simply failed to appreciate their significance or if I repressed the knowledge somehow. Because all I could see was that money coming my way. Lord knows I needed it. So maybe my judgment did get clouded."

"What need?" Twohig jumped in, always a dangerous man around a ruminating witness. "How come you needed money so bad you can't think your way clear to button it up as tight and legal as you can?"

It's a funny thing about friends. They know you so well that they pick up on those little overtones of tribulation no one else can hear. They catch you out. So Morrissey didn't meet his eye right away.

And Twohig knew.

"You've been dipping into client funds." It was a statement, not a question. Almost whispered. Morrissey did not respond at first. Twohig pressed him. "How much are you out of trust?"

Morrissey looked up and saw the disappointment in his friend's eyes. "Nobody's missing their money, Kenny. Every nickel's been paid over when it was due. I'm just short if I had to pay it all out at once, that's all."

"How *much*?" he demanded.

"About fifty-four thousand and change." He said it quietly, and a silence fell over them.

"And change," Twohig repeated at last. "So you hoped the old lady's money would take care of it, is that it?"

"Yes, but she *did* want to give it to me. I never took her money. It's just that the prospect sort of clouded my judgment, like I said."

It was suddenly very important that Twohig understand this. And believe him. *Because it's the God's own truth,* he told himself.

"Christ, Jimmy," he said bitterly. "You picked one of the only capital crimes in this business. You diddled with your clients' money. You might as well have bribed a judge. They find out, it's certain disbarment."

"*Borrowed,* Kenny. Nobody's been deprived of a penny." This sounded hollow even to him, but he pushed on. "They're all down payments I'm holding on house closings. The real estate market's strong, and I can replenish the account with new deposits in time to close on the old ones. It'll work out."

"You better hope the market stays hot till you square things. It turns south, and you're fucked."

"You think I don't know this? You think I don't read the goddamn business news every day? But it'll work out, I tell you."

Twohig rubbed his eyes, then reached over to press a button for one of the building's asthmatic elevators. A bell rang and, like magic, one appeared immediately—which was nothing short of miraculous in this rattletrap courthouse. He stepped in and turned to face his client. Morrissey made no move to join him.

"One thing, Jimmy. If you don't get square, don't ask me to stand up in front of Lizzie again and beg her not to put you on the beach. Okay?"

Morrissey nodded as the door slid shut.

Thinking, *Because there wouldn't be any fucking point, and we both know it.*

CHAPTER FOUR

SIGNS

FRIDAY

From the Wyatt Detention Center in Central Falls, Rhode Island, Arthur Patch rode in the backseat of a gray Chevrolet Celebrity. The only other occupant was the driver, a U.S. marshal who had introduced herself as Linda Getzendonner. Clad in a charcoal gray skirt, a crisply starched white blouse, and a navy blazer that hung just right across her square shoulders, Linda Getzendonner was slim, attractive, and openly pleasant—a welcome change, Arthur wryly observed, from the dour porker who had cuffed him wordlessly in the courtoom three days ago and later drove him and a sweating little man named Ariña all the way to Rhode Island in silence.

Getzendonner had come for him at 5 A.M. He didn't know whether the hour was chosen to avoid calling attention to his departure or merely because she anticipated heavy traffic into Boston. Arthur didn't care. The glorious June weather and Linda's fresh good looks made him feel almost buoyant after three nights in Wyatt. As the Chevy whizzed northward he watched the billowing sunlight suffuse itself through the swags of cloud draped across the horizon.

Soon he felt emboldened to strike up a conversation through the wire mesh.

"Great day," he offered. Always a good beginning.

"Umm," she agreed.

"You do this a lot, hauling us thugs to court?"

"A lot." She eyed him in the rearview mirror.

"I have to tell you," he said. "After growing up with Matt Dillon on *Gunsmoke.* You're not exactly what I expected in a U.S. marshal. But I bet you hear that all the time."

"A lot," she said again, still watching him.

"I'm gonna put this down to my conversational charm," he said, undeterred. "I'm sure you're much more tight-lipped with your other fares. Or are you always so chatty?"

"A lot." She was smiling now.

"I knew it," he said, nodding in mock satisfaction. "I'll have you slipping into two-syllable words any minute."

"Maybe," she said, and her smile blossomed into a full-blown grin.

So it went. She would answer direct questions with straight answers, yet she volunteered nothing. But then, so far as he could recall, neither had Matt Dillon.

They had a clean shot north to Boston. It was still too early for much commuter traffic, even on the usually sclerotic Southeast Expressway, and they soon found themselves off the freeway and headed up Congress Street. Arthur watched as the little park at Post Office Square, a tidy oasis of green with brick walks and a trellised arbor, slid by on his right.

Getzendonner took a left on Water Street and then cranked the wheel hard to the left again, descending a ramp into the underbelly of the ancient, gray-stone building that housed the post office and the federal courthouse. She slowed for a security guard, who waved her through with a nod of recognition. Turning to the right as she approached a shipping dock, she wheeled left again and stopped before the lip of a heavy steel garage door. She activated a button on the visor and waited as the door rolled up. When it cleared the roof of the Chevy, she eased forward into a concrete chamber not much larger than a double garage. She shut off the engine and sat motionless until the big door had rumbled shut behind them.

"This is the sally port," she said as she opened her car door. "You have to wait here a second." It was an explanation, not a command; the rear car doors had no inside handles.

Arthur watched her proceed to three oil drums arranged to the left of the only other door in the chamber. Painted bright orange, the drums were propped up at an angle like chubby cannons trained on the Chevy. Each drum lid had a saucer-sized hole cut in the center, with a rubber grommet fitted like a collar around the opening. Getzendonner opened her purse and removed her automatic. Leaning over, she inserted the gun barrel into one of the drum holes and ejected the cartridge clip into her left hand. She straightened, hitched the strap of her purse higher up on her shoulder, and carried the gun and ammo to the other side of the door. There, mounted above a keypad and a bright red scramble button, was a rack of small steel boxes like miniature bus station lockers. She turned one of the extruding keys and opened a locker door. She shoved her weapon and ammunition inside, locked the door, removed the key, and dropped it into her purse. Turning her attention to the keypad, she punched in a code and tilted her head toward the grille above it. Arthur could not hear what she said into the squawk box, but after a brief exchange she turned and walked smartly back to the car.

"What's with the drums?" he asked as he climbed out of the car. She was holding the car door for him.

"They're clearing barrels," she explained, slamming the door after him. "Filled with sand. So you can clear your weapon in safety."

"Then you lock them up?" He stretched to relieve the stiffness from the long ride.

"No weapons allowed in the courthouse," she said. "In case you haven't heard."

He paused to look around him at the security cameras and motion sensors mounted on the bare concrete walls and ceiling.

"Why do they call it a sally port?"

"Search me."

When she got to the door, she stared through its Plexiglas window and waited. He heard the metallic click of a solenoid echo off the concrete walls. She shoved the door inward and stepped aside to let him enter first.

Arthur passed into a tiled hallway. To his left he saw a small room with a table and chairs and a camera mounted on a tripod. A booking room, Getzendonner explained. She led him around a corner to the right, past two holding cells, each large enough to house several prisoners.

"Not here," she said. "We have a segregated holding area for you up ahead."

"For the special guests?" he asked with a smile.

"Something like that. For women, usually. And protected witnesses."

It was a single, tiny cell, a miniature version of the other two.

Instead of bars it had wire mesh, like hurricane fencing, only made of much heavier metal and slathered with thick gray paint. Stainless-steel benches were bolted to the two concrete-block walls on either side, and a waist-high metal divider across half the back cut off most of one's view of the toilet.

She closed and locked the door after him. He noticed two television cameras on the wall behind her and another scramble button between them. She smiled at him through the mesh.

"I'll be back for you later," she said brightly. "You might have to wait here a while. I'm sorry, but it's still pretty early for the lawyers."

"Thanks for the good company," he said. "You've got it all over that first guy, the tubby one, what's his name—Burke?"

"Byrne," she corrected. "We aim to please."

And then she was gone, the tails of her blazer bobbing gently behind her as she walked away.

Arthur looked around him in the little cell and inhaled disinfectant. He stared through the metal toilet seat. The bowl was empty and dry. He tried to imagine what kind of security risk standing toilet water might pose, but he got nowhere.

Deciding to do his best to relax, he sat down on one of the benches and tried to make himself comfortable. The seat was hard, but the coolness of the steel felt oddly soothing. For the moment he was safe, he knew, safer than he would be on the street, certainly, safer even than in Wyatt. But he knew he would have to do a power of thinking to maintain his thin margin of safety.

It was Friday, the last day in what had been a nightmare of a week. Monday morning he had spent with the lawyer, Grutman, who acted as if they were actually meeting to discuss his legal options for the contempt hearing on Tuesday. But the subtext of their conversation was deafening over all that lawyer talk. For he knew, and Grutman knew he knew, that Arthur's real agenda was to convey to Larry, through the lawyer, that he had nothing to fear from Arthur. He would never testify, he repeated to the owl-faced lawyer. He would serve the time. He had been as blunt as he could be, short of coming right out and saying that he could think of no quicker way to end up dead than to testify against Larry Coniglio. He needed desperately for Larry to understand that. And to buy it.

The discovery that he hadn't made the sale came upon him gradually, for it took time to grasp the significance of the stranger.

Arthur had watched the stranger enter the restaurant early that same evening. His face was as white as lard and pocked by eyes so close together they made him look cross-eyed. His shrunken frame swam in an oversize brown suit. Ignoring the hostess as he looked the place over, the man had stuck out his hand to Arthur and introduced himself as Jerry Something. His eyes were fugitive, glancing over Arthur's shoulder instead of looking at him directly. He seemed fascinated by the kitchen's swinging doors.

"This La Vucciria?" the man asked, still not looking at Arthur. He butchered the pronunciation, rhyming the first syllable with "moose" instead of "mooch." "Do I got the right place?"

"Yes," Arthur answered. "I'm the owner, Arthur Patch." The stranger made him feel uneasy, but he wasn't sure why.

"Yeah, Artie. That's it," the man said, finally drilling Arthur with a look in the eye. "Larry sent me."

"Did he?" Arthur answered, and he grasped at once the reason for his own uneasiness. It was the man's tentlike suit and his complexion, so oddly chalklike at summer's end. *It's a prison pallor,* he realized. *He's just out of jail.*

"Yeah. I'm the rep for Beamon's. You know, the sign people? We make the neon signs."

"I don't understand," said Arthur, his voice tight. "I never ordered a sign."

"Well, that's why I'm here," the stranger explained, shoving his hands in his pants pockets. "To fix that. I'm the sales rep, see? Here to talk about signage."

Arthur shrugged. "But I've *got* a sign, right out there in front. I don't need another one. There must be some mistake."

"No mistake," the stranger said, shaking his head. "Larry said you need one, and I should talk to you about it. You're not tellin' me Larry's got it wrong, are you?"

"No. I mean, I don't know about that. I'm just telling you Larry never mentioned it to me." *Is it possible,* he wondered, *that Larry is only muscling me into a deal he has a piece of?*

"Well, that's Larry for you," the stranger said, trotting out a smile that never reached his eyes. "Never says more'n he's gotta, right?"

Was he kidding? Most of the time Larry ran on like a nervous weatherman.

"He said I should talk to you," the man continued. "About a sale. 'Cause when I show you what we can do for you, I know you're gonna agree. Come on out front a minute, and I'll show you."

The man beckoned by twisting his upper body toward the door, and Arthur saw the rear of his jacket interrupt its vertical fall to fold itself over a sizable lump at the small of his back. With terrifying suddenness, Arthur realized that Larry had decided not to count on Arthur's vows of silence. He froze for a moment, the blood pounding in his ears.

Then he made up his mind. "Okay," he said. "Give me a minute to check on my sauce in the kitchen, and I'll join you." He looked over the man's shoulder. "Joanne!" he called.

The hostess looked up from her reservation book by the door. With two fingers he summoned her to them.

"Sauce?" said the stranger, his nostrils contracting as he seemed to take in the aroma of the place for the first time. "You mean, like spaghetti?"

"Something like that," said Arthur as Joanne approached. Taking the measure of the man now, he smiled at him. "Maybe I could get you something from the kitchen? A nice porterhouse, maybe? On the house, of course. For a friend of Larry's."

He watched the man's facial muscles sag as he wrestled with temptation, then shook it off. "Nahhh, I better not. Hit and run, you know." He grinned, first at Arthur, then Joanne. "I got a lotta signs to sell."

"Sure," said Arthur, smiling back. "Joanne, can you see that, uh—Jerry, is it?—that Jerry gets something to drink while I check in the kitchen? He's here about the sign."

"Sign?" said Joanne, bewildered.

The stranger nodded. "That's right. From Beamon's. Hey," he called to Arthur, who had started toward the kitchen. "How long you gonna be?"

Arthur lifted both hands and waved them vaguely. "A minute, Jerry. Just a minute."

Arthur banged through the swinging door, walked straight through the kitchen, sidled past Jonathan leaning over the prep table, and left the restaurant by the rear door. By the time he hit the alley he was running hard, and he didn't stop running until he reached Tremont Street, two blocks away. Once there he grabbed a cab in front of Hamersley's Bistro. Sinking back in the car seat, he massaged the stitch in his side and fought to catch his breath. From out of nowhere came the sudden urge to vomit. The fear, he realized. He fought it off.

"Where you go?" asked the black driver in an accent Arthur couldn't place.

He didn't know. "Just drive," he said, waving his hand. "I'm not sure yet."

The driver grinned at him. "You in one big hurry for a man who don't know where he go."

Arthur snorted absently to give him that one.

A dispatcher's voice crackled on the cabbie's radio. In Creole. *Haitian,* he thought inanely. *That's what the accent is.* As he felt the car pull away from the curb, Arthur closed his eyes and tried to figure out where to go.

South Boston was out of the question, since Larry's people would undoubtedly know to watch for him at his apartment. He didn't know how much they knew about his family and friends, so he didn't feel he could risk going to any of them. In the end he settled on the Holiday Inn on Cambridge Street. It was sufficiently nondescript, he knew no one there, and it was only ten minutes' walk from the federal courthouse, where he had to be at eleven in the morning. *Definitely* had to be there, now.

To make sure no one traced him through the cab (unlikely, he realized, but he was taking no chances), he told the driver to loop toward the southwest and drop him at Copley Square in the Back Bay. From there he mingled with the parade of young people ambling past the boutiques and buzzing bistros on Newbury Street, and hurried east. Crossing Arlington Street with a nervous look back over his shoulder, he entered the Public Garden.

He was numb to the Garden's summer charms. The gathering darkness welled up first under the trees before spilling out onto the Garden's walkways. Striding briskly through the thin grass, he turned north to keep the Boston Common on his right. The wild panic was no longer roaring in his ears, and he sat down on a wooden park bench to weigh his options.

Larry obviously had chosen not to trust him to keep his mouth shut. And just because he had failed once to shut it for him did not mean he would give up trying. That left federal custody, but for how long? It did not seem like much of a haven. If anything, Arthur would probably be more at risk in prison, which had to be full of men who ached to ingratiate themselves with the likes of Larry Coniglio. Nor could he testify against Larry. His restaurant encounter with the killer notwithstanding, Arthur was not about to throw in with the feds, for he did not relish making a new life for himself in the Witness Protection Program. *Doing what?* he asked himself. Besides, he knew Larry and his friends had long, long memories. They would pursue him to the hinges of hell. And Larry's undoubtedly extensive contacts in the law-enforcement community did nothing to instill confidence in federal protection.

No. He needed to find a way to get the feds off his back and convince Larry that he posed no threat to him. He didn't have much to work with.

Stumped, he stood up and headed northwest, leaving the Garden to head up Charles Street. He was passing the gaslit shops at the bottom of Beacon Hill when he stopped dead, like a man transfixed. *Extensive contacts in the law-enforcement community.* A few paces in front of him stood two valet parking attendants, smoking idly in front of Ristorante Toscana, but Arthur's thoughts were far from that handsome dining establishment. He was back in South Boston, a year earlier, smelling the stale beer and old piss of an Irish pub called the County Cork. A brief conversation involving three men at the bar. And an odd name. What was it? Flukes. Yes, that was it. Flukes.

One of the parking attendants turned his way with a questioning look, and Arthur's attention snapped back to the present. He resumed his hike up Charles Street. By the time he had left the soft lights of Beacon Hill and emerged into the glare of the Charles Street T-stop, the glimmerings of a plan had begun to take shape in his mind. He turned right and headed east up Cambridge Street toward the Holiday Inn.

It presented a lackluster façade that seemed at home with the forbidding, precast state office buildings up the road. He took a room. He had a moment's anxiety when the desk clerk swiped his overburdened credit card for authorization, but if the card was maxed out the computer didn't know it yet. She smiled at him as he signed in, then gave him a plastic key and directions to his room. He passed a raucous banquet room where, a blue banner proclaimed, the Massachusetts Paralegal Association was holding a convention. He hurried to his room and locked the door behind him. Looking about him, he took comfort in the room's undistinguished appointments and his anonymous surroundings. Then he lay back on the bed to do some hard thinking.

By the time the sun rose he had fleshed out his plan. It was thin, chancy, he knew that. And it was bottomed on two assumptions he had never tested. With the Boston telephone directory on his lap, he waited fitfully for the start of the business day. Then, at a little past nine, he cleared his throat and placed the call from the phone next to the bed. He'd had the number memorized for an hour.

"Federal Bureau of Investigation. How may I direct your call?"

Arthur took a deep breath before responding. "Agent Flukes, please." He closed his eyes and hoped.

"I don't believe he's in yet, sir. Is there anyone else who can help you or would you like his voice mail?"

Arthur smiled. He *was* an agent. His first assumption had passed the test. "Can you connect me to his, uh, squad or whatever it is?"

"One moment, please."

He heard three rings and another voice came on the line, male this time.

"Tevlin here."

Arthur's heart raced. "Lemme talk to the Fish," he said.

There was a short silence on the other end of the line. Then Tevlin spoke up. "I'm afraid I don't understand," he said. "The fish?"

"Flukes, asshole," Arthur said harshly. "He'll know who it is."

Another pause, a mind being made up. "Flukes isn't here," Tevlin said, his voice more tentative now. Then a corrective belligerence. "You got a name?"

"You just tell him I called. Can you handle that?"

Arthur hung up without waiting for a response.

Promising, he told himself as he wiped his sweating palm on the pillowcase. This Tevlin character hadn't actually given anything away, but he hadn't acted as though such a call was beyond the realm of possibility either. So the second assumption was still alive. Nothing like a hundred percent, but promising.

He checked his watch. Nine-twenty. His appointment with Grutman and Judge Biddle wasn't until eleven, but he planned to get there as early as possible in case Larry had dispatched the Welcome Wagon. He could waste no time. Besides, he didn't know whether the FBI could trace his call back to the hotel. He assumed they weren't looking, but he'd be stupid to stick around and test *that* assumption. Better hurry.

Using hotel stationery he found in the desk drawer, he hurriedly jotted his note to Danielle Gautreau and stuffed it in one of the envelopes. He folded the sealed envelope in half and wrapped it in a second note, this one to Joanne. Then he stuffed everything in another envelope, addressed to Joanne at the restaurant. On the back he wrote, "Joanne, Give $20 to the person who delivers this—AP." His last act, on leaving the hotel, was to deposit the envelope and two twenties with a taxi driver who was waiting under the porte cochere to pick up a fare. The cabbie checked the address, the message on the envelope, and fingered the two bills before looking up at Arthur and nodding his agreement. Arthur then took off to walk up Cambridge Street to Post Office Square.

And now, three days later, as rising noise levels from the command center of the U.S. marshal's office signaled the arrival of other staff, he waited impatiently for his appointment with the new lawyer Danielle Gautreau said they had found for him.

CHAPTER FIVE

CALL THE FISH

It was pushing ten-thirty when Kenneth Twohig left his client outside the SJC courtroom, and Jimmy Morrissey was thinking hard about whether he should finally get some breakfast. The thought of greasy eggs and more coffee did a number on his seditious stomach, so instead he lumbered over to 45 Milk Street, where he took the elevator to the seventh floor. Hanrahan, Gordon, Morrissey & Palmer, it said on the door. It wasn't actually a law firm, just a loose association of sole practitioners who shared space and clerical staff.

"Law offices," sang Taffy, their spike-haired girl Friday, as she snapped her gum into the phone. She took down a message with a lot of *uh-huh*s and *yeah*s and *gotcha*s. She gave Morrissey her usual high five without looking up from her padful of pink message slips. Morrissey made straight for his office and eased himself into the wooden desk chair. It creaked at him in agony.

He knew he should be attending to business. His Lawyer's Diary lay open accusingly right in front of him, and he dimly recalled that he had a deposition scheduled for the afternoon. But he was still too wound up from that business with Twohig and Lizzie Mallow. He just needed a little time to chill, he told himself. An emotional breather. Then he'd get a grip.

Forgetting for the moment that he might actually get suspended (a big one to forget, he had to admit), his practice was very busy.

Which is okay, he told himself, *when you consider the alternative.* But his cash flow had slowed to a trickle. Too many contingent-fee cases, for one thing, which were fine if and when he settled a case, but they did not keep the wolf out of the freezer while he was waiting. The flat fees he got up front for criminal defense work tended to get spent right away, and if he couldn't plead them out early he ended up facing a mountain of work for no additional money. So it was operating cash he needed, not work. Not to mention that little problem he had just been discussing with Twohig about the shortfall in his client trust accounts. Bleak, was the word for it.

Then, like the fairy godmother, Taffy was standing in his doorway with the good news.

He gaped stupidly at her for a moment. He was inured to her hair colors *du jour* (Orange Crush, today), and this wasn't the first time he'd seen the bottom half of her ensemble, which featured a twelve-inch miniskirt, white knee socks, and black Kombat boots. It was today's top that grabbed him. She seemed to have shown up for work in her underwear. What looked for all the world like a teddy was covered only by a chartreuse matador jacket, unbuttoned. Her lingerie item was beige, *nude* he thought they called it. He couldn't tell if she had just pulled the jacket on as she rolled out of somebody's bed or if she was way out front of the fashion curve.

"Ya walked right by this one, Jimmy," she said, chewing violently as she waved a message slip at him. "New case in the federal court."

Morrissey reached out eagerly for the slip and spotted Danielle Gautreau's name and number. The box for URGENT had been checked. Though he was delighted by the news, he was also a little puzzled. Notice of federal appointments usually came directly from the Federal Defenders Office, not the prosecutor. Taffy seemed to pick up on his confusion.

"What a huffy one!" she said, the timbre betraying irritation. "I tell her you're not in yet and she goes, 'When do you expect him, it's urgent,' and I go, 'I don't know, he's in court this morning,' and she's like, 'Which court?' Uh, right. Like I should know. So I go, 'I don't know, I can have him call when he gets in.' What else can I say, right? Then she says she wants your cell phone number."

This made him grin. He didn't even carry a pager. He should make it *easy* for them to find him? "What did you tell her?" he asked.

"Well, I don't want her to think we're some cheesy outfit, behind the times, like. Which I don't know if we aren't, by the way. So I tell her, 'I'm not allowed to give it out,' which gets her more worked up."

"I'll call her."

She shook her head. "I don't know how you do it, Morrissey. It was me, I'd let her stew a couple days just to teach her a lesson."

But Taffy didn't need that federal money. The feds paid decent counsel fees, and with reasonable alacrity. Unlike the Commonwealth, which paid pocket change—when it felt damn good and ready. He noticed she was still standing there, even though he had the phone in his hand to call Dani.

"Is there something else?" Not more boyfriend trouble, he hoped. With this most recent one she'd gone almost nine months now without needing a restraining order.

"It's Mr. Volkert. He wants you to call him about his case."

Morrissey closed his eyes briefly. *I should fire the guy,* he thought. *I really should.*

Paul Volkert was a mousy little engineer who worked out of the head office for Bell Atlantic. After a lifetime of breathtaking insipidity, Volkert had finally endured one too many games of bike-messenger roulette as he crossed Franklin Street on his way to work one morning. Looking up to see a bicycle bearing down on him from the wrong direction, he first had jerked back and then, with a flare of crisp decisiveness Morrissey was sure he had never brought to anything in his whole paltry life, he had plunged his umbrella into the spokes of the front wheel. The messenger, a punk with a pistachio Mohawk and an earring the size of a Gothic door knocker, did a half-gainer over the handlebars. He broke both elbows when he hit the pavement. Wait till the casts are off and give him a Financial District jury, Morrissey figured, and he could skate him on the criminal charges. Shit, the jurors would send him Christmas cards. Volkert, however, had since reverted to type. Brimming with remorse and fearing against all reason that he'd get jail time, he wouldn't leave his lawyer alone. Morrissey *would* fire him, too, if he hadn't already spent his fee.

He promised Taffy he'd call him. Once she was out the door, he crumpled Volkert's slip into a ball and banked it off the file cabinet into the wastebasket. Then he called Dani.

At nine-thirty the next morning he was waiting in the interview room of the marshal's office to meet Arthur Patch face to face. Morrissey sat on what resembled an old-fashioned diner stool while examining the wire mesh that would separate him from his new client. He preferred the solid plastic used at the state prison in Walpole; here there was no protection from getting spat on when you came with bad news.

Arthur entered his side from the right. Morrissey was not sure what he'd expected. Some trembling wiseguy wanna-be, perhaps, shitting his pants at the prospect of snitching out Larry the Rabbit. But if Arthur was scared, he couldn't tell it from those unwavering baby blues sizing him up through the chicken wire. Dani might have thought this was a friend of the friends, but Morrissey learned she was wrong.

Boy, was she wrong.

Almost six hours later Morrissey was at the U.S. Attorney's office on the ninth floor of the same building. There he was escorted to a windowless conference room. One look around told him all he needed to understand why they were spending the annual GNP of Senegal to build a new courthouse over on the Fan Pier. The stained ceiling tiles were sagging, the eggshell-plaster walls were dinged up and greasy-looking, and the surface of the wooden conference table was scarred by gouges and burn marks. Under a grimy photograph of Bill Clinton, a cast-iron radiator gave off flakes of silver paint and way too much heat as it banged out the metallic backbeat from Sam Cooke's "Chain Gang." They probably couldn't wait to move into the new building in a few months.

Morrissey cooled his heels for twenty minutes until the door opened and Arthur was led in. He was escorted from the S-elevators by a fine-looking young woman who, Morrissey was astonished to learn, was a U.S. marshal. After they had said good-bye like old friends, she left the two of them alone.

Arthur, Morrissey noticed, was out of the coveralls now and wearing a brown wool jacket with a natty knit tie. He looked poised, relaxed even, as he took a seat beside his lawyer at the table.

"How'd you get the threads?" Morrissey asked, seeking to put the man at ease in case he was more jittery than he appeared.

"My partner brought them over for me," he explained. "Marshal Getzendonner let me call."

"Partner?" *Gay?* he wondered. *Or has this become the trendy way to say* girlfriend? *Did I miss the demise of 'significant other'?* "You mean a girlfriend?"

"Hardly. She's a lesbian. Joanne Balzer. She's my business partner, in the restaurant. She's the one who got my note to Gautreau."

Morrissey considered for a minute. He hadn't thought about a partner. "She aware of your banking arrangements with Larry?" he asked. " 'Cause whether she is or not, she shares what the law calls joint and several liability for the debt. And believe me, where Larry's concerned, your joints can get pretty several in a hurry."

Arthur smiled wincingly at this. "She will now. I'm going to have to make it up to her."

He fell silent. Morrissey changed the subject. "You still sure this is the way you want to go? They don't bite, you could really piss 'em off."

Arthur twisted his smile. "What can they do, put me in jail?"

Morrissey chuckled. "Ah, yes. The celibate life—*if* you're lucky. But there's more to it than that. There's all kinds of ways they can get even. Hey, this is the Organized Crime Strike Force you're dealing with. The provisional wing of the DOJ. They think they're on a mission from God. They're used to dealing with people who think murder is a form of alternative dispute resolution. So they play for keeps. And if they decide you're just stirring shit with a stick—*plus* getting some of it on their own people—they can be very rough. Maybe even put out the word that you're givin' 'em Larry after all."

Arthur shrugged. "Larry's already decided I might do that. No, this is the only way. The FBI needs to believe it would be worse if I *do* talk—and I need their help with Larry. I'm in a tight spot."

Morrissey couldn't argue with him there. There was nothing else to talk about, really, until Dani got there. So he asked about the restaurant. He had always thought Sicilian food was what you got in any of the joints in the North End, at least until the Yuppies started demanding white sauces and pesto.

"No," Arthur explained. "The cooks there are Southerners, it's true. From Calabria and Abbruzzi, even some from Sicily. But the food is mostly bastardized Italian-American. Gooey eggplant parmesan. Overloaded lasagna. It's the food of exiles, prepared and served with contempt. 'Sicilian' is a term they use to describe pizza with a crust as thick as a hockey puck."

"You mean that's *not* Sicilian pizza?"

"No. Chicago pizza, maybe. But not Sicilian."

"So what's Sicilian food, then? Goat hair and olive oil?"

"Ah," he said, sitting back in the chair, his features softening as his eyes shone. *Oh shit,* Morrissey thought, his heart sinking. He had seen such expressions before. It was as if he had tripped a land mine and had precious seconds before getting fragged by a burst of Arthur's almost palpable obsession with Sicilian food. But before Arthur had the chance to edify his lawyer, the door opened and Dani strode into the room with two middle-aged men in tow.

Morrissey had known Danielle Gautreau for several years, and he'd always figured her for a primly idealistic and zealous prosecutor who ate and slept by *The U.S. Attorney's Manual.* (He pictured her on her deathbed murmuring: "Must . . . file . . . brief . . .") But there was no denying she knew her business. She was extremely bright and impressively well-educated. Out of Swarthmore College and the London School of Economics, she had graduated from Yale Law School and spent four years feeding the beast at Royce & Bell before going public. And as for looks, well, she was a knockout, a stunner. Long blond hair, huge green eyes, her features pulled smartly together by a model's classic bone structure. A trim figure, too, with long, graceful legs extending from a very fetching caboose. It was this last that had led his pal Twohig, with a bow to her English schooling, to dub her the London Derriere. As a consequence Morrissey could never look at her without having to stifle an urge to start humming "Danny Boy."

He knew the two men as well. Stanley Prout was Dani's boss, a glib lawyer who headed up the Organized Crime Strike Force in New England, while Ryan Butters was special agent-in-charge for the Boston field office of the FBI. Prout was tall and bald, with a fleshy bead of cartilage drooping from between his nostrils. He affected squarish wire-rims and double-breasted suits. To a project rat like Morrissey, he had always come across as a bureaucratic prima donna. *Thinks the Lord picks his nose for him,* he thought. *If he was a painter, he'd put his signature in the middle of the canvas.* He'd been topping the ball for years, making slight but steady progress in his career.

Butters, on the other hand, looked like the Marine he'd always be: short, solid, pugnacious. Even allowing for his gray brush cut, the top of his skull was as flat as the deck of an aircraft carrier. It amused Morrissey to believe he had hammered it flat by butting down doors as a young field agent. Butters was Prout's right-hand man, which, since Prout was left-handed, gave you a pretty good idea what an effective team they made. The two of them sat together at the other end of the table, while the insistent radiator behind them gave voice to their evident displeasure. Morrissey viewed their presence as a good sign, because he and Arthur would need a lot more juice than Dani alone could bring to the table.

Dani sat directly across from Morrissey and unsnapped her attaché case to remove a yellow pad, which she positioned on the table in front of her. She pumped a ball-point pen into readiness and held it poised above the pad. All business.

"So," she said briskly, her eyes on Arthur's. "I understand Mr. Patch is prepared to make a proffer. I'm sorry it had to come to this, but if we can reach a rough understanding today, he'll be able to go home tonight. We're here to listen."

Arthur's expression didn't change much, but Morrissey could see he was furious. Which was understandable, of course. This woman had busted in on his tidy little world, turned him upside down, and tried to shake him out like a sack of turnips. Without so much as a thought for his convenience or privacy, she'd hauled him in to get at Larry—put his life in jeopardy, in fact—just because Arthur had borrowed money from the man. A piece of horribly bad judgment, Arthur would be the first to admit, which had put him in Larry's clutches and thus in Dani's crosshairs. What did she expect? That he'd be eagerly panting to see her, like a dog with its leash in its mouth?

Fearing his client's anger might make him say something really stupid, Morrissey jumped right in.

"Before you start thinking two-stage proffer, you need to understand something here. In his note to you Mr. Patch indicated a willingness to provide valuable information, and he will. But he is *not* offering to testify against Larry Coniglio. On that issue his position is unchanged."

It was her turn to get mad. Morrissey watched her eyes narrow as color reached her cheeks. "In that case," she said, flipping her pad like a Frisbee into her attaché case, "you're here under false pretenses. And you've wasted my time. *Our* time," she added, and Morrissey realized she must be feeling embarrassed in front of her boss. She stood up.

The two men with her, Morrissey noticed, were still in their seats, waiting. Morrissey was about to weigh in again when Arthur spoke for the first time. "Don't you want to know what *kind* of information I have to offer you?" he asked, his voice tight with resentment. "It may not be what you wanted when you started cranking this meat grinder, but at least you might *listen* to me. What have you got to lose?"

The two of them glared at each other in silence. Morrissey checked out the other two. Butters was stone-faced, giving nothing away, but Morrissey noticed a faint smile playing at the corners of Prout's mouth.

"Let's hear him, Dani," said Prout. "We've gone to all this trouble, we might as well listen."

She waited a couple beats, as if to stress she was only doing this at her boss's behest. Then she sank slowly into her chair again. She said nothing.

Morrissey put his hand on Arthur's arm to keep him quiet and made the pitch.

"My client has information which suggests corruption within the Bureau's Boston office. At the special agent level."

He now had their complete attention. The nascent smile vanished from Prout's lips, and Butters folded his arms across his chest in a revetment of bone and flesh. *We're not a witness anymore,* Morrissey realized. *We're the enemy, and they are closing ranks.*

"What *is* this shit?" demanded Butters, his mouth turned down like a man who'd just discovered a turd in his picnic basket. Prout was silent, but Morrissey knew the flunky was only amplifying his master's voice.

"The corrupter," Morrissey went on, ignoring Butters and focusing on Prout, "appears to be one Thomas Crimmins. Tommy, to his friends. Ring any bells? You indicted him almost a year ago, and he's been a fugitive from justice ever since."

"Don't be a smart-ass, Morrissey," said Prout, a sour look on his face. "Just get on with it."

"Okay. It's August 16, 1997. Your grand jury has handed up sealed indictments against a whole slew of mobsters, including Tommy and his partner, Phil Hinkle. And various assorted Italians from that *other* gang. Top-secret arrangements are made to coordinate the arrests so everybody will get swept up together. It almost works, too.

"But not Tommy. He's disappeared. Vanished. Rumors abound that he was tipped off about the indictments."

Morrissey talked right at Prout now. "You, Stan, you pooh-pooh all that to the press. Tommy will be apprehended, blah blah. Almost a year later he's still out there somewhere."

"Assuming he doesn't call in dead," Butters added with a smirk.

"Oh, he's alive, all right," said Arthur, and all eyes switched to him. "He's alive because he got a head start and then got himself out of town before you pounced. He was tipped."

"How do you know that?" Dani demanded.

"Well, I guess I don't *know* he's still alive, because nobody's seen him since he split. But I do know he was tipped."

"I repeat," she said evenly. "How do you know that?"

Arthur paused briefly and smiled at her. "That," he pointed out, "is the very information I'm selling. You can't expect me to give it to you until we have a deal, can you?"

"No," she said, shaking her head. "Way wrong. We need more than that. I'm not buying a pig in a poke. You've got to give me enough to demonstrate it's worth our while to talk business with you. So far you've given us nothing but speculation. *That* I can read in the *Globe* or the *Herald*."

"I can give you a name," said Arthur. "For starters."

"What name?"

"The name of the agent who made the tip."

"And who would that be?"

Arthur looked over at his lawyer. Morrissey nodded. Arthur turned back to her.

"Martin Flukes."

It got very quiet for a minute. Even the radiator shut up. Arthur and Dani stayed fixed on each other while Morrissey scrutinized the other two for some hint of—what did he expect to see? Surprise? Concern? Outrage? He wasn't sure what he had expected, but they were giving him nothing. Flat lines from both of them. Not a damn thing.

Danielle exhaled noisily. "Anybody can come up with the name of an FBI agent." She snapped her briefcase shut, then looked up at him. "Mr. Patch, you've given me nothing here."

Lawyer and client had reached the point they had discussed in some detail. The point where Arthur had to shoot his wad. But before he did, Morrissey figured he'd better talk price.

"All Mr. Patch wants," he told her, "is for you to leave him alone, and to find a way to do it without making Larry the Rabbit any more suspicious than he already is. It's not so much."

He said this for Prout's benefit, not hers, because he knew she didn't have the authority and because, if Arthur was right, she wouldn't know what was going on anyway.

She looked bemused. "You're not hearing me, Jimmy. He hasn't given me anything I can work with."

"Okay," said Arthur with a faint sigh, as if he'd finally decided to spill the beans. "Go back to August 16. About four P.M. I'm in the County Cork over on West Broadway, waiting to meet a wine distributor. He's late. I have a beer at the bar. Tommy comes in with a guy he runs with sometimes. I forget his name—Shaun something."

"Crowe," offered Butters.

"Yeah, that's him. Crowe. Anyway, they go up to the bar about five stools to my left and stand there a minute. I thought they were waiting to order, but then the bartender goes over to them and Tommy gives him this gesture, as if to say, 'Well?' "

Arthur demonstrated this by twisting both palms open upward and giving an irritated dip of the head.

"The bartender says, 'Call the Fish.' Tommy just looks at him, and the guy says, 'That's the whole message. It was 'Call the Fish.' " Arthur paused.

"Call the fish." Dani repeated dryly. "Is there more?"

"Yes, there is. Tommy said something to Crowe, and then walked over to a pay phone on the wall by the men's room. I saw him dial a number and talk quietly for a minute with his hand cupped around the mouthpiece. Then he gets loud—and angry, turning his back to me and cursing into the phone. I couldn't pick up much beyond the fact that he was mad as hell, but I did hear him yell, clear as can be, 'We had a deal, Flukes!' That was the only thing I could make out. A minute later he hung up and left the place with Crowe. I never saw him again."

"And neither," Morrissey joined in at this point, "has anybody else. Am I right, Ryan?"

But Butters wasn't saying anything. He was watching Arthur very closely.

Morrissey picked up the thread of his client's story. "The next day, the seventeenth, you execute the arrest warrants and go public with the indictments. Hinkle and most of the others get taken down at once. But Tommy's nowhere to be found. Hey, I hate to bring the bad news, but it looks to me like your guy Flukes put a bug in his ear so he could take off. Somebody ought to investigate, don't you think?"

Dani, he noticed, was agitated and incredulous, but his interest was in her two companions, who remained expressionless throughout.

"That's it?" she cried, exasperated now. "That's what you're offering? 'Call the Fish' and somebody yelling 'Flukes' in a barroom?" She shook her head in disgust.

"I looked Flukes up in the Boston phone book," Arthur said. "You know how many I found?"

Dani shrugged.

"None," he said. "Not a one."

"He doesn't live in the city," Butters finally spoke up.

Arthur looked over at him. "You're not getting my point. It's a very unusual name."

"And a kind of fish," Morrissey added. "But I wouldn't expect a meat-and-potatoes guy like you to know that."

"*If* he heard it right," Dani pointed out.

"I heard it right," Arthur responded evenly.

Dani looked at him, shaking her head again. "Do you think," she asked slowly, "that we would impugn the integrity of a trusted agent like Martin Flukes on the strength of what you've given us today?"

There was still no visible reaction from Prout or Butters, and Morrissey saw that it wasn't enough. He could see the whole thing starting to slip away from them. They weren't buying it. *Time,* he said to himself, *I tried to set the hook.*

"Maybe you look," he pointed out as innocently as he could, "and you'll find some *documentary evidence* that would corroborate Flukes's relationship with Tommy Crimmins."

Dani tipped her head slightly to one side and stared at him in perplexity. "Documentary?" she asked, as if floundering to imagine how Morrissey could be so obtuse. "What are you talking about? If he did what you're suggesting, you think he'd leave a *paper trail*?"

"Oh, you never know," he said, looking past her and right at Prout. "A fellow knows what he's looking for, he might find some paper."

His eyes widening just perceptibly, Prout locked on to Morrissey, and suddenly Morrissey saw that he got it. *He gets it—that I know,* he thought. *Which means I do know what I know. And that Arthur's right.*

Meanwhile, Ryan Butters, his mind a flooded engine, was glaring at Morrissey with unconcealed hatred.

Gotcha.

CHAPTER SIX

PAPER TRAIL

"What's there to 'think over,' Stan? They had nothing! What the hell is going on here?"

Stanley Prout was out of the chair now, his buttocks planted on top of the hot radiator and his feet crossed in front of him. He lolled like a priest, with his laced fingers resting on top of his genitals. Soon the heat on his rump would be too intense, but for the moment it was pleasurable. He smiled indulgently at his angry assistant.

"It's enough to trigger an inquiry," he told her. "Under the regs the threshold for instituting an informal inquiry is pretty low. We have to look into it."

Danielle did not back down. "Look into *what*? Some uncorroborated and scurrilous story that links an agent to Tommy Crimmins? Stan, this guy is desperate to come up with *anything* that will keep him from testifying. His credibility is just about nil here."

Prout expanded his avuncular smile. "Then he probably wouldn't make much of a witness, would he?"

She ignored the sally. "So you want to cut him loose? Jesus, this will turn about six months of work into garbage. You can't *do* this, Stan!"

Prout stood up and plucked the hot fabric of his trousers away from his toasted flesh. "Relax, Dani. I didn't say he was off the hook.

I just said I'd look into it and give it some thought. Nobody's made any decisions yet."

He glanced at Butters, who watched his every move like a cat.

Danielle lifted her arms and let them flop against her sides in dismay. "I don't believe this," she said. She looked up at her boss. "What are you going to do, then? Bring in the Office of Professional Responsibility? That could take *months.*"

"Oh, I don't think we need to go *that* far. Not yet, anyway."

"I think you *do,*" Danielle said. "If there's enough to trigger an inquiry, the book says OPR should be in on it."

Prout's eyes snapped at hers. "I'll be the judge of that," he said sharply, ice in his voice now. "For the moment, all you need to keep in mind is that this business is on hold. Am I being sufficiently clear?"

His change of manner confused, then angered her. "Quite," she replied coldly. She picked up her bag and walked out the door.

Quite? Did I really say "quite"? As she headed up the harshly lighted corridor, she lingered with dismay on her toothless parting retort. *How inanely English of me. As if the jerk were one of my dons.*

During the walk back to her office, she tried to bring perspective to what had happened today. Morrissey had made his absurd proffer, of useless and unreliable information, and Prout had sat up and taken notice. That was the gist of it, and it made no sense. Stanley had then gone on to extract an elaboration of Arthur's demands for release and covert protection of some kind. She wasn't sure if she ought to take seriously Arthur's claim that some sign salesman had shown up to kill him, but it was clear Arthur did. Now Stanley was telling her to sit on her hands while he looked into the allegations—all while disregarding his obligation to bring in the OPR, Justice's branch for investigating its own personnel. It was all very confusing. At least, she consoled herself, Arthur was on his way back to Wyatt for the time being.

She was turning in the doorway of her own office when the thought froze her. She looked vacantly in the direction of her cluttered metal desk, images spinning before her mind's eye.

Could it be true? That Martin was corrupted?

It seemed inconceivable. The man must have over thirty years of service with the Bureau. Why would Prout give credence to such a thin charge? And if he *was* going to treat them seriously, why would he proceed with half measures to investigate them? It made no sense.

"You think they know?" Butters asked, tentatively. "Or are they guessing?"

"Don't be ridiculous," said Prout, his manner dismissive. "It doesn't matter. Even if they don't know, they know enough to guess. That's bad enough."

Butters squeezed his chin as he thought. "I find it hard to believe Flukes could be so stupid. What would possess him?

"Who knows? Sometimes a handler gets too tight with his charge. It gets personal. You know how it goes. And they both came from the neighborhood. Maybe it's just a case of working too close to the bull. Anyway, see that Martin gets transferred out of here. Someplace *far* away." He smiled to himself as he considered the options. "Brownsville, Texas, comes to mind. Special liaison to INS or something."

The two men were silent. The radiator knocked. Butters spoke. "Maybe we should just wait a few weeks and tell 'em we looked into it and there's nothing there. You know, give out something like we've established that Marty was out of town when the indictments came, so he couldn't have tipped anybody off. Then tell 'em, thanks, but no thanks for the info?" He looked up questioningly at the other man.

Prout twisted his features into a grimace of sour contempt. "You don't get it either, do you, Ryan? Morrissey isn't offering to trade '*info.*' Don't you see? He's *threatening* us with it. If we don't give him what he wants, he'll take it public."

Butters frowned back at him. "Well, I gotta go with Dani on that one, Stan. Even if Marty did tip Tommy, he wouldn't be dumb enough to leave tracks."

"Christ!" Prout hissed through his teeth, looking at the ceiling in exasperation. "What *is* it with you people? Of *course* he wouldn't. That's the *point*! And Morrissey knows it. That's precisely why he's giving us that little poke about a paper trail. He's telling us he knows Flukes is not a rogue agent, acting on his own, and that if anybody gets an opportunity to look hard at our files, they'll discover just what kind of relationship Tommy has with the Strike Force."

"Had," Butters reminded him. "It ended when we indicted him."

"That," snorted Prout, "depends on whether Patch's story is true. Here's the bottom line: if we don't give them what they want, they'll spread it around and the resulting uproar in the media will force the Department to conduct an investigation. Which will uncover all *kinds* of paper on Crimmins. *That's* the paper trail Morrissey's hinting at. All of Top Echelon, the whole informant program, will come unraveled."

"Can't have that," Butters agreed, shaking his head.

Prout put trembling palms together prayfully and raised his eyes skyward in thanksgiving. "It *thinks*!" he said wonderingly. "At long last."

Butters looked hurt. He said nothing, waiting for Prout. The latter pursed his lips and, holding his hands behind his back, rocked back and forth on his heels. Neither man spoke for some time. The radiator knocked again.

"I think," Prout announced at last, "we give them what they want. It's not so much, when you think it through. Really, now, Ryan. You've met the guy. Do you think he'd flip?"

Butters frowned, Prout's insult forgotten. "You mean would he testify about Larry? No way. He's a tough little fucker, I'll give him that. He'd sit out the time."

"That's what I think, too," said Prout, nodding knowingly. He sat down and laid his right ankle on top of his knee. "Even this attempt on his life hasn't budged him in that respect. So add it up. Odds are he'll either serve the eighteen months or Larry whacks him. Either way, Dani gets nothing out of him. So we lose *nothing* by letting him slip. Why risk calling his bluff?"

"Makes sense to me," said Butters. "You just gotta convince Dani."

"The hell I do," said Prout amiably. He wriggled his toe to ease the bottom of his oxblood loafer off his heel, watching it dangle from his toe. "This is my team, and I call the plays. That business about dragging in the OPR." His tone turned contemptuous as he shook his head at her obstinacy. "For Christ's sake, that's the *last* thing we need. Obviously, she's not somebody we can trust on this thing. She's too much of a stickler for her own good. And *way* too emotional. No, we deal directly with Morrissey on this."

"What'll you tell Dani, then?"

The question seemed to amuse him. "Why, nothing. The matter's under investigation, and she's to stay away from it. Meanwhile, though," he added, serious again, "we have to think of a way to provide Patch with some air cover vis-à-vis Coniglio. Morrissey's right. We can't just shove the man out the door, and say, 'Good show, lad! You're a stand-up guy. At least we tried.' Larry would be even *more* suspicious. No, Mr. Patch needs a cover story to explain his release—and we need to think of somebody who can convince Larry to pull in his dick."

"Fuck Patch," snarled Butters. "The little bastard wants out, let him shift for himself."

Prout pulled back and laid his palm across his breast in horror. "Ryan! I am shocked, *shocked* that you should suggest such a thing! We are the United States government and you are an agent of the Federal Bureau of Investigation. We do *not* consign American citizens to the tender mercy of animals like Larry the Rabbit. Besides," he added with a sly smile, "he would then have no alternative *but* to go public with whatever he has on us. Fuck him, indeed!"

"So how do we do it?"

"Well," said Prout, looking up at the ceiling as if reading the answer off the yellowed tiles, "it appears that Shelley Grutman is still counsel of record for Mr. Patch—not to mention being Larry's missing middle finger. And Grutman has filed an appeal from Judge Biddle's finding of contempt. His argument is a transparent bit of sophistry, I grant you, but it might give us an opportunity. You see, Shelley also filed a motion to stay the order pending his appeal. Fat chance. Biddle will not smile on the motion, but he *is* aware of the nature of our recent communications with Mr. Patch. Suppose we explain to the good judge—most confidentially, of course—that Patch has agreed to provide valuable information to this office but cannot appear to have done so, not even to his putative lawyer. And maybe I let on that we would not be outraged if the court were to grant the motion to stay, thus releasing Mr. Patch pending his appeal of the contempt order. You know us lawyers, Ryan. We're a dilatory breed. If no one's pressing, it can take us *months* to brief and argue an appeal. God knows, Grutman will do everything *he* can to delay it, and we've certainly heard nothing here today that would make us want to expedite the matter, now have we?"

Prout grinned at Butters. Butters grinned back.

"A few months down the pike," Prout continued, "and who knows? Passions subside. Larry cools off. We have other fish to fry.

(Forgive me, Flukes.) Danielle is then working in, oh, say, the Bank Fraud Division—I like to think of it as the Nome, Alaska, of the U.S. Attorney's Office."

Butters laughed.

"And then, when everyone is tired to *death* of the whole thing, we talk to Grutman about dismissing the appeal and vacating the order of contempt. We merrily go off to find another way to take down Larry the Rabbit. What do you think, Ryan?"

"It's slick," he said. "I like it."

"The other part of the deal," he stressed, "is your department." Elbows on the table, Prout pointed both index fingers at Butters. "You have to figure out someone—an agent, one of your informants, *somebody*—who can convince Larry to back off. Counselor Morrissey has made it quite clear that Patch's information will not go to the grave with him. You know anybody who could speak persuasively to Mr. Coniglio? Preferably without suggesting that we're trying to protect an informant?"

"Sure." Butters beamed back at him. "I know just the guy. Phil Hinkle."

Prout looked puzzled. "Correct me if I'm wrong, Ryan, but isn't Mr. Hinkle in jail at the moment? Because *we* put him there?"

"Yeah. And still trying to figure out why. He and Tommy were a team, remember? In every respect, including their deal with us. So he's an asset, too. I'm sure he still thinks he can work something out with us on the charges. So, I tell him that it's in his and Tommy's interest that Morrissey doesn't blow up Top Echelon. I mean, it *is*, isn't it? And I tell Hinkle he should get word to Larry that he and *Tommy* want him to leave Patch alone."

Prout smiled broadly. "Why, Ryan. Just when I despair of you, you come through like this. It's absolutely ravishing! Mr. Patch hails from South Boston, just like Tommy and Hinkle, who might well have reasons of their *own* for wanting no harm to come to the poor fellow. And, rumors of war aside, we know Tommy does enough business with Larry and his bunch to get such a request honored. Especially if Patch is back on the streets and no immediate threat to Larry."

Prout pushed his chair back and pulled himself to his feet. "You're a beautiful man, Ryan. I could kiss you."

Butters's smile faltered a moment, as if he feared the man might actually do it.

CHAPTER SEVEN

STOP THE PRESSES

To understand what happened with Eddie Felch it is necessary to know a little bit about how things get done up at the Supreme Judicial Court. If a lawyer has a matter pending before the full court and they're ready to issue a decision in the case, a clerk calls to give notice that the decision is being released. They'll even read out the bottom line over the phone—affirmed, reversed, or whatever. Then the lawyer can send someone over there to pick it up immediately or download it off the Internet after one o'clock the same afternoon. Otherwise, it just gets dropped in the mail and the lawyer receives it when the post office sees fit to deliver.

That is how it works in the *full* court. But a lot of the Supreme Judicial Court's business gets done in the single-justice session. The matters handled there tend to be nuts-and-bolts stuff that does not command a lot of general interest. Such as pretrial appeals from the denial of a motion for preliminary injunction. Or the Commonwealth's request for leave to appeal to the full bench from an order suppressing evidence in a drug case. Who cares, right? Consequently, there are no courtesy calls from the clerk when a single justice hands down a decision. It just gets put in the mail.

Except that bar discipline is also handled in the single-justice session. Those orders get mailed, too. And sometimes a reporter happens to be up in the clerk's office checking the docket for some reason or another when the single justice's order gets entered. Or maybe it's not serendipity at all, just a clerk with a grudge deciding to tip one of his cronies in the press that there's a disciplinary action worth a peek. Under circumstances like these it's possible—though pretty rare—that a reporter could actually get the news before the respondent.

That's the accused lawyer. He's the respondent. And so it happened, somehow, that Eddie Felch learned before either Jimmy Morrissey or Kenneth Twohig that Lizzie Mallow had decided not to suspend Morrissey after all. In fact, it was from Felch that Morrissey first got word of the mercy vouchsafed him. Of course, that was not exactly how the *Globe* reporter put it when he called. Eddie wanted to know if Morrissey wished to comment for his story on the public reprimand he'd just received from the Supreme Judicial Court.

So Morrissey didn't even get a chance to savor his deliverance before he had to defend himself on a different front. He had figured all along a reprimand would get play only in the *Massachusetts Lawyers Weekly*, the local lawyers' newspaper. Its editors tended to bury the discipline reports in the back of the B section, where the more ghoulish of his brethren pawed through them with obsessive fascination, the way people linger over obituaries right after they turn forty. An appearance there was embarrassing, humiliating even, because one's friends and enemies at the bar would pick it up, but the public at large seldom got wind of the news. So it did little real damage.

Coverage by one of the big papers was something else altogether. All Morrissey needed was a spread in the *Boston Globe* about how he'd been caught trying to fleece some little old lady in a nursing home. From Charlestown, no less—his home turf. No matter how false, a story like that would drain off a lot of his business in the neighborhood, and there was no telling what kind of intangible harm it might do in pending cases, Such as his high-stakes poker game with Prout and Dani. As a result, hearing from Eddie Felch, four days after meeting Arthur Patch, that Twohig had won the day with Lizzie Mallow was not what he would have called unalloyedly good news. It was the medium, not the message.

The *Globe* ran Felch's column on the first page of the metro section twice a week. It was a flip, often mean-spirited little bagatelle, favoring astringent opinion and derisive anecdotes over the hard news Felch had once picked out of stubborn sources like a coal miner working a seam. Fortunately, Morrissey had known Felch since his days covering the police beat in the district courts when they were both just starting out. Because they had this shared history and decent rapport, Morrissey figured he stood a chance with him on this one.

"Eddie," he begged, "you don't want to go with this. It's just a technical mistake blown all out of proportion by those fanatics up at the board of bar overseers."

"Can I quote you on that?" Felch asked, immediately taking up the slack. Morrissey could hear his fingers clacking away on his computer keyboard.

"No! I mean yes—Jesus, *I* don't know." Morrissey struggled to figure out how it would play, but he was no spinmeister. *Juries are my medium, not ink.* "Look, can we go off the record here a second?"

"Sure." The clacking stopped. "But the story's too good to bury for old time's sake, Jimmy. You gotta understand that."

"There's no story here, Eddie," Morrissey urged, his plea feeling limp even to him. "I just didn't realize I shoulda got her another lawyer to do the will. She really *did* want me to have the money."

"Could be, Jimmy, but the old lady's dead. So we only got your word on it. How can I *not* go with this? It's juicy—and timely. Remember, two weeks ago? When the AG said he was gonna form a special unit to deal with abuse of the elderly? According to my editor, the topic is hot."

"Abuse!" he spat. "If you knew the old harridan, Eddie, you'd agree *I* was the one got abused!"

"So let me tell your side of it." Morrissey could almost hear the grin break across Eddie's face. "Tell the people what she was *really* like."

"No thanks," he responded dryly, despairing a little. "There's nothing I could say that would change how it's gonna look on the page. You know that, Eddie."

"Well," he said, "I just wanted to see if you had any comment before I start writing it up. I'm sure Ms. Vyshinsky will give me something I can use."

"You're a nasty little guttersnipe," Morrisey said. "You live off roadkill, Felch. You're tub scum. We go back a long ways, you and me. You don't have to do this."

Felch laughed. "But I *do.* Jimmy, you know I got a job to do, just like you. Hey, you'll look pretty in ink. And we'll both get over it."

"No, we won't. Not me. I have the Irish Alzheimer's."

"I'm afraid to ask."

"We forget everything but the grudges."

He laughed again. "That I am *gonna* use. But seriously, Jimmy. I got no choice here. The story's too tasty to pass up. You know the rule: if it bleeds, it leads. And I've been working dry holes for the last six months. I gotta go with what's at hand."

What's at hand. And that's when it occurred to him. That, like Arthur, he might have something to swap.

Just like Arthur.

"Suppose," he inquired, "just suppose I got something very juicy and very heavy. To trade, I mean."

"Like what?" Morrissey heard the sound of lips sucking on a cigarette.

"But it's gotta be way, *way* off the record. Just material to point you in the right direction. You can't even use me as an anonymous source."

"I can live with that," he said, "but it'll have to be pretty big if you expect me to drop this story. Pretty *fucking* big."

"It *is* pretty fucking big," Morrissey assured him.

"So are my ears. Let's hear it."

It was time for second thoughts, and Morrissey entertained them. But not for long. You don't worry about getting too close to the edge when you're already in free fall, and he knew that Eddie, whatever else he might be, was a man whose confidence he could trust. Without it he couldn't do business. *Kind of like a lawyer that way,* he thought. So he took the plunge.

"A name. Tommy Crimmins."

Eddy was quiet on the other end, as if he expected Morrissey to say more. Then he came on sarcastic. "You're gonna tell me where he's buried, is that it?"

"No, I'm gonna tell you he's a snitch. For the FBI."

"Oh, Christ, Jimmy!" He sounded disappointed in him. "That rumor's been kicking around for a couple years now. It should have been strangled in its crib. The feds even got a tape with Francesco Coniglio joking about it, that's how ridiculous it is."

"And?" Morrissey pointed out. "Where's Francesco now? He's gonna die in a federal prison."

"True enough," he admitted, "but that doesn't make him wrong on this one. Jesus, Tommy's gotta be the most powerful gangster in the whole city, now that Francesco is out of the game. Or at least he was till he disappeared. That puts him way beyond snitch material, kiddo."

"And I'm telling you, you ought to take a hard look at how he *got* so big. Think it through, Eddie. Francesco goes down, and Tommy ends up on top. Then, what's left of the Boston Mafia begins to regroup under Larry and, pow, it gets hit with this new set of indictments. Tommy, too, but him they can't find. These developments are related."

"Doo-doo-doo-doo, doo-doo-doo-doo." Eddie Felch was humming the theme from *The Twilight Zone.* "Of course! I see it now, Jimmy. It all fits!"

Morrissey ignored the derision. "Like you said, Eddie. The guy's the biggest bad guy on the block right now. And he hasn't even been *ticketed* in twenty-five years. Ever since he got out of the can in the early seventies, he never took a pinch. What do you *think* makes him so lucky?"

Felch snorted. "You don't need to look under cushions at the FBI to account for *that.* What about his significant brother? He's the *governor,* for Chrissakes. And DA before that. You don't think that would give him some cover?"

"Not with the feds, Eddie. Jackie Crimmins's influence doesn't extend that far."

He still didn't sound convinced. "You're telling me Tommy gave them the Italians so he could run the show? And then the government indicted him anyway?"

"Yes, something like that. Maybe he outlived his usefulness."

"Rumors, Jimmy. Nothing more."

"More, Eddie. I got information Tommy was tipped by somebody in the FBI that the indictments were coming. So he could jump ship."

Felch was quiet now. Thinking. Finally, he asked, "What kind of information?"

"Nothing you can print," Morrissey pressed. "But it's a hell of a lot more than a rumor. I got an eyewitness. And a very reliable guy, not some guinea lowlife. He listened to Tommy's side of a call from an agent the day before the fibbies started making arrests. So at least you know the rumors are true. You're the ace reporter—or you used to be. Dig into it. You might get lucky. *Pulitzer* lucky."

This last was a bit over the top, Morrissey knew, and Eddie snorted into the phone to show him he shared that assessment. But he said nothing for a long time, and Morrissey just waited.

"You wouldn't be making this shit up, would you?" he asked at last. "To screw an old friend?"

Like you were ready to do? he wanted to say. But instead he said, "It's all true, Eddie. Seek and ye shall find—if you know where to look."

He was silent again. Then he said, "I'll need the agent, Jimmy."

It was now Morrissey's turn to be silent. This was getting close to home. "You can't print it. You can't even show it around. *And* you kill the story on yours truly."

"Scout's honor. It's killed. And nothing on the agent. Not unless I can get the name from somebody else. But I gotta have the name. Like you said, I need to know where to look."

Okay, he said to himself. *If they spring Artie, it will happen fast, a lot faster than Eddie could ever get anything out of the Strike Force.*

He gave him the name.

"You're shitting me."

He assured him he was not shitting him.

"Martin Flukes," he said wonderingly. "Who'da thunk it? Okay, it's a deal. Pleasure doing business. And Jimmy?"

"Yeah?" *What now?*

"Stay out of the nursing homes. It leaves a bad taste."

Morrissey let him have the last jab, and he was gone. He heaved a big sigh of relief. He'd dodged that one. He figured it was pretty safe, too, because nobody was going to confirm that story. Nobody in the Strike Force would, certainly, and Eddie wouldn't even know to ask Arthur, who'd have the sense not to answer anyway. So in this exchange, by Morrissey's calculations, he'd just cut himself a pretty good-sized watermelon.

When he thought back on what happened later, he realized it was not that he had overestimated Eddie's journalistic ethics. He had just underestimated his talent.

CHAPTER EIGHT

THE WELL

Tommy Crimmins could feel the weight of his heels settle slowly into the wet sand, which was hard packed by the pounding of the surf. Looking out at the early-morning horizon, he could distinguish no break between the colors of sea and sky, just a leaden monochrome as far as he could see. He watched a wave break and its lacy verge race toward him to foam and fizzle around the tips of his shoes. Then the sucking sound of the backwash and the clatter of trailing pebbles, the last of the water sluicing out again in slender rivulets around the bigger, unbudgable stones. He felt a sympathetic tug seaward in the pit of his own stomach. As if seeking a mooring, he sank the point of the spade into the sand like a bollard and gripped its stirrup handle with his right hand.

So he stood for some minutes, filling his lungs with the chill salt air and his ears with the susurrus of the rolling surf. Then he eased the spade out of the sand and swung it over his shoulder. He turned on his heels to his right and walked a hundred yards to the base of a headland that interrupted the beach. A lopsided shoulder of gravelly soil and tufted grasses, the headland was topped by a small stand of stunted white pine bent hard away from the water by the prevailing winds. He stopped briefly at the base to look up, then glanced back over his shoulder. Nobody anywhere. Driving the blade of the shovel into the rising terrain, he began to haul himself up the side of the headland, scrabbling for footing as crumbled soil and rock tumbled behind him.

When he reached the top he felt winded, but not too much. He leaned for a moment against one of the trees to rest, looking out at the waves rushing against the southern shore of Long Island. *Fifty-nine and still fit,* he said to himself with grim satisfaction. *But don't push it.* He snugged his watch cap on his head. He checked the pager to make sure it was still clipped securely to his belt. Dragging the blade of the shovel behind him now as he breasted the pine branches, he started looking for the blaze that marked the well.

He couldn't find it. He frowned. This was the spot, no doubt about that, and he carried a vivid image of his hatchet biting into the trunk, slashing off the bark and leaving the moist, creamy yellow of the blaze glistening in the sunlight. Where the hell was it? His confusion was already giving way to percolating irritation when he heard the impatient honk from the parking lot above the beach. *Shut the fuck up,* he muttered. Suddenly, all he could think about was the *swock* of the spade against the side of her face, the jaw caving in, the impact traveling the length of the ash handle and right up his arms to sing in his shoulders.

Then he saw it. It was a flinty gray now, of course. After almost four years, he should have anticipated that. Only a candy-ass townie like him would have expected the blaze to retain its live color. He felt the rage bleed out of him as he made his way to the leeward side of the marked pine. Though the tree was a large one, he had to hack off a few of its lower limbs to clear enough room for him to dig through the brown needles that carpeted the ground beneath it.

The digging was easy, the sandy soil soft and friable. The work was pleasurable even, in the way small amounts of hard physical labor can be to a man who doesn't have to do it for a living. In less than ten minutes he felt the blade scrape against the hard surface of the box, and when he brushed the soil away he could see the dark green of the garbage bags covering it. Another three minutes and he had the top exposed, the dirt along the sides mostly gouged out. He tried to wrench it out of the hole, but the box wouldn't budge. Positioning the spade along one end of the box, he pressed his foot down on the top of the blade to drive it in. Then he bore down on the handle and gently levered it out.

Leaning the shovel against the tree, he knelt on the bed of needles and tore away the garbage bags. He was hunched over a heavy plastic lunch box, bright yellow and swaddled in three layers of garbage bags. The box was the thermal kind you might pack for the beach with a container of Blue Ice to keep the food cool. The tension lock gave way smartly, permitting him to raise the top like the lid of a miniature coffin. He heard the honking again, three short blasts this time, but they triggered no response as he stuck his hand inside the box.

He extracted a white bundle the size of a brick. The whiteness was its wrapping, a CVS Pharmacy shopping bag cinched by two rubber bands. Zippering the bundle into the pocket of his windbreaker, he shut the lunch box and laid it back in the hole. Still on his knees, he used the side of the spade like a grader to scrape the loose soil back into the hole. When it was filled, he stood up and proceeded to scatter handfuls of pine needles over the scarred earth. Rubbing his hands to clean them, he surveyed his handiwork. It wasn't perfect, but then there was nothing of value or danger left to be found anyway. And he had dug many more wells.

He grasped the shovel in his right hand like a spear and, taking the route he had come by, slid down the bank of the headland. He walked back up the beach and climbed the path through the dunes to the empty parking lot.

Empty, that is, except for the big blue Lincoln that idled, nose out, at the head of the path. Without looking at the passenger, who had watched his approach through the rear widow, he walked straight to the trunk and raised its unlatched lid. He reached in and grabbed a white hand towel, still folded and bearing the name of a motel in Stamford, Connecticut. He used the towel to clean the soil from the shovel, which he then stowed in the trunk, wedging it between the driver's-side wall and a cardboard box that held his barbells. He slammed the lid, tossed the towel into a litter barrel at the head of the path, ascertained that his hands were unsoiled, and slid into the driver's seat.

Mavis watched him settle in. Then her attention was reclaimed by the game of solitaire laid out on the screen of the portable computer open on her lap. "What took you so long?" she asked, sliding a virtual queen on top of a black king. "I been starving to death out here."

He didn't look at her. He unzipped his jacket pocket and pulled out the bundle.

"You need to learn," he said, still not looking at her as he worked the rubber bands off the bundle and slipped them like bracelets over his left wrist, "not to draw attention. You honk next time, I'll give you something to honk about."

She was quiet, watching his small, delicate hands unfold the CVS bag and reach inside. Out came two packets of crisp new bills, one containing fifties, the other twenties, each packet almost an inch thick. He tore off the wrappers and, licking his fingers, counted out three hundred in twenties and another three hundred in fifties, all of which he added to a wad from his pants pocket. He rolled the rubber bands off his wrist and around the packets of bills, then stuffed them back into the CVS bag.

When he removed his hand this time, he was holding a clear plastic sandwich bag. He opened it and slid its contents, a collection of plastic cards, into his other hand. A valid New Hampshire driver's license, with photo. Credit cards: Visa, MasterCard, Mobil, Sears, Kmart, Staples—dummies, all of them. A library card from Nashua, New Hampshire. A card indicating membership in AAA, genuine. He was beginning to stuff them into his wallet, piling the ones they replaced on the dashboard, when she spoke again.

"What about me? You gonna give me a new ID, too?"

He still did not look up. "You never had to use the first set I gave you. They're still good."

As she shifted her hips on the seat and adjusted the position of the laptop, she continued to watch his hands.

He picked up a Styrofoam cup nestled between the seats and removed its plastic lid. Holding the cup by the edge against the dashboard, he swept the discards into it. He held it out to her.

"Take out that little scissors of yours," he said, motioning with his head toward the purse at her feet. "Cut these up in tiny pieces and then pour them out the window when we get back on the road."

She stared at him for a few resentful seconds, then closed the laptop's jaws with a heavy click. Rising from her seat, she twisted herself around to face the rear. She managed to ease the laptop onto the backseat, nudging two of his hardbound military histories to the side in the process. A bottle of vitamin pills bounced off and rattled on the carpeted floor. Once resettled facing front, she rooted in her purse for her nail scissors. By then his wallet was back in his pocket, and the bundle had disappeared.

"So who are you now?" she asked as she started snipping bits of plastic into the cup. "You better tell me so I know what to call you."

"Thomas Holte," he said. "You just change the last name. And I live in Nashua now. Otherwise, just like before."

"Okay, Thomas Holte from Nashua, New Hampshire," she said without looking up from her work. "Take me someplace for breakfast. I'm starving, for cripe sakes."

He put the car in gear and started wheeling the Lincoln out of the lot. A few minutes later she was shucking the snippets out her open window. The wind whipped them away and they swirled like light snow in the wake of the speeding car.

She chose a small boxcar diner, the two of them facing each other in one of the vinyl booths that ran along the front window. When the waitress returned with her order, Mavis refilled her cup from the individual coffeepot left on the table, then stirred in copious amounts of cream and sugar.

Tommy looked down at her breakfast with disgust, at the prefab square of frozen hash browns, sweating grease, and the runny whites of eggs congealing on the cold plate around strips of noxious bacon the color of dried dog turds. Eggneck. That's what his brother Jackie used to call it, the snot of undercooked egg whites. He looked away and rubbed a porthole through the condensation on the window, grateful he had finished his yogurt and wheat toast before her food arrived. The gray sky was starting to spit a little now, stinging drops that left cursive trails like snail spoor down the surface of the glass.

He slid out of the booth and stood up.

"Where you going, Tommy?" she asked, nervous in the way she always was now, whenever he left her side. "You gonna be long?"

Fishing in the pockets of his windbreaker, which hung from the hook on the end of the seat, he said, "I'm going to the crapper. What do you think?" He pulled out his book of crossword puzzles and brandished it before her as if in further explanation. Then he strode off, leaving her to her caffeine, to her American Heart Association Special, with its animal fats and nitrates.

Because he spent longer than he had intended, absorbed in the puzzle, it was almost fifteen minutes before he returned to the booth. The table was clear now, thank God, but he saw at once that her face was not. He looked into Mavis's red, puffy eyes, smeared with running mascara, and watched her look down to avoid his gaze. Yellow corkscrew curls drooped like tassels over her face. *Oh, Christ,* he said to himself, groaning silently. *Here we go again.*

"What is it?" he asked, struggling to contain his annoyance.

"Nothing," she snuffled, staring through the glass into the pelting rain, which had picked up while he was in the can. Then she gave up and turned to look at him, her face sagging, the lower lip trembling. "Oh, Tommy!" she blurted. "They killed them! They—" The rest was inaudible, as she hung her head and sobbed.

Startled and confused, he shot a quick glance over his shoulder. A waitress was taking the order of a couple with a baby three booths back. Two women in nurses's uniforms were pulling on jackets at the cash register. Nothing out of the ordinary. He spun back to face her.

"What the hell are you talking about?" he demanded. "Who got killed?"

She looked up at him, grief and hopelessness etched in her features. "Erol and Cookie. They got rid of them, Tommy. Like they were stray cats." She broke down again.

He stared at her, still lost for a moment, then he understood. He could feel the pent-up fury eddy inside him, like too much swirling water for the tiny drain in a basin, about to flow over.

"You *called* somebody," he hissed through clenching teeth. "Who the *fuck* did you call? What's the matter with you, anyway? I can't even take a dump, you gotta call Boston?"

"Just Janice," she went on, tears cutting channels in the pancake makeup. "The FBI told her they sent them off to the pound. *Months* ago, they said. Before, they wouldn't tell her anything when she called. Now it's too late. They as good as killed them, Tommy. In a pound, I mean. The dogs all get kennel cough and end up dead in a few weeks."

She bawled noisily.

He considered. "You dipshit," he said evenly. "It coulda been a setup. To make you call her." He shook his head. "How much clearer can I make this? There can be no contact. None. Zero. Unless it's through me. You're gonna put me back inside with this shit."

"It wasn't collect, Tommy. I used change I got from the waitress. And I called her at work. What's the difference, anyway? We're leaving here today, you said."

"The *difference* is you leave a trail," he said coldly.

Sniffing, she lifted her hands off the table and looked about her, searching for something. He understood, handing her a paper napkin from the dispenser. She blew her nose.

"I'm sorry, Tommy. But Jesus. I been worried sick about the dogs. Not knowing and all. You know that. Ever since we left like that and they got to the apartment before I could reach Janice. And now—" She waved her left hand at him vacantly, and he filled it with another napkin. She wiped her eyes. "I don't have any family left, Tommy. You know that. Just my dogs. And they're *dead,* Tommy. *Dead.* And you, you don't care. You don't care what I been going through!"

Yet more waterworks. And more napkins. At the moment, she looked every bit of her forty-three years.

" 'Course I do," he said, sighing. "You gotta keep the two things separate, is all. The dogs I understand. I'm sorry about that. But I can't have you leaving bread crumbs. They may be stupid fucks, but you're makin' it easy for them. You understand?"

She nodded slowly, still snuffling. "I'm sorry, Tommy."

She looked vulnerable, a repentant child now, and he felt a tiny erotic charge arc across the distance between them.

"Plus," he added, softer now, "we get settled you can get new ones." He bent down to catch her eye. "Puppies in the house, Mavis," he said, smiling now. "Think about it. Bound to pick you up."

"Really?" she asked, hope dangling before her. "And a house?"

"Promise," he assured her. Knowing he'd regret it.

CHAPTER NINE

A BIG PICTURE GUY

A lot of them thought Larry Coniglio didn't know about the snickering, about the bad-mouthing that went on behind his back. They were wrong. Someday they'd find out just how fucking wrong they were.

It went way back, beginning in the early seventies when they were just getting rolling in Somerville and he was nothing more than Francesco's little brother, the short one with a head for numbers. Larry, they said, tagged along to keep Chicco's knot for him. To maintain the count. Because he could keep the numbers in his head like a Jew. He knew the odds and the splits and the expected takedown in the numbers and dice and barbut games; knew precisely what the cut should be from guys who put ginch on the Avenue in the South End or money on the street out of bars in the Zone. Maybe a guy's light on the weekly envelope and you think he's shorting you. Was a Winter Hill bookie backing bets? Or a stalker in Chelsea skimming the vig? You wanted to know, you went to Larry. He knew how to figure it. He kept the knot, all right, and Chicco (who couldn't do numbers for shit) had always understood the value of his little brother's services. Truth was, they'd have been robbed blind without Larry. And Chicco never would have moved up.

But he did, of course, in 1978. Right after Anthony "Tony Boots" Buscemi got clipped as he stepped out of his Eldorado in an underground garage in North Station. Nobody knew for sure who took Tony Boots off the board, but then nobody gave a shit either. The old man was past it, turned greedy and ungrateful in his old age and losing turf to the Irish, whose quickness to violence stunned even the wiseguys. Guys everywhere welcomed the news that the big man in Providence had given the Office to Chicco, making him underboss in charge of all greater Boston.

Those were the glory days on the North End, the best of times for the brothers. Chicco made peace with the Irish, the feds were still running around busting crap games, and the state cops were either jerk-offs or on the tit. The money kept rolling in. True, no one ever described Francesco and Ilario as partners; Chicco had made another man his *capo*, and Larry's role at the Office was sufficiently junior to supply continuing grist to his detractors. Still, it was Larry who knew the ins and outs of the layoff network and Larry who kept track of the money lent to the Irish at one or two percent and put on the street in Southie and Dorchester at three or four. Chicco had long been carrying his own knot by then—a wad as big as a roll of toilet paper—but some of the guys still belittled Larry as the one who peeled off the crispies when his big brother wanted to flash a little green. The word among the backbiters was he was still just a numbers guy, with no head for serious business and no balls for wet work. A cutman for the combatants. Chicco's towel boy. Not a *man,* you see.

Was it just because he'd never personally cracked a guy? That he never had to do it hands on to get made, like the soldiers? Larry could feel the pressure of his rage build behind his eyes whenever he thought of those sniggering assholes. Made guys, shit. How many of them had lost a finger, had it blown off in an ambush while trying to hustle their brother to cover behind a lunch counter? And hadn't he ordered his share of hits even if he hadn't personally supplied the muscle? They wanted personal? They wanted hands on? Just let him catch one of them yapping, that's all he asked. Christ, he *thirsted* for it. Just a chance to catch the look in their eyes as he put a fucking cap in their ear.

The good times soured when the feds took Chicco down in 1990. Larry had tried to talk to him about wires, about the mikes they were aching to get in his places, but Chicco, who never could understand how the RICO statute worked, had laughed him off. Now he was inside, for good most likely, and in the lean years since then Larry had done what he could to keep things together and to rebuild. The fealty of the rank and file was anything but solid, but at least he had no open challengers, the guys biding their time to see if Larry could hold on and maybe get the franchise with the blessing—so tantalizing, yet so elusive—of the big man in Providence. Given the disarray and widespread incompetence of his own people, Larry had been forced to sub out blocks of heavy work to Tommy, who had consolidated his own grip on the D Street Gang out of South Boston and brought discipline to the Irish—if you could use those two words in the same sentence. Irish discipline? It was like you're talking pan-Slavic solidarity. Not that Larry and Tommy didn't have tension between the two of them. After Chicco's takedown the Irish began moving aggressively into traditional Italian turf, especially with bookmaking and loan-sharking.

Larry bided his time. He prepared. Then he began making his initial moves to reestablish the old Italian hegemony. To put Tommy back in his place—namely, the Irish neighborhoods of South Boston, Dorchester, and the South Shore. When the time was right Larry had his people speak to Tommy's people, had them explain how it was going to be in the rest of Boston. To operate outside their traditional territory, they would have to lay off a piece of the action to Larry. Bookies would pay rent on their telephones and a cut of the take for use of the betting wire. Irish shylocks would deliver a quarter of their gross, right off the top, to the Office.

"The Office?" Phil Hinkle had objected. "I thought it closed down with Francesco."

"We're having a grand reopening," Nick Tramontana replied. "And you're all invited." Larry had rocked with laughter to hear him tell it.

It was working, too, guys hauling in rent and tribute, independents like the Irish squawking but paying. Those who didn't he'd reach out to, sit down with them. No bullshit, either, his message simple: "Go get my fuckin' money." And they did. He was putting it all back together. It was going to be his city, just like it had been Francesco's, and Tony Boots's before him.

Then his people fucked up. Got too regular in their habits, hanging all the time at a steakhouse called Aufiero's down on Causeway Street. The feds got a mike in the place and they jabbered like Chatty Cathy—just like Chicco before them. Hence this latest round of indictments and arrests. Sure, the feds couldn't touch him and they missed top guys like Nick and Peetie (thank God), but they took out most of his middle management. Indicted some of the Irish, too, including Hinkle and even Tommy himself, though Crimmins had disappeared. Picked up his girlfriend and screwed. And Larry? He was left to pick up the pieces again while the feds diddled the grand jury to hound his ass.

Stanley Prout. Danielle Gautreau. Ryan Butters. Their names were sour on the tongue. It was like they were right there in the booth with him, ruining the fine burn of the *grappa* after his noon meal in Donna Lucia's on Prince Street. That cocksucker Prout, making cracks to the press about how, with Larry following Chicco, the Mafia was "wading in the shallow end of the gene pool." Ha-ha. Prout. A little Yankee pissant with a book of rules and his lawyer tricks. He'd never be able to keep stride with Larry. Because Larry saw more. The big picture stuff, that's what Larry did. Shallow? He'd like to show him shallow.

Larry was still luxuriating in the fantasy of a shallow grave in the tall grasses along the Mystic River when Pietro approached with Sheldon Grutman in tow. Larry snapped into focus.

Round-faced and round-eyed with round metal-framed glasses, the lawyer had a damp gray forelock that drooped over his forehead. He wore a navy blue suit and a blue-and-white polka-dot bow tie. *Never trust a Jew in a bow tie,* Tony Boots used to say. *It means he's ashamed of his people and he wants you to think he's something else.*

"Shelley," said Larry, gesturing to the other side of the booth, "you having a little brandy? The *grappa* here is real good."

"No thanks," said Grutman as he took a seat. Then he paused, cocked his head to one side, and smiled. "Wait a minute. Why not? Maybe I will. Good news you should celebrate, even in the middle of the day."

Larry caught his son's eyes and, with a dip of the head, dispatched him to fetch the waiter. Then he turned and looked into the beaming face of his lawyer.

"You say you got good news?"

"I do indeed," said Grutman, proudly. "And I think you're going to be pleased."

He waited for a response from his client, but Larry only watched him impassively.

"It's about Arthur," Grutman continued. "The judge has stayed his order pending appeal." Grutman's smile broadened. "Arthur's being released, Larry."

Larry's eyes took on a feral intensity as he focused hard on his lawyer's words.

"Released?"

"Yes. I moved for a stay of the order finding Arthur in contempt. And Judge Biddle granted it. Pending appeal."

"Pending appeal?" Larry frowned, trying to think this through. "He gets out, but you lose the appeal and he's back in the shit. Right?"

"I suppose. Sure." Grutman tasted the *grappa* and grimaced. "Whoa! Strong stuff!" He held the little glass out at arm's length and examined it respectfully. He blinked rapidly a few times before continuing. "But we're talking time here, Larry. It could take several months, maybe a year or more, to get a decision out of the court of appeals. A lot can happen to an investigation in a year. A *lot.* Meanwhile Arthur's off the hook. And so are you."

Grutman glowed with a sense of accomplishment.

"It's rare to win one of these, on a contempt," the lawyer went on. "A motion to stay, I mean. Judges usually leave the guy in jail—unless he's a reporter or something. But you know?" he added with an air of muted self-satisfaction. "I think I got to him a little with my point about self-incrimination. It was something of a novel argument. Anyway, it feels good, Larry. Cheers!"

He raised his glass and drank. Larry looked over at Nick, who had materialized to stand beside the booth on Grutman's side. Grutman followed his gaze, then swung back toward Larry with a puzzled look on his face. Less certain now.

"He's back on the street already?" Larry asked. "After only, what? Six days inside?"

Grutman set his glass down and leaned forward a little. "Larry," he said, earnestness in his voice, "this means Arthur poses no threat to you now. At least, until such time as the court of appeals rules. He can't hurt you."

"Yeah?" Larry said. Thinking, *He's scared. He's scared I might do the guy and he'll get his clean Jew fingers dirty.* Larry enjoyed watching him sweat a little. Because Shelley was just like Prout. He couldn't see the big picture. "But how do I know he didn't already talk, when he was inside?"

Grutman shook his head. "Couldn't happen, Larry. They couldn't have taken him to the grand jury without telling me. *I'd* know."

Larry puckered his lips in thought, his eyes flicking over to meet Nick's.

"That just means he didn't testify, right? It don't mean he didn't talk to them. Give 'em information, like."

Grutman lifted both palms and his shoulders in wonderment. "*What* information, Larry? He's only useful to them as a witness, not as an informant. Think about it. What kind of information could Arthur give them about your business? He had none, right? All he could tell them was he took money on the shark. That's of zero investigative value. No, Larry. It's only Arthur's *testimony* you have to worry about. And there can't be any testimony until the court of appeals acts."

Larry watched carefully as his lawyer argued for Artie's life. Larry looked for a tell, any indication there was something else going on. But he could detect nothing. He looked up at Nick again.

Nick shrugged, raising his eyebrows slightly. "I gotta go with Shelley here, Larry," he said. "Artie knows shit about business. He's just a witness."

Larry looked back and forth at the two of them. Squinting. Thinking. Pietro glided into place beside his left shoulder and stooped over him. "Shaun Crowe is here," he whispered into his father's ear. "From Phil, he says. You want him?"

Larry looked up at him, confused. "He's here? Now?"

"Yeah," Pietro explained. "He showed up at the club and said he needed to see you. I had 'em send him over here. Wasn't that okay?"

Larry frowned, then nodded. He looked over at his unhappy lawyer once again and rubbed the pad of his index finger around the rim of his glass. "You're right, Shelley," he said, to put him out of his misery. "He's just a witness. And one hell of a cook. You ever eat at his place there, in the South End? La Vucciria, it's called. Real Sicilian food, the genuine article. I'm tellin' you, Shelley, you'll love it. We'll go there sometime, you and me, and you'll see for yourself what I'm talkin' about. Right, Nick? Am I right or what?"

"You're right, Larry."

Grutman shoved his chair back and got to his feet. "I'm sure you are," he said, pulling a money clip from his pocket. "I look forward to it."

Larry raised both hands and shook his head. "No, no, Shelley. You can't spend your money here. You just keep up the good work."

Grutman left, with Pietro following him. Nick settled into the lawyer's place across from Larry and lit a cigarette.

"You did the right thing there, Larry," Nick said as he expelled smoke toward the ceiling.

"Did I?" Larry twisted his mouth into a smile. "What'd I do?"

"Hey, Larry! Gimme four, big guy!"

The booming voice belonged to Shaun Crowe, a big, black-haired Irishman with a massive jaw that always needed shaving. He loomed over Larry with his right hand raised for a high five. Larry, who resented Crowe's stale joke at the expense of his missing middle finger, just glared at him, letting him stand there a minute with his hand in the air like some jerk about to take an oath. Then Larry nodded in the direction of the seat next to Nick.

"Great to see you, Larry," said Crowe as he sat down. He looked around the room, lightly slapping his hands one at a time on the tabletop. *Ba-bap.* "Nice place here. Food good?"

"You stay away from the fish, yeah."

"I never eat fish 'less I'm in South Boston," said Crowe. "You ever try the Fish Pier?"

"The dock? You mean get it off the boats?"

"No, no. It's a little fish 'n' chip place. Right on East Broadway. Fish Pier, they call it. Best fish in town. Since Kelly's Clam Shack closed, anyway. You wanna try it."

Larry tipped his head to give the point.

Crowe laid his forearms on the table and leaned forward. Business now.

"Listen, Larry. I got this request from Hink. A personal favor he wants to ask you. Not business, just a favor for a friend."

Larry placed one hand over his other on the table before him, feeling every inch the don of his fantasies. He vouchsafed an indulgent smile to the supplicant in front of him and waited.

"Hink has this friend, see," said Crowe, leaning closer still. "Actually, he's a friend of Tommy's, too. A *good* friend. So anyway, this friend needs some assistance and Hink, well"—Crowe smiled and raised his hands in a gesture of helplessness—"he's a bit *preoccupied* at the moment. You can understand. And Tommy's not exactly in a position to help either, you know what I'm saying?"

Larry eyed him, nodding gravely at the misfortune that had befallen their mutual friends.

"I believe you know the guy," Crowe continued. "You eat at his place a lot, they tell me. Artie Patch. You know him, right?"

Larry's eyes widened. He nodded. *Twice in one day?*

"A Southie guy. Old friend. Goes *way* back. Well, it seems Artie's got a hair across about somebody leaning on him. Some fallout over business shit, I suppose. Anyway, he comes to us for help. Now, of course, we'll help. But Artie says the fella threatening him is Italian. A guy, he thinks. Showed up at his place of business and scared the shit out of him. Now Hink, he says, Whoa, I don't wanna go messin' in somebody else's business if it's Italian. Not 'less I clear it with Larry. 'Cause suppose Artie's right. Suppose it *is* a guy, that's got a hard-on for Artie. Then we don't mess with it without the okay from Larry. You know what I'm saying here?"

Crowe paused for a response from Larry, whose mind was whirling. A pinwheel in a storm.

"You wanna know if one of our guys is muscling Artie?"

"Hink wants to know if there's some reason he shouldn't look after an old friend, is all. A very *good* friend. Of his and Tommy's."

"This ain't business?"

"No, no," Crowe shook his head. "It's completely personal. This'd be a favor, a *big* favor to Hink. And Tommy."

A silence fell over the two men while Larry figured.

"You understand they been hauling Artie's ass before the grand jury?" Larry asked at last.

"Yeah, I hear that." Crowe shook his head in dismay at the way of the world. "You'd think they'd leave the civilians out of it, wouldn't you?"

"They don't understand *shit,*" Larry said bitterly. "They been tryin' to pump him for shit on . . . on one of the guys, but I keep hearing Artie's a stand-up guy. That what you hear?"

"That's what I hear," Crowe said, nodding gravely. "A stand-up guy."

"You vouch for him?"

Crowe looked hard into his eyes. "Better than that, Larry. I mean, I could, but that ain't what I'm here to do. I'm here to tell you *Hink* vouches for him. And Tommy, too. Artie's a stand-up guy."

Larry smiled. "How *is* Tommy, Shaun?"

Crowe smiled back. "In the wind, Larry. In the wind."

Larry sat back and, after catching Nick's eye briefly, bowed his head slightly. "You tell Phil for me. Tell him he don't need no permission to protect Artie. And he don't need to do it neither. 'Cause

I'm the one's gonna see nobody fucks with him. You with me here? Artie's a friend of mine, too, and with Phil and Tommy vouching for him, he's solid with me. A hunnert percent. *Nobody's* gonna lean on him. Okay? That good enough for you?"

Crowe's smile spread into a grin as his hands slapped the tabletop again. *Ba-bap.* "That's terrific, Larry. It'll take a load off Hink's mind, I can tell you that."

"Phil's got enough to worry about, he shouldn't have to worry about this," said Larry, resting one hand on top of the other again. "Tell him my heart is with him in his time of need."

The three men—Larry, Nick, and Pietro—had more *grappa* and coffee after Shaun Crowe left them. They chewed it over, Larry's decision, and the consensus was that he was right.

"I always said he'd never talk," Nick reminded them through a scrim of smoke. "He was just too scared. This'll be all right."

"It's not that," Larry said, shaking his head. "Anybody gets too scared you can't trust them. No, it's these other two things together. Shelley bein' right that Artie's only good to them as a witness, and Phil wanting him left alone. We don't need no fuckin' trouble with the Irish right now, for Chrissake, so what the fuck? Why not give 'em what they want, 'specially with Artie out of jail and he ain't in a position to hurt us? You get the word to Spunt."

"The only thing I can't figure," interjected Pietro, "is why do they give a shit? I mean, what's Artie to Phil and Tommy? Why are they vouching for him?"

Tramontana pulled a fleck of tobacco off his lip and examined it. "Kid's got a point, Larry. When Artie needed green he went to you, not the homeboys. Why the sudden interest?"

"I think," said Larry, the big picture looming again, "it prolly *is* a personal thing with them. And maybe Artie come to me for the money 'cause he didn't want his own people to know he was in the hole. Some Irish honor crap, I don't know. 'Sides, he got to know me, a regular customer and all."

It gave him a little hum of satisfaction when he thought about it that way. That when Artie needed help, he had turned to Larry. Not to Tommy or Phil, the hometown boys. To Larry. Who had outmaneuvered even Tommy.

"You know," he said, his tone meditative, "if it was Tommy in the can and Hinkle who screwed, I mighta figured it the other way. Tommy you gotta be careful with. The only place you'd wanna turn your back on that icy fucker is at Mass. But Phil? Phil's nice people, like you say, Nick. Him you can trust. Am I right?"

"You know how to read 'em, Larry," Tramontana agreed.

"You're fuckin' right there, Nick. I tell you, I got a fifth sense about these things. Phil's nice people. But Tommy? Use him for heavy work, sure, but watch out."

Grinning now, Larry directed his attention to Pietro. "So you call Artie tomorrow and tell him to hold us a table for Friday night. Tell him I got a powerful hunger for some *involtini di pesce spada.* You join us for a little swordfish, Nick?"

Tramontana made his RSVP with a nod.

"Then tell him there'll be three of us. But remember, Nick. Make sure we stay on top of Shelley and this appeal thing. He has to go back inside, we gotta rethink our position here. Am I right or what?"

Nick Tramontana assured him that he was.

CHAPTER TEN

JUNIOR G-MAN

When the phone call came, Randy Zullo was midway into his post-jogging routine. Let his suitemates stuff themselves at lunch. He preferred to put the noon hour to good use—when the weather was halfway decent, anyway—by running down the Embankment Road to the Esplanade and along the Charles River. There he would put in six or seven hard miles before winding down with stretching exercises in his office. He was leaning with both hands against the closed door, one foot in front of the other, and savoring the burning pressure on the muscle of his left calf, when the telephone cheeped at him like a day-old pullet.

He finished his count, pulled a clean towel off the hook on the back of the door, and wiped his face. Whipping the towel over his neck like a scarf, he tugged on it with both hands as he strode to his desk and picked up the receiver. He perched with one haunch on the edge of his desk. The indicator light on the set, he noticed, belonged to his direct line. The private one.

"Hello," he answered.

"Hey, tough guy," said a familiar voice. "It's your favorite voice from the Fourth Estate."

Zullo smiled in recognition. "The Fourth?" he asked. "Isn't that the bankrupt estate? According to public opinion polls, anyway."

"Hey, hey. Do I bad-mouth *your* profession?"

Zullo barked a laugh. "All the time, Eddie. What are you talking about?"

"Oh, in *print*, sure," said Eddie Felch, sighing theatrically. "You can't hold that against me. It's just business. But not to your face, Randy. Never. Never such perfidy. So how's it going? Spring any career pederasts from Bridgewater this week?"

"Ah, Eddie. You have no sense of perspective. There are things in this life that bring home to you what's *really* important. Life-changing experiences, you know? Like this morning. There I am, driving up Route 16 in that god-awful damp rain, feeling sorry for myself. Stress at work. Stress at home. And I pass a cemetery. I see gravediggers lowering a casket in the rain. All of a sudden I'm flooded with gratitude, Eddie. I see things in perspective. Thankful that I can sit indoors and make my living on the phone."

Eddie laughed as Zullo sidled his way around the desk, lifting the phone cord to clear the family photographs propped up on the surface, and made his way to his chair. Once he had settled in, the two friends chatted amiably for several minutes, about acquaintances, politics, boxing. But when the reporter finally got around to business, Zullo was hardly shocked. Eddie Felch did not call in the middle of the day to make small talk.

"Phil Hinkle?" Zullo repeated, feigning surprise. "The man is wrongly incarcerated, on trumped-up charges. Quote me on that, will you, Eddie?"

"Fuck Hinkle," said Felch.

"No, thank you." he said brightly.

"It wasn't an invitation, Randy. Jesus, control yourself. And it's not Hinkle I wanna talk about. It's his partner. I refer, of course, to the missing desperado."

"Tommy's in the wind, Eddie. So what can I possibly tell you about him? Besides," he added with a grin, "I hear he took two in the hat."

"And *I* hear he was government issue. An asset. Can you shed any light on that?"

Zullo felt his muscles tense up, and he focused his attention sharply on his interlocutor's questions. "Come on, Eddie," he said, forcing a chuckle. "The *Herald* floated that corpse a couple years ago. There was nothing to it then and there's nothing to it now. What is this, a slow week? You're looking for filler?"

"No, it's just that the story won't die."

"That," Zullo suggested, "is because it's what you guys call a 'good story.' So you *want* to believe it. Not because it's got legs."

"Well," Felch persisted, "I got a new source—a damn good one, too. Not some get-a-lifer. Somebody who overheard him talking to the FBI the day before he decamped. I even got the name of his handler."

"Yeah?" Zullo prompted, with as much nonchalance as he could muster. "And who's that?"

"Sorry. Can't say. Confidential sources, you know. So I figure it's a story worth working for a while."

Zullo laughed at him. "Eddie, you're so full of shit. You got nothing, I can tell. Come on, what do you want from me?"

There was a pause on the line. Gravely now, Felch said, "I want a heads-up, Randy. Pal to pal. This story is eating at me like some parasitic wasp. I know Hinkle's your client, and you can't go shooting your mouth off, even on background. This I understand. So I'm not asking you to tell me anything he told you. I just want you, bein' an old friend and all, to tell me, based on what you might know but can't say, am I sticking my dick in the wrong barrel here? That's all. Save me from a lot of pointless work. Or tell me to keep digging."

It was Zullo's turn to pause. He saw before him Hinkle's expression in the lockup some six months ago, his bum eye twitching more wildly than ever as he listened to his lawyer explain that this was for real. That his indictment and arrest were no charade staged to provide him cover with the boys. The government planned to press forward with charges of conspiracy to murder, extortion, bookmaking, and racketeering. If the surveillance tapes came in, the charges would be almost indefensible, and would likely net him a three-digit sentence. Hinkle had raged at the treachery of the FBI and his own lawyer, those huge fingers clutching and wrenching with all his considerable might at the shuddering steel mesh, the lawyer fearing for one horrifying moment he might actually rip away the barrier between them, until the guards burst in and hauled him away. Perfidy? Eddie didn't know the *meaning* of the word.

Felch brought him back. "Randy," he said softly, "I'm taking comfort in your silence. Tell me I'm not out of my gourd on this one."

Making up his mind now, the lawyer chose his words carefully. "Let me put it this way. I know nothing from any informed source that would suggest you're on the wrong track."

Felch was slow to respond. "Do you have any reason to suggest I'm on the *right* track?"

Zullo shook his head. "Don't overstay your welcome, Eddie. A negative is as much as I can give you and still sleep nights. Okay?"

"Then again," Felch mused, ignoring his friend's reticence, "Tommy could be a government agent without Hinkle knowing it. In fact, that's probably more likely. Or Hinkle might know it. And he might even tell you what he knows—or suspects. Would you say he qualifies as an 'informed source,' Randy?"

Zullo was careful again. "I'd say Mr. Hinkle's a guy who, if he told me something about Tommy, I'd sit up and listen."

"So," Felch reasoned out loud, "either Tommy *is* a junior G-man or Hinkle isn't sure he's not. Otherwise, you'd tell me to forget it. Am I right?"

Zullo smiled. "I can't add to what I've already said."

"So I should continue to dig?"

"Oh, dig, Eddie," Zullo said, laughing. "Dig."

"Yowzah, boss. Ah'll git raht on it." He dropped the clowning. "I owe you one, fella. And hey? If you should hear of somebody who decides to take anything public—assuming there *is* anything to take public—tell them to talk to me first. Okay?"

"It's a promise, Eddie."

And he was gone.

Zullo examined the state of his feelings over his exchange with the reporter. Disturbed, yes, because he knew he had skated right up to, perhaps even slid over, the line marking off the outer boundary of his client's confidences. But there was more to it than that. Something in Eddie's choice of words had intrigued him. Recasting the situation in a possibly productive manner, like the crack of a door admitting a tiny sliver of light into the gloom: Yes, it was in the words.

Junior G-man. Government agent.

Agent?

Why not? What had they done for Hink lately?

CHAPTER ELEVEN

THE WHALE

(From the *Boston Globe,* July 3, 1998)

U.S. Admits Crimmins, Hinkle Were Informants

By Eddie Felch
Globe Staff

Facing threat of contempt from an angry federal judge, prosecutors today acknowledged that two Boston men under indictment for their alleged top leadership role in organized crime had worked as confidential informants for the FBI for more than two decades.

The government's astonishing admission confirmed many of the allegations made by one of the defendants, Philbert J. Hinkle, in a sworn affidavit filed with the federal court two weeks ago. Hinkle and the other informant, Thomas Crimmins, are two of the defendants indicted last year on federal charges ranging from racketeering and gambling to extortion and murder. Crimmins, who is the brother of Governor Jackie Crimmins, has been a fugitive since the indictments were issued.

Assistant United States Attorney Stanley Prout, who heads the New England Organized Crime Strike Force, made the announcement following a ruling by Judge Henry E. Biddle. Biddle had ordered Prout to appear personally before the court and respond to the allegations in Hinkle's affidavit.

Hinkle and Crimmins, Prout told a packed and stunned courtroom, had "provided periodic and sometimes valuable information regarding the operations of certain criminal organizations" for over 20 years. In addition to other information, Prout told the court, the two men had given "material assistance" to FBI efforts to place hidden microphones at the business headquarters of convicted Mafia kingpin Francesco "Chicco" Coniglio. The tape recordings made there constituted key evidence at Coniglio's trial six years ago, when he was convicted of multiple racketeering charges. Coniglio is now serving an 85-year sentence in a federal penitentiary.

Prout insisted, however, that the FBI's relationship with Hinkle and Crimmins had been terminated more than two years before they were indicted. Prout also vehemently denied Hinkle's claim that the two men were promised immunity from prosecution in exchange for their cooperation.

In his affidavit, Hinkle claimed that his FBI handler, Special Agent Martin Flukes, and other unnamed federal officials had told him and Crimmins they could continue their illegal operations as long as they didn't "clip anyone." Prout scoffed at the claim, telling reporters after the hearing that the FBI "is not in the business of giving anyone carte blanche to commit felonies."

Hinkle's lawyer, Randall Zullo, disagreed. "These guys aren't stupid," Zullo said. "Immunity was the price they extracted from the government before they agreed to cooperate. Now the government has reneged on its promise."

Zullo also denied that the government had ever taken steps to end its relationship with the two men. "Six weeks before he was arrested," Zullo told reporters, "Phil and Tommy had dinner at [Agent] Flukes' house in Wellesley, and the three men drank a toast to their continued collaboration. If anyone ended this thing, nobody told my client."

At a pretrial hearing last week Zullo asked the court to dismiss the indictment against his client on the grounds that Hinkle had been promised immunity by the government. "The only 'criminal' enterprise my client was ever a part of was one run by the government," Zullo argued to the court. "He was granted immunity and then entrapped."

Hinkle and the other defendants, alleged Mafia lieutenants Joseph Cacchiotti, Ettore Coli, and Anthony LoPrete, have also asked the court to rule that tapes of intercepted conversations among the defendants and others be excluded from evidence at trial because Hinkle's and Crimmins' status as informants was not disclosed when the government applied for the warrants authorizing the electronic surveillance. Crimmins, according to court documents, was actually present during some of the taped conversations, most of which were overheard at Aufiero's, a popular Italian restaurant on Causeway Street.

Under federal law and Justice Department guidelines, electronic eavesdropping—considered the most intrusive of investigative techniques—may be authorized only if the government convinces a judge that other methods won't work. One less intrusive alternative, according to Suffolk University Law Professor Clive G. Stickney, is the use of informants.

"At the very least," Stickney explained, "the informants' existence should have been disclosed when the government applied for the warrants. Even without revealing their identity, the government probably could have made a convincing case that the use of informants who are unwilling to testify is a much less effective way to gather evidence than planting a bug."

But failure even to mention that informants existed, Stickney suggested, "gives the defense a strong argument that the tapes were made illegally."

That failure touched a raw nerve here, since the judge who signed the challenged warrants, Judge Biddle, has also been assigned to conduct the trial.

Clearly angered by the government's failure to make the disclosure before the warrants were approved, Judge Biddle announced that he will permit defense lawyers to examine some of the government's investigative files so that they can determine the nature of the informants' dealings with the government and the extent to which higher officials knew about it.

Citing long-standing government policy, prosecutors had previously refused either to confirm or deny whether Hinkle and Crimmins were informants. Visibly angered, the judge ordered the head of the Strike Force to appear and answer his questions or face jail for contempt of court.

After several days of open confrontation and behind-the-scenes negotiations involving officials from the Attorney General's Office in Washington as well as Prout's superior, United States Attorney C. Morton Atwater, the government decided to forgo a threatened appeal of Biddle's ruling and instead to comply with the order. Prout's extraordinary admission came this morning.

In a related development, another lawyer said today that he will seek to overturn the conviction of Francesco Coniglio, the government's marquee prosecution in its war against organized crime in Boston. Coniglio's lawyer, Sheldon Grutman, announced that he will file a motion to set aside his client's conviction for the same reason urged by the defendants in the present case—that tape recordings used to convict him were illegally obtained because the government had failed to reveal the participation of the informants.

The U.S. Attorney's Office in Boston has been aswirl in controversy ever since Hinkle first made his revelation two weeks ago. The controversy has centered not on the long-standing practice of using criminals as informants, but on permitting those alleged to be the leaders of one of Boston's most powerful crime organizations, the D Street

Gang, to do business virtually free of government interference.

"Tommy Crimmins wasn't some lowlife minnow they used for bait," remarked one federal prosecutor who asked not to be identified. "He was the whale. Who uses the whale to catch the small fry?"

But Buck Quarles, a former FBI agent and now head of an Atlanta-based private security firm, defended the government's actions. "The target was always the Italian mob, because the Mafia is the only outfit organized on a national scale. The Italians were taken out almost completely in Boston, leaving only a disorganized band of leftover goons to run the show. If these guys gave them the Mafia, then the deal was worth it."

Attorney Wallace Segal disputed this. A former state prosecutor now in private practice, Segal said he spent much of his public career trying to make a case against the elusive Crimmins. According to Segal, whatever usefulness Crimmins and Hinkle had for the government ended with Coniglio's arrest eight years ago. "That put the Irish gang on top and without question made Tommy Crimmins the preeminent gangster in the city of Boston."

Segal believes Crimmins attained his position by using the FBI to take out his competition, first by going after Coniglio and later by going after the Mafia men who sought to take his place. "Look what happened when the wiseguys tried to regroup and reclaim their old turf," Segal pointed out. "Tommy sold them out again, triggering this latest round of indictments. He was getting far more from the government than they were getting from him."

"Don't think for a minute," Segal added, "that the FBI was running Tommy Crimmins. He was running the FBI."

The U.S. Attorney's Office and the Justice Department may never do business the same again, according to an official in the Boston office who spoke on condition of anonymity. Atwater, the U.S. Attorney, is reported to be so furious he's considering dismantling the Strike Force, and the Justice Department has ordered the Office of Professional Responsibility, its internal investigations unit, to look into possible misconduct at the FBI's Boston field office.

"Everyone's deeply embarrassed by this mess," the source told the *Globe*. "I suppose it's a risk you run. Like the old saying—if you're going to dine with the devil, you better bring a long spoon. Well, somebody didn't."

Segal seemed to take ironic satisfaction in the developments. "Just think," he mused. "All those years Tommy seemed magically untouchable. And we thought it was his brother's clout. No wonder the feds haven't managed to catch him since he went on the lam. Just how hard do you think they're looking?"

CHAPTER TWELVE

THE RAINSTORM

"P*hil*bert?" Larry Coniglio read out loud without looking up from Eddie Felch's news story. "You mean like the nut?"

From his perch beside him in the backseat of the big Chrysler, Nick Tramontana chuckled softly. "Maybe his mother couldn't decide between Phillip and Bertram. Maybe she split the difference."

Larry looked over at his companion and frowned. "What the fuck you talkin' about?"

"I'm talkin' about Philbert J. Hinkle. Just like you." Tramontana turned his gaze to the front of the car, catching Pietro's eye as he did. Riding shotgun, Pietro had screwed his head around to look into the backseat. The driver was a Zip, a recent arrival from Sicily, and Larry had taken a shine to him. He was a short, swarthy man in a tweed cap who had to crane his neck to see over the wheel. Its tires whispering through the lashing rain, the Chrysler held the rail position in the southbound lanes of the Tobin Bridge.

"Madonna with crabs," muttered Larry with a sigh, returning to his paper.

"Thing I don't get," Pietro piped up, "is how come Phil got arrested. If he and Tommy got a heads-up on the indictments, like he says."

Tramontana chuckled again. "He said he thought he had more time. To get things in order, he says. It was in the paper he signed."

" 'Leftover goon!' " Larry lowered the paper to his lap savagely, his falling arms crumpling the newspaper. "Asshole calls me that?" He slapped at the newspaper with the back of his hand "Who is this asswipe, anyway?"

Grim-faced, Larry turned to his right and stared out the window at the freight cars hunching in the rain below them along the open flats at the mouth of the Mystic River. The four men rode in silence for several minutes before Larry spoke again.

"Cocksuckers. We used to sit around and laugh at the shit they were putting out. Rumors and shit. It was a joke, Tommy bein' a snitch. You know what I'm sayin' here?"

"Looks like it was," Tramontana suggested. "To *him.*"

"Well, it ain't to Chicco, I can tell you that. Cocksuckers sold him out. Both of 'em. One you could see, almost. But *both* of 'em? No way, you'da thought." Larry shook his head gravely. "Never saw it coming."

Larry resumed his gloomy vigil at the side window. Then he snapped his head sharply back to face Tramontana.

"Was it *just* two of them?" he asked with more animation. "You think Crowe was in on it, too?"

Tramontana considered this briefly, his eyes narrowing to slits. "Nah," he said at last. "Tommy and Phil gave up their own people, too. Not just ours. That's what he says in the paper he filed. So they wouldn't spread it down through the ranks."

Larry shook his head again. "We gotta talk to Chicco."

Three miles away, in the same steady rain, Arthur Patch wheeled his Dodge Caravan onto Tremont Street in the South End. He was hauling the morning's fresh fish and produce. He'd managed to score some remarkably good-looking tuna steaks—sushi-quality, in fact—and he'd finally found a California supplier who could furnish wild fennel on a regular basis. But like Larry the Rabbit, Arthur let his thoughts linger over Eddie Felch's story. And Stanley Prout's humiliation before Judge Biddle.

Couldn't have happened to a nicer guy, he told himself. Yet the whole business made him too uneasy to bask for long in that bit of good news. What, he wanted to know, did all this mean for the arrangement he had made with the prosecutors?

He turned south on Upton Street, and then made the awkward entrance into the narrow alley behind the restaurant. The frost-heaved asphalt looked greasy from the rain, and the overflowing Dumpster told him he'd have to get on the phone to his councilman again. He brought the van to a stop next to the yellow kitchen doors and shut off the engine. He laid his arms across the steering wheel and sat motionless. The rain, its trajectory no longer interrupted by the van's wipers, streamed down the windshield like children out a schoolhouse door.

He thought.

They had struck an uneasy truce with Stanley Prout, he and Morrissey, the lawyer. The judge had released him while Shelley Grutman's appeal from the contempt order wended its torturous way up to the court of appeals—a journey, Morrissey had assured him, Prout would do his best to prolong. And Grutman—well, Grutman had puffed up like a peacock out on the town, caught up in the delusion that his own magnificent lawyering had redeemed Arthur from federal clutches. Which was fine with Arthur; let him pass that along to Larry. Let them believe—*please* let them believe—that Arthur's deliverance stemmed from their own efforts. And not from Stanley Prout's machinations.

Despite the information Arthur had pretended to offer them, Prout's forbearance was clearly understood by both sides as a commodity purchased with the currency of Arthur's promised silence: he would tell no one else what he had told them about Tommy and Flukes, and they would leave him alone. Yet this currency had devalued precipitously over the past couple weeks, what with Hinkle revealing far more than Arthur had ever dreamed was going on. And if Arthur's silence had been rendered worthless, would Prout and Dani land on him again with subpoenas and court orders? To make him testify against Larry?

Or was it so worthless? Hinkle was now claiming he was tipped off about the indictments, as Arthur had told them, but the government strenuously denied that. That meant, did it not, that Arthur's story of Tommy's phone call from the County Cork still retained the power to embarrass Prout and his people? That must give it *some* value?

And what about Larry? The FBI guy—what was his name?—had assured him that Larry would leave him alone, but how could he say that with any certainty? Butters, that was it. Ryan Butters. The smug bastard had refused to explain how they had convinced Larry to back off. A real box of chocolates, that one. Arthur did not like having to place his faith—and his ass—in the hands of a dumb ox like Ryan Butters.

And yet there was Larry, showing up all smiles and spouting hearty congratulations at the restaurant the night after Arthur's release. Fell on his food like always. Downed the swordfish with customary gusto and brayed over the *pasta con le sarde,* grunting his vociferous approval of the unsalted *pecorino* flown in from Palermo. His lips glistening, Larry had even promised to stop the clock on the vig—at least, he pointed out, " 'til this legal crap gets straightened out." And all the while Nick Tramontana, looking creepily amused as always, just sat there watching the two of them in silence as he picked at his food in slow motion.

Not what you would call a stable situation. A definite improvement over federal detention in Rhode Island, he had to admit. But, no, not a stable situation.

Jimmy Morrissey tore another sheet off the legal pad on his desk. He crumpled it into a ball and tossed it back over his shoulder, where it rolled to join a half dozen other rejected drafts on the office floor.

Coming up with the right wording was a pain in the ass.

It wasn't so easy, this targeted direct-mail business. Oh, it was fine if you were one of those factory ships—the big television advertisers with their publicity people and copywriters and focus groups. They sucked in the clients with ads full of smarmy sincerity and intimations of bogus expertise, then referred them out for a cut of the fee to meatball lawyers lower down the food chain. Who in turn would butcher the file. What was the expression? *You hold 'em, I'll skin 'em.* That was it, all right. And in the process they were ripping off the lion's share of the lower-end personal-injury practice, the life blood of little guys like him. Was it any wonder he was hurting for paying clients?

So, as a client-development opportunity, direct-mail advertising held considerable attraction for Morrissey. And some promise, thanks to the unwitting complicity of the city's blue-nosed mayor. But the form of the letter required a deft touch and, as he would be the first to admit, the written word was not Jimmy Morrissey's forte.

He had tried something like it before, with modest success. Culling the names of automobile-accident victims from police reports in neighborhood newspapers, he had sent out tasteful letters extending his heartfelt sympathy and crying his wares like a fishwife. He'd even included a helpful list of do's and don'ts for dealing with insurance adjusters—unscrupulous vultures, the pack of them, who preyed on the vulnerability of recent accident vicims. Which was why they needed a lawyer.

He had had similar success targeting people arrested for driving under the influence. Put together an especially sweet deal out of the Somerville District Court, where a cooperative clerk magistrate found ways, while granting bail on weekends, to put in a good word and pave the way for Morrissey's own self-recommendation. But the clerk had taken early retirement last year—in the midst of some niggling brouhaha over petty-cash receipts—and without someone who could drop his name to the clients before they got lawyers on their own, business from his driving-under mailings had dwindled to next to nothing.

But this new mayor? Well, she presented a new vista of opportunities. Elected in part on her promise to eradicate pornography, strip clubs, and prostitution from city life, she had launched an aggressive campaign to drive the hookers off the streets. Nothing new there, really, except that she did not target the working girls themselves or even the pimps. Operation Squeeze went after the customers.

Arresting the johns and bullying the newspapers into publishing their names had a certain feminist appeal that went down well in the wealthy wards, while the terror of actually getting arrested and having one's neighbors read all about it in the *Brookline Tab* or whatever dampened consumer confidence among the white hunters on Massachusetts Avenue in the South End and the businessmen out slumming in the Combat Zone.

Not entirely, fortunately. By forgiving an old (and uncollectable) legal bill owed by a compositor at the *Herald*, Jimmy was getting the list of arrestees faster than the newspapers could publish them.

Which brought him to this, his agonized undertaking to craft a letter of solicitation. He needed to strike just the right tone of delicacy, manly comradeship, and the promise of aggressive but discreet advocacy by James A. Morrissey, Esq. It wasn't easy.

Especially given everything else that was weighing on his mind.

Like the shortfall in his client accounts. Or clients calling up every now and then to ask what all this was about, him being publicly reprimanded by the supreme court. But what his thoughts really sought out, unbidden, like a tongue returning to the socket of a missing tooth, was the subject of Hinkle's affidavit and Prout's astonishing revelation.

He had thought he'd tied up that bit of business quite nicely with the deal they'd struck for Artie. What did these latest events augur for the future? Would Prout see it as less of a good deal now that Hinkle had given away the store? Maybe, if Prout reneged and started harassing Artie again, Morrissey would get a little more of that well-paid federal work to help cover his monthly nut.

Nah. Chagrined, he realized that was pretty unlikely. Prout and his entourage would be tied up in knots for months trying to deal with the aftermath of Hinkle's sudden attack of logorrhea. Judge Biddle and the boys from Justice—maybe even Janet Reno herself—would see to that. Prout must be running around with his hair on fire.

The thought made him smile.

He had to hand it to Eddie Felch, though. The wily little bastard had triggered all this. Morrissey had told him about Flukes, and within a week—without burning Morrissey as the source of his information—Eddie pops up as the guy to break the story that Hinkle is going public. Eddie had explained how his off-the-record conversation with Randy Zullo, Hinkle's lawyer, had planted the seed for Hinkle's decision to go public about his dealings with the FBI. And once Hinkle made his decision, well, it was only natural to give the scoop to Eddie.

And Morrissey? Should he feel guilty? For exposing Artie to a vindictive Prout who now had little to fear from Artie's own veiled threats to go public? Morrissey's quailing conscience raised a brief, monitory finger before it was bullied into submission.

Nah. See above. Prout was way past worrying about Artie. Guy had to be fighting to keep his job.

Jimmy Morrissey, on the other hand, was not past worrying about his cash position. This nerve-wracking business of juggling funds from one account to another to cover obligations to his clients as they came due—well, it was taking its toll. He knew a reckoning was looming, and he wasn't ready for it.

He needed money.

With a sigh, he returned to drafting his Dear John letter. . . .

"It's a tribal thing," the governor said, standing with his back to his interlocutor as he held the curtain aside to stare out the window. Rain streamed down the glass like rippling sheets of cellophane. Eddie Felch sat in the governor's cavernous office, awed by its colossal size and the majesty of its appointments. Jackie Crimmins had left him sitting before his modest partner's desk (was it Curley's? Coolidge's?) to walk to the windows and peek out at the little park. Bowdoin Street had been turned into a shallow sluice by the heavy rain.

But Eddie wasn't looking at the rain. This was his first visit to the governor's private sanctum, and his eyes feasted on the almost laughable grandiloquence of the place. The dimensions alone were spectacular—it was forty by forty-five, Jackie told him, with twenty-foot ceilings—and its marble floor was softened by a single vast carpet specially manufactured in Manchester, England. The three interior walls were wainscoted to a height of ten feet in Honduran mahogany, toothbrushed back to its original, surprisingly light sheen during the recent restoration. Above the wainscoting ran a circuit of now lacquered portraits of previous occupants. Two full-length couches and a coffee table were positioned before an unlighted fireplace, carved of the same mahogany, that Jackie seemed to avoid—because, Eddie suspected, a mantel seven feet high showed his diminutive stature to disadvantage. A gigantic conference table ran along the wall of floor-to-ceiling windows, which were draped by tasseled tapestries held open just wide enough for Jackie to do his rain gazing.

The governor turned around to smile the big one down at Eddie. "Let me tell you a little story," he continued, clasping his hands behind his back. Felch felt a reflexive urge to take out a pen and pad, but he knew better.

"When I was a lad growing up in the project, we played a lot of baseball. Church-league stuff, you know. In my neighborhood you played for St. Monica's. Nothing so well heeled as Little League today. Because we were poor—this was in the project, remember. The McCormick. First public-housing project in the nation. This was before the word 'project' became a synonym for urban decay and failed social engineering and *fin de siècle* anomie."

Jackie stopped and smiled to himself as he rocked back and forth lightly on his heels, pride apparently redirecting the course of his recollections. He pulled himself back. "But that's getting off the point," he said with no apology in his voice. "The point *is,* we were poor, and if we had a baseball with its hide still in once piece—well, we felt like little plutocrats. It's the stuff of Norman Rockwell, is it not?"

Felch nodded uncertainly.

Jackie pushed on. "Except one day some rambunctious little urchin with a pellet gun shot out all the streetlights on Preble Street. Every one of them. A scandal, it was.

"Enter Edso Clohissey. A red-faced old darlin' of a policeman—looked like your stereotypic Irish cop straight out of a Pat O'Brien movie, he did. But mean, mean as a constipated Republican—assuming that's not redundant. So anyway, Edso confiscated our baseball and he told us we wouldn't get it back until we produced the culprit."

Jackie threw his brush-cut head back, which showed his faintly jug-eared physiognomy to momentary disadvantage, and laughed at the memory. Felch found himself staring once again at the governor's tie, a broad floral extravaganza in nine distinct colors (he had counted them) that clashed heartily with everything else about his understated appearance. The man was a four-decade medley of coiffure and couture: haircut from the fifties, gray suit with skinny lapels from the sixties, large outrageous tie from the seventies, comfortable Vibram-soled shoes from the eighties. Only the nineties were neglected. Or did the pager clipped to his belt take care of that?

"Edso got nothing, of course. Sure it is, we felt the loss of that ball like a phantom limb, but nobody so much as raised the *subject* of ratting out the little hooligan. Who, naturally, we all knew and blamed for our communal misfortune. We went almost three weeks without a proper ball to play with. Finally, Father Zielinski took pity on us and gave us a respectable used baseball. He was the pastor of Our Lady of Czestochowa, you see, the Polish church over on Dot Ave, and I suppose he *was* motivated by pity to some extent. I suspect it was also because he knew the miscreant was a student at his parish school. The boy would suffer enough at the hands of the Felician sisters who ran it."

Jackie stopped, checking to see that he had his listener's attention before modulating to the sentential. He bobbed a finger at Felch, and spoke gravely, intensely. "Whatever. The point is this, Edwin. WE DON'T INFORM."

Felch had the familiar feeling that the room had suddenly become too small for the two of them. He managed to hold Jackie's gaze as he waited for him to resume. When he did, his tone was softer, his voice lighter.

"I suppose it goes back to the Troubles and our long history under the yoke of a colonial power, when lives depended on the inculcation of such an ethos. It's injected in us, Edwin. It's not something you can extirpate with blandishments like leniency or ready cash. We. Just. Don't. Inform."

Then, like a kneeling suitor opening a delicate velvet box before his beloved, Jackie produced a tiny, private smile so wonderful Felch could not imagine how he had ever loathed the man for all those years.

"And that," Jackie said in almost a whisper, "should help you understand two things about this whole business. One," he said, holding up an index finger, "is that I will never, ever discuss publicly—or even privately, outside the family—anything about Thomas. Except, of course, to say that he is my brother, and I love him. And that most of what you fellows like to print about him is fabricated or exaggerated by my political enemies in an effort to tarnish *me.*"

Jackie paused just long enough to let his first point settle before proceeding.

"Two," he said, aligning his other index finger alongside the first, the thumbs touching, "it makes it *unthinkable* that Thomas could be an informant. He is not a snitch. It's just not in him."

Again, Felch felt transfixed by the intensity of the man, whose lips trembled slightly as he spoke. He realized he was being granted a privileged glimpse into something more personal, more private than Jackie Crimmins had ever allowed him before. Despite himself, Felch felt awed. Honored. It frightened him for a moment, this power the man had to sweep him in like that. So he pushed it away, retreating to a more comfortable mode of relating.

He became a reporter again.

"What about Hinkle, then?" he asked "He's Irish and he *admits* he's an informant. What's that do to your tribal theory?"

It worked, for the brief connection between them snapped cleanly, as Jackie reverted to the big grin and scuttled back into the shell of his public self. He sank into his chair and laid his forearms along its arms as he looked hard at the reporter.

"And Hinkle will have to live with himself. Oh, it's not that the race is immune, Edwin. I never meant to suggest that. The Sassenach, after all, did manage to find informants among us. Even Parnell was betrayed. But there are none of them in our family. That I can assure you. Never were, never will be."

"Prout's admissions to the judge notwithstanding?"

"Stanley Prout?" Jackie's lips quivered in an effort to suppress his mirth. "I'm surprised at you, Edwin. The man's an unscrupulous poseur. Swims in the warm water of his own good opinion of himself. Why, he even investigated *me*, once!"

Whereupon Jackie raised his eyebrows and both hands, palms up. *QED,* read Felch, who laughed out loud.

"Not to mention, I suppose, the fact that he was the protégé of your Republican predecessor," Felch tossed in.

"Republicans," Jackie said in a musing tone. "Republicanism is nostalgia with attitude. They yearn for the days when the Yankees and all those tight-sphinctered Good Government types kept us sweaty ethnics in our place. Fortunately, we outbred them. *And* outwitted them. Look around you, Edwin."

Jackie's eyes made a sweeping motion toward the portraits ranged above the wainscoting. Staid old men, painted in formal poses, none of them known to him. They all looked like . . .

"Yankees," Jackie supplied, as if reading his mind. "There's not a Catholic or Democrat in the lot. All of us parvenus are hung in the hallway, never here in the sanctuary itself. Do you think I should change it? Maybe hang Silent Cal himself next to the men's room?"

"Well," said Felch as he pulled himself to his feet, "I don't think it would make him break his silence. But I'm no decorator. It's been real, Jackie, but as usual I come away with nothing. Sometimes I think it was more fun when we were enemies. I couldn't get any information then either, but at least we could trade insults."

Jackie laid his open palm against his breast in mock injury.

"*I*? Insults?"

Felch grinned. "You told my editor if I had any integrity I would fall on my pen. That my prose suffered—'irremediably,' was the word you used—from a weak grounding in your beloved Greek and Latin."

"And mining the same vein, you called me the Ablative of Means. As if I were some political fix-it man, a go-to guy for the venal. So I guess it was something of a draw."

The two men smiled at each other. The only sound in the room was a sudden gust of wind and rain that shivered the windowpanes.

Without troubling his smile, Jackie stood up again. "I suppose," he said with a sigh, "I'd better get back to piloting the scow of state." He extended his right hand to the reporter, who shook it. "But don't forget what I told you, Edwin. We don't inform."

"You don't?" inquired Stanley Prout. He had rotated his chair a quarter turn to his right so he could clip his fingernails into the wastebasket beside his desk.

"No, Stan," Danielle Gautreau insisted. Declining a chair, she stood before his desk, clutching her shoulder purse to her side. "I *don't* understand. When they get bigger than the people they can give you, you cut them loose."

Prout looked across his shoulder at her. "But Dani," he said with an indulgent smile, "that's exactly what we did. Why the hell do you think we indicted them?" He snapped the nail on his left pinkie and shook the paring into the basket.

"No, Stan. That's several years too late. You protected them too long. Let them *use* you too long. And it'll be a continuing embarrassment to all of us."

When he looked at her this time it was with a harsher glint. He folded up the clipper and dropped it into his desk drawer. He pushed it shut.

"Perhaps," he said, "you should cut to the chase here. Just what is the *point* of all this? And what does it have to do with your transfer to Bank Fraud? I thought that was what you wanted to talk to me about."

She stared at him with a harshness of her own. "I'm not going to Bank Fraud, and you know it, Stan. You want me out, and you're going to get your way. So I'll leave, don't worry. But I want you to know that I know what happened here. You scuttled my investigation of Larry Coniglio—*months* of hard work—just to cover up how badly you guys had overplayed your hand with Tommy. Your prize asset. But it's all coming out anyway. So I hope they fry your ass."

He gave her a pitying smile. "You mean your little feckless foray after the hapless Larry the Rabbit? Or should I say hopless? *Hopeless* is more like it. And putting the screws to some straight-arrow squid fryer Larry took a liking to? Christ, Dani, your 'investigation' wasn't going anyplace anyway. He would never have talked, you know. Didn't you glean at least *that* much from your dealings with Arthur Patch?"

Prout paused before administering the *coup de grâce.* "You know what your problem is, Dani girl? You have an instinct for the capillaries. I scuttled *nothing.*"

She looked stung, but not for long. She shook her head in disbelief, her hair shifting lightly on her shoulders as she did so. "You know," she said, "at least Arthur Patch was just what he pretended to be. He didn't deal in the bullshit you peddle."

She opened her purse and fished through it for something.

God, she is a looker, he thought as he watched her extract an envelope. *She'd be perfect if she could keep her mouth shut. Well,* he corrected himself with a secret smile, *maybe not* all *the time.*

"There," she said, letting the envelope fall on his desk. "My resignation. Enjoy the coming shitstorm, Stan."

She turned and headed for the door.

"Dani," he called after her. She stopped and turned back to face his beaming visage. "A word to the wise, sweetheart. Let sleeping dogs lie, if you know what I mean."

She took a beat before returning his smile. "You mean let lying dogs sleep?"

"Whatever."

She left. His gaze lingered over that taut ass of hers as it vanished from view. *What a shame,* he said to himself. *The girl's all sphincter.*

But she was right about the coming shitstorm. There would be hell to pay, of that he had no doubt. U.S. Attorney Atwater had been on the phone with Main Justice all morning. Butters had been summoned to FBI Headquarters for "talks." They would come up with something to stanch the flow. All the muck-a-mucks had too much egg on their face, and DOJ would respond with something dramatic to shore things up. The only question was what it would be.

He had no idea.

The storm lashed the hunching city hard from the northeast, rattling windows that should have brightened Morrissey's tiny office on Milk Street and Jackie's grand one at the State House on Beacon Hill. The wind slapped sheets of stinging rain against the windshields of Arthur's van and Larry's big Chrysler. Even the thermopanes of the federal courthouse shuddered from its gusts.

Stanley Prout wondered what kind of bomb Main Justice was

about to drop in his lap. Arthur Patch pondered how he could ever pay his debt to Larry the Rabbit and keep the U.S. Attorney away from his door. Larry the Rabbit dreamily conjured the image of his Zip chauffeur leaning over Tommy Crimmins with an electric drill or a soldering iron. Jimmy Morrissey racked his brain for ways to raise the cash he needed.

Governor Jackie Crimmins just looked out into the rain and whispered, *Keep your head down, Thomas. Wherever you are, keep it down.*

CHAPTER THIRTEEN

INTO THE SLUSH

The volume on the television was set at a low murmur, just barely loud enough for Mavis to follow from her perch at the foot of the bed. Poking free from a beige dressing gown stamped with splotches of indistinct roses, her bare knee was pressed against her right cheek as she daubed violet polish on her toenails. The TV remote lay on the bed beside her foot. She managed to apply the polish in deft, smear-free strokes even as she monitored closely the turning of letters on *Wheel of Fortune.* Vanna White glided in stately counterpoint to the manic giddiness of the bouncing contestants.

Over Mavis's right shoulder and as far away from the set as possible in the little hotel room sat Tommy Crimmins. He had settled himself in the room's only easy chair, which he had shoved into the corner, pinning a furl of drapes against the wall. He shifted irritably, swinging his legs onto the bed in an effort to get comfortable. The pager dug into his side a little, so he slid it a forward on the belt until it fetched up against a belt loop. He read from a paperback book propped up on his lap.

The book was *Endurance* by Alfred Lansing, and this was at least the third time he had read it. Stoically ignoring the low babble from the television, he riffled ahead to find his favorite scene. Shackleton had just given the order to abandon the *Endurance,* as the ship's tortured timbers screamed from the pressure of the pack ice that was slowly crushing it. His soot-faced men stood before him, preparing to haul the three lifeboats through the heavy slush toward open water. To impress upon them the need to travel light, Shackleton cracked open the heavy Bible Queen Victoria had given him before he sailed. With a flourish he tore out two pages—one bearing the Queen's personal inscription, the other the Twenty-third Psalm. He folded the loose pages into his pocket and grandly dropped the Bible into the slush at his feet. Then he set off to lead his men on a plodding march to the open sea.

Tommy loved that scene—the best passage in one of the best books he knew. And it was true, every bit of it. That was the best thing about it. For Tommy could not abide fiction. Novels and plays and movies about shit that never happened. Fiction, all of it. But this, Shackleton and his doomed expedition to traverse Antarctica in 1914, was as real as it got. Real the way he lived his own life. On a life-or-death basis, one day at a time. And like Shackleton, he would make it.

He looked up at Mavis. With her lips parted slightly and staring straight ahead, she was caught in the TV's tractor beam. Tommy despised television, with its ridiculous cop shows and soap operas and those idiotic sitcoms that made him edgy. Her game shows were stupid, but at least they weren't fiction. He heard a spattering of applause and watched one of the contestants hop up and down like Dan Quayle at that first press conference after Bush chose him as his running mate.

The network went to commercial and Mavis thumbed the remote. Tommy scowled and redirected his focus on Shackleton, but as she took her channel tour the dissonant slivers of sound kept breaking his concentration. He let the book drop on his legs and leaned back, looking up at the water-stained ceiling tiles.

What a dump.

The Hotel Alva just three blocks off Times Square was discreet and anonymous, and its largely gay staff and clientele made it unlikely anyone would ever suspect him of patronizing the place. But it was a dump. Not too bad a dump, mind you—the elevators worked fine and the lobby had once been grand—but the halls stank of mildew, the beige carpets were threadbare, the towels raspy and napless. And the rooms, with their pea green walls and fuzzy, bile green furniture, were depressing as hell. Maybe a walk would—

"Tommy." Her voice was low, surprised. "You gotta look at this. It's *you*!"

He brought his head down to see what she was talking about. There on the screen was that picture, the one the Boston papers always ran, of him in three-quarter profile, looking grim in his watch cap and a Pit Stop Diner sweatshirt.

What the fuck?

"Turn it up," he demanded.

Mavis bent her head down and pressed a button on the remote. The picture disappeared and he was replaced by some vacuous starlet on *Entertainment Tonight.*

"What the hell are you doing?" he barked. "I said *up*!"

"I'm trying," Mavis whined at him as she stabbed at the remote. "I musta hit the wrong button."

Dipshit.

The picture flicked forward twice, then three back, and his brother's picture filled the screen now. Smiling that big, shit-eating grin of his, Jackie was standing on the State House steps with his shiny black shoes together and his hands clasped behind his back. *Still looks like a fucking altar boy. The eager CYO president waiting to welcome the monsignor.* Shaking his head and working his mouth soundlessly—declining comment, no doubt.

Mavis finally managed to raise the volume.

". . . declined comment," said an unseen announcer. "Today's announcement by the Justice Department capped a week of speculation after an admission by the government that Thomas Crimmins and his business partner, Phil Hinkle, had been government informants for more than twenty years."

Jackie's image gave way to an old one of Hink, his huge body upholstered in a tight blue suit. He was descending the steps of Suffolk Superior following his arraignment on a state beef that got dismissed four or five years ago. Hink grinned and waved to photographers, the big guy's charm still intact.

"Some observers expressed surprise at the size of the reward for Crimmins," the announcer continued as his pretty-boy face supplanted Hinkle's. "However, others suggested that the three-hundred-thousand-dollar figure would go a long way to counter suspicions that the FBI had no real interest in catching the fugitive. As one knowledgeable defense attorney put it, that much money can paper over a lot of embarrassment."

The guy smirked and turned his head to his right. "Kendra?" A perky blonde smiled back at him, her eyes widening. "I should hope so," she said. Then she moved on to another story, about some shenanigans by New York's egotistical mayor.

"Shut if off," Tommy said quietly.

She did. *Plink.* The picture imploded, leaving a small white dot before disappearing completely.

"Fuck and a half," he said softly.

She turned back to face him, her bare legs now hanging off the end of the bed.

"A reward, Tommy?" Her voice trembled. "All that money. What are we going to do?"

Oh, Jesus. This crap he didn't need. He had enough on his mind without Mavis freaking out on him.

"Listen to me," he said slowly. "Did you see the whole story? I mean, did you miss any of it when you switched over?"

Frown lines intersected the curls that fell across her forehead. "You mean when I was trying to turn it up?"

"No, no." *Jesus.* "When you first turned to the news. Did you get all of the story?"

She narrowed her eyes and chewed at her underlip in thought. "I think so. Yes!" She opened her eyes wide and looked straight at him, a slow-witted pupil grasping the solution to a math problem. "I remember now. There was the tail end of some story about flowers in Belgium or something, when I turned over. Then they started on you—with your picture and all. But it doesn't really look much like you."

"So *you* weren't mentioned? No pictures of you, right?"

She looked terrified as she shook her head. "Do you think—"

"Shut up and let me think a minute."

Tossing *Endurance* on the bed, Tommy sat back in the chair and directed his gaze over her shoulder. Fucking Hink. Mavis always liked him. The big guy made her laugh. Why couldn't he be more like him, she'd asked. Instead of Mr. Sourpuss. Well, because *somebody* had to tend to business. Hink could be the charmer, jolly the boys along, make like pals with animals like Francesco and half-wits like Larry. *He,* on the other hand, had to be the hard-ass. What did she know about the messes he'd had to clean up after Hink?

Look what Hink had set in motion. Oh, it was understandable, that he should go public like that, facing forever in the can. And Phil was never really inside, never had to do hard time like him. Because God knows *he* wasn't about to go back inside. Never. The smell of piss and stale sweat and disinfectant. And the noise. That was the worst of it, the fucking noise. It was never quiet. No, he'd rather spend his life playing checkers in a feed store in Chickenbone, Iowa, than see the inside of a block like Leavenworth again.

Phil had obviously thought he could air it out for himself alone. He had been careful not to mention Tommy's role in their little joint venture with the Strike Force. But it was inevitable, and if Phil had had a few more smarts he would have foreseen that the feds would have to spit out both of them if pressed hard enough to cough up Phil.

"Tommy."

He flicked an annoyed glance in her direction. She looked tiny, a scared child. He quelled his irritation. He shot her a brief smile and beckoned her to him.

She slid across the bed toward him and put her arms around him, her head in his lap. He laid his hand on her head, his expression serious again.

"Listen," he said. "It's okay. Like you said, the picture doesn't look much like me. I'm a pretty nondescript sort of guy anyhow. And you, they haven't put out your picture. So it'll be okay."

He stroked her hair absently. The two of them stayed there, saying nothing. Not in silence, exactly, for through the window they could hear the traffic? honking, and a siren, and the steady bass thump of a pile driver as New York busied itself to throw up more steel around them.

She checked his stroking with a hand on his wrist. Looking up at him, she said, "Is it true, what they said, Tommy? That you worked with the government?"

When he looked down, there was chitin in his eyes.

"An informant, you mean?" he demanded. "A snitch?"

"Whatever." She held his gaze.

"Not *whatever.*" He spoke crisply, the words bitten off. "That's the whole thing, the word. We don't inform."

"We?" She frowned at him.

"Yeah, we. You, you're what, French?"

"Yes, mostly." She tried on an uncertain smile. "Why?"

"Well, if you were Irish, you'd understand. I'm no informant."

Subject closed. He looked away. Mavis watched him doubtfully, then let it drop.

The palm of his hand lay on her head as he sank into a reverie that took him back to the office at the rear of Dell's, the little joint in the Lower End where he once held court. He was a local hero, then. A feudal lord who kept order in the Town. It was he, with Hink's help, who had tamed the notorious Mullens, an undisciplined gang named for Mullen Square at E and O Streets, where they used to hang out. This brought a little peace and quiet for the residents and left, as a grateful constabulary backed off, a better business environment for his own activities. It was not so surprising, therefore, that during the busing wars in the seventies, the cops had come to him for help to keep the Town from blowing sky high.

By then he was a solid citizen, almost. Everyone knew he didn't drink (it was a weakness he couldn't tolerate and he made a point of staying out of the madness on St. Paddy's Day), and the residents regaled outsiders with stories of how he stomped all over any baboons from the D Street project who tried to deal drugs in the neighborhood. Sure, that changed when the massive profits available from drugs counseled a more flexible position. Even then he stayed neutral: like Switzerland, he just took the gold—in the form of rent paid for the privilege of doing business on his turf. And he still stomped the interlopers.

The office at Dell's was nothing special. A one-window room with three beat-up wooden chairs and an old desk whose walnut veneer had peeled away in random strips, leaving blond streaks to darken with grime. Nothing on the walls. A floor lamp, a coatrack. An air conditioner laboring noisily in the summer; heat pipes banging in the winter. No phone. But there Tommy had granted audience in the good times, with supplicants lined up outside the office like shoes at a mosque. And not just for business, either. It was more than guys delivering his end, rent and such. Sometimes it was a guy needed a job, or maybe somebody's kid needed straightening out. A daughter getting stalked by an old boyfriend with no respect for a court order. Tommy would help. And he'd deliver. Once, even, a family whose little girl went missing came to him. The cops had picked up a suspect they liked for it, but he wouldn't answer questions. Tommy had spent fifteen minutes alone with the guy in his cell. Without laying a finger on him he was able to report with utter certainty that the guy knew nothing.

But all that was gone now—or almost, anyway. Without the heft of his physical presence, he could exert no authority, and the D Street

Gang seemed to be disintegrating. One by one, as their orbits decayed, the men who had revolved around him were spinning off into undisciplined darkness on their own. Further misunderstandings were bound to arise from this business about Hink's affidavit and the government's talk of his cooperation. They'd jump to the same conclusion Mavis had. To the same fiction.

Maybe his future *was* a feed store in Chickenbone, Iowa.

Mavis broke the silence. "What do we do now, Tommy?"

He still looked past her. "We better move on," he said. "We can't go hanging around a hotel fulla assholes with nothing to do but watch TV. They're probably walkin' around trying to memorize my picture. Best check out and move on. So you get packing."

He swatted her ass and pushed her off his lap. He stood up. From the bedside table he plucked his navy watch cap and, slipping two fingers under the fold, worked it around in his hands.

Another thought struck him. The feds had to be fucking nuts. A *reward,* for Christ's sake? Did they think he was so fucking stupid he hadn't taken precautions? They *had* to know what he could do to them. Flukes would, anyway.

But he knew one thing for certain. Every meatball who ever heard of him would perk up at the mention of that $300,000 reward. He smiled with sardonic resolution. *Well, let them try.*

Tommy walked over to the armoire that housed the television and looked down at the plastic wastebasket beside it. He held the watch cap out at arm's length and admired it. Felt it flex when he tugged at it, then retake its shape when he eased up.

I'll miss it, he thought.

He let it drop into the wastebasket at his feet.

Into the slush, you could say. And he plodded on.

PART TWO

No mean person may keep a greyhound.

—Statute enacted during the reign of King Canute

CHAPTER FOURTEEN

GRANDPA DUNPHY'S FLY

Native Americans called the peninsula Mattapannock—a Naragansett word, Governor Jackie Crimmins liked to crack to amused gatherings of the faithful, for *mosquito.* Mattapannock was cut off from the city of Boston to the north by flat marshes and a narrow channel, and it jutted eastward out into the Harbor like a deformed proboscis. Because the peninsula was linked to the rest of the Puritan settlement of Dorchester by a thin neck at its western end, it became known as Dorchester Neck or, more simply, the Neck.

Graced by hilly grasslands freshened in the salt breezes, the Neck supplied rich pasture for the settlers' cattle, which could be kept from straying by a short run of fence across the neck. Springwater was plentiful, and the livestock ambled along a meandering cow path, seeking shade under scattered clusters of weeping willows in the hot summer weather. In such bucolic serenity the Neck lolled peacefully, except for the brief disturbance of the Revolutionary War, for more than a hundred and fifty years.

At the beginning of the nineteenth century, however, the city of Boston was becoming overbuilt. Savvy speculators from Boston Hill saw the Neck as a source of raw land on which to build housing for the burgeoning numbers of city dwellers. In 1803 they petitioned the legislature to annex the peninsula to the city of Boston. Dorchester vehemently opposed the loss of its pasturelands, and it spurned all offers of financial settlement. Less hostile to annexation were the dozen Yankee families who actually lived on the Neck; they stood to reap large profits from the sale of land if they joined Boston.

The residents had another reason to side with the speculators—a grudge over their perceived mistreatment by the town of Dorchester. The only school for their children was at Meeting House Hill in Dorchester, but access to the mainland was via a low causeway at the end of the neck. This the town apparently neglected, exposing it to floods that often turned the peninsula into an island at high tide. So it happened that, with the residents' support, the petition was granted and the Neck was absorbed into the city of Boston without any compensation paid to Dorchester. Given the peninsula's subsequent political history (especially the busing wars of the 1970s), there is much to savor in the irony that South Boston—as the Neck was renamed in 1805—joined the city because of a beef over schools and an abiding sense that it had been slighted by civic authorities.

The resident families and the Boston speculators made out handsomely during the ensuing construction. A toll bridge built across Fort Point Channel afforded a corridor to the city. Over the pasturelands developers laid out a grid as logical as Manhattan's, with numbered streets along its elbowed length intercut by alphabetic cross streets. As if in homage to its rural provenance, the surveyors left the old cow path, later rechristened Emerson Street, to loop anarchically through their tidy plat.

South Boston flourished, but the slights continued. After annexation the residents were forced to maintain their own school, as the Boston School Committee ignored their petitions for financial support. The city also rejected other demands for public improvements. In protest the residents in 1847 sent an angry "memorial" to city authorities. This document boasted that they were not "scum, thrown out of purer material," but respectable citizens without "a single colored family" and only a few "foreigners." And even the latter were from the "better class" of immigrants, not those derided as content to "live in cellars, or congregate together in order to keep warm" along the squalid waterfronts of Boston.

This last was no doubt a sneer at the Irish, whose immigration into South Boston was then but a trickle and confined largely to middle-class artisans and industrious farmers from Ulster. All this changed with devastating speed and effect over the next decade, when the potato famine began to empty the southern counties of

Cork, Kerry, Galway, and Clare. In ten short years 130,000 Irish streamed into South Boston, a community that had shown such promise as a fashionable outpost for upscale young Yankees. The "purer material" scuttled into the ethnic sanctuary of Yankee enclaves like Beacon Hill. And still the flood of Irish immigration continued. The lace-curtain Irish moved into the better homes in City Point, the eastern tip of the peninsula, while the poorest packed into the teeming, pestilential tenements of Little Galway, an area to the west and north now known as the Lower End.

It was out of such shabby lodgings, approximately a century later, that a young trucker named John Michael Crimmins was able to move with his wife, Grace, and their infant son, John Jr. By cashing in a political chip, John was advanced to the head of the list for placement in the spanking-new Old Harbor Village Project.

This was 1938. The first housing project in the nation, Old Harbor was composed of three-story brick buildings laid out around square courtyards just off Andrew Square—the very site of the flooding that used to enisle the peninsula and rile its inhabitants. The complex was later renamed the Mary Ellen McCormick Project, after the congressman's mother, but the locals never took to the new name. While admission was limited to the working poor, rents were deemed high; John paid $22.15 a month for three rooms on the second floor, with heat and running water—exotic luxuries for a young couple whose grandparents had been born in County Cork.

John's taste for porter kept him poor, even when he was working, and Grace managed to stave off eviction and worse by working as a sweat, testing deodorants for the Gillette Razor Company. But neither John's drinking nor Grace's exhaustion kept him from filling her with children. The three rooms were home to a family of nine by 1951, when Grandfather Dunphy was killed in a derrick accident on the docks at the Black Falcon Terminal, just across the Reserved Channel.

Cornelius Dunphy was waked out of his parlor on Pilsudski Way and buried from St. Monica's Chapel at Preble Street and Old Colony Road. At fourteen, Grace's oldest son, Jackie, was given the honor of serving the funeral Mass. His six siblings huddled on both sides of Grace's sobbing figure in the third pew while Jackie, his water-slicked black hair parted cleanly on the right side, glided importantly around the steps of the altar in his immaculate vestments. Perhaps pride in her son worked to soften Grace's grief over the loss of her father, but Tommy was having none of it.

At age twelve, Tommy was Grace's third child, after Catherine, and from the outset her biggest heartache. As he slid his skinny butt off the oak pew and knelt on the padded prie-dieu like the others, he looked away from the altar. He couldn't stand to watch his brother's posturing. *A sacristy rat,* he thought. Then he smiled to himself. *The Sack Rat.* A new nickname for the altar boy. It was all that mawkish piety that got to him. Jackie didn't even clasp his fingers together in prayer like a man but pointed them straight up, the pads touching. Like a girl. This being October, Jackie would probably return the next evening to make a novena with his mother, in devotion to the Blessed Virgin. Tommy shifted his knees irritably.

He detected movement to his left and heard the creak of weight on wood. His father leaned his bulk against the pew back as he raised the kneeler with his instep, then shuffled the length of the pew from the outer aisle. Even before John took his place beside Fawnie at the end of the Crimmins family queue, Tommy could see the sunburn of whiskey below his cheekbones and the bleary glint in his blue eyes. John, Tommy noticed, did not look at his wife. She didn't glance his way either, but a tiny hitch in her soft weeping told Tommy, as plainly as the blackest of glares, that her husband's belated arrival had registered. He was sure his father knew this as well.

Catherine had warned him not to look at his dead grandfather ("It's how you'll always remember him"), but Tommy could not resist taking his turn when the mourners filed past the open casket. With his rouged cheeks and heaps of hair like corn silk, Cornelius Dunphy's head was leonine resting on a starched linen pillow. His face seemed puffier than Tommy remembered, and a little less angry, though his right fist was clenched around his rosary as if he were still wary of the larceny all around him.

It was the other hand that held Tommy's attention. A fat housefly, gravid with the lateness of the season, crawled up the webbing of the old man's thumb before disappearing beneath the starched white cuff. *Wasting no time,* he thought. He pictured the fly's likely itinerary, a colorful route spanning the Widow Piggot's privy and the alley beside Pejewski's butcher shop before touching down in the nave of St. Monica's. He wanted to see if the fly would reemerge, but he felt a pat against his hip from the back of his father's hand. He took the hint and moved on.

After the burial they returned to the church basement, where the air was heavy with pipe tobacco, cabbage, and damp tweed. Fawnie tugged at Tommy's elbow. She pointed with awe at the long harvest table heaped with one-pot dishes brought by sympathetic neighbors. Tommy watched as Mrs. Collins, the baker's wife, used a dish towel to lift the hot lid off a cottage pie. Fawnie began to thread her way eagerly toward the crowded table.

Tommy spotted his father standing in front of the pass-through to the kitchen. He looped around the people crowding the table and edged along the wall to his left toward the clatch of men smoking and talking with John. He was holding forth already, and Tommy wondered if even he would have the gall to tipple in church.

John took a drag of his Lucky Strike and nodded toward the tableful of food. "We were gonna have chicken," he explained, "but it got well."

A couple of his cronies chuckled at this, colluding in the man's shame at accepting the charity of his neighbors.

"The old man would have tucked in to all that by now, you know," John added with a histrionic shake of his head. "Lord knows, Neil did like a touch of corned beef and cabbage." Then he fell silent and hung his head. "Only fifty-four, he was."

With a curl of his lip Tommy waited to see if his father would have the audacity to deliver a public snuffle in memory of his father-in-law. John disappointed him by simply lifting his head bravely and looking resolutely across the room.

Tommy stifled a snorting laugh. *That's where Jackie gets it,* he thought.

"Boys," said John, his voice thick now, "I could use a bit of the fresh air, if you don't mind. Any of you care to join me?"

They did, and the men clomped heavily up the kitchen stairs toward the back door, to the churchyard. There, Tommy knew, a pint of Old Bushmill would be passed around.

He turned his gaze back across the room and sought out his mother. Absently staring straight ahead, Grace was now seated on a folding chair between her two sisters. Uncle Walter leaned over her from behind, whispering into her ear as he rested his hand on her shoulder. Tommy found himself full of puzzlement that she should be so devastated by the loss of a sour old man he himself had learned to avoid.

Jackie entered the room ten feet to her left. With his server's vestments now stowed in the little closet beside the sacristy door, Jackie stood in his school blazer and tie and glittering black shoes.

Tommy watched him stride directly to his mother and squat in front of her, his palms on her knees. He could see his brother's jaws working as Grace raised her eyes to his and smiled back with bleak affection. When Jackie stood up she squeezed his right hand with both of hers. Jackie said something to his aunts, was repaid with smiles, and moved to his left as if working a receiving line. When he reached the far corner, he fluidly eased himself into a conversation between Father Feloney and Ned Quirk, the city councilman. Tommy turned away.

There were now a few breaks in the ring of people girdling the food, so he picked up a plate and made his way along the table toward Mrs. Collins's cottage pie. Just before he reached it, his place in line was usurped by Teresa Carney, a corpulent spinster who lived with her cats a few blocks away on Tuckerman. She was, he knew, an opportunistic interloper, not a friend of the family. She swished her hand across the top of the cast-iron pot, shooing another bloated fly off the potato crust. It lifted off sluggishly and bobbed its way down the table, then alighted on a platter of sliced bread. Tommy was seized by a sudden conviction.

It's the same one! It's gotta be. He hadn't seen a fly in five, six weeks, and now two in one morning? No way.

He took a step back from the table and watched. The fat woman heaped her plate with cottage pie before moving down the table. Others followed her lead: the cottage pie was a popular choice. As Tommy took his secret pleasure in watching them, a grin stole across his face.

"What's so funny?"

It was Catherine, his older sister. Smiling herself between deep-cut dimples like double parentheses, she did not look grief-stricken.

Tommy nodded toward the source of his amusement. "That cottage pie?" he said. "There was a fly on it. The same fly I saw crawl up Grandpa's sleeve. When he was upstairs, I mean. It's on the bread now."

Catherine's eyes widened. "The same *one*? How do you know that?" Her eyes never left the pot.

"Because it's October. How many flies you seen lately? It's gotta be the same one."

"So," she said, smiling again, "they're eating food that was crawled on by a fly that crawled all over a dead man?"

"Yup."

He made the mistake of catching her eye, and they both broke out laughing. Catherine did a better job of keeping hers inaudible.

A moment later Tommy felt a hand clutch his arm, and he turned to face Jackie, who glared angrily at him.

"What's the matter with you?" Jackie hissed, his voice low. "Both of you," he added, though his eyes never left Tommy's. "Grandpa's hardly buried, and you're making jokes over here?"

Tommy looked into his brother's—his dad's—blue eyes and said nothing.

"Look," Jackie continued. "Ma's father just died. How do you think she feels? Suppose it was *your* dad. Or Ma, even. How do you think *you'd* feel?"

Tommy felt the rage prickle up his sides like a popping of warm sweat. Black spots danced in front of his eyes. He stared at his brother, not daring to trust his voice. Then he turned hard on his heels and banged into Father Feloney, whom he pushed past on his way to the stairs. The priest called after him, but Tommy did not hear what he said. He took the steps two at a time, not even breathing until he burst out of the church's front doors to stand on the cement stoop. There he stopped, his hand gripping the wrought-iron railing as he gulped mouthfuls of damp, chill air. With the wind blowing from the east, there was a whiff of brine in it, too.

After a few seconds Tommy rolled, then squared, his shoulders and idly descended the concrete steps. He had no route or destination in mind, and he soon found himself turning off Old Colony Road and heading northwest on Jenkins. At Dorchester Street, the street sign reminded him that Jenkins became Tuckerman at that point, and his thoughts returned to Teresa Carney. A few more strides and he was passing in front of the entrance to her cellar apartment. Four steps below grade, a scrawny yellow cat rubbed its back against her door and mewed at him.

Tommy stopped and stared at the cat. He shot a glance back over his shoulder and saw no one. He realized at once that he could reach Teresa's door without being seen, as the entryway was tucked between the wooden stairway to the aboveground apartments and a thick hedge separating her building from the next one. Without consciously considering the matter, he slipped quickly down the steps and grasped the knob on the door to her apartment. He tried it.

As he expected, the door was unlocked. He and the cat slipped inside the darkened apartment together. He closed the door behind him.

Serves her right, he thought as he waited for his eyes to adjust to the darkness. *Crashing a reception for a man she hardly knew.*

The cat rubbed up against his leg and mewed again. Tommy roughly kicked it out of his way and burgled the place.

He told his friend Hink about it later that evening. He'd hauled off a coffee can full of coins and a few dollar bills—her Christmas money, they figured. They both agreed the heist made a neat addition to their expanding repertoire, but Tommy insisted they avoid funerals in the future. They would concentrate instead on wakes, for many visitations took place at night.

Wake burgling proved profitable for the two of them, so much so that Tommy began hearing talk of the break-ins on the streets and in the stores. So he told Hink they should lay off for a while. Hink just shrugged and went ahead anyway. Two nights later, when the cops took him coming down the fire escape from a room above a drugstore on East Fourth Street, Hink took his first fall. He was a stand-up guy about it, of course, resisting all efforts to get him to implicate his buddy.

Tommy just shook his head, and said, "I told you."

CHAPTER FIFTEEN

A NEAR MISS

The guy at Cushing Restaurant Supply wanted way too much for the used range he had advertised. The restaurant might be showing signs of turning the corner financially, but Arthur knew he had to be careful. He wanted no replay of the miscues that had led him, in desperation more than a year ago, to accept the bogus largesse of Larry Coniglio. No matter how much Jonathan, his sous-chef, complained about the antiquated kitchen range, he was just going to have to make do for a while. Tomorrow Arthur would get someone in again to fix the dead burner at the back.

All this Arthur considered as he climbed into the van on Cushing Street to make his way back from Cambridge to the South End. La Vucciria had begun to make a name for itself as an up-and-coming dining establishment, reviewed glowingly just two Thursdays ago in the *Boston Globe.* He'd come a long way from the early days, when authentic Sicilian fare had rained confusion on his patrons.

He recalled with particular chagrin the initial debacle that had almost done him in. It should have been self-evident, even if Joanne had not been begging him to cut it from the menu, that *pasta con le sarde* was an absurd choice as his signature entrée. It might be the national dish of Sicily, but how could he ever have dreamed that the monochromatic Yankee (not to mention Irish) palate would not quail before macaroni tossed with sardines, anchovies, wild fennel, and currants? Its only true devotee was Larry, and he couldn't even get his son Pietro to eat the stuff. Joanne had been right. It was like trying to hawk liver ice cream.

Eventually, Arthur settled for less adventurous fare. He had great success offering street food as appetizers—like *panelle*, the fried cakes of chick-pea flour sold off the backs of Vespas in Palermo, and *arancine*, balls of rice stuffed with cheese or sauce or spinach, then coated with bread crumbs and deep fried into golden globes. The late-night favorite was pizza *rianata*, topped with onions, oil, a dusting of oregano, and Tiddlywinks of *caciocavallo* cheese. When it came to eggplant, the more traditional *pasta alla Norma* was outsold by his *spaghetti alla coppola*, though he feared it might owe its popularity to a mistaken association with the director of the *Godfather* movies. Most gratifying of all, his patrons had been won over by the wonderful native fruits from the island—the sorbs and medlars, loquats and blood oranges they downed with wedges of sharp *pecorino* at the end of a meal.

Now, he thought as he neared Belmont Street, if he could just put this business with Larry and the U.S. Attorney behind him, his dream of owning a successful and authentic Sicilian restaurant might become a lasting reality.

The looming street sign reminded him that he was just a few blocks east of Joe Rancatore's, whose handmade ice cream he admired greatly. Impulsively, he decided he had time for a small dish of pistachio. Coming to a rolling stop at Belmont, he glanced left, then accelerated forward to make a right turn.

It wasn't really as close as it seemed at the time. He spotted the jogger just after she stepped off the curb and moved into his field of vision from the right. He slammed hard on the brakes and froze, his heart thumping. The jogger, a slim young woman in gray sweats, pulled up short in front of him, then turned to lean both hands on the hood of the van and glare angrily at its careless driver.

Sorry, Arthur mouthed broadly, patting his sternum three times to communicate his own distress at the near miss. Then, watching her green eyes widen slightly with dawning surprise, he recognized her, too. With the yellow hair tightly pulled back and tied into a ponytail, her cheekbones assumed greater prominence as they burned red from exercise and the frosty air. And anger, too, he supposed. He offered a half smile and a propitiating shrug, but she made no response. She just pushed herself away from the van and loped fluidly across Belmont Street in front of him.

Arthur stared at Danielle Gautreau's retreating figure as she turned left on reaching the other side of the road. He was briefly transfixed by a rectangular patch of Day-Glo orange on her back, right in the middle of her gray sweatshirt. She ran off in an easterly direction on Belmont Street without once looking back at him.

A parking ticket. That's what it was, stuck on her back. She had pasted a parking ticket on the back of her sweatshirt to enhance her visibility.

As if she needed anything, he thought as the van eased forward again. And of course she would live in Cambridge. Where they probably had checkpoints to keep out any cars that weren't Volvos or Saabs.

He headed west toward Rancatore's Ice Cream.

She could sense him staring at her. The jerk. Sitting there and brazenly ogling her backside as she ran.

Dani shook off the thought of Arthur Patch. In front of a liquor store wedged into the crotch of the Y where Belmont merged into Mt. Auburn Street, she jogged in place and waited for a break in the traffic. Once the crossing was made, she picked up the pace and ran flat out the last few blocks to the graveyard.

When she reached the high cast-iron gates to Mt. Auburn Cemetery, Dani slowed to a walk. It would be disrespectful to run on the burying ground. With her hands crimping her waist above the hipbones while she caught her breath, she ambled past the redbrick gatehouse that resembled a Romanesque chapel but did duty as an information center. She turned left onto a walkway marked as Acacia Lane. After a couple hundred yards she left the path, scuffled through a carpet of fallen beech leaves, and took a seat on a stone bench perched on the lip of the big pond near the cemetery's eastern boundary.

This being late October, the resident kingfisher was gone, as were the turtles that sunned themselves on the muddy shore in the summer months. The gigantic weeping willow to her right had shaken off its leaves. She let her gaze drift across the pewter surface of the pond, which was wrinkled by an unfelt breeze. On a knoll directly across from her loomed the grandiose tomb of Mary Baker Eddy—pale granite discs of diminishing diameters laid one on top of another to form steps, the last disc forming the base for a Doric colonnade. Dani took a deep breath and tried to relax. Despite her resolution to leave it alone today, she found herself ruminating over her future.

She needed to make a decision, it was true. She could only last five, maybe six months on her savings. Royce & Bell, her old firm, had expressed an interest in her return, but it was the tedium of big-firm lawyering that had sent her scurrying to the U.S. Attorney's Office in the first place. Carrying some senior partner's bag again, one of the schlepparazzi, as Stanley Prout called big-firm associates.

She could probably catch on with the Suffolk County District Attorney's Office. A dismal prospect. The pay cut there would be even larger than the salary jump she'd get if she rejoined R&B. And could she put up with the pathetic conditions in a county prosecutor's office? The lack of resources, investigators, technology? Not to mention the rawest of political elbowing; it was, after all, the Kronk Gym of Massachusetts politics. She had her doubts. The feds had spoiled her, she had to admit. Not to mention the plush life she had known at R&B. It would be a hard adjustment.

A pair of Canada geese waddled up to the brim of the pond just past the willow, then breasted the water without pausing. Plunged right in. Was that what she needed to do?

From her left came a flooding smear of darkness: an enormous cloud of chittering starlings—swirling, changing shape, volitionless—engulfed first a towering copper beach just behind her, then imploded and pulled itself inside out before sweeping her, too, into its coreless vortex. So vast were their numbers that the flock blotted out the sun for a moment, a thickening of black protoplasm, eerily menacing. Then, as swiftly as they had come, the birds moved on. She watched the flock sluice through the bare branches of the big willow like heavy smoke through a screen. Soon the mass disappeared entirely. Sunlight and silence reasserted themselves in the crisp air.

Dani shivered and checked her watch. Three-twenty. Better hustle. She had a hair appointment at four-thirty and Leighton was due to pick her up at seven. Dani hauled herself to her feet and made for the cemetery gates.

One of the first things Dani had noticed about Dr. Leighton Taylor, before they started dating some three months earlier, was the man's superb physical conditioning. Leighton took care of himself, no two ways about it. If the flesh is a cage, he gilded his. His belly was flat and hard, the muscles on his upper arms had definition without unseemly bulk, and his tanned skin shone with a burnished, cinnamon glaze. *The trainers at his health club must covet his body mass index,* she thought as she watched him hand the keys of his Lexus to the parking attendant. Leighton was tall, a big man. A bit, well, *assuming*—if that was the opposite of unassuming.

But that was all right. She tended to scare men, she knew. Most of them tried to cover it. Leighton didn't scare. It brought an edge of excitement to their dealings.

He turned back to her and smiled. It was a winning smile, a little toothy but full of vigor and self-confidence. A broken wing of sandy hair dangled boyishly across his brow. He wore khaki trousers and a brown sport jacket over an azure shirt made of buttery washed silk that lolled across his molded pectorals. Returning his smile, she clasped his arm with both hands.

Huddled against the cold, they walked together up Tremont Street. A block and a half later they turned off onto Upton. She was almost in front of the restaurant before she read the name on the awning and stopped in her tracks.

"We're eating *here?*"

Mystified, Leighton looked down at her. "Well, yes. My broker says it's marvelous. What's wrong?"

Dani stared into the windows, picking up the brilliant white of the linen tablecloths and the flickering flames from the wood oven at the rear.

"Leighton, this is a *mob* joint."

"La Vucciria?" he chuckled incredulously. "You must be kidding. I just read about it. It's owned by a couple from South Boston, not the Mafia. They're not even Sicilian."

She turned to face him, irritated at his belittling tone. "This is my business, Leighton. Or used to be, anyway. I *subpoenaed* the owner once. There's Mafia money in it."

If Leighton was nonplussed by this news, he didn't show it. "Oh, come on, Dani," he said. "By those standards you couldn't eat *any-*

where. Or get your garbage collected, for that matter. Listen, I had to make this reservation three weeks ago."

He tipped his head to the side and grinned, lifting his hands in a gesture of supplication. "My broker told me about it. He says the food's—"

"Marvelous. You said that."

"—and you *said* I could pick the place. . . ."

He trailed off at this, which was voiced in a wheedling tone, a nine-year-old's. She could feel herself giving in.

"I suppose," she conceded, wanting to please him. "I should keep in mind that I don't work there anymore."

"That's right," he said with satisfaction. "You're a woman of the world now, not a crusader."

She didn't care for either characterization, but she allowed him to propel her toward the restaurant with the heel of his hand at the small of her back. A ballroom dancer signaling a turn.

"How's the Caesar salad?" Leighton asked the waitress, his nose, like Dani's, buried in the menu.

"It won't change your life."

They both looked up at her. She was a tall, big-boned woman in her middle thirties, clad in a crisp white blouse and a short purple skirt. Her haircut could have been a knockoff of Leighton's.

"Hey, it's the truth," she said with a shrug. "Don't worry: I'm an owner. We're shorthanded tonight, so I have to wait tables. But that doesn't mean I can't say what I think." She cranked her head to the right to give a nod of welcome to a couple who looked lost beside the hostess's station.

"Well, then why—" Leighton began, in some confusion.

"The Caesar's like the porterhouse," the waitress broke in, turning back to them. "It's okaaay." Her tone belied the claim. "But it's there for people who don't want to eat what it is we do here."

Dani watched Leighton's brow ripple with annoyance. She interceded.

"So what *will* change his life?" she asked with a conspiratorial smile. *Or mine,* she thought.

The waitress made a show of peering sideways down at Leighton. He did not seem amused.

"Beats me," she confessed. "That sounds like a tall order."

Dani laughed, and the waitress joined her. Leighton vouchsafed a half smile and turned his attention back to the menu.

"Are you Joanne?" Dani asked, handing the menu to her. "I'll have the tuna."

"Yes," said Joanne, eyeing her quizzically. "Have we met?"

"I think so," answered Dani, seeing once again the woman's face backlit by the streetlight as she stood on the stoop outside Dani's apartment. "I believe you once delivered a message to me."

Joanne frowned.

"At home," Dani prodded. "From your partner."

Joanne's eyes widened. "That was you? On, what's that street? Funny name. Thing-something? Over in west Cambridge."

"Thingvalla."

Joanne pointed her finger in Dani's face. "You're the prosecutor! Arthur's tormentor!"

Dani dipped her head, giving a little bow. "The same, I'm afraid."

As the two women exchanged tight smiles of appraisal, Leighton's gaze traveled from the one to the other, then back again. "Give me the swordfish," he announced stolidly as he pushed his chair back and rose. He laid the napkin on his chair and excused himself to Dani. Then he looked about the room uncertainly.

"Straight back of the bar," Joanne announced. He nodded without looking at her and headed across the room toward the semicircular counter that arced around the wood-fired oven. Joanne chuckled. "Bailed right out, didn't he? What's Bigfoot do for a living?"

"He's a urologist," Dani replied. Then—inanely, she realized immediately—she added in his defense, "And quite successful, too."

"It figures." Joanne still stared absently in Leighton's direction.

Dani grinned in spite of herself. "Well, I suppose he can be kind of pissy. Not much of a sense of humor, I'm afraid. But he does have other qualities."

"Men," Joanne said, shaking her head. "Hey, I got nothing against them, mind you. We need another gender and, well, they're *it.* But sometimes . . ." She caught Dani's eye and rolled her own toward the ceiling.

"I suppose we do have to make compromises," Dani offered.

"Sometimes I'd settle for opposable thumbs—maybe a prehensile penis, if I was straight."

Dani found her tuna delicious, but the swordfish didn't change

Leighton's life. Instead of the beefy steak he had expected, he was presented with small, scantily breaded chunks of fish snuggled into little hammocks of bay leaves. They were okay, he conceded, but it was plain he had not yet recovered the buoyant mood he had borne into the restaurant. This annoyed her somewhat, but she felt a little guilty about making fun of him with Joanne, so she let it go. He was peering intently at the dessert menu when a man's voice drifted over her left shoulder.

"You're not wearing your parking ticket. Did you get it fixed?"

The voice belonged to Arthur Patch, who stepped into view beside the table as she looked up. She took in the half-handsome head, the squarish chin cleft in the center by a vertical dimple. His alert blue eyes glittered in concert with a guarded smile. Taking her measure. She didn't smile back. He wore a clean white apron. It was of a piece with the way he presented himself—clean, neat, compact. As if he took care to occupy no more space than necessary.

"You seem to have a way of sneaking up on me like that," she responded, somewhat stiffly. "And twice in one day. Should I be suspicious?"

His smile broadened. "Accidental in both cases—at least on my part. Fate seems to to be throwing us together. As for tonight . . . well, you came *here,* remember?"

"I suppose I did," she allowed. The man seemed to be flirting with her, though in a halfhearted way. Was he mocking her or just doing customer maintenance? She glanced at Leighton, who was watching them closely. She betrayed a small smile of her own. "The food is quite good, I must admit. No poison or anything. Or do I have to wait for it to take effect?"

Arthur solemnly raised his right hand. "Scout's honor: no poison. I try to tell myself you're just doing your job."

"*Was,* you mean. I don't work there anymore."

"You left?" His surprise seemed genuine.

"Threw in the towel," she admitted. "It may give you some small satisfaction to know you had a hand in it."

For the life of her, she couldn't explain why she was telling him this. Was she just giving vent to her annoyance with Prout? With Leighton?

"I don't understand."

"You made me see their feet of clay. Or mud—or what have you."

He seemed to consider this. "You mean that business about Tommy? You know, I had no idea it was as big a deal as it turned out."

"I'll bet," she said dryly, her eyes holding his. "You just thought we had a bad apple in the department, is that it?"

His smile returned. "No," he confessed. "I suspected it was more than that. But I never dreamed it was as big as it turned out. I just wanted out of a jam."

"Well," she said with a soft snort, "you got out of it. And me, too."

"What will you do?" He actually sounded concerned.

"Oh, I haven't decided yet," she said breezily. "I have a number of options."

He frowned briefly, then smiled again. "So we don't have any reason to be curt with each other anymore. I'm sorry about this morning. My head was elsewhere. I must have given you a start."

"Apology accepted. And I meant it about the food. About it being good, I mean—not about the poison."

They were both smiling now.

"Are you the chef?" Leighton butted in. Dani recognized the wounded tone of the male feeling passed over in conversation.

Arthur turned his smile his way, seeming to take him in for the first time. "Yes," he said, extending his right hand. "I'm Arthur Patch. I hope everything was all right."

Leighton stared at the offered hand long enough to make a point of some kind, then took it. Dani watched Arthur wince a little from the force of his grip. "Leighton Taylor," he said shortly. He fluttered his other hand over his plate and glanced down at it. "Mezzo, mezzo. Okay, I guess."

Arthur smiled back equably, giving no ground. "Joanne confessed that she might have been a bit flip earlier," he said. "She can be a little salty. Comes right at you. An asset in a business manager but not necessarily in a hostess. But she doesn't mean to offend."

There was something off here, but Dani couldn't identify it. Something different about the guy. She found herself coming to Joanne's defense. "She didn't offend. She's just quick, is all. And we led her on—*I* did, anyway."

Leighton's eyes flicked in her direction, then back to Arthur's.

Arthur smiled at him again. "Well, let me make it up to you. Have dessert with my compliments. And coffee. Both of you. Try the fruit and cheese. We have them flown in from the island."

Was it the way he talked? She realized she had no basis for

comparison: he had never said much during their previous encounters, preferring to sit quietly for the most part and let Grutman or Morrissey do the talking. But whatever it was that made him seem different—maybe just seeing him on his own turf?—she found it oddly disconcerting.

Leighton considered Arthur's offer, as if searching for a way out of some trap. "You don't have *cannolis*?" he asked finally.

Arthur nodded. "We have *cannoli*."

"Then I'll have a *cannoli*," he reported with a satisfied note of soft triumph. "And a decaf cappuccino."

She sensed he was engaged in some contest, as if the two men were bracing each other or something. She turned away from him and smiled at Arthur, warmly this time. She asked for the fruit and cheese.

Maybe she did it to spite Leighton. She wasn't sure. Leighton gave her a blank look.

They spent the night at Leighton's Marlborough Street apartment. He was, as before, an attentive and responsive lover, but she found the sex more aerobic than joyful, calling for concentration instead of inducing abandon. She realized they had not succeeded in rebuilding the rapport lost somehow during those interchanges with Joanne and Arthur. As he slumbered beside her, she found herself trying to figure out just what had taken place at the restaurant. What was it about Arthur that Leighton had found challenging—or had goaded him into challenging Arthur?

And why did she care? *Did* she, for that matter?

She recalled how Arthur had almost run her over that afternoon. He was featured in the last filmy image that floated over her as she sank into sleep—a vision she found oddly comforting in some way. There was Arthur's face, framed by the windshield of his van, bearing a penitent expression as he soundlessly made his apology. *Sorry*, he had mouthed, gently patting his breast with the splayed fingers of his right hand, right over his heart. An odd, almost effeminate gesture; a confiding display of his own fright and distress.

It was a winter sun, slanted and weak, that filled the room when she awoke in the morning. Leighton had left the bed already. The bedside clock advised that it wasn't seven yet, so she assumed he had left for the health club. She pulled herself up into a sitting position and flung the covers aside. She had almost padded her way through the door to the bathroom before she identified the black lump on the dresser she had just passed. It was his wallet. She paused in the doorway.

"Leighton?" she called in the direction of the living room.

Getting no answer, she walked back toward the dresser in puzzlement. Beside his wallet lay his car keys. A full money clip and some pocket change. An American Express receipt. Then the bewilderment left her and she smiled.

Of course. He was jogging. The AmEx receipt, she noticed, was for the dinner they had eaten at Arthur's place. She remembered Leighton signing it with a flourish and turning it facedown on the little tray on which Joanne had delivered the check. Idly, she picked it up. It took a moment for the omission to register, but when it did she was surprised by her anger.

The good doctor had left no tip.

Wreaking his revenge, she was sure. All that money he made in his fashionable Brookline urology practice, and he stiffs the help in a restaurant. And the message? Trifle with Leighton Taylor and he withholds his largesse. Keeps his uro-dollars. And why? Because of a little badinage with Joanne at his expense? Some ineffable macho exchange with Arthur? Did he think he'd "lost" because she took Arthur's advice about dessert?

But whatever it was, it was irredeemably petty, betokening a vein of meanness that had never shown itself so baldly. She was surprised she had not detected it before.

Doctor Thug.

Dani was gone before Dr. Leighton Taylor returned from his early-morning run. He just missed her.

CHAPTER SIXTEEN

ALMOST ALIVE

NOVEMBER 27, 1978

It took Tommy a solid hour to make the drive up to Cape Ann, but it was only prudent. A meeting anywhere in the Boston area would be too risky. They settled on Gloucester, so he headed up the Northeast Expressway, took 128 east, and got off early onto 127, taking the back way through Manchester and Magnolia. By the time he spotted the harbor as he entered Gloucester, he was playing once again in his head the telephone conversation with the one person who could have persuaded him to talk to the guy.

What's he want?

He didn't take me into his confidence, Thomas. He just asked me to get the message to you. He wants to sit down and talk.

I don't see any percentage in that.

All you have to do is listen to him, Thomas.

Why?

You know him, after all. And he's a man I trust.

Why should I trust him?

Because you have nothing to lose—and you may discover a way to get out of the hole you're digging for yourself.

Tommy had snorted, but with insufficient contempt. He didn't know why he listened to Jackie, and he understood even less why he was acceding to his request. The two brothers had maintained a civil but wary distance for several years now, ever since Tommy stopped bothering to pick up his paychecks for that bullshit maintenance job in the South Boston courthouse. It was a no-show position anyway, a sop Jackie had thrown his way just after his release from prison—as if a long pull on the public tit was going to turn him into a solid citizen (read: sucker). After that, they'd see each other occasionally at family events, Christmas and such, but that was about it. They moved in different circles, that was all. He was in business, overseeing a number of ventures; Jackie was in politics, naming fire hydrants after dead Irishmen. Yes, different circles. It was as simple as that.

In the end his own curiosity got the better of him. What could the guy have to say to him? He called the number Jackie'd given him and somehow here he was, four days later, at dusk with the sea air full of winter and the slap of high tide in his ears, waiting at the cut. The drawbridge was up so some white-haired asshole on a pennant-festooned launch could churn his way toward the shelter of the slips along the Anisquam River. Tommy drummed his fingers on the steering wheel.

When the drawbridge was lowered and the gate raised, he accelerated slowly up the Boulevard and looked for the Fisherman. And there he was, right where the guy said he'd be, on a cement pedestal just this side of the seawall. In a verdigris oilskin and fisherman's floppy hat, the Fisherman had his back to the town, leaning on a ship's wheel as he gazed benignly out at Ten Pound Island. He looked like something Jackie would hang a wreath on.

Tommy pulled the Regal into a parking spot along the seawall. The last of the daylight was melting into the still-bright surface of the harbor, laid out before him like a plate of hammered silver. He shut off the engine and looked around. There was only one other car parked at the seawall, a dozen slots farther down and empty. He glanced at his watch. Twenty minutes early and alone, just the way he liked it. Turning his head to the right, he bent forward. With his left temple touching the top of the steering wheel, he groped up behind the dashboard with his left hand. It was still snugly in place, the cool metal reassuring against his palm. Just a precaution. He was ready for him now.

Tommy sat up straight again and rubbed his palm on the skirt of the seat to remove any dust. Then he cranked down the window and breathed in the chilly salt air. A parka-clad father and daughter were taking turns peeking through one of the coin-operated telescopes mounted near the railing that ran along the seawall in front of the Fisherman.

He didn't mind waiting. He felt it gave him a bit of an edge to watch the other side arrive. It also afforded him a last opportunity to rethink what he was doing here. What did he have to gain? He was at the top of his game, really, the number-two man in the crew, after Mellet. He and Hink both. The two of them were the eyes and ears and muscle, the discipline, for the D Street Gang, and his own reputation as somebody you didn't fuck with was secure in the neighborhoods. It wasn't just the knowledge that he was dangerous, the fear of brute force. A lot of the guys could supply that—and who better than Hink? No, it was more than that. He had come this far on leadership, the air of command he brought to his work. And smarts, of course. But also something else, too, something harder to describe.

The touch. That was it. He had the right touch. The right touch for the particular situation. It was a gift, when you thought about it. And he had it.

Like that business with McGinty that Hink liked to go around telling everybody about. McGinty the hardhead. McGinty the Catholic Memorial football star and Vietnam war hero, big as Hinkle, and maybe tougher. Decided to take a stand, like he was back in Khe Sanh or something. Till Tommy applied the touch.

Charlie McGinty traded on his Purple Heart and athlete's fame to put together the hometown financing to buy Crikey's, a beat-up saloon on Elkins Street, just down and around the corner from the Edison plant. Crikey's was the kind of place where, if some guy passed out, a fight would break out over who got to finish his drink. But a look at the books told McGinty that Crikey's did a tidy bar business. Most of the patrons stayed away from the food unless they were legless, but McGinty figured to correct this deficiency by putting his wife in the kitchen (they moved into the flat above the place with their seven-year-old son). He hoped gradually to build up the joint as a friendly stop-off for the working stiffs on their way home from the electric plant and the Conley Marine Terminal to the east, and to reach out to the residents of the three-deckers closer to Broadway. The only thing he didn't reckon on, when he bought in, was the laundry at the back.

The laundry consisted of a card table and a folding chair just a few steps from the door to the men's room. Every Thursday and Friday the table's surface was taken up by a gray metal petty-cash box, a manila envelope, an open bottle of Harp, and the skinny forearms of a bitter-faced little guy with a flat nose and a clean white dress shirt. His name was Heller. Heller ran the laundry.

How it worked was a guy would come up and endorse his paycheck and hand it to Heller. Heller would count out cash from the box, give it to the guy, enter the amount on a deposit slip, and stuff the check into the envelope. At closing he would laboriously total the amounts of all the checks on the slip and slide it into the manila envelope. He would put the sealed envelope in his waistband, the cash box in the trunk of a maroon Nova, and his bony rear end behind the wheel. The Nova would climb out of Southie by heading north on the Southeast Expressway, then across the Tobin Bridge to the first Chelsea exit. There Heller would make an after-hours deposit at a small neighborhood bank.

Heller's several counterparts also made deposits at the bank. The bank dutifully posted the checks to a business account held in the name of a nondescript corporation. Thanks to a junior bank officer who had the circumspection not to examine too closely the corporate resolutions presented by the man who opened the account or his personal identification, the corporation was an anonymous dummy. Each week the bank executed a standing order to wire all but a nominal balance to an out-of-state bank, which would relay the funds to yet another account somewhere else. And so on. The funds would be schlepped about electronically until they landed dizzily in some unexceptionable account belonging to some seemingly legitimate business. Which paid its taxes like a good citizen—with clean, virtually untraceable funds. All in all, a tidy arrangement for everyone concerned, including Crikey's, since the opportunity to cash a paycheck before going home to the missus was a magnet for bar business.

Except McGinty didn't want it. Move it somewhere else, he told Heller. Crikey's was a family business now, and McGinty was not about to sully his hard-won reputation by laundering the take for Mellet and his crew. So just move on down the road. Heller's efforts to explain that Mellet did not want him to move got him nowhere. Equally unavailing was a visit from three toughs dispatched to reason with the man; McGinty tossed them out the front door like discarded pillows, trailing stuffing. So Mellet told Tommy and Hinkle to take care of the problem.

McGinty was holding three cases of full Budweiser long necks, one on top of the other, when they entered Crikey's early in the morning. McGinty was big all right, massive through the chest and even taller than Hink. His round dumpling of a face was dead white and punched with dark button eyes like a pig's. He paused briefly to watch them trundle toward him between the bar and a row of tables stacked with chairs. Then he went on about his business. He carried the beer cases out from his body with ease, as if they were no more than a cafeteria tray bearing his lunch. Setting them down on the floor behind the bar, he started filling the cooler without looking up. The beginnings of a bald spot showed through his curly red hair as he bent to the task.

Tommy felt a sudden urge to crack him just for the disrespect, but Hink stuck to the agenda, starting right in with the easy schmooze, the friendly grin. McGinty eventually stopped work to listen to him, his pale face expressionless. Twice he shook his head; once he said, "I'm not interested." After several minutes of this, Hink sank onto the barstool next to Tommy and lifted both hands in a grand gesture of helplessness.

"You hearin' this, Tommy?" Hink asked, sighing. "Mr. McGinty here is some kinda loner. No appreciation for the community at all, far as I can see." His tone was still amiable, like an amused adult who can't jolly a child into sharing his strawberry Popsicle. But Tommy knew from the rippling of his jaw muscles that Hink was ready to take him on as a physical challenge—King Kong meets Godzilla. Tommy looked into McGinty's flat swinish eyes and saw that no beating was going to convince this guy. They'd kill him first, and Mellet wouldn't want that much aggravation.

The front door banged open and the three men turned toward the sound. McGinty's kid came bounding in. Long-legged for seven and skinny, he had his father's shock of orange hair, one lock of which bounced up and down against his forehead as he ran. He heeled when he saw his father had company so early, the bar not even open yet. Hink spun his stool a quarter turn toward the door to square around. He shot the kid a wide grin.

"Hey!" he said brightly. "Gotta be Charlie's boy! Give us five, big fella." He raised a big paw and his eyebrows in unison. The kid froze briefly, then timidly extended his palm to take the meat of Hink's playful slap. "What's your name, huh?"

It was very quiet while the kid considered the question. "Charles," he said at last.

"Just like your old man!" Hink declared, beaming at the kid. "Looks just like him, too. Don't he, Tommy?"

But Tommy didn't answer. He was watching McGinty. Saw his eyes soften and soak up fear like a parched garden greeting a summer rain. And he knew he had him.

"How's he look to you?" Hink persisted, still admiring the shyly grinning boy as he tousled his hair.

"He looks . . . almost alive," Tommy answered, his eyes never leaving McGinty's.

Almost alive! On the drive back from Crikey's, Hink threw his head back and roared, then pounded his fists on the dashboard. "Oh, yeah. He looked *almost alive* all right. But his old man sure didn't. D'ja catch his face? Jesus, Tommy. Where'd you come up with that one?"

Tommy had just shrugged. "Sometimes," he explained, "you gotta get 'em to think outside the box."

"Huh?"

"McGinty figured he knew the rules of engagement. So I just gave him the impression there weren't any. No limits. You know what I mean?"

"Oh, yeah," said Hinkle, nodding vigorously. "I know what you mean. So does McGinty. His shit'll be loose for a week. And Heller's Harp will be on the house, you wait and see."

And he chuckled happily all the way back. Just the way he did every time he told the story. *Almost alive.* It became a catchphrase, a shibboleth. *Tell him he looks almost alive,* guys would advise each other when discussing the discreet application of leverage. It was all part of Tommy's touch. As was the end of their ride that morning, when Hink got quiet for a second and then cocked his head to peer over at Tommy from the passenger seat.

" 'Course, it *was* just an impression, right?"

It was Tommy's turn to say, "Huh?"

"That business about no limits, I mean."

Tommy had waggled his fingers on the steering wheel as he looked over at him. He stared hard into his partner's eyes until Hink looked away. "Of course," Hink said, opting to answer his own question. "Just an impression."

But Tommy said nothing at all.

A gray Ford stole into his reverie from the left, its tires grinding pebbles as it eased into the parking slot in front of him. The driver got out and walked toward the rear, trailing his fingers along the Ford's trunk lid. He paused briefly in front of Tommy's Regal. Slowly rolling his shoulder muscles, he glanced up at the Fisherman and then panned the Boulevard behind Tommy. He was tall and heavy with much of his weight jiggling about his waist. He had a long, thick neck and sloping shoulders. *Cokebottle,* Tommy thought, recalling the man's nickname as an adolescent. He wore high-top running shoes, a dark green sweatshirt, and a baseball cap to cover his balding pate. He stepped quickly to Tommy's door and shoved his right hand into the open window.

"Tommy," he said, showing a mouthful of perfect teeth. "Long time, eh?"

"How are you, Marty?" Tommy replied as he shook the soft hand of Special Agent Martin Flukes. "They treat you good?"

When he let go, Flukes laid his forearms on the windowsill and bent forward. "I can't complain," he said. The smile broadened as he added, "Well, I could, but it wouldn't do any good. But yeah, they treat me okay."

Tommy eyed him carefully, biding his time. *Leave it up to him,* he thought.

Flukes finally figured this out. "C'mon," he said, encouraging him with a jerk of his head. "Let's take a walk."

Tommy paused briefly at this unanticipated suggestion, thinking fast. Then he tugged at the door handle. Flukes stepped back to let him open the door. He climbed out of the Regal and, zipping his jacket, trailed Flukes to the sidewalk. He noticed purple heads of ornamental kale planted in the flower bed that encircled the Fisherman.

When they reached the seawall, Tommy felt the bite of the cold wind off the harbor. It carried a film of spray with it. He crossed his arms over his thin jacket.

"You wanna check me for a wire, Tommy?" Flukes asked with a grin. " 'Cause I'm not wearing one here."

"Nah. I'm not gonna give you anything anyway."

Flukes chuckled knowingly at this and kept walking, in the direction of Rockport, a road sign indicated. At the far end of the seawall stood the Tavern, an enormous barn-shaped restaurant with its dining-room lights distinctly visible through the picture windows facing the men as they walked. Another gust off the harbor plastered Tommy's jacket against his torso. He pulled up short as Flukes pulled the hood of his sweatshirt up over his cap.

"I'm not dressed for nautical adventures, Marty. You want me to freeze my nuts off? Let's go back inside."

He headed back to the Regal without waiting for a response. Flukes watched him, then shrugged faintly and followed. As Flukes ducked and twisted his head away to lower himself into the passenger seat, Tommy briefly ran his left hand under the dashboard again. Satisfied, he wiped his hand on the door's upholstery and sat back. He skewed his body slightly in Flukes's direction. Again, he waited for Flukes to start it off.

"So Jesus, Tommy, how long's it been? I don't think I've seen you since before you went inside. That makes it what, nine, ten years?"

"Eleven," Tommy corrected. *As if you didn't check the file before coming here.* Tommy would never need to check the date he entered a federal penitentiary. It was a fixed lodestar in his memory, as unforgettable as a graduation year for other men.

"Eleven *years,*" Flukes said, shaking his head in wonderment. "Christ, it seems . . . Well, whatever. I remember being really bummed out about it at the time." He was looking out at the harbor now, at the dots of light that were starting to sequin the shoreline as darkness descended. "I shouldn't be saying this. I mean, a guy in my position and all. But you know, I always used to look up to you when I was a kid." He turned back to look earnestly at Tommy. "No shit, Tommy. And when I heard about that armored car thing, and how some pug was spilling that you were the guy that brokered the heist plan—well, I felt kinda bad."

Flukes rolled his eyes up toward the roof of the car in disgust. "Will you listen to me? 'Kinda bad'? Shit, I was *bummed.* And who could I tell? You know what I'm saying?"

Tommy didn't answer. He remembered Flukes in a church-league baseball uniform, his dirty face full of awe as Tommy handed the kid an Eskimo Pie at Kelly's Clam Shack. Hanging around Hink and him when they were just tough guys on the corner. But he didn't answer.

"That's partly why I asked Jackie to call you. Jeez, he's really coming on, though, isn't he? In the State House now and making a name for himself. You get to see much of him?"

"We're brothers, Marty."

Expecting elaboration, Flukes waited a moment, but Tommy's silence held. So he pushed on.

"Thing is, things are changing fast. It's not like it was in the sixties, Tommy. Everything's gonna be different. You gotta change with it, or you're finished. So I come with a warning and a business proposition. Because the Italians are getting restless and the Bureau's got a new tool, a new statute on the books that's gonna take down the LCN."

Tommy snorted. How many times had he heard crap like this? And La Cosa Nostra was still alive and well.

"This is different, Tommy," Flukes insisted, shaking his head. "You gotta listen." Flukes paused for effect. "First, we been getting word from different sources that Francesco is losing patience with your guys. He's had it with Mellet. He thinks the guy has been hosing him and doesn't have a very good grip on his piece of the show anyway."

Francesco must be reading my mail, he thought wryly.

"Word is," Flukes continued, "he might make a move. If there's a war, you'd be one of the first to get hit. You gotta know that."

Tommy smiled at this.

Flukes said, "Listen, you weren't around when your guys had their own war, against each other. You were inside then. That probably kept you alive, for Chrissakes. They killed each other off like rabbits. The *Herald* used to keep score: they ran a sidebar with the daily bag of Irishmen, like it was Vietnam. Till everybody got sick of it, and Mellet ended up on top. But if you hadn't been inside, do you think you'd have survived all that? Probably not. Or maybe you would have made it; you were just a tough guy then. But this time you're right up there, next to Mellet. If the LCN makes a move, you'd be high on the hit parade. Am I wrong about this? 'Cause if I am, you should let me know."

Of course he wasn't wrong. But Tommy felt no intimations of a looming war with Francesco, and he reckoned his intelligence on such matters was at least as good as the Bureau's. But all he said was, "So what?"

"Another thing," Flukes persisted, ignoring the question. "It's a new ball game now. We got this new guy, Stanley Prout? That's running the Strike Force, and he's serious about taking down the Italians. It's a national thing, happening everywhere. Comes right out of Main Justice in DC. With the new statute, RICO. You heard of it?"

"The Racketeer Influenced Corrupt Organizations Act."

Flukes nodded. "I'm impressed, as always. Well, Prout's targeting Chicco and his top guys. He's gonna get 'em, too. This is not like all those other times, Tommy. This is big, and it's different."

"What's that to me?" Tommy asked. "I should go whimpering off into a hole somewhere, maybe, 'cause the feds are coming?"

"You're missing my point here, Tommy. Prout's not after *you.* He doesn't want the Irish guys. You're strictly local. No national organization like the Italians. He wants Francesco and the LCN, as part of this nationwide takedown I'm telling you about. So I'm not here to give you a heads-up about Prout. I'm here with an *opportunity.* Something for *our* side."

He was smiling again. Our side. He meant the Irish. The neighborhood. Southie.

"What kind of opportunity?"

"Well, think about it. If Prout takes Chicco off at the knees, if he can wipe out the Mafia's whole upper management—who *benefits*? Who moves into the vacuum, Tommy?"

"Mellet?" There was a malicious slyness to Tommy's smile.

"*Fuck* Mellet!" Flukes sounded exasperated, but Tommy reckoned it was just part of the pitch. "Mellet's a meatball, and you know it, Tommy. How much longer is he gonna be around? He's living on borrowed time, and he'd never have the vision to seize the opportunity I'm discussing here."

"You're losing me there, Marty."

A young couple appeared on the sidewalk in front of them. Flukes waited as, arm in arm and huddled against the cold, they ambled past the Regal.

"Look," he said, "I've been talking to Prout about you. Telling him what a good guy you are. Wild, sure, but okay where it counts. I told him how you helped keep the lid on the Town when they started with the forced busing. How you don't allow drug dealers in the neighborhood either. And how, thanks to you, people can walk down the streets at night—unlike the 'Bury or the South End, for example. And that the two of you should be able to do business. 'Cause you've got something in common."

"Something in common. Me and . . . Prout, did you say?" There was a sardonic edge to his voice.

"*Yes,* damn it. You and Prout. He wants to take Chicco off the board. I figure you wouldn't mind having him out of your hair as well. Prout wants Chicco and his boys so bad he can taste it. He'll deal, Tommy. I mean it."

"Deal," said Tommy harshly, screwing his face up in fury. "You think you're gonna flip me, Marty? Is that it? Make me a snitch?"

"No, no, Tommy. I—"

" 'Cause I don't inform. You can just get your ass out of—"

"Goddamn it, will you *listen,* for Chrissake? Nobody's talking snitch here. You see me offering you a few bucks and packet of blow? Hear me out. I'm talking *business.* I'm talking favor for favor. A joint venture. Purely business, okay?"

"What business?" Tommy spoke in a monotone.

"An exchange of intelligence, that's what I mean. A pooling of resources and, like, *data.*" Flukes seemed pleased with his word choice. "Like I said, nobody's interested in D Street. Here's what I'm authorized to offer you. You listening?"

Tommy said nothing, but his attention was riveted on Flukes, who started counting off on his fingers as he spoke.

"One, we keep you abreast, as we learn it, of whatever is going down out of the North End. You'll know as soon as we do what Chicco and the wops are up to.

"Two, we're offering to take out your principal competition—the Italians. Which leaves you a clear field.

"Three, we leave you alone: no feds looking over your shoulder, raiding your games, or taping your business meetings. A little room to move, you know?

"Fourth—and this is really on the QT, Tommy, abso*lute*ly just between me and you, okay? *We tip you if the local cops initiate any major hostile activity.* Boston PD, the Staties, whatever. You got, in effect, a license to operate free of any serious interference. Oh, a little nickel-and-dime annoyance, maybe—that stuff's bound to happen just to keep people from getting suspicious. The price of doing business. But nothing major. You get a free hand."

Tommy remained immensely alert. "And in exchange?"

Flukes pointed his index fingers at Tommy. "Nothing about your outfit, Tommy. Nothing at all. Just stuff about our common enemy. We want Chicco. You do business with him. You're always meeting with him. He trusts you. You can get in to him, closer than we can ever get. We want to know what he's doing, and what he's gonna do after that. Where his meets are, so we can be there ahead of him. He takes a crap, we wanna know where and what color toilet paper. We gotta know everything we can about his people, his organization, top to bottom."

Tommy was adding it up in his head, but it didn't compute. They didn't need him for that. The guy was leaving something out. He had to be.

"Drop the other shoe, Marty. What else?"

"A natural outgrowth," Flukes said with a sheepish grin. "Follows from what I said."

"Yes?"

"Yeah. We gotta get a wire in Chicco's place of business. Michelangelo Street. And we need your help to do it. 'Cause we haven't been able to get near the place."

Tommy's anger was palpable in the front seat of the Regal. "You want me to wear a fucking *wire* while I talk to Francesco Coniglio?"

"No, no!" cried Flukes, who was waving his hands in front of his chest. "And we're not asking you to *plant* one either. It's just that we don't have anybody's ever *been* inside Michelangelo Street. We need somebody who can sketch it out for us, the layout, in detail. To go back in later for the answers to any questions we might have about the floor plan. For more details, basically. We have to know everything there is to know about the interior of that place. About its doors and windows. Electrical fixtures. What kind of ceiling tiles they got. We're talking low-risk stuff here, but stuff only somebody on the inside can give us. 'Cause once we know how to get into Chicco's office—how to get in and out when we need to service the wire—we will get the goods to put him away. Forfuckingever. Count on it."

Flukes sat back now, the pitch complete. He'd shot his wad. He was watching Tommy, who remained quiet for some time. It had started raining, small beads running down the windshield as the two men sat in silence.

"Suppose," Tommy said at last, "we do a deal and it all works out like the dream you're peddling. What happens then? You come after *me* next?"

"Tommy," Flukes said, his tone pitying. "This is the United States government here. Not some hack with the Suffolk County DA. We're calling this our Top Echelon program. You'd be the biggest thing in it. We don't mess up an asset that large."

"Nobody comes after me?"

"Long as you don't clip somebody, I can't see that happening."

"I'd need more than that, Marty. More that what you can *see hap-*

pening." Tommy paused before enunciating slowly and carefully. "Does this come from the top—that they won't come after me later?"

Tommy could see Flukes making up his mind whether to say it out loud. The agent peered out into the dank gloom over the harbor for a moment, then turned to face Tommy. "It's from the top, Tommy. Long as it's not a murder beef, you get a free ride."

"All the way to Prout?" Tommy seemed to raise his voice a little.

"All the way to Prout," Flukes said, nodding gravely. "But more important, it goes all the way to *me.* I mean, if something goes rotten—a new director or somebody at Main Justice decides to welsh on the deal—I *personally* guarantee you'll get a heads-up. Before anything comes down, I mean. At the very *least* you'd get a head start."

Silence again, broken only by the rumbling of a passing eighteen-wheeler, its refrigerated trailer bearing a Gorton's Fisheries logo.

Tommy said, "I'll give it some thought, Marty. S'all I can say for now."

"I understand, Tommy. Just let—"

"It's very complicated. I'd have to have Hink in it with me, if I agreed to do business. Gotta have Hink."

If this surprised Flukes, he didn't let on. The agent just nodded placidly.

Tommy smiled at him. "You guys are something else," he said, shaking his head in astonishment. "You're offering to let me run an illegal operation—loan-sharking, gambling, protection—in exchange for information. That's a big, big step, Marty."

Flukes's smile was smug. "We're gonna do big, big things, Tommy. So let me know." He pushed open his door and climbed out of the Regal. He looked back in at Tommy. "Just give me a call at that number Jackie gave you. Ask for me and tell them your name is Braddock. Got that? Braddock."

"Braddock," said Tommy as if to himself. "I'll think about it."

"Good to see you again, Tommy."

But Tommy was too preoccupied to respond, so Flukes slammed the door and made for his own car. Tommy sat staring out at the harbor as the agent drove away. Checking his rearview mirror to make sure the guy was clear, Tommy leaned forward under the dash and shut off the tape recorder. He ejected the miniature cassette and slipped it into his shirt pocket.

He started the Regal and began the drive back to the city. It wasn't until he was passing the first Somerville exit off I-93 that the idea came to him. Why not expand the deal Flukes was offering him? Why limit it to Francesco and the wops? Sure, D Street did a lot of business with the LCN, despite a little friction at the edges now and then. Taking out Francesco would free up a lot of turf for D Street. But in that case the beneficiary would be Mellet, not Tommy.

Why not give up Mellet first?

And so it happened. On a hot evening some nine months later, Brian Mellet, the reigning chief of the D Street Gang for over eight years, was arrested in his Somerville home and charged with fixing races at the Wonderland Greyhound Track in Revere. Someone supplied the attorney general with information to prove he'd been feeding buttermilk to slow down the favorites and chocolate to goose the dogs he bet on. Mellet's sources within the state constabulary could determine only that the tip had come to them from the FBI, and from the feds they could learn nothing further. But he knew in his bones that the ultimate source had to be someone inside his outfit. As he was cuffed in the courtroom after receiving an eleven-year Walpole sentence, Mellet extracted from his faithful lieutenant—and now successor as gang boss—a promise to ferret out the snitch who had put him away.

"I want his fuckin' face in a baggie," Mellet hissed as the respectful trooper waited politely for him to say his good-byes. "The rest of him you throw on a Dumpster in the Lower End—alive if possible. Swear it!"

Tommy swore it.

CHAPTER SEVENTEEN

ANIMAL RIGHTS WEEK

I don't want anything fancy," the patron said as he handed his menu to Arthur. "Just give me some spaghetti with red sauce."

"Which of the sauces would you like? Today we have—"

"Whatever," the man interrupted with a shrug. He turned his attention toward his luncheon companion.

"No," Arthur said, struggling to throttle his irritation. "Not 'whatever.' They're different sauces. The *pomodoro* is a cooked sauce based on *'strattu,* a special kind of tomato paste we make on the premises. The *carrettierria* is with raw tomatoes. So they're very different."

The patron, a pudgy bespeckled man in double-breasted pinstripes, glanced up at Arthur, then back across the table and raised his hands as if to say, *What's with this guy?* "What*ever,*" he repeated. "It's all the same to me." His companion handed her menu to Arthur, who took it without looking at her.

Arthur felt his irritation growing. "You said you're a lawyer, right? Would your clients trust a lawyer who said 'whatever'?"

The patron stared back at him in pop-eyed wonder, but Arthur couldn't stop himself now.

"Of course not," he continued. "Because you understand your work requires precision, attention to detail. The ability to draw distinctions. Like, like—between a corporation and a partnership, right? Well, my work's the same way. These are distinct sauces."

"I just want it red, okay? Red sauce. On my spaghetti. Is that too much to ask, for crying out loud?"

Arthur had his mouth open to reply when he heard Joanne intervene from his right. "Of course not," she said with a placating smile. Her foot came down on his and ground harshly on the tops of his toes. It was all he could do not to cry out. "Let's try the *pomodoro.* It's simple but intense. I know you'll like it. Right, Arthur?"

Her smile was withering. "Yes," he said, feeling sheepish for getting after the guy. "That's a good choice. I'm sure you'll enjoy it."

Within seconds Arthur had hobbled through the swinging door and into the sanctuary of the kitchen. Brad, the prep cook, was deftly making a finely minced hash called a *battuto* by chopping carrots, onions, and celery together. His chef's knife clacked on the big white cutting board. At the range Jonathan was adding calamari rings to a fish sauce bubbling in a sauté pan. He shook the pan and shuffled it back and forth over a licking gas flame. Arthur was hoping Joanne wouldn't follow, but she was right behind him.

"What the fuck's the matter with you?" Joanne Balzer demanded as the door shuddered back into its rest position.

No one ever described Arthur's business partner as "pretty" or "attractive"; such frivolous modifiers shivered in her daunting shadow. Hands on hips, Joanne stood an inch taller than Arthur, with square shoulders and powerful, no-nonsense legs, though she carried no more weight than her solid frame was built to support. Her thick cinnamon hair was cut short, brushed up at the front and just reaching her earlobes at the back. Her features were mobile and expressive, dominated by quick, skewering brown eyes above a sharp nose that turned up as if spurning her upper lip. Sometimes she scared the hell out of him.

Getting a whiff of powder, Jonathan and Brad looked up to witness a skirmish between the bosses. But it was no contest, a rout. Arthur held up his hands to repel a scolding that was no longer needed. "I know, I know," he conceded. "The guy just got to me, is all. I mean, why pay these prices if you don't give a shit?"

She shook her head. "No, Arthur, you have it backwards. It's why give a shit if he'll pay these prices."

He dropped his chin to concede the point. "You're right, you're right. This is a business, not a cooking class. I should stay in the kitchen."

She exhaled heavily. "Some business. Have you seen this?" She thrust a sheet of paper at him. He took it from her. "The meat bill wasn't paid last month. Last week it was the wine distributor. Arthur, we're gonna be bleeding red ink all over the balance sheets." She gestured toward the sheet of paper. "And how come we have to buy such expensive veal anyway. What is it, massaged by Japanese monks or something?"

Arthur examined the invoice. He grimaced sympathetically at the balance due. "It's baby beef, really. *Vitellone.* A little older than veal, and it's not just penned up and fed milk. I'll pay it."

"You mean it's free range, like that anabolic poultry you order? Stuff that's too *fit* to eat?"

Carlotta came barging in behind Joanne. "Where's my seafood linguini?" she called out.

"Coming up," Jonathan answered. He threw in a handful of raw shrimp and gave the pan another shake.

"I suppose it *is* free range. But the flavor's richer and more authentic. I suppose it's more humane, too." Arthur shrugged off the final benefit as serendipitous.

Carlotta bellied up to the range and began filling a bowl with soup from the heavy pot at the back. Brad resumed his chopping, his ponytail bobbing in rhythm.

Joanne was unappeased. "So this is animal rights week? You better not go vegetarian on me, Arthur Patch. I'm not gonna let you run us into the ground because you decide to offer nothing but weird broccoli hybrids or something. I'm still recovering from that sardine pasta thing."

"Hey," piped up Brad, the vegetarian. *Gratitude,* the lettering on his T-shirt pointed out, *Is an Anagram for "I Get A Turd."*

"Oh, *please,* Bradley. Don't go ideological on me. The way I figure, if God wanted us to be vegetarians, how come He made animals out of meat?"

"Speaking of meat," Jonathan jumped in, "I had this idea for tonight's *osso buco*?" He dropped mussels and clams into the sauté pan and covered it. "Arthur, you listening?"

"Is that mine?" Carlotta asked him, bowl of soup in hand.

"I figured it might be interesting to add something besides artichokes to the veal shanks."

"That's just specious. If meat's so wonderful, how come He made vegetables better for you?"

"Like what?" Arthur asked warily. Jonathan Mildig had an undeniable talent, but he sometimes squandered it on silly "creations." Like an immature claret (good nose, no finish), he just needed aging.

"*Better* for you? Are you kidding, Bradley? You lay off the meat, your circular system gets out of shape. Take all those joggers, grim as cadavers, coddling their blood vessels with tofu and St. John's wort."

"Now don't just reject it out of hand, Arthur. Give it some thought. I'm suggesting fiddlehead greens."

"Then Thanksgiving rolls around and they eat like human beings for a change, and what happens? Stroke City. Those pampered arteries burst on them."

"Fiddleheads?"

Joanne raised her arm and made a muscle, her voice sinking to a masculine growl. "No, sir. You gotta flex them arterial walls. Build vascular tone."

"Can I *please* have my linguini?"

"Fiddleheads? Did he say fiddleheads?" asked Joanne, switching targets.

"Yeah, fiddleheads." Jonathan sounded resolute, as if anticipating ridicule. Using a long-handled sieve, he scooped linguini out of a pot at the rear. He let it drain as he lifted the cover off the sauté pan, then dumped the pasta on top of the seafood. "If you time it right, they would come out emerald green. Plus they'd add some welcome crunch to the texture." He shook and shimmied the pan across the flame.

"No, no." Arthur shook his head vigorously. "Absolutely not." He watched as Jonathan slid the pan's contents into a serving bowl and sprinkled parsley over it. He handed it to Carlotta. Arthur stepped aside to let Carlotta back out through the out-door with her soup and pasta, then spun back to face Jonathan. "You didn't already *do* it, did you?" he demanded suspiciously.

"No, I was just thinking it—"

"Because I still remember when you decided to marinate the rabbit in lime instead of lemon."

"It gave it a Caribbean twist!"

"Speaking of rabbit—"

"Jonathan, this is a *Mediterranean* restaurant. Sicily and the neighboring islands. *Not* Barbados."

"Speaking of rabbit, your pal Larry the Rabbit is coming to dinner tonight."

Silence fell. Arthur turned to face Joanne, his abdominal muscles clenching.

"His son called," she continued. "Why does he always give the impression that some nameless village is missing an idiot?"

"Peetie?" he asked weakly.

"The very same. He left a message on the voice mail. Daddy, he says, wants to talk a little business with you."

"Terrific." The knot in his viscera got tighter, if that was possible.

Her bird-quick eyes held his own. "Arthur, what 'business' can Larry have with us? Is this like that guy who wanted us to buy a sign? Can't we get rid of him somehow?"

It's time, he thought. *Fess up and get it over with.*

"I have a confession to make. You're not gonna like it. It's pretty awful."

She didn't respond.

"I borrowed money from Larry. For the restaurant."

Joanne gaped at him. Brad's knife stopped clacking. Jonathan turned to face him. Arthur took them through it, through the dark days when the restaurant was about to fold and no bank was would put up any more working capital. How Larry was always there with cooings of support for the restaurant. With his feelers in the community, Larry also knew Arthur's suppliers were having difficulty getting their bills paid. Arthur had resisted his offers of help at first, but when the shortfalls threatened to close the place down, he had relented. And now, as Larry's people liked to put it, he was on the shark.

When Joanne finally spoke, there was an icy fury in her voice. "You have it wrong again, Arthur. You're not on the shark. *We* are—because I'm your partner. I can't even walk away without losing everything I've put into the place. So excuse me if I don't express my gratitude for your decisiveness. Especially since *I'm* supposed to be handling the financial end. Why couldn't you stay in the fucking kitchen, like we agreed?"

"I'm god-awful sorry, Joanne." He felt swamped with self-loathing. "I just saw the whole thing, my dream, going down the tubes, and I—"

"Wait a minute! This is making sense now. That's what that business with the grand jury was all about, wasn't it? It wasn't about stuff you overheard when Larry and his goons were in here eating."

"No, the U.S. Attorney learned about the loan somehow."

"And I believed you. Jesus, I'm so naive." But she didn't mean that at all; she meant he was an asshole.

"I'm *sorry,*" he pleaded. "They wanted me to tie Larry directly to loan-sharking. Something about a 'predicate offense.' To make a

RICO case, they said. I never did understand it, but I knew it was suicide to testify."

"So just how much did *we* borrow?"

Arthur flinched at the sonic italics. "The loans total forty-two thousand. And almost all of it is still owed. The vig is so high I haven't been able to pay down much principal."

"Vig?"

"Sounds like a laundry detergent," Brad volunteered.

"The vigorish. The interest on the money. It's five points a week."

"A *week*?" Her mouth actually hung open a little. When Arthur didn't respond, she looked away. "Jesus," she muttered. "No wonder the butcher's not getting paid."

"Will we?" asked Brad. "Get paid, I mean?"

"Yes," Arthur promised. *God willing.*

Jonathan piped up. "Will they come in and take over the business? Isn't that what they do if you don't pay? I mean, besides breaking legs and stuff."

Arthur glared at him. "Not always," he said. "They don't take over a business unless they think they can make some money at it. That was my biggest misjudgment. I figured our profit margins weren't big enough to interest them. And we're too small-time to be much use for laundering money. So I figured it would just be a high-interest loan. God knows, we needed the cash. And there was Larry, coming in to wallow in the pasta and wishing us good luck. So . . ."

He raised his hands in a gesture of helplessness.

"So you decided, on your own, to jeopardize all of us," said Joanne. "And now?"

"And now I have this terrible feeling that Larry actually *does* want the restaurant. I didn't figure on him being such a gourmet."

"Oh, *please*," she said, twisting her mouth in disgust. "If you served the guy a tortilla, he'd blow his nose in it."

"No doubt about it," Arthur agreed grimly. "The man's a moron. But he *thinks* he's an epicure, an authority on Sicilian cuisine. This from a guy, mind you, who grew up calling spaghetti sauce 'gravy.' Oh, he once spent a week in Palermo, but he never went back because he found out how scared he is of flying. So, what's he want? From the not-so-subtle hints he's dropped, I think he wants a piece of the restaurant—with me as his indentured servant. He wants to cultivate his self-image as a culinary bon vivant. To greet his pals at the door and preen himself as he moves between tables like a hearse through a crowd. Slapping people on the back and telling them to order the eggplant, he's tasted it and it's good tonight."

Joanne, quiet now, seemed lost in contemplation of this prospect. "Jesus," she said at last. "Imagine filing K1's with Larry the Rabbit."

Arthur snorted. "Oh, he'd never appear as an owner of record, but I take your point."

"You couldn't go to Tommy? At least he's hometown. I can't imagine him wanting a restaurant. I mean, he really *is* a vegetarian, right?"

"Hey," Brad protested. "Guilt by association."

"I doubt it," Arthur said. "He's supposed to be something of a health freak, but I believe he eats meat." He looked at her. "And you *know* why not Tommy. I would never go to him."

"Because of that business with your uncle? You keep letting your personal shit get in the way of good business, Arthur." She shook her head. "First with Larry, now a customer who just wants his red sauce. I don't know about you sometimes."

Arthur said, "I wouldn't have known who to approach in Tommy's crew anyway, and Larry was right there, at my elbow at least once a week."

She eyed him for a moment. "Too bad. At least Tommy's among the missing. Would that we could say the same for Larry the Rabbit."

Would that we could. Arthur stared at his shoes. Joanne strode out of the kitchen in an understandable huff. Brad and Jonathan pointedly let him be as they busied themselves with handling the tail end of the lunch crush. Arthur spent several minutes trying to concentrate on the order of battle for dinner, but his thoughts kept leaping ahead to his scheduled tête-à-tête with Larry Coniglio.

Five minutes later Joanne came back into the kitchen. "Arthur," she said, "I don't know just what to do with how pissed I am."

"I'm sure you'll think of something," he said with a feeble smile.

"No doubt," she said dryly.

To his relief, the kitchen door swung open. Carlotta was back.

"Whew," Carlotta said. She feigned a knee-sagging stumble and clutched at the steel table. "The lunch crowd is finally kaput. Except for the couple at seven; the guy says he's still waiting for a spaghetti with red sauce. I'm gonna make myself some coffee and take a load off. Anybody want some?"

Arthur was the only one to take her up on it. She bounced back out on her way to the coffee station.

"Teach her how to make coffee, willya?" Joanne pleaded. "She puts so much foam in the lattes I always get this urge to shave my legs."

"I like it that way," Arthur said. "Would you mind handling that barbarian who wants his generic red sauce? I'd like a minute to drink my coffee outside. Maybe soak up a little melanoma on Tremont. Who knows, maybe I'll actually come up with something that'll get us out of this mess."

"Why don't you hit up Gordon for a loan while you're over there?" she suggested. She referred to the owner of Hamersley's Bistro, the upscale competition around the corner on Tremont. Hamersley's was arguably the most fashionable and successful restaurant in the South End.

"Another dry well, I'm afraid. They've hit a bit of trough themselves. I ran into Gordon on Friday and told him I heard he had a fire. He held a finger to his lips, and whispered, 'Tomorrow.' "

Joanne's eyes widened. "He's gonna torch it?"

Arthur laughed and headed out the door. It felt good to have Joanne back on *her* heels for a change.

Arthur sat on a concrete stairway to an apartment building that fronted on the south side of Tremont Street. He put the saucer on the step beside him, took a sip of coffee (Joanne was right about the foam), and placed the cup back on the saucer.

It was ridiculously warm for November. The sky was so blue and the air so clean it made him think of the squeak of fingers on a dinner plate hot from the dishwasher. Feeling the warmth of the sun on his face, he laced his fingers behind his neck and bent his elbows backward in a stretching motion. He squinted across Tremont at the chic storefronts and rival restaurant marquees. Impeccably restored apartment buildings basked in the early-afternoon sun with him, the high light burnishing sand-blasted facades of pudding stone and red brick. The heat felt wonderful, revivifying after days of chilly weather. When he shut his eyes a blood orange stain soaked through the thin curtains of his eyelids.

The sun wasn't enough, however, to burn out the image of Larry Coniglio. That one lodged deeper, hunkered down in the cold and the dark, where Larry wiped the grease off his chin and mournfully shook his head over the burden of Arthur's debt service. While Peetie's boredom grew truculent and Nick Tramontana looked on with laconic amusement at the whole comic opera.

Arthur shook his head and blinked his eyes open. From his right he watched the halting approach of a muttering derelict. The man shuffled along in oversize gray trousers, the cuffs piled up on moldy, laceless wing tips. A red corduroy vest with brass buttons flashed each time his flocked overcoat swung open. He wore a yachtsman's cap with yellow braiding, set at a rakish angle. Decked out in his musty finery, his complexion the mottled red of a pomegranate, he reminded Arthur of a seedy ringmaster in some provincial circus.

The man talked to himself while his hands semaphored wildly before him. Tears, Arthur noticed, streamed from the man's eyes and cut smeared furrows through the grime on his cheeks and jaw. Arthur looked away lest his attention be misread as an invitation to conversation. Almost out of eyeshot on his left, a woman with a dog on a leash pulled up short, apparently with the same motive.

The derelict stopped and turned in Arthur's direction. He braced himself for some unpleasant encounter, but the man's eyes were focused on nothing in his immediate environs. Unseeing, he continued to jabber with breathless urgency, the words fired through a windmill of dissociated gestures. Nothing he said was audible.

The man suddenly stopped talking, his head cocked to one side in a listening pose, as if his invisible interlocutor had modulated to a different frequency. He made a quarter turn to his right and began to resume his journey. Then he froze again.

He was alert to his surroundings this time—frantically alert, in fact—for he was obviously transfixed by the dog in front of him. The man remained motionless, staring at the animal as if his immobility alone kept it from ripping his throat out. The dog, which sat on its haunches just fifteen feet away, cocked its own head in mild curiosity. Then the woman spoke up.

"It's all right. She won't hurt you. And anyway, I've got the leash." She raised slightly the hand with the leash wound about it. "See?" She offered a reassuring smile.

The derelict remained in place, his eyes darting feverishly. Then he turned smartly on his heels and lumbered off in his herky-jerky manner in the direction from which he had come. In the right pocket of his overcoat, Arthur noticed for the first time, the man carried a plastic liter bottle of Perrier. The springwater sloshed as he walked.

In the better neighborhoods, it occurred to Arthur, even the bums drink designer water.

It wasn't until the man was a quarter block up the street that Arthur and the woman turned away from him to face one another. They smiled. The unspoken complicity of the moneyed, the sane.

She was pretty, a young African-American in her late twenties or early thirties with hair that fell to her shoulders in gold-banded corn-rows. The lenses of her gold-rimmed glasses glittered like coins in the sunlight. She bent her smile toward the dog still poised on its haunches beside her. Arthur got to his feet out of politeness.

She said, "I don't know whether to be grateful she scared him off or ashamed that he found her so terrifying. The poor guy!" They both looked off in the direction he had taken, but he had vanished.

Arthur shrugged. "Who knows *what* he saw. Your dog doesn't look all that vicious."

A greyhound, Arthur noticed for the first time. The dog was sleek and muscular, with a heaving rib cage that embossed its brindled hide. It made him think of an Olympic sprinter—you knew it could run like the wind. The animal gave Arthur the same look of harmless curiosity that had terrified the derelict.

She made a scoffing sound. "Bella? She wouldn't harm a soul, really. If a burglar ever broke in, she'd show him where to find the silver."

Arthur asked, "She's a greyhound, isn't she? I've seen them at the track, but I don't remember ever seeing one up close." He smiled. "She's not even gray."

"It's a common mistake. The name has nothing to do with color. It comes from an Old English word meaning dog hunter."

"Was she a racing dog once?"

"Oh, yes." It was as if he'd thrown a switch or something, given the way she snatched at this conversational gambit. "All greyhounds are bred for racing now. The good ones race. Those that show no great promise are destroyed. The ones that do show promise run races for a couple of years and *then* get destroyed."

"So they all get killed?" He had never given the matter any thought before.

"Unless they are among the very few kept for breeding purposes, yes. They all get killed."

Arthur made a sympathizing face.

She said, "That's why we have to save them."

"We?"

She eyed him carefully, as if searching for ridicule. When she continued, there was a wariness in her voice. "Yes, *we.* This is not some cult, you know. We just rescue the dogs." They exchanged polite smiles, and she was off again. "But all the same, we're a committed group, we who keep greyhounds. There are thousands of us. We're organized all over the country, local groups in almost every state. To find foster parents for the dogs. Like Greyhound Friends, right here in Massachusetts. It's found homes for more than six thousand dogs. We have national clearinghouses and linked websites for exchanging information. Check out Greyhounds Anonymous on the Net, it's a trip. Plus adoption agencies almost everywhere. You see, these dogs are very sociable and people-loving creatures. Very well suited for elderly people and apartment dwellers. They're gentle and calm, and hypoallergenic. They sleep about eighteen hours a day if you let them."

"Doesn't sound like a bad life to me," Arthur said.

Her expression soured.

"I'm sorry," he added quickly. "I didn't mean to make fun. It's like the old saying—you know the one I mean? *I wish I was the man my dog thinks I am.*"

She brightened again and laughed. "Ain't *that* the truth," she said. "But it's serious business to those of us who rescue the dogs. You know Bo Derek, the actress in *10*? Well, she's heavy into hounds. Believe it or not, these dogs never even get a chance to be a puppy. They start out in mass-production kennels, like they were laying hens or something, till the breeders decide which ones will live to run. Sometimes . . ."

But Arthur wasn't listening anymore. He was suddenly three miles away, on Castle Island at the farthest edge of South Boston, strolling counterclockwise along the parapet that girdled Fort Independence. It was a windy Sunday in June, and Arthur had just turned from watching the threadlike pedestrian causeway that unspooled itself toward the southwest to enclose Pleasure Bay. A mammoth shadow swept over him. It was a jumbo jet, rising off the water from Logan, so close the shuddering growl of its engines set off a responsive drone in the pipe railing he was clutching. He stared up at the plane's underbelly. He could have counted the rivets.

Still deafened by the roar, he had turned to resume his walk. It was then he spotted the woman. She was a tall blonde wearing heavy pancake makeup and eyelashes the size of epaulets. Like a charioteer pulled along by a pair of leashed dogs, she had her other hand wrapped around the arm of her male companion. The dogs were greyhounds, he realized now, but he had given it no thought at the time. He had been too absorbed by the shock of recognizing her companion. Tommy Crimmins had flicked blue eyes his way and passed him by.

". . . and greyhounds are the only dog mentioned by name in the Bible," the woman rattled on. "Did you know that King Canute made the killing of greyhounds a capital offense just like murd—?"

"Excuse me," Arthur interrupted her sharply. He put the pads of his fingers to the sides of his head and stared down at his feet. "I . . ." His voice trailed off. It was as if he could feel the slop of thought against the sides of his skull. And then the beginnings of a rush of excitement.

"Are you okay?" she asked him, concern in her face.

He raised his head and smiled straight at her as he raked his left hand through his hair. "Yes, I'm fine. Listen, can we back up a minute? You were talking about how you guys are really *committed* dog owners? Did I get that right?"

She hesitated, eyes narrowing, then squatted to put her arm around Bella. "You don't *own* a fellow creature. They are nonhuman animals, you know. But yes, we're committed. There's an urgency that builds a sense of community among hound lovers. It comes from feeling, well, *embattled,* I guess is the word. After all, nobody's going around and systematically destroying cocker *spaniels.*"

"But suppose you lost one. Then what?"

She was nonplussed for a second. "Lost? You mean, like died?" She seemed to hug her pet a little tighter. The dog panted joyfully.

"Whatever. But unexpectedly anyway. You'd replace it, right?" He corrected himself. "I'm sorry. I mean replace *her.*"

She was making an effort to be patient with him, he could tell. "Of course I would," she responded, as if choosing her words carefully. "You return to what you love. Besides, you're constantly aware that the whole breed is being exploited for profit—slaughtered even. If I lost Bella, you wouldn't expect me to go out and get a *gerbil* now, would you?"

She shot him a sideways, pitying smile. He couldn't help himself.

"Hey, watch it," he protested. "I'm a charter member of the Gerbil Protection League."

CHAPTER EIGHTEEN

IT TAKES A VILLAGE

Hello."

"Danielle Gautreau?"

"This is she."

"It's Arthur Patch."

A silence. Then, more crisply this time, "How did you get this number?"

"The same way I got your address last time—the night before I went into the clink and sent Joanne to give you the note: you're in the book."

Arthur leaned against the reservations podium beside the cash register and smiled over at Joanne. She rolled her eyes away from him. Joanne still needed convincing. He hoped Dani wouldn't be such a hard sell.

"I may need to do something about that," said Dani, but Arthur sensed a softening of tone. "Is this a social call?"

A social call? He felt his heart flutter in his rib cage like a trapped bird. He shook off the incomprehensible sensation. "No, no. I have a business proposition. I'd like to sit down and talk to you about it."

She was silent again, and he felt the stiffness return. "How could there be any business between us? I thought you understood: I don't work there anymore."

"I did understand. It's not prosecutor business I'm talking about.

Not directly, anyway. I want to propose a . . . a financial venture, I guess you'd have to call it. A pooling of resources toward a common end."

It was as if he could hear her processing all this.

"If you think I'm going to buy out Larry's position, forget it. I can't afford it." He was about to chuckle appreciatively at her little poke, but she pushed on. "What end could we possibly have in common?"

"Three hundred thousand dollars." He paused for emphasis. "That's the reward they're offering for Tommy Crimmins. I think I know how to find him."

This time, when she spoke, he thought he heard a humoring smile in her voice.

"Then what do you need me for? Go claim your reward."

"I didn't say I knew *where* he was. I only said I knew *how* to find him. But I don't know exactly what steps to take. I mean, the mechanical stuff. You know, law-enforcement techniques and all that. That's what I mean by pooling resources."

She seemed to snort at this. "Do you think I'd exploit my former position—violate my oath, in fact—by disclosing confidential information to earn a *bounty*? Besides, I never had anything to do with Crimmins. The handling, the charges, nothing. I should have thought *that* was apparent," she added with some asperity, "given what happened with you and Morrissey."

"It sounds to me," he said, "like you've answered your own objection. You don't know anything confidential that would be of use to me. Please, understand me here. I'm not after confidential information. I want something much more general. Like I said, the nuts and bolts. Investigative stuff. Scuttlebutt. How to go about it and all. Nothing confidential."

She was quiet again, so he kept going. "Look-it, the money interests me. The reason for that is obvious to both of us. And I figured it might interest you as well, you being out of a job and all—thanks to some extent to Tommy. Isn't it at least worth discussing?"

He waited, deciding to make her sit with the silence this time. Lifting the phone cord out of the way with his left hand, he let Joanne get by the podium to conduct a couple of early diners to a table. He leaned his back against the wall.

"You still there?" he asked finally, tired of waiting for her.

She said, "Tell me something."

"What?"

"Anything you like. Whatever you figure is likely to convince me you're onto something. Why is it you think we could find him?"

We. He liked that. "You remember Tommy's girlfriend, the one who split with him?"

"Mavis something or other."

"Mavis Riley," he said. "Well, she was a dog lover. More specifically, a greyhound lover. She had two of them when they left. But they left on such short notice she had to leave them behind in her apartment. You remembering any of this?"

"It was in the papers," she said, and he could tell she was choosing her words with care. Was she afraid he'd think she was revealing information she had learned in her former position? "I remember she left the dogs behind. The part about them being greyhounds escaped me. So what?"

"Eddie Felch interviewed a neighbor of hers for one of his columns shortly after the couple disappeared. She went on about how much Mavis loved her dogs and how out of character it was for her to leave without them."

"That rings a dim bell."

"Well, what happened to them?"

"The dogs?"

"Yeah, the dogs. Where are they now?" When she didn't answer right away, he added, "What would the FBI do, in the usual course, if it seized two dogs while searching a fugitive's apartment?"

"They'd have no reason to keep them, obviously. It's not like they would have any evidentiary value. Eventually, they would get rid of them."

"How? Turn them over to the SPCA? Try to find them a home?"

"That I doubt. As a group, FBI agents aren't much on sentimentality. They don't exactly run with the animal-rights crowd. No, they'd probably dump them with some pound. Maybe even put them down."

"Is that some barnyard term? Do you mean destroy them?"

"I mean kill them. Which is probably what would happen at a pound, too. They don't get many takers for full-grown dogs, and after a while they destroy them. Why? Are you shocked?"

"No. That's what I figured, too."

"Then let me repeat my prior question: So what?"

More customers had started to arrive. Arthur picked up the base of the phone and walked farther away from the podium. He switched the phone to the other ear.

"So these were greyhounds. I just had a long chat with a hound lover here. Then I spent three hours in the public library and on the phone researching greyhounds and the people who rescue them. These people are a tight group. Committed, you might say."

"I believe I've heard something to that effect." Her tone was flat—*un*committed, you might say. "I recall activists getting arrested for disrupting dog races, but that was awhile ago."

"There's even a website on the Internet called Greyhounds Anonymous. As if they think of themselves as positively addicted to the creatures. It's just an inside joke, I'm sure, but a telling one, don't you think? So picture it this way. You're a middle-aged lady who's a fool for greyhounds. You have two of them. You love them to pieces. Then one day your louche boyfriend gets indicted, finally, and he suddenly whisks you away to a life on the run. Might even seem romantic to a woman who was probably attracted to him in the first place because he's such a bad boy."

"*Louche?* Did you just say *louche*?" There was a smile in her voice now.

"Yeah. It means, like, not straightforward."

"I *know* what it means. It's just . . ."

She stopped, and he felt a sharp flick of annoyance. "What's the matter?" he asked. "You figure it's too big a word for a lowlife on the shark?"

A tiny pause this time. Then she said, "No, it's just the notion of describing someone like Tommy as louche. Sort of like—oh, I don't know. Like calling Godzilla *pesky*. Or Bill Clinton a flirt."

"No," he said, offended now. "That's not what you thought. You can't get past it, can you? Past seeing me as some meathead who gets his jollies hanging around wiseguys?"

"Why should I listen to this?" He could hear her getting angry, pulling away. "You called *me*, remember. Suddenly you're accusing me, telling me what I'm thinking. I don't need this kind of—"

"Wait!" he said quickly, before she could hang up. *Whoa,* he told himself. *Keep it on track.* "Please wait. A truce, okay? I'm sorry. Let's stick to business. To the girlfriend. *That's* what's important here. Remember, Tommy picks her up at work and she has no time to do anything about the dogs. So she has to leave them. Later that day, according to the papers, she called her girlfriend and asked her to pick them up. But it's too late. The FBI is already there. Mavis is devastated by this. So put yourself in her shoes for a minute. What would you do?"

"Make a donation in their names to Angel Memorial?" Still miffed.

"No," he said, blowing right by her sarcasm. "*You'd replace them.* Get another dog or two. And not just any dogs. They'd have to be greyhounds. Oh, not right away, of course. Not while he's actively running. But he's been gone more than a year now. Eventually he'd have to settle down someplace. And that's when she'd replace them."

"And you figure," she said, jumping in, "you could trace her through this network of like-minded dog lovers."

"Like I said, they're a tight group. It's a possibility, don't you think?"

He heard nothing for a moment. Then she said, "You're being awfully free with your information here. How do you know I won't just pass this tip along to my friends back in the Strike Force? Assuming they haven't thought of it already."

"Because," he said, "that way you wouldn't get the money. Think about it. Three hundred large split three ways."

"*Three* ways?"

"Joanne. She's on the hook to Larry, too, you know."

She was quiet now, but he was grinning in triumph. She was talking about the split.

"Personally, my opinion is you gotta let a guy do what he's gotta do to catch up with himself. You know what I'm saying here? On account of he don't ever get square if he can't go about his business."

Larry Coniglio lifted and opened both hands, then gave a little sideways tip of his head to concede the objection he was about to voice. "I know what guys say. They say you don't collect what's due, you lose respect. You're not lookin' at a lotta pictures of dead presidents when you're spose'ta, nobody takes you serious. I know all this. But me, I'm a realist, Artie. I'm a practical man. I appreciate you gotta get your business on its feet. Plus I know you had this other shit on your mind, this grand jury thing. And besides, I like you. This is a personal thing here, you and me. You're nice people. Helluva cook.

So I give you extra time. I even stop the clock on the vig. You tell me: I been patient here or what?"

Arthur said, "You've been very patient, Larry. And I appreciate it."

Peetie coughed from Larry's right, a deep bronchial hawking that told of respiratory infection. Larry hunched away from his son, a protective arm curled over his plate. "The fuck's the matter with you? I'm *eating* here, for Chrissake. Cough the other way. You wanna give me the bourbonic plague or something? Jeez."

Peetie turned away and coughed again, grimacing from the pain in his chest. Larry picked up his oyster fork again and turned back to Arthur.

"Hey, Artie," Nick Tramontana said. "How come you never got couscous? I mean, I don't see it on the menu so I wondered. They got it in Sicily, you know."

Arthur was surprised by Nick's uncharacteristic interest in culinary matters. "I've tried it," he said, "but my customers just didn't take to it. I think they're too used to the Moroccan version, with the lamb. We'd tell them it was fish and they'd just move on down the menu."

"You could try putting some chicken in it, too."

"There's no chicken in Sicilian couscous," Arthur pointed out.

"The fuck there isn't."

"No, really, Nick. I—"

"Look," said Nick, his neck reddening. "Don't tell me about couscous. That's the way my *nona* used to make it, and she got right off the boat from Trapani."

"All I'm saying, Nick—"

"Hey!" Larry dropped both hands on the table and the crockery clattered. "I'm talkin' about my fucking money here."

Nick glowered at Arthur. "He's tellin' me my *nona* don't know from couscous."

"No, I'm not, Nick. I'm—"

"Money! M-O-N-E-Y."

Arthur listened in suspense, but Larry's spelling was perfect.

"Okay?" Larry waited until he had their undivided attention. " 'Cause here's where the snot hits the wall. A loan's got a life, Artie. It's like milk which can go bad. It's got a pull date says when it's time to come off the shelf. And you're past your pull date, Artie. That's how come I gotta start the clock on the vig again. We gotta talk about the future."

Arthur watched Larry bend over his plate again. Pinioning a veal shank with a thumb and forefinger, he rooted in the hollow center with the skinny fork. Like gouging the jelly out of an eye socket. With a soft grunt of triumph, he extracted a gobbet of marrow, swiped it across the plate to sop up sauce, and popped it in his mouth. He added a crust of bread and an abstemious slurp of red wine before closing his eyes to savor the churning mouthful. Arthur pictured the sloshing of soiled laundry in a washing machine.

Larry set down both the fork and the wineglass. He blotted his lips with a napkin, which he then crumpled and dropped on the table with a leaden flourish. He leaned back in his chair. Finished. His place at the table was littered with marrow bones, the linen flecked with tomato sauce and spattered with grease spots and purple wine stains. It looked like a mass grave.

"So," he resumed, looking up and across the table at Arthur, "it's a question of where's the money coming from to pay me back? This is what I ask myself. Does Artie have some golden boat's gonna truck in the money? And you know what I answer myself? I tell myself, do chickens have lips? That's what I say. So talk to me, Artie. Do chickens have lips?"

Arthur smiled respectfully at Larry's witticism. To his right a still-pouting Nick Tramontana took a deep, face-buckling drag on his cigarette. He sent the smoke in a fine stream toward the ceiling. Arthur decided this was not the time to call attention to the restaurant's no-smoking policy.

"No, Larry," Arthur admitted. "Chickens don't have lips. But they do have ears."

Frowning, Larry seemed to treat this as a trick question. Was he trying to remember if he had ever seen ears on a chicken? Arthur hurried on lest Larry think he was being a wiseass.

"They can hear, Larry—and so can I. I hear things that may be to our mutual advantage."

Larry just stared at him. Peetie hacked again, doubling over so much Arthur winced for him.

Arthur said, "Based on what I hear, Larry, I'd like to talk to you about a kind of, well, a *workout* on the loan."

At this Larry shook his head in fake sadness, a reasonable man beset by importuning naifs.

Leaning forward slightly, Arthur hastened to make himself clear. "I'm not talking about restructuring the debt, Larry. I know we're past that. I have something more comprehensive in mind. A straight-up swap. I trade you a piece of information. In return, you forgive the loan. Wipe it off the books completely. I figure what I have to trade might be worth it to you."

Larry was positively amused now. He looked around the table at his confreres and grinned. "You hear that, Nick? Artie's in the information business now. What do you think it could be, this forty-thousand-dollar rumor?"

With a lift of his hands and shoulders, Nick joined the fun. "Don't sell the guy short, Larry. Maybe he's got a forwarding address for Jimmy Hoffa." All four of them laughed, even Arthur, though Peetie's laugh was more careful than the others'.

Now. "Nothing that rich," Arthur said. "But suppose I had an address for Tommy Crimmins? Would that be a piece of information that could square things between us? I mean, once and for all?"

There was no mirth in the silence around the table now. Larry glanced quickly at Nick, then back at Arthur. Arthur struggled, with bomb-squad intensity, to maintain eye contact with the man, and waited. An ill-starred Carlotta appeared at Larry's right. Larry waved his hand in an irritated gesture of dismissal. Arthur shook his head at her, and she flounced away.

Larry said, "This ain't no fuckin' joke here, Artie. That mick's got more enemies than Carter's got Little Liver Pills. So don't go jerkin' my chain, you hear?"

"I hear, Larry. And I'm not jerking your chain. I swear."

"Tell me straight up: You know where he is or not?"

"No, but I think I know how to go about finding him. It might take some time, but I've got a lead that I think will lead me to him. *If* I can get the breathing room and there's something waiting at the end to make it worthwhile."

"And that 'something' is I eat your marker, is that what you mean?"

"Yes. And the breathing room is you stop the clock on the vig again. I can't run down my lead *and* keep the restaurant afloat if I've got to pay you five percent a week at the same time. I need a moratorium, is all."

"Suppose you come up with jack shit?"

"Then," said Arthur, "you're right back where you started. I still owe you the money and you start collecting the vig again. You've got nothing to lose, really. A little time—"

"And five points a week," Larry reminded him, his eyes narrowed.

"True," he agreed. "But look at the upside."

He watched Larry marshal his perplexities. A large-mouth bass rising to circle something that seemed to flutter helplessly on the surface. Trying to draw himself a picture while maintaining eye contact with Arthur. Finally, Larry reached out and rested his left hand on the back of Tramontana's chair. "Arthur," he said, his eyes on Nick now, "you give us food for the belly and now food for thought. Let me cerebrate on this for a while, and we'll talk again."

Cerebrate? Larry the Rabbit was threatening to *cerebrate*? Had he been trapped in the john with nothing but a *Reader's Digest* opened to "Increase Your Word Power"? Arthur stood up to leave them. "Whatever you say, Larry. I hope the food was to your liking tonight."

"A-one, kiddo," Larry said, making an "O" with his thumb and forefinger. "Took me back, I gotta tell you. It took me right back."

To what? Maverick Square? But Arthur gave a little bow to acknowledge the compliment and slipped away.

It wasn't until he was back in the kitchen, with the door shut behind him and his back against the fridge, that he allowed himself to start shaking. After a moment Jonathan turned away from the range to grin at him. "So how did Larry the Rabbit like his surf 'n' turf," Jonathan asked. Then, taking in Arthur's demeanor, he added, "You okay, Arthur?"

Brad looked up, too.

Arthur took a deep breath and let it out. He nodded. "Just a chill there for a minute."

"Something Larry said?"

"More like something I said." Thinking, *What have I let myself in for*? He frowned. "Surf 'n' turf? What are you talking about? He had the *osso buco*."

"With an oyster." Jonathan was beaming now.

Arthur just stared at him. Then he got it. "You didn't."

"Sure did," he said proudly. "Hawked up an oyster and spat right in his veal. Carlotta carried it off like it was the head of John the Baptist."

Arthur gawked at him, but not for long. He laughed until the tears came.

"Beats the hell out of fiddleheads," he admitted when he was finally able to speak. It was Jonathan's first triumphant creation.

"I think of all the guys that they hate his guts," Larry was saying to his two remaining table companions. "Oh, it'd be fucking sweet! To be the guy that found that skinny cocksucker. And put an ice pick in his ear. Personally."

Nick nodded his approval. "No doubt about it," he said. "It would put a little spine in the whole outfit."

"A little? It would go right up and down the line. Stiffen discipline all the way to Providence. *Everybody'd* know who did it."

"Especially Uncle Chicco," whispered Peetie through his laryngitis.

Nick chuckled. "He'd declare a national holiday from Fort Worth."

Larry laughed shortly. "Would he ever."

Gripping the sides of the table, he hauled himself to his feet. He reached into his jacket pocket and pulled out his knot. Usually, he ate on the cuff at Artie's, the guy owing him and all, but he was feeling magnanimous tonight. He peeled off four hundreds and tossed them on the table. All the while he smiled, picturing Francesco, eighty-two years to go on his sentence, as he trudged the yard at the federal facility in Fort Worth. He could hear him, too, hear that smoke-ravaged voice that could eat the paint off the Tobin Bridge, when the news of Tommy's treachery first reached him.

"I want him," Chicco had said, the way they told it. "The first lady says it takes a village? So make her one. Turn him into a fuckin' crowd."

CHAPTER NINETEEN

SCRATCH TICKET

Jimmy Morrissey looked up from the police report to survey the countenance of his client. Dermot Tump showed him a sweet, quizzical smile, like a kindhearted schoolmaster too unworldly to control a classroom. His bald head, round and rosy, glowed warmly beneath the harsh strip lighting of Morrissey's office.

Morrissey sighed. "Why don't you just tell me what happened, Dermot?"

The client made a show of pursing his lips and spoke carefully in a light voice. "Well. I was sitting at the bar, sipping their watered whiskey and minding my own business. Just watching the show, you know?"

"At the Purple Papaya," Morrissey interjected tonelessly. He referred to a notorious strip joint just north of the city on Route 1. Context was needed here.

"The very place. And Ginger—she's the performer in question—well, she's really on tonight. Guys are hooting and hollering like crazy. Plus I notice she's been smiling and giving me the eye during her whole routine. I'm getting the come-on, you know what I'm saying?"

Oh sure, he thought. *Must happen all the time.*

"Anyway, she gets to the part near the end where she's coaxing tips out of the guys, right? You know, prancing around on the bar, and squatting down so guys can tuck dollar bills under her G-string."

This came with body English, first a sideways rocking of his shoulders, then a slight hunching to signify a squat. "And under that other thing—you know, the strap that like, ties the whole thing around her waist. She starts at the far end so by the time she gets to me there's so many flapping dollar bills it looks like something oughta be strung up over a used-car lot. You get the picture?"

Morrissey got it. He nodded.

"So she gets to me and she sorta swings her can in my direction as she squats down—presenting a profile, like—and I go to give her my tip. Then all hell breaks loose. Next thing I know Ginger's yelling and some goon appears out of nowhere and starts dragging me towards the door. Me, I'm hollering, too, because I left money on the bar. And the goon—"

"Hold it. Wait a second." Morrissey held up both hands as if stopping traffic, his head cocked to look down at the desk. "The police report says you were *groping* under the G-string."

"I was making change for a twenty! And when I . . ."

But Morrissey wasn't listening anymore. He pressed the pads of his fingers against his temples and silently cursed his lot. Cursed his clientele. Despite his pleasant, favorite-uncle visage, Dermot Tump (nee Tumpowsky) was a career petty criminal. This was no Professor Moriarty come to life: the first charge Morrissey had defended him against—seven, eight years ago now—was for selling knockoffs of designer watches. On that occasion Morrissey was able to convince a judge that anyone who hadn't picked up the misspelling of "Rolex" on the dial was probably dumb enough to believe the watches were authentic. Tump had been less lucky in subsequent scrapes. He once had done nine months for theft after stealing a fetal heartbeat monitor from a public health clinic. He mistook it for a karaoke machine.

Feeling hopeless now, Morrissey realized he would never be able to dig himself out of his hole with the fees paid by Tump and his ilk. Fees paid, that is, by his usual clientele. But he accepted Tump's three hundred dollars and gave him a slip of paper bearing the date of his scheduled court appearance. He escorted him to the elevators with as much dispatch as his client's loquacity permitted.

On the way back he passed Taffy's station. She was playing hearts on the computer screen in front of her as she jabbered into the bobbing telephone headset. He heard her mention Brad Pitt. She clicked her mouse to pass two hearts and the queen of spades to a virtual opponent named "Terri." With her other hand she languidly held out three message slips. These he bore gingerly, as if they were pink letter bombs. He went into his office and closed the door. Once at his desk he laid the slips down carefully before him.

The one on top was from his wife, Phyllis. She would be late getting home. No need to call. He crumpled the slip and read the next message.

Call Rory Concannon. Morrissey felt a hot prickling of fear along the nape of his neck. He'd been ducking his calls for several weeks now. And a letter just this morning. A subway train operator for the MBTA, Concannon had a fractious manner that no doubt served him well in his post as a steward in the Carmen's Union. He was also the principal beneficiary of his late mother's estate. In that capacity Concannon had exhausted much of his meager store of patience waiting for Morrissey to administer the estate. Morrissey couldn't close it out because he had cashed the mother's CDs in order to replenish a down payment he was supposed to be holding for the sale of another client's two-family in Brighton. Robbing Peter to pay Paul, he told himself when he was being honest about it. He was grimly aware that if you hope to stay afloat on your clients' escrow funds, you have to watch out for heavy weather. Concannon, he realized with chagrin, was a storm cloud gathering head. He had better deal with the man.

"What a coincidence, Rory," he said as he fished in his wastebasket. "I've got your letter right here in front of me."

"I wanna know what the holdup is with the money." Concannon spoke in a gruff half shout, the voice of a man used to making himself heard above the keening of wheel on rail in confined spaces.

"I thought we went over this," he said in what he hoped was a tone of sweet reasonableness as he ground the handset into his ear. "I need a release of estate tax lien from the Department of Revenue before I can file my accounting. I've applied for it, but it hasn't come in yet. You know how these bureaucrats oper—"

"I got this nephew's a law student up at Suffolk. He says there shouldn't be any taxes on an estate this small."

Morrissey paused, but not for long. "Did you say Suffolk? Good for him! It's my alma mater, you know. But I'm afraid it's a little more complicated than that, Rory."

You have no idea *how complicated.*

But Concannon would not be deflected. "He says even if there was taxes, you could pay out some of the money as long as you keep enough to cover the tax."

"Rory, I'm—"

"I'm not trying to bust your chops, Jimmy, but it feels like I'm getting the runaround here. It riles me up when that happens. Just ask anybody who knows me. I become a real prick."

"You are what you eat."

"What?"

"I said, you're far too sweet. You know, the kid may have a point there about making partial distributions. Let me do the math and see if it's not possible to get some of the money out. I've got a jury of six waiting in Somerville at the end of the week, which is just eating me up, but after that . . ."

Morrissey got him off the phone—and off his back for another week or two—but he knew he was going to have to do some more juggling.

It depressed him to think about it. You make one bad decision, dipping into the client accounts once when you're having trouble covering your monthly nut. But you settle a tort case the next week, and with the fee you collect you put back what you've taken. Clean, no problems. Unfortunately, the absence of problems turned out to be the real problem: it made it even easier, the next time he was short, to dip again. Then, when new funds of his own were slow to materialize, it was like he was a rat in a maze, scurrying from one client's money to another's, just to keep a step ahead of their most pressing demands. And falling further behind. After almost a year of this, he was getting frazzled. He felt old and exhausted. Fried.

Not exactly what he'd planned, of course, when he entered law school. In the fall of 1971, fresh out of the Coast Guard (the Vietnamese were attacking and he wanted to, well, guard the coast) with tuition money from the government, he had a headful of throbbing visions of his own future. These were the ones he shared with Phyllis Cronin, a long-haired sylph with brown eyes so soft and warm they were like peeking into a hidden inglenook, all cushions and comfort. In the third-floor apartment on Mission Hill they would lie naked and sweating on his used mattress and talk through the sweltering summer nights. He could tell her then. How he would be a crusading defender of the underdog about to be crushed by the machinery of the state. He would ally himself with up-and-coming politicians who championed progressive causes. They would live modestly but cleanly in a tidy white house with red trim, up north someplace, like Danvers or Wakefield.

They sustained him, these visions and Phyllis, through four arduous years as a part-time law student. He got by on federal grants and loans and driving a cab out of his uncle's garage in Everett. Shoveling snow in winter. Doing paralegal work for a workers' comp mill in North Station. They sustained him through the horror of watching his old neighborhood, proud, scruffy Charlestown, eat itself up in rage and hate when the buses started rolling through Monument Square to carry Irish kids to schools in urban graveyards like Roxbury and the South End. They even sustained him when he got his degree and learned there were no public defender jobs open to someone with his meager qualifications. His uncle sent him to suck up to a politician-pal, a greasy bagman who twiddled maroon suspenders with rubescent nudes on them. The man opened doors to the Suffolk County District Attorney's Office. There he spent six years as an ADA, prosecuting major crimes by the time he left. When his Irish boss lost his bid for a fourth term to his archrival, the scion of an Italian political family from East Boston, Morrissey was broomed during the ritual cleansing that followed.

Forced to hang his own shingle, Morrissey had struggled to build a practice. Phyllis's job as a social worker with the Department of Human Services had helped carry the couple through the financial trough of those early days, and they had made it. Over the years he had switched offices from time to time, flitting in and out of partnerships and looser associations as business changed and collegial relationships shifted beneath him like the uneasy grinding of tectonic plates. They bought a single-family house halfway up a hill on Vinal Avenue, a few blocks off Union Square in Somerville, which was far too urban and dense and industrial to qualify as one of the northern suburbs of his fevered dreams. But it had all been endurable, and the dreams still flickered dimly.

Until this, the mortal shame of kiting his clients' funds to keep the business from cratering on him. It was all very depressing indeed.

Like a scratch-ticket junkie, he allowed himself to sink into the warm bath of his recurring fantasy of redemption. The one that would solve all his problems. He just needed an angle, was all, some way to crack open the secret. There had to be a way to earn that big reward.

It was eerie, the feeling he got when he saw the name on the last message slip. Was it coincidence? Synchronicity? What was that line Phyllis had just quoted him, what, two nights ago? "A coincidence is a spiritual pun." Who said that anyway? And what did it mean, for that matter?

Whatever. It augured well. Morrissey lost no time returning Goff's call.

Rollo Goff was assistant postmaster for the South Boston office. Morrissey had twice defended him, without much success, against charges of driving while intoxicated, and Goff was still scraping to pay off Morrissey's fee for the last go-around. (Another one of his high-end clients.) Dangling a hint that he might be willing to forgive the unpaid balance on his fee, Morrissey had noodged Goff into making certain discreet inquiries of one of his letter carriers.

"This is Goff."

"Rollie? It's Jimmy. Tell me you've got good news, buddy."

"Hold it a second," Goff said, and Morrissey heard the heel of a hand scrape across the mouthpiece and muffled voices in the background. When Goff came back on the line, he spoke in a hoarse whisper.

"I think it's a dead end, but you tell me. I talked to Roger Coakley. He was the regular carrier assigned to that route when Mavis took off. By the way, you weren't the first to think of this. The FBI talked to him, too, about a month after she split. He told them, just like he's telling me now, that he hardly ever saw her. She worked days, he reckoned. And he said he couldn't remember anything unusual about her mail. *Nada.* Zip."

Morrissey's spirits plummeted. A shotgunned partridge, trailing feathers. So much for synchronicity.

"But then I had this thought," Goff continued. "It's her workin' days that gets me thinking. Maybe, I say to myself, maybe she's home on Saturdays, and Coakley I know don't deliver Saturdays. So I talked to the girl who has the Saturday route. A moonfaced broad named Lourdes Escobedo. No shit, Jimmy—affirmative action. What can I say? Anyway, you should be proud of me. I'm way ahead of the FBI on this one. They never thought to interview her. And guess what?"

"What, Rollie?"

"Lourdes and Mavis? They talked. Not bosom pals, now, but occasionally they exchanged words. And Lourdes remembers one bit of mail she used to get. It was some kind of newspaper thing. The reason she remembers, it was big—outsized, we call it. Like *Rolling Stone,* you know what I'm saying?"

"She subscribed to *Rolling Stone*?" Morrissey was incredulous.

"No, no. Just shaped like it. Which is why she remembers it. Anyway, it was like her hometown paper. She never knew the town though. But it came every Saturday, and Mavis used to look forward to it, she remembered that."

Maine, Morrissey recalled, his hopes rallying. There was a twitching yet in that downed bundle of feathers. *Somewhere up in Maine.* He yanked open his bottom desk drawer and grabbed a manila folder. He laid it on the desk and opened it.

"But then comes the bad news, Jimmy," Goff continued, as Morrissey leafed rapidly through the contents of the file. "The dead end. Three, four months before the broad takes off, the paper stops showing up as part of her Saturday packet. So Lourdes figures she either stopped subscribing or maybe they changed the ship day. One day she's talking to her on the stoop and Lourdes asks her how come she doesn't get the paper anymore. And Mavis just smiles at her, and says, 'Why pay for a subscription when you can get it on-line for free?' "

Morrissey halted his search and listened intently.

"So," Goff added, "looks like you been done in by these fucking computers. Just like us, with this goddamn e-mail and shit. We're takin' the hit every which way over here."

Disappointed, Morrissey pushed the file to the middle of his desk. Goff kept talking.

"Too bad. I'm not sure what kind of angle you were hoping to work, with the mail and all. She must have left owing you a fair piece of change."

"About fourteen hundred," Morrissey ad-libbed halfheartedly. He had told Goff he was trying to track Mavis down because she owed him a sizable legal fee. He chose the amount Golf still owed him—to give him a little poke, was all.

"What kind of work she have you doing?"

Everybody's curious about Mavis.

"Sorry, Rollie. Client secrets. You wouldn't want me telling people what I did for *you,* would you?"

" 'Nuff said, Jimmy. I understand completely. I'm sorry I couldn't be more helpful, but there you are."

"I appreciate it, Rollie."

They nattered on about nothing for a few more minutes, with Goff promising he'd get current with his payments on Morrissey's bill and both of them knowing he wouldn't see any more money until the day Goff got pulled over again.

For several minutes after hanging up, Morrissey sat thinking. His angle was to focus on Mavis, not Tommy. She was the weak link, he was sure of it, and taking her with him had to be one very large mistake on Tommy's part. It would be like dragging a grappling hook behind him. She was bound to screw up even if he didn't.

Morrissey also supposed it was a good sign that the feds had thought the same thing. It made him think he was at least running down the right alleys, even if this one had proved a dead end. In fact, with that business about the hometown paper, he had learned more than they had, all because he had had the sense to turn to an insider who knew what questions to ask and of whom. And when Goff mentioned the hometown paper, his spirits had flared brightly. There was an outside chance that Mavis, once resettled, might reup for the paper. Under a new name, of course, but if he could get his hand on the paper's list of subscribers (they'd probably sell it to anybody) and focus attention on the new ones? Well, who knows, he might have gotten lucky.

But it really was a dead end. She didn't need a subscription if it was free on-line. It was not a way to track her down. Of course, once dead in the hand, the idea looked less appealing than it had in the bush. Tommy was too crafty to let it happen. If the FBI and Morrissey could figure it out, so could Tommy, and the likelihood of his permitting Mavis to lay a trail by reviving her subscription had to be close to zero.

It was ironic, really. The very thing that put an end to his inquiry—the paper's availability on the Internet—meant she could follow the news from home in the safety of cyberspace. Nobody could track her down through her computer connections.

Unless . . . Morrissey sat bolt upright and stared at the dead computer screen in front of him.

Unless you turned it around. If you can't bring Mohammed to the mountain . . .

He clutched at the file and pulled it toward him. His morgue file, he called it. It had begun as a dossier containing the results of research he had done in the morgue at the *Boston Globe,* courtesy of Eddie Felch. In the bowels of its offices over on Morrissey Boulevard (no relation, alas), Morrissey had risked a debilitating allergy attack from lurking spores of mold to dig out everything the paper had printed about Mavis Riley. She had enjoyed a brief notoriety during the first months after her flight with Tommy, and the *Globe* had run several stories about her. There was a long piece in the Sunday magazine on the "Irish Moll," the middle-class, middle-aged divorcée from City Point who kept company with a stone killer. There was even a column dripping with the acidic fruits of an interview her ex-husband had given to Eddie himself. Morrissey had since supplemented the press clippings with material gleaned from other sources. The court papers on her divorce from Ernest Riley. A bland, unrevealing credit report from Transamerica (no recent credit cards). Worthless stuff from the registry of motor vehicles.

Morrissey grabbed a yellow pad and made a list, in whatever order they came to mind or appeared in the file, of the things he knew about her. Tall. Relatively slim. Blond (as far as anybody knew). Forty-three years old, forty-four now. Grew up in a small town way up in northeastern Maine. Kept dogs. Worked for Millbank Tweed, a mail-order distributor of high-quality women's clothing—the WASPy kind, from the look of its catalog, that appealed to entitled Wellesley matrons and peppery Beacon Hill preservationists. She had started out taking orders on the phone, later graduating to handling customer queries and complaints on-line. Good worker, according to her supervisor, though she had to be warned about Net crawling on company time.

There was something else that tugged at his memory. Something her ex had said about her. Morrissey shuffled papers until he laid his hands on Eddie Felch's column. He ran an eager finger down the page. Only child. French-Canadian family. Way up north. Grew up eating lobster because up there it was cheaper than buying bologna. Father drove a truck for a logging company. Parents dead.

There. He picked up the sheet of paper and read the Edster's spite-filled prose.

> This was not your Technicolor wiseguy's bimbo, with the balconies out to here and hanging all over the boyfriend among the swells at Joe Tecce's. "She was quiet, a homebody," Ernie Riley insisted. "Not exactly a risk-taker. And she was tight as bark on a tree."
>
> How tight? Dredging fountains for pennies, perhaps? Recycling Kleenex?
>
> "Naw, just everyday cheap. She had the most organized coupon wallet you ever saw. And God help you if you blew hard-earned cash on scratch tickets."

Morrissey slipped the article back in the folder and closed the file. He rocked back in his chair and whistled breath out his nostrils. There *had* to be a way to work that. Here was this pretty ordinary lady—as ordinary as could be expected of someone who sleeps with a gangster. With a lot of insecurity around money. Understandable, given her background. Comes from low-income, depressed area up there, folks deceased. Riley, her ex, hadn't helped matters much. Tending bar in Braintree somewhere, he had scrabbled at the margins, pissing away paychecks by betting against the spread on the Patriots when he was swacked. She doesn't get much out of the divorce—a seven-year-old Civic and their apartment in City Point, the rent payments all hers now. She drives to work in Quincy every day wondering what she'll do if the car dies.

Enter Tommy, and her worries are behind her. He flashes more money in an evening than she sees in a month—and, as these guys go, he's not flashy. For three years she cooks for him and hangs out with him, secure in the knowledge that all the money she needs is right there, in his pocket, and plenty more where that came from. She can relax at last. As much as anybody could relax around a ticking psychopath like Tommy Crimmins.

And then he snatches her away from all this and hauls her off into the great unknown of life on the lam. Exciting at first, maybe. But after a while? Put to one side how nerve-wracking it had to be, always wondering if the FBI is about to drop down on you like Freddie Kreuger every time you open the door. Or how they've got you cold for harboring a fugitive or obstruction or some such felony. Forget all that. She's got to be terrified of something happening to Tommy. She's totally dependent on him in a way she never was in Southie. If they collar him, and even if she's left out of it, where is she then? A thousand miles from anybody she knows, most likely.

And flat-pocket broke. Crowding fifty. With no money, no job, no prospects. No future this side of a federal penitentiary.

The bottom line was he had an anxious woman, especially about money. Who reads her old hometown newspaper on-line. There had to be a way to tap into that. A way to get her to contact *him.* And he knew just what might make her come to him.

Money.

He smiled as these shards of information and inference began to reconfigure themselves into a glimmering mosaic in his mind. Not quite a plan yet, but the fragments, the rough outline of one. Morrissey sat up straight and rolled his chair up to the desk. He began to flip through the file again, looking for the marriage certificate that accompanied her divorce papers. There were two things he needed. The name of her hometown. And Mavis Riley's maiden name.

CHAPTER TWENTY

HOUNDBYTES.COM

Looking out the window of the smaller bedroom, the one she used as a study, Dani watched the angled morning light weave a shimmering moiré through the imperfections of the old glass. Her eye traveled across the side yard. A few fallen oak leaves whistled and eddied through the narrow corridor that separated her two-family from the one next door. Once again her mind threaded its loopy way from the sight of her neighbor's fire escape to the stanchions in her father's milking parlor.

She couldn't account for it. It might have been the color of the rusting steel or the odd tilt of the fire escape's rickety members, she wasn't sure. But the zigzag lines of the descending steps inexplicably conjured the cockeyed V of stanchions before being yanked perpendicular and locked in place about the necks of the milk cows. She could picture the Holsteins headed into the stanchions, always in the same order, their rumps in symmetrical alignment, tails swishing. Milking machines like chromium bagpipes skirling out an old man's wheeze in the predawn. She could even smell the rich odor, trailing a surprising emotional force, of sweet manure and hay and warm milk.

A pair of raucous crows darted across her field of vision. The association broke up and dissipated. Dani willed herself back into focus. It was a long way from this two-bedroom apartment on Thingvalla Avenue to her father's hardscrabble farm in Vermont's Northeast Kingdom. She was surfacing from an intense day at her computer, burrowing into a cyberculture she had never imagined existed. And suddenly there she was again, her imagination replacing the restored maple floors of the bedroom with the coarse, three-inch fir planking of the milking parlor. In a barn that leaned so far to the southwest it was as if only the clothesline running back to the farmhouse kept it standing.

Funny, when she stopped to think about it. Look at her. Valedictorian of her high school class. Basketball star. Honors student in college. A Fulbright fellow with ten years of higher education at two hotshot universities and an Ivy League law school. Law review. Recruited, feted, hired by the biggest, the fanciest white-shoe law firm in the city—where, it turned out, the work was so irresistibly yawn-inducing she'd toyed with the idea of having her jaw wired shut. Chucked it for a position in the United States Attorney's Office. There she tried more cases in two years than the younger Royce & Bell partners would see in a lifetime. Eventually she second-chaired the four-month criminal trial that put away Francesco "Chicco" Coniglio, the Mafia underboss for all of Boston. And now? She'd come to—what?

Well, to this, apparently. Out of work and reduced to surfing the Net to see if it made sense to join forces with a dubious cook who wants to track down a mobster to claim a reward. And as she sits here, she gets flung back to the sights and smells of West Barton, Vermont, by a peek out the window at a fire escape. It was as if former selves were layered over her like old paint—a little scratch on the surface and another one peeked through and reclaimed her.

She smiled to herself and gave a little snort.

Danielle Gautreau, bounty hunter. Her newest avatar?

Please.

She stood in the doorway and peered into the tiny office just past the ladies' room. He didn't notice her at first. He sat at the desk with four hardcover volumes arrayed in front of him, two of them opened, one sprawled across the computer keyboard. She was able to make out the title on the spine of one of the unopened books. *La Cucina Tradizionale Siliciana.*

Cookbooks?

Arthur frowned unhappily as he flipped over a page in the book immediately before him. As he did so, he bit down on his lower lip in concentration, the way Bill Clinton did at press conferences when he wanted to look resolute or empathetic. A lock of dark hair lay across his forehead. With a sigh he closed the book. He reached for the one on the keyboard and folded it shut, too. He piled the books in front of him and lifted the stack with both hands.

It wasn't until he came to his feet that he noticed her. His blue eyes widened in surprise, then narrowed as a smile creased his face. He eyed her as if she were a gift-wrapped package, but it seemed more a ritual of delight than ogling. Beneath her dark green down jacket, open now, she wore a man's button-down white dress shirt, neatly pressed and tucked into her jeans, which were cinched with a wide leather belt. Her hair was tied in back the way she wore it for running. She smiled back at him.

"My," she said. "He reads Italian, too. Or should I have expected that?"

He paused, as if filtering for irony. "No, not really. I can find my way around menus and cookbooks, is about all."

Her smile broadened. "You serve food made from recipes out of cookbooks? Isn't that like plagiarism or something?"

His frown returned, and he stared gloomily at the volumes he was holding. "No, I'm just licking my wounds." He set the books upright on a shelf against the wall to his left. He let them lean against a row of other hefty tomes. Several were dictionaries, she noticed. He turned back to face her. "How would you feel," he asked her sourly, "if you just learned that somebody like Nick Tramontana knows more about your business than you do?"

She could feel herself pull away at the mention of the name, but she held her tongue.

"He tells me Sicilians put chicken in their couscous. I tell him he's wrong—it's all fish and seafood. But"—he nodded toward the books—"it turns out he's right. I never knew it, because apparently nobody serves it that way in the restaurants. In Sicily—with chicken, I mean. Aggravates the hell out of me. I mean, Nick Tramontana! As if the guy *cared.* And I have to listen to him maundering about his grandmother, how *she* used to make couscous."

He shook his head slowly, then refocused. "Hey, where are my manners? Have a seat. Let me take your coat." He came around the desk and pulled a chair away from the wall and positioned it in front of the desk for her. After a tiny hitch of hesitation, she laid her vinyl briefcase on the desk and sloughed off her jacket. Shaking her head at his outstretched arm, she slung the jacket across the back of the chair. She sat down.

"I didn't realize you still had such convivial relations with Larry and his entourage." It felt prissy to say it but, damn it, that's where she was. The man expected her to go into business with him, after all.

He took his own seat. His tone was matter of fact, but with an edge. "Let me explain. If you're into Larry the Rabbit for five figures, you make nice. You don't spurn his custom. And you sure as hell don't screen his table companions. You understand what I'm saying?"

"You make *so* nice you discuss variations in regional dishes?"

"If it comes up, yes. The health of my business depends on Larry's forbearance at the moment. Not to mention my physical safety, in case you've forgotten. So I make as nice as I have to."

She thought about this. He was right, of course. It was just that such relationships were so alien to her own experience.

Or were they? She rummaged briefly through her own dealings as a prosecutor. With informants. With defendants flipped into co-operating witnesses. Dealers, gamblers, bookies, junkies, leg breakers—murderers even. Not exactly a savory bunch, she had to concede.

But never socially, God help her. Not like this. Dining with them. Then again, if she was being honest with herself, she had to admit she had no reason to believe Arthur Patch was anything other than a financially strapped businessman who had borrowed money from the wrong people. Hadn't Judge Biddle said just that to her, the day she'd come to him with Arthur's note?

Best to let it go.

"Whatever," she said blandly. "But if you find out why he's called Larry the Rabbit, let me know."

He smiled. "You mean, besides his last name? Do you know what the Sicilian word is for 'nickname'? It's *injuria.* Which also means harm, injury. You don't pick your own; other people choose them for you and they're usually meant to be insulting."

She considered this. Picturing Larry the Rabbit in mid-hop brought a smile to her lips.

But back to business. She pulled her bag onto her lap and groped for the zipper. "I've been doing some digging into these dog people you—"

She faltered when she took in the blotter on the desk. It covered most of the desktop not already occupied by the computer screen and keyboard. Involuntarily, she leaned forward to examine it.

The blotter was, in effect, a huge memo pad, a thick stack of tear-off sheets of blank white paper. Two-thirds of the top sheet were densely filled with columns of minute, crowded handwriting. The obsessive care taken to inscribe as much miniscule lettering on the sheet as possible reminded her of a diary the DEA had once seized from a crystal meth freak, a cranked-up dealer with a ruinous taste for product. She looked up at Arthur and gave him a puzzled look.

His smile was sheepish. He offered a guilty shrug.

"May I?" she asked, even as she spun the blotter around to examine his scratchings. The blotter's columns were lists of words, hundreds of them in no particular order, followed by almost indecipherably tiny phrases she was able to identify as definitions of the words. She ran her eyes down the words in one of the columns.

> *Felucca, pomatum, scholia, picaroon, ventricose, bandeau, villeity, apograph, looftah, clyster, greengage, ephebe, cembalo, perlustration, costive, dengue, blatherskate, ancilla, retrorse, culm, objurgatory, syncope, pelmet . . .*

She glanced sharply at him again. "You looked them up? And then—"

"Wrote down the definitions for them," he finished for her. "Words I come across as I read. I jot them down on my bookmark, then add them to the blotter later. When I get a few minutes, I look them up." He bobbed his head toward the dictionaries on the bookshelf. "Then I write down the definitions. It helps me remember them. Well, some of them anyway." An embarrassed smile, as if he feared she would pity him.

This didn't fit, somehow. She wasn't sure what to think. "What do you do when the page is filled?"

He raised his eyes toward the ceiling and flexed his neck, like a small boy's diversionary tactic. "I throw it away," he said. "Then I start on a new one."

Her smile was teasing as she bent over to inspect the blotter again. "Will I find *louche* on here?"

He smiled back, looking confident again. "I don't think so. But it probably was there once, many sheets ago. I'm not a *total* ignoramus, you know. I even went to college. Three years of it, as a matter of fact."

"Really?" Curiouser and curiouser. "What did you study?"

"Humanities," he said, and she detected another change of tone, an aural blush. "You know, liberal arts." Then, "Did you think it was culinary school?"

His question came out subtly defiant, and he straightened up as he asked it.

"No, not at all." She hoped her smile carried no trace of irony. There was a fragile defensiveness to the man, a vulnerability in his manner she found oddly touching. "But this"—she gestured toward the columns of words—"this is, well, it shows discipline, I guess."

He shrugged. "Or obsessiveness. That's Joanne's take. I can't really argue with her."

"Maybe both," she offered.

They looked at one another in silence. He looked away after a moment, using both hands to shove the keyboard off to the side a little more. She felt herself recalibrating her impressions of the man, a shuffling of colors and patterns after a shake of the kaleidoscope. She was still watching him when he spoke.

"You said something about digging."

Briefly holding his glance as well as her silence, she rubbed her thumb along the vinyl bag. Then, businesslike, she grasped the zipper tag and pulled, its metallic whisper a ground note to her voice.

"Quite a little world you stumbled into," she said. "These greyhound people. I spent some time on the Net learning about them. I started with that Greyhounds Anonymous site you mentioned, but there are others. Lots of them. And yes, these people seem pretty tight."

"As in, closely tied to one another?"

"Exactly." She reached into the bag and pulled out a bundle of papers half an inch thick. It was bound together by a heavy black binder clip. "Stuff I printed out," she indicated. "They're a subculture all their own. But just how did you expect to go about finding Mavis in it?"

He leaned back in his chair and crossed his arms over his chest. "Well, I'm not really sure. I thought there must be some way to get at membership lists for these local organizations. And then, you know, maybe take a look somehow at the new members, those who came in in the last year. Because I'm sure she wouldn't use her old name."

"These people do not strike me as trusting of outsiders. You think they're going to just send us their lists if we ask?" Her look was almost pitying.

"No. I figured there must be some sort of electronic clearinghouse for this kind of information. And that you might know how to get access to it."

"If you're the federal government maybe. With subpoenas and unlimited manpower and all the time in the world. No, you're going to have to find her on *that* thing."

She bobbed her head at the terminal on his desk.

"My computer?"

"Yes. You've got one, I notice. Can you use it?"

She saw him stiffen again. "A little," he said. "We keep our financial records on it and do some purchasing on-line. Plus we use this program called Cato to coordinate our catering business. It's pretty nifty, actually—the Cato program, I mean."

She seemed not to be listening. Paging through her bound pages, she said, "I did two things today. First, I learned everything I could about greyhounds and the groups of people who keep them and rescue them. Then I dug up as much as I could find on-line about Mavis Riley herself. Your hunch was right in one respect, at least. She's very much into the 'movement,' if that's the right word. She was actually a member of one of the Massachusetts organizations."

"You found that out already?" Arthur looked positively awed by this revelation. "How?"

"Luck, really," she confessed. "One of the first things I did was join it." She twisted her mouth into a sardonic grimace. "I joined a *lot* of them. I'm not sure what I've let myself in for. But the point is, they—the local outfit, I mean—immediately e-mailed me their most recent news bulletin. An organizational alert they call *Barks.* These people can get pretty cutie-pie and cloying, I have to tell you. Stay in there too long and you come out with diabetes. Anyway, it's full of stuff. Photos, poems, doggie gift ideas. Anecdotes. Touching testimonials for dogs gone by. Plus upcoming events and news, especially about this referendum they're trying to get on the ballot here, to outlaw dog racing."

"Maybe I can get Larry to sign it." He grinned as he said it.

"Right. He probably *owns* several kennels. So this bulletin—the

November *Bark*—comes with a header listing the addressees. A column of e-mail addresses two pages long. Take a look."

She squeezed the binder clip to release it and handed him two sheets of paper.

"You see the one I underlined? The address *mavisriley at hotmail.dot com*?"

He stared at the page. "This is her? No shit?"

"It's her. I checked."

"Checked?"

"There are look-up directories. Peoplefinders. On the Web, I mean. And they'll give you e-mail addresses if they have them. So I just looked up Mavis Riley. They still give her old street address in South Boston. And right after it is her e-mail address."

"Mavisriley at hotmail.com."

"The very same. So we know she was a member. Which tells us—"

"It's not still good, is it?" His eyes were quite wide. "The address, I mean?"

"Hardly," she said brusquely. "But I checked it anyway. I sent a message to her address. It came back undeliverable." She could read disapproval in the slight dip of his eyebrows. "Relax. I did nothing that might spook her if she actually received the message. I just forwarded a piece of spam, an e-mail joke I had received. And there's nothing in my e-mail address to give away who I am. Anyway, she didn't get it. As an address it's a dead end. But it tells us other things."

"That she's tied in to these people," he added, nodding now.

"More than that. It also tells us she's pretty comfortable using a computer and finding her way around on-line. Which fits with other stuff we know about her. Did you know she left a PC behind in her apartment when she took off?"

He nodded. "She used one at work, too. Part of her job. I saw this *Globe* story where her boss had to get after her about using the office computer to log on to the Internet."

"Saw it. And her dogs, too. The ones she abandoned. Don't forget them. Did you catch their names?"

"Erol and Cookie. Also in the *Globe*."

"Odd spelling for 'Erol,' don't you think? It was on the collar. Missing the usual extra *r*—like in Errol Flynn."

"Or Errol Garner."

"Who?" But he waved her off with a shake of his head, and she proceeded. "The curious spelling she chose rang a bell. Remember the ads? On television?"

He frowned back at her.

"Erol's Internet! You never saw them?"

He shook his head.

"They jumped out at me. So oddly informal. Kept making me think of other combinations. You know, like Phil's Airlines. Inspires no confidence whatsoever, does it?"

He grinned. "Or Earl's Mutual Funds?"

She smiled, too. "Precisely. Who knows? It's probably an acronym anyway. Erol's, I mean. But wherever the company got its name, it's a cut-rate ISP."

His stare was uncomprehending.

"An Internet service provider," she translated for him. "The computer equivalent of a local phone company. Erol's is like America Online, only smaller and cheaper. And then there's Cookie. A cookie, you ask? It's the name given to the little bits of data a web server drops into your own computer when you visit their website. It's like an identification tag so you don't have to reintroduce yourself every time you return to the site. Virtual bread crumbs. It can also be a way to track your surfing habits, but that's another story."

His frown deepened. "That's a pretty complicated derivation for such a common name. I mean, *Cookie*?"

She pursed her lips and tipped her head to one side as if to give the point. "By itself, yes. But given the other stuff, it's not off the wall. Like her job, and Erol, and having a home computer—and don't overlook the nature of her e-mail address. Hotmail dot com. Hotmail is a free Internet service offered by Microsoft. You download your mail right off the Web. Perfect for getting mail at the office, because you don't have to use your office address, where a snoopy supervisor could easily read it. Hotmail is just the thing for somebody whose boss doesn't want her making personal use of her computer on company time."

He had an overloaded expression on his face. "Where is this going? Do I really need to know all this computer stuff?" he asked.

"No. I'm merely making the point that this woman has a certain level of amateur sophistication around computers. Which suggests to me that, in addition to replacing her dogs, she's likely to reestablish electronic communication with these hound people. Maybe we can pick up her trail there. So . . . let me introduce you to *Houndbytes dot com.*"

She watched his shoulders sag, but she pushed on. "That's: *Houndbytes* one word, *bytes* with a *y*. See what I mean about cutie-pie? Well, look at this."

She handed him a thick stack of papers, stapled together. He ran his eye down the first page, then looked up at her questioningly.

"This is right off the *Houndbytes* website," she explained. "You have before you, in forty-one scant pages, a list of all the messages posted on the *Houndbytes* bulletin board in the last ninety days. It's a rolling list. Stuff gets dropped after it's been on for ninety days. Here."

She stood up and sidled around next to him at the desk and leaned over the documents. She pointed to an entry. "Look at this," she said.

Free to good home....... **-Candi, the frustrated** 13:28:07 11/16/98
•Re: Free to good home..... - **JP** 11:09:12 11/17/98
•Re: Free to good home..... - **Anonymous** 11:23:58 11/17/98)
•Re: Free to good home..... - **Candi** 13:28:01 11/17/98
•Re: Free to good home..... - **Leah and Angela** 09:09:00 11/17/98
•Re: Free to good home..... - **Ellen, Roger+Kewpie** 21:02:42 11/16/98
•Re: Free to good home..... - **Constance and Nancy** 16:54:11 11/16/98
•Re: Free to good home..... - **Darlene's Mom** 14:45:08 11/16/98

"The first line," Dani went on, "is the title of the original message. 'Free to good home.' 'Candi the frustrated' is apparently trying to get rid of a dog. If you want to read her message, you just click on it and it pops up on the screen. Meanwhile, over here—" As she leaned over to point, her arm brushed his shoulder and she broke off. She felt the warmth of him through the shirt. She pushed on. "Listed below the message are the responses, like JP's, and further indentations indicate responses to his message from Anonymous and then from Candi herself. And so forth. You see? People go by their first names here. Or, in the case of Darlene's Mom, by her dog's name. And who knows if the names are real? All this is followed by the date and time of the message. You with me here, Arthur?"

"Yes, I think so. How do they communicate? By e-mail?"

"Yes. You join up, like I did, and provide your e-mail address. The website receives your message and electronically posts it on the bulletin board by referencing your chat name only. Your anonymity, should you care, is maintained."

Arthur lifted the stack of papers and riffled it with his thumb. "All this, in just ninety days?"

"Oh, that's just the *list* of messages. The *thread*, it's called. Their titles, if you will. The messages themselves, if you printed them all out, would generate at least a page each. That's a lot of activity over three months. And *Houndbytes*, I hasten to add, is not the only site running a bulletin board for greyhound lovers. I just picked this one because it seems to be the biggest, the most popular. And best maintained. But there are others. A couple of them even host real-time chat rooms."

"So," he said, his eyes narrowing, "you figure she would start looking for new dogs on the Internet, and we could catch her at it?"

"No, no." She waved off the thought, then leaned back down over the table, their shoulders touching this time. "She's probably already done that."

"Not necessarily."

The voice came from the door, and she lifted her head toward it. Joanne Balzer filled the doorframe, her right hip leaning against the jamb. "Hi," she said, waggling a handful of fingers at them. She lifted her eyebrows suggestively when her eye fell on the touching shoulders. "Isn't this cosy? Where did you leave Bigfoot?"

Dani felt herself redden. "Out in the cold, I hope. And good riddance."

"Smart move. You mind?" Joanne stepped into the room and pulled out Dani's unoccupied chair. "I do seem to be on the hook for the loan that brought us all together in the first place." She sat down.

Dani looked back at Arthur. "I see. The third share you mentioned."

He smiled and lifted his hands in a gesture of helplessness.

"As I was saying," Joanne proceeded. "Not necessarily. About Mavis, I mean. Getting new dogs right away." She crossed her legs and made herself comfortable. "I'm just extrapolating from my sister's reaction, when she lost her cat. Garbage truck. Messy. The pallbearer had to use a shovel. Anyway, it took her a long time to even think about replacing Goehring."

"Goehring?"

She raised her right hand like one being sworn. "I kid you not.

She's got a weird sense of humor, my sister. Must run in the family, 'cause I always thought it was a great name for a cat. Captures the utter boorishness at the heart of every one of them. But the point is it must have been, oh, six, eight months before she brought home a new kitten."

"What did she name it?" Arthur asked. "Goebbels?"

"Nubbers. Go figure. But we digress. The thing is, you gotta allow for time to grieve. It's not like a toaster, you go buy a new one when the old one blows. With a pet you need time. So would Mavis, I assume."

"It's already been over a year," Dani pointed out. "Isn't that long enough?"

"No!" The voice was Arthur's, and it was almost a shout. He was flipping rapidly through the papers Dani had handed him. "Where was it? The time doesn't matter, you see. We don't find her by looking for dog swaps. Joanne's right about the grief stuff. We focus on that. I just saw this entry here, somewhere. Yes! Here."

He stabbed his finger at the page, then heavily pressed down on the pages he had folded back to reveal the entry that interested him. He read aloud. " **'Katrina—I know your pain!!—Tina.'** "

He fixed them both with a look of triumph, but they stared back blankly.

"Don't you see?" he demanded. He glanced down at the page again. "There must be two dozen responses to Tina's message. They *respond* to grief!"

Dani said, "I checked that message, Arthur. Katrina's 'grief' is about living with a dog that's inadequately housebroken. And Bonnie, she's been there. Pathetic stuff."

Arthur made a short, dismissive glance to the side, an unmistakable gesture of impatience. "No, you don't understand. It doesn't matter what Katrina's problem is. These people respond to one another's misfortunes around their animals. And Mavis knows that her two dogs, the irreplaceable Erol and Cookie, were lost to the FBI. That's the hook. We tap into *that.*"

"How?" Joanne asked. "You're gonna look for a message here you think is from her, and respond to it?"

"No," said Arthur, sitting back and smiling now. "It has to be the other way around."

He jerked his chair forward and looked from one of them to the other. "Listen. My name is—Miriam, okay? I'm going through this horrible divorce from my total asshole of a husband. Call him Kirk. Kirk the Jerk. Well, Kirk and I can agree on *nothing*. And now the pig is just ripshit because the court has kicked him out, letting me live in the house, which he thinks is his 'cause he's the one who signed the mortgage checks. And what does he do, the bastard, the worst thing he can do to me short of just killing me outright—which he'd love to do, by the way?"

He paused and made a windmill of his hands to encourage an answer.

Dani grinned. "He'd take the dogs."

"No," said Arthur, shaking his head gravely. "He'd *kill* the dogs. Christ, he'd *butcher* them. Leave their mutilated bodies behind for me to find. Smear the walls with their blood and—"

"Easy, Arthur," said Joanne, both hands in the air as if to hold him at bay. "Down, boy. We get the picture already. Then what?"

Arthur beamed at them, and spread his arms. "*Then* I'd want to tell the whole world my terrible story. Especially the dog lovers. Especially the *greyhound* dog lovers. Because they would feel my pain, they'd *know* my pain. I'd splash it all over this bulletin board"—he jabbed the papers with his first two fingers—"and then wait for their sympathetic responses."

He stopped. The two women stared at him expectantly.

"You don't think Mavis would be one of those to respond?" he asked. "Assuming she's as wired into these people as Dani thinks. How could she *not* respond? Miriam's horror would have to sound like a painful echo of her own loss."

"And you figure," Dani jumped in, "that she might respond in a way that would permit us to identify her? To say this 'Gloria' or 'Magnolia' or whatever she'd call herself, is the Mavis Riley we're looking for?"

"It's worth a shot," he said. He turned his chair slightly to face the screen and, with an aura of fixed purpose, he squared the keyboard to align it in front of him. He made a click on the mouse and Dani watched the screen as pixels gradually assembled themselves into a ship's wheel, the logo on the homepage of Netscape Navigator. "What was the address of that website again?"

Feeling a tiny jolt of excitement herself, Dani spelled out *Houndbytes.com* for him once more.

"But," said Joanne, her brow rippled now, "even if you locate her on the bulletin board, how would you ever find her from there?"

"Don't know yet," Arthur admitted. "But at least we'd be talking to her. That's a lot closer than we are now."

His fingers clacked across the keyboard. Dani watched them admiringly. Small hands, a cook's, displaying a physical intelligence—dexterous and supple and efficient. Clean. Neatly clipped. She lifted her gaze to his profile, to the line of his jaw. Found more to admire.

What am I letting myself in for? she wondered.

CHAPTER TWENTY-ONE

UNCLE ARMY

PUBLIC NOTICE
Commonwealth of Massachusetts
The Trial Court
Probate and Family Court Department

Barnstable Division — Docket No. 980324

ESTATE OF ARMAND DENIS TREMBLAY

Pursuant to Massachusetts General Laws Chapter 194, § 1 et seq., the undersigned James M. Mulcahey, as the duly appointed Public Administrator for Barnstable County, hereby gives notice that on May 3, 1998, **ARMAND DENIS TREMBLAY** died in Provincetown, Massachusetts, possessed of goods and estate in the County of Barnstable. **ARMAND DENIS TREMBLAY** having left no will and leaving no surviving spouse or identified heir in the Commonwealth of Massachusetts, the undersigned Public Administrator on May 12, 1998, took out letters of administration in the Probate and Family Court Department, Barnstable Division, that he might faithfully administer the Estate of **ARMAND DENIS TREMBLAY**.

Based on information from the personal effects of the deceased, the Public Administrator has reason to believe that **ARMAND DENIS TREMBLAY** was born in Aroostook County, Maine, on or about August 8, 1928.

Notice is hereby given that the personal and real property in the Estate of **ARMAND DENIS TREMBLAY** has been appraised and assigned an approximate value of One Million, Seven Hundred Fifty Thousand Dollars ($1,750,000). No heirs have claimed a right to inherit under the Estate, and the Public Administrator has no knowledge of any persons entitled to bring such claims. If the Court determines that the deceased left no kindred, his Estate shall escheat to the Commonwealth of Massachusetts.

Persons related by blood or adoption to **ARMAND DENIS TREMBLAY** may be entitled to make a claim of inheritance against the Estate. Claims and inquiries shall be made on or before January 21, 1999, to James M. Mulcahey, Public Administrator, P.O. Box 447, 210 Main Street, Barnstable, Massachusetts 02630. Telephone inquiries may be made to (508) 394-4555.

Dated: November 19, 1998

James M. Mulcahey

By order of the Probate
and Family Court
County of Barnstable

Jimmy Morrissey admired his handiwork for a moment before Taffy intruded.

"So what file is this for?" she asked, still standing there after handing him the typed draft. "And who's this Mulcahey fellow when he's at home? I couldn't find him in the Lawyers' Diary."

Jimmy Morrissey looked up at her. She kept her eye fixed on his, gum snapping as she masticated. There was no way, it occurred to him, for an adult to chew gum in your presence without telegraphing disrespect. Contempt, even.

"That's because he's not a lawyer," he said, thinking fast now. "Mulcahey's a court employee. A clerk, like. And it's a new matter. Open a file."

He watched the gum shift cheeks like a squirrel moving around under a blanket.

"Then who's the client?" She leaned over to read from the draft. "This Tremblay dead guy? Sounds like a hockey player."

He thought for a second. "No. It's Mulcahey. I'm his counsel on this. Just list him as administrator of the estate. I'll take care of the rest."

"Okie-doke." She turned and left the office. Static cling held her short maroon skirt up in the back, exposing the lower quadrant of a buttock encased in black tights.

"Close the door, willya?" he called after her. She did.

Jimmy examined the notice again, more closely this time. It struck just the right note, he thought. An appropriate measure of legal mumbo jumbo leavened by the mention of big bucks. Eye-popping, that. He especially liked the bit about how the money would go to the state if no one claimed it. He congratulated himself on his deft touch. It would eat her alive to think of all that coin slipping down the public drain, disappearing forever.

It had cost him more than seven hundred dollars, not counting long-distance phone calls, to come up with the information that led to this. That was how much Darla's bill came to. Darla Carpenter, a small-time skip tracer out of Portland, had done work for Jimmy in the past, running down deadbeat husbands and chiseling debtors. Mavis Ouellette, Jimmy had told her, was born and raised near the small town of Benedicta, in Aroostook County, that big lumpy corner up on Maine's northeast border. Full of diseased timber and granite outcroppings and about forty-seven people, was how Jimmy remembered it, the year he and Phyllis had driven up Route 1 to visit the Maritime Provinces. No big surprise to learn she had fled the area right out of high school. He only wondered what it was that made her want to keep reading the hometown paper.

Because she sure didn't leave much family behind. None, to be precise. He'd directed Darla to do a search of the public records for Aroostook County—births, deaths, marriages, divorces. Court dockets, too, both civil and criminal. Mavis, it turned out, was born in 1954, the youngest of the three children from the marriage of Henry Ouellette and Jeannette Tremblay. The other daughter was stillborn; her brother, Louis, had died in infancy—crib death, according to the records. Henry died of congestive heart failure in 1968. Jeannette followed in 1973, about three years after Mavis fled south. No other Ouellettes around, according to the records. In fact, there hadn't been any in the area for the past twenty-five years.

Which made attempts to interview friends and neighbors of the family a largely bootless exercise. Even the old homestead, a rattletrap clapboard house two miles outside Benedicta, was abandoned now, wind-ripped with the windows knocked out, the front door hanging from one hinge. But somehow Darla had lucked onto a retired deputy sheriff in Presque Isle who remembered the family.

The Ouellettes were a ragtag skein of Frenchmen who had drifted down from New Brunswick in the early twenties. Loggers and fishermen; laborers toiling in processing plants and sawmills. Mavis, the deputy recalled, was a tall, good-looking girl who dressed and talked a little trashy. A bit on the wild side, hanging with tough boys who were more inclined to talk hot cars and hotter pussy than high school sports. When she took off not long after the father died, the deputy was not shocked. He harbored little hope for her future.

So much for the Ouellettes. There wasn't any place else for Darla to go with them. She was already making for the door, she related to Jimmy, when the deputy asked if she might be interested in the other side of the family. Jeannette's people, that is. The Tremblays. And Darla could tell from the deputy's smirk, a crooked seam in a face coarsened by white bristle, that he was hoarding some salacious tidbit. It must have been burning a hole in his larynx.

Jeannette had one brother, so far as anyone knew. His name was Armand Tremblay, and he was born over in Alagash. Army, as he was called, showed up around Benedicta in the mid-sixties. A rounded, doughy man in his early forties, he held himself out as a dealer in antiques. He lived with the Ouellettes for a couple winters—it's how they count the years up there, Darla explained, in winters, and who could blame them? Then he moved on.

It was the circumstances of his moving on that the deputy was aching to divulge. Army got picked up for soliciting sex from someone he mistook for a prostitute in downtown Presque Isle, the closest thing to a city up that way. The prostitute turned out not to be a prostitute at all, but a sales rep for Johnson chain saws who had stopped off at a local taproom to buy himself a short pull for the road. The rep was vociferous in his rebuff, and Army ended up in the county jail with a split lip and a swollen left ear and facing arraignment on vice charges. Army jumped bail and was never heard from since. A return to the courthouse, Darla reported, revealed that Jeannette had posted Army's bail in April of 1968. Did Jimmy want her to keep looking for Armand?

He did not. The details Darla provided gave shape to the amorphous scheme that had hunkered in his head for last few days. Jimmy savored the irony, how the plan played off the disciplinary charges made against him in connection with Maryann Nee's will. Kenny Twohig had faulted him for failing to publish notice likely to reach those with an interest in Nee's estate. Well, he'd publish a notice that would make Mavis Riley come right up out of her chair.

Uncle Army was gone. Disappeared. Given the circumstances of his decampment and Mavis's own sudden departure, she probably never saw or heard from him again. That would be his working assumption, anyway. So Jimmy could make of him what he would. As a gay man Uncle Army would not likely have children, which would make Jeannette, his only sister, his heir. If she predeceased him, his niece, Mavis, Jeannette's only surviving offspring, would become his next of kin—and his only heir if he died without leaving a will. Under Massachusetts law, anyway.

So let's put Uncle Army in Massachusetts. Provincetown would be a nice fit—a mecca for gays and lesbians, and littered with antique shops. Give him a little property. A couple antique stores—and a bed and breakfast, a profitable resort inn over on the East End. The way Cape Cod real estate has been selling (especially in P'town), such properties would translate into a seven-figure estate. Kill him off sometime in the middle of 1998. No will. No local relatives. What would happen then?

The truth was, Jimmy didn't know. As Twohig had explained to Judge Mallow up there in the supreme court, Jimmy didn't do a lot of probate work. But after half an hour spent perusing Judge Dunphy's *Probate Law and Practice,* he learned that each county had a public administrator whose job it was to probate the estates of those who died leaving no kin in Massachusetts. They get themselves appointed administrator, marshal and liquidate the assets, pay any creditors, and try to notify next of kin. By statute, public administrators are appointed by the governor. Given the exigencies of the situation, however, Jimmy decided to make the appointment himself.

Preparing the magnificent public notice he now held in his hand was Jimmy Morrissey's first official act as public administrator for Barnstable County.

Well, maybe not quite the first. He needed a business address first. Taking a drive down to Barnstable, the county seat for all of Cape Cod, Jimmy had rented a mailbox under the name of James M. Mulcahey in a Mail Boxes Etc. store on the lower end of Main Street. Establishing a Barnstable telephone number in the same name required a little more ingenuity. Eventually he was able to prevail upon an old high school buddy to let him bring another line into his dry-cleaning store in Barnstable. He activated the call-forwarding feature on the new phone, so that incoming calls would be automatically rerouted to another new line—this one installed in his Boston office, where it bypassed reception and Taffy—and eventually spilled over, if he wasn't around to pick up, into an answering machine. Both the answering machine and the new phone itself were stashed away in his credenza—out of sight but within easy reach from his desk. The answering machine was nothing special, right off the shelf at any Staples, but its features did include caller ID. So did the new phone itself. He was counting on that.

He had only to make arrangements to publish his legal notice in the *Presque Isle Gazette,* the lone newspaper in Aroostook County to publish an on-line edition. Then he could just sit back and wait for her to see it. And ring him up.

But hold it. Would she see it? He felt a cold splash of disappointment as he thought it through. It would never happen. She might still be reading it on-line—he was counting on that, after what he got out of Goff and what's her name, Lourdes—but that didn't mean she'd see the ad. One's eye did not chance upon a legal notice when reading a publication on the Internet. It might happen with a hard-copy of a newspaper, as you paged through it, but not on-line. There you don't even *see* the item, not unless you first bring it up on the screen by clicking on the caption for "Classifieds" or "Legal Notices."

And for the life of him, he could see no reason why Mavis would want to do that. Reading the hometown news was one thing. But job postings, apartments to rent, legal notices? Not a chance. He had to find a way to make her want to go there.

In the end it was so simple he had to smile. It was right there in the notice. The big bucks. A missing heir. The drama of almost two million dollars there for the taking—or disappearing forever into the coffers of the Commonwealth of Massachusetts. That wasn't just a legal notice.

It was news. And it shouldn't take much to get a small-town paper to treat it as such—right on the front page if he played it right.

Jimmy Morrissey dug out the number and made the call. Two rings. Three. Then the receptionist.

"*Presque Isle Gazette.* How may I help you." A real Down East twang.

"Give me the news desk, please." He cleared his throat to summon his interview voice.

CHAPTER TWENTY-TWO

AN UNDISTURBED DARKNESS

Tommy claimed she liked to stay up late because she was scared of the dark. Like a little girl, he said. But it was never the dark. Even as a little girl, Mavis had no fear of the dark. Tommy just got it wrong. Like he did with the dogs.

He had no time for the dogs, he said, because they were craven. It was his word, craven. She even looked it up once, when she got dragged along on one of those dreary library trips of his so he could read his blessed *New York Times.* It meant *cowardly, contemptibly faint-hearted.* He called them that, she supposed, because they cringed whenever he raised his voice or lifted his hand around them. Well, no wonder. When you thought about what their lives must have been like? Boxed in those kennels and denied any warmth of human interaction? There was nothing craven about an animal's conditioned response, stuff that was caked on by years of degrading abuse. What would Tommy know about such things?

Craven, indeed. The man didn't know the meaning of the word. Oh, he maybe knew what the *dictionary* said it meant, but in the real world? No way. Craven was a nine-year-old girl lying in the dark and hoping it stayed dark. Who hears the wind whip against the drafty farmhouse and listens with limbic alertness for the creak of footsteps on the floorboards. It's not fear of the dark that presses down on her in the night. It's the fear of *light.* The light that leaks into her bedroom from the hall lamp as the door opens, then grows into an icy wedge on the floor, a maggot-white stain the Creep sidles into. He just stands there for a child's eternity, with his face backlit so you can't see it, while his eyes get accustomed to the dark. She can hear him clearly enough, hear his low wheeze, the rheumy rumble of his breath. The pressure in the air tightens up. Lying as still as she can under the mildewed blankets, she feels a little bead of impacted terror in her solar plexus, feels it billow and swell before bursting into a savage light that routs the dark, sends it scurrying away from her in all directions. And then he would be all over her like a bluebottle fly on old meat.

That was craven. And that she never resisted or cried out. That she could never speak of it, not even to her own mother, whose bedroom was just down the hall and you'd think she'd have to see or hear or my God just *know,* because it was going on right there in the house, and wasn't he her mother's own father before he was her grandfather? But Mavis never spoke of it, in the mornings afterward. Watching her mother's rigid back as she hacked furiously at the breakfast fry in the skillet, the little girl felt a mysterious tension between mother and daughter. A twisted fairy spell. She knew in her marrow it didn't come from herself alone.

No, as Mavis was to say later on, when she was hundreds of miles away from there, they didn't sing "Kumbaya" in *her* house growing up. In its sun-haunted kitchen she would have to watch the Creep shovel breakfast into his lipless mouth. *Girlie,* he'd say, *pass us the salt.* But he didn't have to say anything. He could beam a kind of lazy menace with a half smile, his eyes the color of a Milk of Magnesia bottle. Waggling his silverfish eyebrows. No, she knew better than to speak of the pungent intimacies he brought in with him to the bedroom. With the light.

Dead never looked so good.

She heard them on TV now, on the talk shows like *Oprah* and *Sally Jessy.* Grown women talking about stuff that happened to them as little girls—stuff like what the Creep did. But they didn't remember it at the time, they said. They had repressed the memories until recently.

Don't I wish, she thought. *I could have used some of that repression myself.* But apparently it wasn't going around then. Not way the hell up in Maine, anyway. She pictured a process like using serious cold to preserve sperm—or even dead people, she'd heard. What was the word for it? Cryo-something. Your brain would just flash-freeze the tears and terror into hard chunks and pack them in a subzero vault. Until somebody came along who was stupid enough to crack open the freezer door to let in the light and thaw them out. But why? If you have to pick a frozen dog turd, would you thaw it out first?

When Mavis was eleven, her Uncle Army gave her an old radio he'd picked up at an estate sale. It was an old-fashioned RCA Victor, a big boxy console made of wood, with huge knobs and genuine tubes inside that gave off a lambent light—a harmless glow that did not disturb the dark. She set it up next to her pillow, between the bed and the wall. Late into the night, after the Creep had left her in the ravenous silence, she would turn it on low and wheel the red needle along the dial in search of music from faraway stations—Wheeling and Bowling Green, Little Rock and Tulsa. She would listen to talk of strange places like Greasy Creek and Licking River. With her tearless cheek pressed against the warm walnut veneer, she soaked up country songs of loss and heartbreak. They were stylized songs, sung in blessedly alien accents, a catch in the throat to color the phrasing. Like Jesus with the water and wine, they could change her desolation into an honest yearning.

Especially Patsy. Oh, how Patsy could cry! "I Fall to Pieces" and "She's Got You" and "Walkin' After Midnight"—they were a fever to Mavis, boiling through her veins, burning and cauterizing. "Crazy" was her favorite, with Patsy squeezing out the pain of a hopeless love like paste from a tube. With that big, wraparound voice, Patsy seemed to hold her quivering soul in the hollow of her hand, in a sanctuary where she felt relief. Because Patsy Cline could break the jam and let the crying out.

Grandpa Tremblay died in his sleep on her twelfth birthday. When she first learned of this gift—there was no other word to describe it—her deadened religious faith flared for a moment, only to gutter once again when she tried to reconcile his peaceful death with what had happened to Patsy, her flying into a mountain and all. No mumbling priest was going to convince her of the divine justice in *that.*

Watching other girls enter puberty with her only deepened her suspicion that she was unspeakably different. Their curiosity about sexuality seemed quaint, unreal even; they raised timid questions, revealed tiny glimpses of their astonishing ignorance. Were they just being coy? Acting like good little girls? Set against her own foul knowledge, their whispered wonderings cut an unbridgeable divide between their innocence and her own dank shame. She made no friends among them.

It was different with the boys. If she felt less worthy than the girls, she felt nothing but contempt for the teenage boys who sniffed after her with such naked desperation. She preferred them, though. You always have enough stature to deal with those you find contemptible, and with the boys she was not swamped by the paralyzing otherness she felt around the girls. The boys' childish groping was puppylike, pathetic even—but welcome on that account, after the Creep's casual brutality. They brought no light with them when they came to her; they craved a furtive darkness. Theirs was a need she could understand and manipulate, and they used each other together. Now, years later, she would scour the old hometown paper for word on the fate of those horny woodchucks. The bits she gleaned—alcohol-related deaths on lonely back roads, arrests and court appearances reported under "Crime Notes"—served to validate even as it muted her original contempt.

Mavis packed up the shame and hauled it with her when she moved to Boston after high school. For several years she moved around, slept around, worked here and there. In the late seventies she met Ernest Riley. Ernie tended a bar in Braintree and rented an apartment in the City Point neighborhood of South Boston. He was a soft dumpling of man, with a bloodhound's jowls and a belly like a popover, but he had a kind of cheesy charisma. He could make her laugh, too—no small feat, and God knows Tommy sure didn't bother these days. She and Ernie started keeping company, and soon she moved in with him.

Ernie was less needy than the boys back home, largely self-contained in a way she welcomed. She knew he was small-bore. As her mother would have put it, he could use a little hurry in his uptake. He wasn't exactly the ambitious type either; his idea of the good life, she told him derisively near the end, was a luxury doublewide and a bar tab. Yet he promised a bit of stability for a life that had known little of that. She landed a good job with the catalog people at Millbank Tweed, and with the two incomes life wasn't so bad. She even married the guy.

The only difference between dating and marriage was—well, nothing. And then it got worse. Ernie's drinking picked up, and with it the gambling. She'd learned to be careful about money—if you came from as far down as she did, you held on to what you got—but nothing prepared her for the devastation Ernie would bring down on the family fisc. If he was into some bookie over the Super Bowl, he was into her purse in the morning. She had to stop using the joint bank account entirely, learning instead to stash out of his reach what little money she could set aside on her own. And the booze just got worse.

Once, after a few years of this, she managed to bundle him off to Beach Hill, an in-patient treatment center in New Hampshire known in Southie as the Irish Alps. Thirty days later he came back cured—spun dry, buffed up, his game together. But not for long. He practically lived at the bar now, and she noticed how he looked down over his shoulder when he walked, like a man with a dog at his heels. But he had it under control now, he insisted. He was having a run of rotten luck, was all. *Sure,* she'd replied. *You've just been having a bad decade.* Always quick with a retort, he gave her a shot to the mouth. As a couple they were circling the drain, she could see that, but his was the name on the lease for the apartment and it was scary to make the break.

Tommy changed all that. She'd seen him a few times in the bar where Ernie worked, always coming in with Hinkle, the big loud one. Then she started noticing him around the neighborhood, too. Tommy was quiet and trim. Trim? Lord, if the Church awarded a plenary indulgence for neatness, he was really knocking the years off his stay in purgatory—assuming he got that far. She found herself luxuriating in those sand-washed blue eyes of his, the ones that said *Impress me* to men, but something else altogether to women. To her anyway. She thought a lot, now, about what that something else was. It was an imperturbability he radiated. Solid, unmovable. Let the waters break over him, he'd still be there, quiet and trim. She liked that. There were no dogs at *his* heels.

He noticed her, too, she could tell. But she never thought anything would come of that. And nothing did, not until the day after Ernie fattened her lip for telling him about his bad decade and she bumped into Tommy coming out of a convenience store in Perkins Square. He just said hello and offered to buy her coffee, and soon they were standing outside on the street, watching the 7 bus make the wide turn onto East Broadway, the two of them drinking coffee and chatting about nothing. She noticed he kept looking at her lip.

Did he do that to you?

She just shook her head, swatting the question away like a fly, but he wouldn't let it go.

Did he do that to you? He repeated the question word for word, with no change in his inflection. More of the blue seemed to leach out of his eyes as he asked. He looked hard into hers and a stillness settled over him as he waited.

She nodded.

You deserve better than that. You want shut of him?

She was suddenly frightened, knowing what people said about him. He must have picked this up because he smiled at her. A clean, economical smile.

All I gotta do is tell him to screw. He'll pack his Irish luggage and be out of there before you finish your coffee. Like I said, you deserve better than that.

She felt herself melt inside, a marbling of relief and desire. She sensed he was offering more than assistance, but she knew enough not to show anything. Not anything, that is, except a sly smile of her own.

Irish luggage?

He smiled back.

Green garbage bags.

She laughed.

Ernie was gone in the morning, his Irish luggage bulging as he humped it out to his car. The lawyer Tommy found for her got the divorce through the court in record time. Soon afterward, Tommy started stopping by in the early evening, just to check up on her. And talk, during longer and longer visits. She always treated him real welcome, as her mother used to say, and she made a point of stocking something nice to cook in case she could convince him to stay for a bite. Sometimes he did.

She knew people would laugh now to hear her say it, but the start of her relationship with Thomas Crimmins was the closest thing to an actual courtship Mavis had ever known. She expected hell on a stick; she got a soft-spoken man whose wooing proceeded at what was, in her considerable experience, a glacial pace. This had the effect of making her both intrigued and anxious, and suspicion hovered at her shoulder like an overly attentive waiter. It crossed her mind that he might not like women that way, but the pull of him was too strong for that to be the case. Still, she grasped intuitively that it would be a fatal mistake to try to take matters into her own hands.

So she waited, and he came around. His sexuality, she discovered, was of a piece with the rest of the man: quiet and trim. She found she could deny him nothing—and didn't want to. She missed the rush of power that used to come when she could reduce Ernie to a mass of whimpering protoplasm. Tommy never got that lost in it all. But she also didn't have to assuage her ex-husband's macho craving for assurance that she'd had an orgasm. Tommy just ignored the issue, as if it were her business. She took this as a token of respect, holding her responsible for her own come, as he was for his, and expecting her to take it how and when she pleased. She liked that. And if he seemed casual and blunt about sex, well, at least it was straightforward. She didn't have to divine what he wanted. She didn't see it as an assertion of crude power over her, but as an expectation that she could take care of herself. She liked that, too. It gave her a measure of dignity.

They didn't live together. Tommy had his condo on the waterfront in Squantum, and Mavis stuck to the apartment in City Point. Partly, that was because it suited her. She had her job, through which she was eventually inducted into the sodality of computer users, and with Tommy picking up the tab for dinner every night—or bringing by expensive groceries when she cooked for him—she was able to make do comfortably on her income. He would show up almost every evening, shortly after she got home from work, and they would have supper together. Sometimes they would go out afterward, walking maybe or to a club, and then he'd drop her off at the apartment while he went about his evening's business.

Tommy had a lot of his own reasons for not living with her, but mostly it was the dogs. He suffered them in her space, even walked them with her around Castle Island and along the Strandway or on Carson Beach, but he plainly had no time for them. He never kicked them out of the way, as Ernie had done, but she could tell he had no patience. Let alone the love she bore them.

It was a love they requited, passionately and unconditionally. Such was their principal attraction: Cookie and Erol asked for nothing in return. The knowledge of what she had saved them from at the hands of the kennel owners, from destruction or starvation or experimentation, added piquancy to her relationship with them. She liked to think it was what they had in common, for like her they had been liberated from degrading origins.

Which made it all the more painful to leave them behind to follow Tommy after the indictment. When Tommy called her, she tried to cobble together a hasty plan for her friend Janice to care for them—she had even hoped against hope to be reunited with them one day—but the FBI won the race to the apartment. They seized everything, including the dogs. When Janice did show up, they grilled her mercilessly. They refused to respond to Janice's subsequent calls for information about the dogs. Months Mavis waited, in an agony of dread and uncertainty, for news of them. She knew how the parents of missing children must feel. And then the devastation of learning the truth: that the FBI had murdered them when they could find no use for them.

How she got through that time she'd never know.

Two months ago Tommy had finally made good on his promise to let her adopt new greyhounds. They had just moved into this bungalow in Arcadia, a featureless little town about sixty miles inland from the Gulf Coast. It was a quasi-permanent stop, Tommy said, so she was able to convince him there was no reason to delay the adoption. She'd called around. With its many dog tracks, Florida offered them a decent choice of rescue shelters. Of course, they needed one that didn't ask too many questions or insist on a home visit, as some of them did (evoking an outburst of F-bombs and swearing from Tommy). She found them at last, two needle-nosed darlings, and there was color in her life once again.

So here she was. With no job to give structure to her days, she found herself drifting back to the nocturnal habits of her youth. She would stay up all hours now, sitting at the tiny kitchen table, the one with the half-moon scars along the edge from a previous tenant's cigarettes, the dogs at her feet. The darkness in the room was relieved, but not disturbed, by the soft glow from the screen of her laptop computer. Her eyes were fixed on the screen, where the pixilated images gathered form and reconfigured themselves in crisp colors as she nestled her bare feet under Dapple's warm belly. Or was it Bernadine's? She eased a disk into the CD-ROM drive so she could listen to Patsy on the earphones. Every once in a while she ran her hand along the side of the computer. She could feel the same soothing warmth she remembered from Uncle Army's old RCA Victor. In an undisturbed darkness.

CHAPTER TWENTY-THREE

A DIRGE FOR HILLARY

Dani stomped the new snow off her boots before stepping in through the back door. She sloughed out of her down jacket, then plucked off her stocking cap. Arthur watched as she shook her mussed hair into alignment; it settled over her shoulders in blond waves set afire by the snow-bright sunshine behind her. Standing there in jeans and a heavy red flannel shirt, she laid full claim to his attention, and he was staring stupidly at her. When he noticed her looking inquisitively back at him, he snapped to. He smiled and took the coat and cap from her.

"Go on through to the kitchen," he said as he shut the door behind her. She started down the corridor. He watched her briefly before hanging her garments on one of the coat hooks mounted along the wall. Then he turned to follow her.

She hesitated in front of the double saloon doors before pushing on through. She stopped just inside again, as if to get her bearings, and he almost banged into her when he entered. She glanced back at him over her shoulder.

"Something smells good in here," she said, smiling. "I thought you were closed on Mondays."

"We are," he said, moving past her toward the cooking range. "I thought we might like a little brunch first."

He bent over the oven door and pulled it open. Using the end of the towel tucked into his waistband, he reached in and slid the skillet toward the front. He shook it gently by the handle to check the eggs for doneness. "A couple more minutes," he announced. He shoved the pan back in and shut the oven door. Dropping the end of the towel, he turned toward her.

She had pulled up a stool to the stainless-steel table between them. From her perch she looked about the kitchen. She tossed her hair again.

"How come La Vucciria?" she asked, then caught his eye.

"It's the name of the famous open-air market in Palermo. One of the most mouth-watering sights in the world." He began to slice a loaf of bread that lay on a board on the table. "It's just a tiny piazzetta, with the sun blocked by all these reddish awnings, but it's bursting with a display of plenty that's so . . . *baroque*, I guess, that you feel overwhelmed. And ravenous. When I came to naming the restaurant, it seemed the perfect choice."

His slicing finished, he set the knife aside and reached up to the rack above them. He took down four dinner plates, laying them out on the table beside the breadboard.

Dani frowned. "Are you expecting company?"

"No, just us."

He stooped over the oven again and this time came up with the skillet, which he set down on the table. He slid a palette knife around the inner edge of the skillet, easing its flexible length under the food to make certain none of it stuck to the bottom. Satisfied, he laid one of the plates facedown on the top of the skillet and, keeping the flat of his left hand on the back of the plate, flipped the skillet upside down. The frittata slipped out cleanly onto the plate. He repeated the process with another plate, and the frittata now lay upright. He placed the steaming dish next to the breadboard.

As he set the skillet aside, Dani leaned over to sniff at the frittata. She made approving noises.

Arthur returned with a plate filled with tomato slices, olives, and a wedge of cheese. Setting it before her, he asked her what she wanted to drink. Water was fine, so he fetched a bottle of mineral water and two glasses. He sat down across from her and cut the frittata into pie-shaped servings. He dished one up for her and passed the plate of cold food.

"This is wonderful," she mumbled through her first mouthful while reaching for an olive. "What's in it, besides potatoes?"

"Parsley and red onion. A few capers on top. That's about it. Come back in the spring, and I'll make you one with fresh fava beans. It's my favorite."

"Is it supposed to be burned on the bottom?"

"Shhh," he said.

They ate in silence for a moment. Arthur admired the beautiful woman who was enjoying his cooking. He found himself wishing she'd still be around come spring, but he knew better than to hope. He felt a neurotic need for something to talk about. Something safe, like business.

"So," he said lightly, "what's your prediction? You think 'Miriam' will have many messages of support yet? We could start a betting pool."

She looked up at him, good humor traveling along the smile lines that radiated out from her eyes. "You'd lose. I already checked. She had thirty-four this morning when I left my place."

Arthur laid his fork down on his plate with an audible clink. "No *shit*?" This was more than he had dared hope. These people really *did* stick together. He felt excited. It was actually happening. He slipped off the stool and onto his feet.

"Let's go see," he said. He left the food on his plate and Dani staring after him.

He waited impatiently for his office computer to boot, then for the modem to dial up. When the connection was finally made, he logged on to *Houndbytes.com* and clicked through to its "Hound Talk" bulletin board. Once there, he scrolled swiftly past message headings that afforded a skimming glimpse into a cockeyed netherworld of New Age bromides, animal-rights manifestos, and cheerful advice about the heartbreak of dog shit. He ignored queries and answers on subjects like shredded pillows and diarrhea, aromatherapy for osteosarcoma ("It really works!!!"), dire news of dog tracks opening in Spain and Vietnam, websites hawking knitted doggie vests for cold climates, pet-friendly hotels, something called a Greyhound Underground Railroad (a support group of some kind?), the hidden dangers of chicken bones, avoiding tapeworms and broken toenails, how acupuncture can cure coprophilia, the perils of fascistic obedience training, and scores of e-hugs for brave new adopters. Down he scrolled until he reached the lurid title of the message he and Dani had posted Saturday morning:

He slaughtered Hillary!!!!!.......... — **Miriam** 9:28:07 11/21/98

He was proud of their handiwork: the vindictive ex-husband (Kirk the Jerk), the carnage he made of the dog, the soulful plea for support from a grief-stricken woman—even the way they'd finessed her sudden appearance out of nowhere ("I never had the courage to go on the board before. But this . . ."). And there, listed below the message heading, were the responses "Miriam" had evoked from fellow greyhound aficionados.

Forty-seven of them.

This amounted to an average of more than two an hour since "Miriam's" message was first posted.

"Jesus," Arthur said, his voice barely above a whisper. "How are we ever going to figure out which one is Mavis—if she *is* one of them?"

As she leaned over to read the screen, Dani laid her hand on his left shoulder and squeezed softly. Arthur felt the warmth of her touch course through him.

She said, "I've given it some thought—on the way over here, mostly. Where's that *Houndbytes* newsletter? The one they e-mailed us when we registered?"

Arthur dug under the papers on his desk and produced it. He watched her examine it. He wished she'd put her hand back.

She didn't look up. "Okay. First, we print out the list of replies. Then, while you start downloading each individual message and printing it out, I'll compare the names of those who sent messages against the names on the heading of the newsletter. See?" She held the newsletter under his nose. "The heading gives full names followed by matching e-mail addresses. We should be able to match the name of almost everyone who responded with an e-mail address."

Arthur looked back over his shoulder at her in confusion. Ignoring him, she pointed at the screen.

"There, for example. The fourth message. See it?

Arthur saw it.

• Re: **He slaughtered Hillary!!!!!** – Candi 10:12:27 11/21/98

She pointed at the newsletter in her hand. "I'm willing to bet you that's Candace Russell, address candir@aol.com. Candi uses America Online."

Arthur still didn't get it. "I can't *imagine* Mavis leaving an e-mail address. It would be too risky."

"That's precisely my point," Dani said shortly. "If you recall when we signed up, we were given the choice of not having our e-mail address used or given out, if we wanted anonymity. I agree with you; Mavis wouldn't give it. But I suspect many would, maybe most—as we did. Well, that means, for our first pass anyway, we can safely eliminate any message that came from somebody whose e-mail address *is* listed on the newsletter." She poked the newsletter. "Beginning with Candi."

Arthur nodded. "Of course. You're right. That's brilliant. *You're* brilliant." He grinned up at her.

Her eyes were on the screen. "Well, let's get to it. Start printing."

After running off the list of messages for her, Arthur began the laborious process of downloading, then printing, each cyberdirge for Hillary. Before he had finished, Dani reported that they could confidently eliminate thirty-two messages because their senders could be matched with names and addresses on the newsletter.

"Plus four others," she added. "The ones from men." She frowned. "Well, maybe only three, since Sam can swing both ways—as in Samantha. I could be mistaken, but I can't see Mavis using a man's name here. Though it *would* be clever."

"For that matter," Arthur reminded her, "you don't know if this Candi is really a woman or a man posing as one. Who could tell?"

"Fair enough," she admitted. "But this is just our first cut, so it can be rough. And it makes sense to take the genders at face value. We can backtrack later if we strike out with what we've got."

"You mean sex," he corrected. She cocked her head to stare at him, and he rushed on. "*Gender* describes categories of nouns, not people. The right word is *sex*."

He felt his ears redden as he watched her eyes billow with amusement.

He said, "Using *gender* when you mean *sex* is an abomination."

In for a penny, in for a pound.

"Jeez," she said, the corners of her mouth quivering now. "I forgot I was dealing with Mr. Words here. I didn't realize you had a thing about grammar, too." She nodded in the direction of the word-soaked blotter on his desk. "I wouldn't want to end up on the desktop."

Arthur struggled to suppress an altogether different image of her on his desktop. He smiled back at her. "Hey," he shrugged. "What can I say? I gotta be I."

She paused, her eyebrows arching, then laughed out loud. He joined her.

She said, "I suppose I shouldn't talk. I was the kid who used to cringe at the split infinitive at the beginning of *Star Trek.*"

Summoning a fake resonance, Arthur began to intone. "You mean, *To boldly go where . . .* ?" He broke off with a visible shudder.

She was beaming. "You, too?"

"How could you ever take Captain Kirk seriously after that?"

"Kirk the Jerk?"

They grinned at one another in silence, Mavis all but forgotten for the moment. The silence between them stretched out and grew until it assumed a presence like a third person in the room, unacknowledged but discomfiting. Then Dani broke it and returned to her list.

"So. Grant me the presumption that she wouldn't assume a new . . . *sex.* That brings the number of messages we can eliminate to thirty-five. Which leaves an active pool of twelve messages. We should focus on those."

Arthur nodded in agreement, wistfully regretting the return to the mundane. "I guess that makes sense. Unless there's something in the content of any of the eliminated messages to suggest they should be returned to your 'active pool.' "

"Agreed. But first, let's examine the twelve in the pool." She used her fingers to tick off their salient characteristics. "We know—assume, anyway—that they're women, one. Two, they have greyhounds. Three, they responded sympathetically to 'Miriam's' plight. And most interestingly, four, they don't want anybody to know who they really are or how to get in touch with them. And all this we know before we even *read* their messages."

"Let's pull them," said Arthur, theatrically rubbing his hands together. He reached over to the printer and retrieved the forty-seven sheets of paper that bore the printed responses to 'Miriam's' lament. "Call out the names. Shoot."

Dani ran her finger down the list of names that weren't crossed off on the newsletter. "Alison, Alice, Cathleen. Sheila, Jane, Patti. Lucia, Karen, Carol, Julie. Marie Jo and Lori."

She had to repeat them a few times as Arthur leafed through the messages, but within a few minutes he had separated all twelve from the remainder. There followed some ten minutes of silence as the two of them greedily read their way through the selected messages. Dani finished first and Arthur could sense her waiting quietly for him. When he finally put down the last message, he looked up and read the bleak disappointment in her face.

"I know," he conceded. "Not much there, is there?"

She reached forward and used her forefinger to slide one of the messages toward her. She read it aloud in a bored monotone. *"I'm so sorry for your loss. I hope memories of the sweet times with Hillary will be a comfort to you—Patti."* She picked up another. *"Ariel and Jade will 'cross paws' tonite for Hillary, knowing she is in a field of wildflowers chasing all the bunnies she can until she can be with you again!!!—Karen P.* What are we supposed to do with crap like this?"

"I know," he said again, glumly.

She sucked air in and let it out despondently, then held her chin as if tugging at a goatee. "Let's read the other ones." She made the suggestion without enthusiasm.

He agreed and they did, but their second tier of messages was no better. Again, they found generic consolations, sometimes coupled with bland assurances that the sender had "been there," too. A couple were punched up by spare accounts of dogs having to be put down or expiring quietly of geriatric disorders. But nothing striking. No intriguing personal revelations. And nothing at all that might suggest the sender was Mavis Riley.

It was Arthur who broke the lengthy silence that followed. "We have to get them to reveal more detail about their own lost dogs."

She continued to stare at the computer monitor, on which a screen saver etched a complex series of interlocking pipes, a mindless Escher without the loss of perspective. "How do you propose to do that?" Her tone was flat. "You can't exactly ask for gory detail."

"No," Arthur agreed. "We have to make them—her—*want* to tell us. And she has to think it's her idea. There has to be a hook."

"A hook."

"Yes, a hook. An emotional hook. Think it through. Emotionally, what do Mavis and 'Miriam' have in common? Besides grief and desolation—and maybe rage at the killing of the dogs." It came to him then, and he felt himself picking up steam as he talked. "What is the secret feeling they share about this?" Arthur caught her eye and held it hard. "You're Mavis. You had to leave your dogs behind. You didn't provide adequately for them. And then they're dead because of it. What are you feeling?"

"That's easy," she said. "I feel guilty. More guilt, even, than anger. I let them down."

"Yes!" He was grinning now. "These are creatures you *rescued,* for Christ's sake. You once saved them from a fate like this. And thanks to you, look what happened to them. You feel *horrible* about yourself!"

Dani was smiling now, too. "And so does 'Miriam.' "

"Of course. She should have known Kirk the Jerk would pull something like this. He used to threaten to kill the dog. Because he knew what would hurt her most, and she would have to know he knew it. But . . ."

"But she missed it somehow. And she left the dog unprotected."

"Poor Hillary."

"Poor Hillary, indeed."

They smiled at one another for a moment.

Arthur turned to face the computer screen. "Let's take a crack at it."

They haggled over the wording, the right tone, and it took them the better part of an hour to come up with a draft message. Arthur read it aloud off the screen.

Thanks for Hillary . . . BUT . . . .—Miriam

Thank you—all of you, for your kind messages of sympathy!!! They mean so much to me. If only I was worthy of it!!!!!!!

My soul burns with the horror of knowing I am not!

Many of you have written to tell me you know what its like to lose your baby. But it wasn't your fault!

You see, I failed Hillary. That's what makes it so shameful and awful. I failed her.

I knew what Kirk was like. I knew what he was capable of. He told me many times that he would hurt her. Yet somehow I left her alone and unprotected, knowing what he was capable of.

It was as if I just *abandoned* her! And she died a horrible death because of me.

I thought I did a loving thing when I rescued Hillary and brought her into my home. God gave her into my care and I failed her completely. That's why your kind words can't stop the hurt. That's why I feel so worthless and shameful and alone. I don't think I can ever forgive myself. Maybe Hillary can, wherever she is now. But I can't.

So alone now . . . Miriam

When he finished reading, Arthur looked up over his shoulder to get Dani's reaction. She stared fixedly at the screen and said nothing.

"Is it too much?" he asked uncertainly.

She shook her head. "No," she said. "I don't think so. That ought to do it. I can't think of anything else to add."

"Is there too much risk in sending it? I'm thinking about that reference to her abandoning the dog. Do you think it could scare her off?"

She thought, then shook her head again. "No, I don't think so. It seems to come naturally out of the rest of the message. And it might just trigger a response."

"So," said Arthur, his index finger raised and cocked over the mouse. "Should we send it?"

She said nothing for a moment, then nodded. "Yes," she said. "Send it."

Arthur depressed his index finger. Pulled the trigger. The click was barely audible. The message disappeared from the screen, the image replaced almost immediately by a small blue box. Like a Burma Shave sign by the roadside.

Your message has been delivered.

Her hand was gripping his shoulder again. It was less gentle this time. Her fingers dug in a little as the two of them stared at the monitor.

CHAPTER TWENTY-FOUR

STAR 57

TUESDAY

Thanks for the card," Phyllis said, when Jimmy picked up the phone. Hearing the yawn in her voice, he could picture the tremor of her jaw whenever she tried to stifle one. "How come you didn't wake me?"

Morrissey smiled. He could still see her lying asleep in their sunshot bedroom as he tiptoed back in to slip the card under her pillow. "You get to sleep in on your birthday. Is there something you'd like to do tonight? Visit your mother? Ride to hounds?"

He heard a sleepy intake of breath. "Oh, jeez, I don't know. You turn fifty-one, you feel a little yellower in the tooth. Suggest something."

He grinned and took a little poke. "You know, a little vindaloo always hits the spot on a cold night."

"No Indian," she said quickly, so fast she almost finished before he did. Like a rim shot hard on the heels of a bad joke. *"Can I be of helping?"* she asked in a passable imitation of the waiter at the Delhi Deli. "Forget it. Not a chance."

"Well, you could spackle your face and join me at that new pricey place you said you wanted to try. What was it called—Ulna or something?"

"Radius."

"I knew it was some kind of bone."

"You're being deliberately perverse."

"I'll make it up to you. Seven o'clock?"

"Better make it seven-thirty."

"Good. That'll give me a chance to pick up your present."

"I'm afraid to inquire." She sighed, but there was a smile in her voice at last.

"I met this guy? Says he can put me on to some bootleg tapes of Barry Manilow outtakes. Real raw stuff—we're talking basement recordings here."

She laughed. "You bastard. You know I only like him cleaned up, with strings to sweeten the line."

He chuckled. "Like me, you mean? Happy birthday, babe. Gotta pee. I'll see you at Ritalin."

"Radius."

"Right." He laughed and hung up.

Morrissey did have to pee. He hauled himself to his feet and was through the door before he heard the ringing again. He craned his neck to get a glimpse of Taffy in the outer office, hoping for some kind of signal to identify the caller, but she was engrossed in a phone conversation and didn't notice him. He waded back into his office and picked up the phone on the third ring. Except all he heard was a dial tone—and *still* there was a ringing.

It sank in then. It was the new phone, the one in the credenza. The muffled tone should have tipped him off. He shut the door behind him and hurried to the credenza. Pulling the cabinet door open, he reached in and picked up the handset. He pressed it to his ear while still in a half crouch before the credenza.

"Mor—Mulcahey here." A close call. He'd received three recorded messages on the Barnstable line so far, but all of them were from commercial heir finders prowling for a commission. This was his first live call on the line, and he'd been caught flat-footed.

There was silence on the line. A hollow hum, actually. He thought he'd better help.

"Hello," he said. "This is James Mulcahey. Can I help you?"

He heard an intake of breath, then a voice. "Um, I think so. I read your ad in the paper? The *Gazette*?"

It was her. He didn't know why he knew, but he was sure of it.

"Yes?" he said encouragingly. He sank to his knees and peered in at the LCD readout on the answering machine. The light was wrong. He couldn't make out the phone number.

She said, "I, ah, I'm a relative of Armand Tremblay. His niece, actually. And I saw your ad. Could you tell me a little about his, the estate?"

"Of course." He reached in and wrenched the machine toward the edge of the credenza shelf. The LCD became readable. "Oh, damn," he said out loud.

The LCD sneered at him.

Not Available. Nothing. Not even a fucking area code.

"What?" said the voice on the phone.

"Uh, sorry," he said, recovering. "I dropped my file. There. I'm ready now. You were saying . . . ?"

There was another pause on the line, then the tentative voice again.

"You said in the paper that Army, Armand left a lot of money."

"Not exactly." Morrissey decided he'd better sound like a real probate lawyer, crisp and pedantic. "Some money in bank accounts, but most of it was in real estate."

"Oh, I see." She sounded distinctly disappointed. "You mean it's all tied up, like?"

Mistake. She'd need liquidity. "It *was,*" Morrissey corrected, ad-libbing as he backtracked. "But I was concerned that the properties might be vandalized if they were left vacant too long. So I got the court to issue a license to sell. I sold the last of the three on Thursday. A bed-and-breakfast and two antique stores. Auctioned off inventory, too."

"So it's cash?"

"Yes, it's cash. But let's go back to this relationship you mentioned. You are his niece, you say?"

He heard a scraping noise, as if someone were moving a wet tongue over the perforations in the mouthpiece. Then he heard nothing at all.

"Hello!" he almost shouted. "Are you still there?"

She was. "I have to call you back."

"Is there a number where—"

But the line was dead. He, or something at her end, had scared her off. He felt crushed that she was gone. From his kneeling position, he sat down on the backs of his legs. He delivered a straight left to the credenza door, and it slammed shut.

False alarm. The guy coming out through the library doors wasn't Tommy after all. Same color jacket, was all. The phone was still swaying in its cradle, but Mavis was too rattled to pick it up again. Good God, her armpits were sopping! She wasn't cut out for this kind of secret stuff. She hiked up her purse, snugging it up against her collar, and walked down the handicapped ramp to the bicycle stand where the dogs were tethered.

When she sat down again, Dapple and Bernadine nosed into her lap, nuzzling her hands to beg a scratch. Pawhandling, she called it. She obliged them, but her mind was back at the pay phone and her eyes were canvassing the old portico of the town library. Watching for Tommy.

She was still shaking. Maybe this wasn't such a good idea. How could she ever claim the cash anyway? It would be incredibly risky, and maybe downright dumb, to show up in Massachusetts again. The Cape was safer than Boston, to be sure, and presenting herself as Mavis Ouillette wouldn't ring the kind of bells the name Mavis Riley would. But still. Plus she'd have to kennel Dapple and Bernadine until she got it all straightened out and had the cash in hand. But these were details, small stuff compared with the biggest obstacle.

What would she do about Tommy?

It went without saying she couldn't tell him. God, he'd kill her if he thought she wanted to leave him. With a tiny shiver, she realized that usually banal statement might be literally true in her case. That's what they all said about him, after all, that he killed people, and if she had never asked about his business, he never troubled himself to deny the rumors either. So, if she were going to claim the money, she would have to manage to slip away from him without his knowing she was gone until she was beyond his reach. *Way* beyond it.

And that was a big problem. The logistics were formidable enough. You don't jump on a bus with two greys in tow. Not even a Greyhound bus, she thought with a grim smile. No, you needed money. And she had next to none.

Not that they were hurting, as a couple anyway. Tommy always had plenty of cash. He had enough of those "wells" of his, he once explained, to keep him fat and happy far past his—or her—life expectancy. But he was careful not to let her get her hands on much of it. Tightfisted? Lord, that wallet of his must have been made of vampire hide, the way he avoided exposing it to the light of day.

No, if she were going to cut and run, she'd need to get together a small stake of her own somehow. And she couldn't count on doing so with Tommy's money.

Tommy turned skinflint was precisely what bothered her so much about living on the run with the man. Was it because he was afraid she'd abandon him? God knows, she still loved him. He had entered her life and rescued her from a deadening cycle of degradation and penury—rescued her as surely as she and her fellow greyheads rescued dogs. But everything had changed after the indictment. A scary year of life on the road, then settling here in Florida. In a sun-bleached wide spot in the road, full of crackers. And this newfound miserliness of his. It was more than annoying and humiliating; it made her terribly anxious. It fed into her own recurrent nightmare: that something would happen to him—a heart attack, an accident, anything—and she'd be stone broke and left on her own. Less than on her own, come to think of it, for she'd still be a fugitive, facing years in prison if she were caught. And how could she *not* get caught without him?

Oh, there was one thing. His "insurance," he called it. A leather shaving kit in which, he told her, he kept tapes that would protect him—and her, if something should happen to him—in the event he was ever caught. Tapes embarrassing to certain officials. But what did that mean? And how could she do anything, take so much as a single step, without money.

Which was what made her think hard when she saw the ad in the *Gazette.* The idea that there might be a way out of all this, if she could just figure a way to play it.

Well, it occurred to her, even if she never got the cash or the nerve together to take the plunge, it couldn't hurt to check it out. As long as she was careful. As long as she made certain Tommy was safely occupied when she called the lawyer.

She had resolved that much by the time Tommy came out of the library and paused above the steps to the portico. His right hand was raised to shield his eyes from the sun as he panned the parking lot looking for her. With his other hand he fished in his shirt pocket for his sunglasses. She waved at him from her perch on the bench. Spotting her, he descended the steps and started walking in her direction.

Mavis stood up so she would be ready to leave when he reached her. She coiled the leashes around her right wrist and the greys slid into place, one on each side of her, warm against her legs. They were so full of love, the greys. She flashed on that poor woman whose husband had killed hers. Miriam, her name was. Mavis knew just what she was going through. God knows, she'd been there.

As Tommy stepped from the street to the curb, she felt a flood of shame that she hadn't responded to Miriam's message. The poor woman!

Tommy was a few paces away now. She smoothed her slacks with the flat of her hand and stretched a tight smile across her face.

Not Available. What did that mean, Morrissey wanted to know? An unlisted number, for Christ's sake? A block on caller ID? He had never expected a home phone; a pay phone seemed much more likely. Not this.

Because it was her, he was sure of it now. Armand Tremblay had only one niece, and her name was Mavis Ouillette. Of course, his caller could have been an imposter of some kind, a confidence trickster hoping to claim the inheritance, but that struck him as very unlikely. The documentation needed to make the claim stick would daunt the craftiest bunco artist. Plus this woman seemed genuinely tentative. No, he'd been talking to Mavis Riley. And she was gone.

Would she call back? She said she would. And the prospect of ready cash seemed to have overcome the pulling away he'd picked up when he told her it was in real estate. Yes, she might call back.

But that wouldn't do him much good unless he could inveigle a phone number or something out of her. Dicey business, that—trying to gag an anxious fugitive into revealing her whereabouts. Which was why he'd preferred the technical solution in the first place. Until it flopped.

Not Available.

But wait. Of course! If it was a technical problem, there ought to be a technical solution. And for that, he needed assistance from someone who knew technical stuff about the phone company. And didn't he know just such a person?

Paul Volkert. His nervous client, the unlikely cavalier who had thrust his doughty umbrella through a bike messenger's spokes. An engineer of some kind, Volkert was, toiling away in the tangled circuitry of Bell Atlantic. If Volkert didn't know, he'd know someone who did.

Morrissey half crawled the four feet from the credenza to his desk. His fingers were scrambling through his Rolodex before his butt hit the chair. Volkert picked up on the first ring.

"Paul, it's me, Jimmy. Jimmy Morrissey."

Volkert did not speak for a moment. When he did, he sounded terrified.

"Is it bad news?"

"What? No, of course not. Why would you think that?"

"Because you never call me. Even to return *my* calls. So I naturally thought . . ." The fear had given way to petulance. Morrissey had to admit the guy had a legitimate beef.

"As a matter of fact," Morrissey said, "it's good news. I spoke to the DA this morning and he seemed amenable to a CWAF." Morrissey hadn't had the conversation, but he was confident he could obtain such a disposition.

"Qua . . . ?"

"CWAF. Continued without a finding. You pay the bike freak a modest sum by way of restitution. The court continues the case for six months or so. If you stay out of trouble in the meantime, the case gets dismissed. Finis. *Verstehen sie?*"

"Oh, that sounds good." Morrissey could almost hear Volkert's pores drinking up the relief. Then anxiety resurfaced. "But what if there *is* more trouble during the six months?"

Morrissey would have laughed if he weren't feeling so desperate. Suppose she called back now?

"Paul," he said cuttingly, "it took you almost sixty years to get into *this* trouble. I gotta figure you're good for six months."

"I suppose." Volkert didn't sound convinced. But enough about him.

"Listen, Paul. While I've got you . . ."

Morrissey led him through a heavily edited version of his problem. A divorce client with an estranged husband who she believed was harassing her with late-night hang-up calls. Morrissey had suggested she have caller ID installed on her phone, but the number always came up "Not Available." Unlisted, he figured. Was there a way around this? Wasn't there a pen register or something Bell could put on her phone?

"A pen register?" Volkert asked, authority in his voice now. "Pen registers only track outgoing calls. You must mean a trap."

"Is that what you call it?"

"Yes, but traps are passé, Jimmy. It's all Star 57 now. Much more effective."

Morrissey was puzzled. "You mean Star 69? *That* I've heard of. Isn't that where you punch in Star 69 and get the number of the call you just missed 'cause you were on the throne or whatever? I don't think I want that."

Indeed he didn't. He could think of no quicker way to spook her than to ring her right back after she hung up.

"No, no," said Volkert. "If the message you're getting is 'Not Available,' Star 69 wouldn't ring through either. And by the way, 'Not Available' doesn't mean it's an unlisted number or that the guy has a block on the caller ID. If that were the case, you'd be getting 'Confidential' or 'Unlisted.' Maybe 'Private.' "

"So what does 'Not Available' mean, then?"

"It signifies that the call was made from a cell phone or a non–Bell Atlantic pay phone. Or it could be a computer-generated call, like from a telemarketing firm, but that seems pretty unlikely, if the calls are in the wee hours. No, it's probably one of the first two. Which is why you need Star 57."

"What's that do?"

"Just tell her to punch in Star 57 after each hang-up. The Annoyance Call Bureau automatically activates a trace on the call. The company charges a modest fee for the service."

"That's all? Just like that?"

"Noooo. That's certainly *not* all. The Bureau won't do anything with the traces until you get three of them to the same number. When the third trace is executed, she'll hear a tape giving her instructions on how to proceed. Because we won't release the number or any other information to the customer. It's only given to the police or some other arresting authority. So we tell her to file a police report and then provide us with the number of the report and the police station involved. Then, if the police ask, we'll give *them* the information—the police, mind you, not the customer."

Morrissey thought it over. Not ideal. Somehow he had to get her to make three calls. And even then, there was no promise Bell Atlantic would cough up the number.

"Paul," he said, "this is a divorce action here, not a crime. She doesn't want to *jail* the guy. How the hell is he supposed to pay child support if he's in the clink? I need to get this info for the divorce case. Are you telling me I can't get it?"

"Of course not." Volkert's tone was pedantic. "A *court* is an arresting authority, too, just like the police department. I'm confident the company would honor a court's duly authorized subpoena."

Morrissey smiled to himself. He was a lawyer. He had a whole drawer full of "duly authorized subpoenas."

"*Confident,* you say? Just how confident, Paul?"

"Well," said Volkert, sounding like he was using only half his mouth, "you could call the Legal Office. Ask for the Subpoena Group. They can give you a more authoritative answer. Let me get you the number."

That's what he needed, all right. An authoritative answer.

Morrissey ended the conversation as soon as he could. With a promise to get right on the DA about that CWAF. Sliding his chair over to the credenza, he opened the little door and picked up the phone.

"Here's to you, Paul," he said to the handset. "Take me to her."

Then he punched the star key, followed by the numbers 5 and 7.

One down. Two to go.

WEDNESDAY

Mavis fingered the phone card in her jacket pocket as she followed Tommy through the library doors. The card, which she'd managed to pick up in the drugstore the night before under cover of buying tampons, gave her twenty dollars' worth of long-distance. It bowed a little when she grabbed it by the edges.

The place was hushed and gloomy, the air dry—just the way she remembered the Aroostook County Library. Long oak tables, goosenecked lamps, ratty armchairs, carousel bookcases filled with paperback mysteries. She had the same sense of imminent suffocation she knew as a high school student condemned to research something very boring. The only bright spots in the place were the two computer screens, gleaming invitingly off to the left. Both computers were in use, but they were huge, antiquated things anyway. Her little laptop could run rings around them.

Tommy moved to the newspaper rack. He pulled out the dowel with the *New York Times* draped around it and laid it out on one of the tables. As he slipped into a wooden chair, she made her move.

"I'm gonna go get a coffee or something. Take the dogs for another walk, maybe. This place is just *too* depressing. You want anything while I'm out?"

He didn't, and she made her escape.

It took her a few minutes to figure out how to use the phone card, but it was clearly better than feeding coins, as she had done the day before. Once she'd dialed the number, she turned her back to the phone so she could keep an eye on the library doors. She breathed deeply and waited.

"Mulcahey here."

The same voice. He even answered his own phone.

"Uh, yes. This is . . . ah, I called you yesterday? I'm Armand Tremblay's niece."

"Yes, of course. Hang on a second and let me transfer this to the phone on my desk. Okay?"

"Okay," she said. She heard a noise, as of someone rummaging around. A complete silence came next, like being place on hold. She waited for the silence to give way. In a few seconds it did, but it was replaced by a dial tone.

Mavis closed her eyes to contain her annoyance. This Mulcahey sounded like a real klutz. Which was okay for him, but it was *her* dime, after all. She raked the phone card through the slot again and redialed his number. He picked up on the first ring.

"Hello!" The guy was almost shouting in her ear. "Are you back?"

"Yes," she said. "It's me again."

"I'm *so* sorry," he said. "I must have pushed the wrong button. I'm *always* doing things like that. My wife says I'm a motor moron. All thumbs."

"It's okay." She pictured a doddering old dear, used to drafting wills and cosseting old ladies. "I do it myself sometimes."

"So you're the niece, eh? I did some checking after your call yesterday. Armand had only one niece. She and Armand would be what the law calls *related by collateral consanguinity.* Which is legal gobbledygook for saying the niece is his only heir if there are no closer relatives still alive. If you can prove you're her, you stand to inherit a nice piece of change."

It made her nervous, this talk of proving her identity. She clutched at the mention of the money instead.

"How much? In your ad you said it might be over a million dollars."

"*Well* over," he said smoothly. "Closer to two million. Of course, that's the gross estate. There will be estate taxes and administrative fees, but it should still net out at over a million."

Mavis held her breath at the mention of all that money.

The man said, "*Are* you Armand's niece?"

"Yes." Her voice felt tiny, like somebody far away.

"And your name is . . . ?"

"Ouillette," she said. "Mavis Giselle Ouillette. I was born in Benedicta, Maine. Armand was my mother's brother."

"And your mother was Florence?"

She frowned. "No. My mother was Jeannette." *What is this?*

"Ah!" said the man. "Just testing. So you *are* Mavis Ouillette. Well, congratulations, Mavis. You're about to become a rich woman."

There was something off here. She could feel it.

"You seem to be getting ahead of yourself," she said sharply. "Don't you think?"

The brief silence suggested he was stumped by her question. She said, "I mean Uncle Army. My uncle? We been out of touch, but we were close once. This is the first I heard of his death. Can't you tell me about him? How'd he die? And where?"

"I'm *very* sorry," the man said. "I must seem very callous to you. It's the nature of the business, I'm afraid. It turns you ghoulish, you know what I mean? I've been getting calls from all kinds of people who want to get their claws on Uncle Army's estate. It tends to toughen the old hide, if you follow me."

"Hmmm." Leaving him there with it.

"Uncle Army died in Provincetown on May the third. Of pneumonia, according to the death certificate. He was in the hospital at the time."

"Was it from AIDS?"

A pause. "I don't know. I never knew the man, you see. I'm a public administrator, appointed to look after the estates of people who don't leave wills and have no relations here. So I wouldn't know."

"It wouldn't surprise me, what I know about him. Poor guy." Uncle Army's face pressed against the surface of her consciousness, filling her with sadness. He was a relentlessly cheerful little man, but always edgy, his fingers twitching at his sides as if, like a quick-draw artist in a Western, he were expecting gunplay. She remembered his kindness, a spot of unhoped-for and transitory grace in a graceless household. When she thought of the old RCA Victor he had given her, she felt a tightening in her throat and feared she might cry.

"A terrible thing, terrible. I'm sorry for him—and for your loss." It was as if the man understood. Then he paused, out of professional respect for the dead, she guessed.

"Ms. Ouillette? Forgive me, but I have a job to do. If you wish to make a claim against the estate—and I hope you do because the money will go to the Commonwealth of Massachusetts if you don't—but if you are, I'm going to need something from you."

"What's that?"

"We'll need you to come to Barnstable, Massachusetts, and present evidence that you are indeed Mavis Ouillette and Armand's niece. I don't know how much of a burden that presents. Where are you calling from?"

She froze for a second before responding. "Ohio. Dayton, Ohio."

"Okay, Ohio. So it *is* a burden. But we can do it at your convenience."

She said, "What if I can't afford to come there? I mean, I'm pretty broke right now. Is there any way I can get money to pay for the trip?"

He obviously hadn't expected that, for he seemed a bit off stride when he answered. "Hm. Let me work on that, okay? Maybe I can talk the court into a small advance. I'd need some kind of documentary evidence that you are who you say you are, though."

"Like what?" She clutched at the receiver.

"Oh, a photocopy of your passport, if you have one. Or some other government-issue ID with your picture on it. Driver's license, that sort of thing."

Her heart sank. All her documentation was in her married name, the name under which she was sought as a fugitive.

"You could fax it to me," the guy continued. "My fax number is . . ."

She pretended to note it and promised to send him something. Before he could ask for anything else, she ended the call.

It was impossible. She could see that now. How could she ever hope to prove who she was without giving herself away? And there was no way to get to Massachusetts. No way at all.

It wasn't until her escape was exposed as a chimera that Mavis realized how much she had been counting on it. It was a flight of fancy before, a pleasant game she could indulge in the dark as long as it remained imaginable, however remotely. Once its impossibility hit home, however, there was no baffle of playfulness to shield her naked need.

Mavis stared across the library's parking lot, the colors of the cars looking rinsed out by the subtropical sun, the merciless light. She was cored out and defenseless, feeling nothing but a familiar kind of deadness inside. She wondered if even the dogs could overcome it.

Does that make three? Morrissey asked himself as he punched in the trace command. At least the last two were from the same phone—of that he was sure. He waited breathlessly for the tape, the message Volkert said you got if they had three traces to the same phone.

A woman's mellifluous voice from the Annoyance Call Bureau told him he had three traces. He closed his eyes in satisfaction and listened as she proceeded to advise him on his options. The message tracked the summary Volkert had given him. All he needed now was to place a call to that number Volkert had given him for the Subpoena Group. To find out how to get his hands on the number and location of the telephone from which Mavis Riley had called him.

He felt good about his morning's work. So good he almost forgot his hangover—the furry one from Phyllis's birthday dinner at Radius. It was those fucking sulfates they put in the red wine, he was sure of it. At least Phyllis seemed to be enjoying herself.

And today, finally, he was, too.

CHAPTER TWENTY-FIVE

IT AIN'T A MORTAL SIN NO MORE

Halogen floodlights sputtered way over on the far side of the vacant lot, along the ridge of the dry creek bed where the backhoe lurched and bucked. After flashing his FBI badge to breach the site perimeter, SAC Ryan Butters buttoned the collar of his trench coat against the cold and hunched into a wicked wind. The temperature had fallen into the low teens, and he was grateful his wife had thought to zip the lining into his coat the night before. He almost tripped over a discarded tire hidden by the weeds as he picked his way across the lot. Bits of airborne jetsam—a Styrofoam cup, a sheet of newspaper—swirled about him in the wind. With a short curse, he had to stop a moment to blink out a speck of dust that had blown into his eye. Once his vision cleared, he knuckled a tear away and slogged on.

Several men stood around the penumbra of light that cut an unnaturally white hole in the darkness. Butters spotted Tevlin, the one standing alone and farthest from the backhoe, and walked toward him. The diesel engine rumbled as the machinery clanged into the frozen earth.

Butters stepped into place beside Tevlin and crossed his arms in an effort to hug himself warm. "Should I be thanking you for bringing me out here on a night like this?" he asked. "Bay *Village*, for Christ's sake."

Tevlin kept his eyes on the backhoe's shovel. "Soon as I heard it was going down, I figured you'd want to be here. Things are happening pretty fast. See the big guy over there, past Velcro?"

Butters squinted across the circle of light at a group of men. He could make out Gower Velcovitch, the skinny tight-ass sent up from Main Justice in Washington. Guys in the Boston office dubbed him Velcro, which was kind of funny because his head was as bald as a honeydew. Velcro was huddled with three or four other agents, his gruesome lackeys from the Office of Professional Responsibility. But Butters didn't see any big—no, wait a minute. Yes, he could see him now. A tall, muscular guy with his hands behind his back, standing off to one side and flanked by two other men. If Butters knew him, he couldn't recognize him in this light, at this distance. He turned back to frown at Tevlin.

"Shaun Crowe," Tevlin prompted, nodding toward the guy.

Butters understood at once. "They turned him."

"Can you blame him?"

No, Butters couldn't blame him. All those years, Tommy had only to fart to send Shaun Crowe running for toilet paper. Hinkle, too. Butters hadn't given Crowe much thought since the day Hinkle promised to send him to tell Larry Coniglio to back off of that wiseass cook, what was his name? Arthur Patch. As far as he could tell, Crowe had gotten the job done.

Crowe was a fairly popular guy in Southie, as gangsters go—and come to think of it, gangsters went pretty well there. He was something of a jock, a hard-hitting amateur boxer in his youth, later a fixture at the Old Harbor Athletic Club and active in coaching Pop Warner football. He had begun as a bouncer at Dell's, where his quickness to violence had impressed Tommy, and he worked his way up to become the guy's principal gofer.

Crowe ran several of the gang's straight businesses, like Flood Square Home Appliance and D Street Liquors. A variety store on Pill Hill, where he collected the envelopes from guys who paid rent to take bets or deal drugs. Eventually, he took over Crikey's, too, after McGinty agreed to sell out cheap. Butters remembered the surveillance photos of them—Tommy and Crowe, sometimes Hinkle, too, but always Tommy and Crowe—having their daily five o'clock meeting. Walking around Castle Island or through Independence Park, or pulling the beach chairs out of Tommy's trunk to sit at Farragut Point or Carson Beach, eyes (and sometimes binoculars) peeled for possible eavesdroppers on the nearby boats.

Crowe inherited the dubious honor of managing the D Street Gang after Hinkle's arrest and Tommy's disappearance. It could not have been easy running things, the envelopes getting skinnier, discipline slipping among shook-up but ambitious wiseguys, everybody wondering who was really in charge—and for how long. All with Tommy phoning it in, no doubt, still wanting things done his way, but without having to suffer the indignity of being on the scene.

And then to have Hinkle drop his bomb. To blow up Crowe's whole world by announcing that he and Tommy had been batting for the other team all those years? *Had* to be devastating. Butters had heard the scuttlebutt. How Crowe had been taking shit from his own people—and worse from the Italians. The taunts, threatened beatings even, as Larry's boys showed up to voice their displeasure at his bosses' role in the dismantling of the LCN and the takedown of Larry's big brother, Francesco. Nick Tramontana himself appearing at the door of the house in Quincy, the one where Crowe's estranged wife and daughter lived, to inquire as to his whereabouts. Downright scary, that.

And then the roll-up three weeks ago. A new round of arrests that swept up the D Street middle management and Shaun Crowe himself. He faced charges ranging from bookmaking to murder, for which the federal sentencing guidelines mandated terms of incarceration counted out in months and easily climbing into the four digits. Left high and dry and dangling, was how it had to seem, with Hinkle singing his lungs out in hopes of some magical release and Tommy on the serious lambrooskie. And Shaun? Poor Shaun couldn't even afford an attorney. So he picked the United States Attorney.

No, Butters didn't blame him.

As if reading his mind, Tevlin said, "Harris told me how it went. Velcro comes in and shows him a picture of his daughter. 'You know who this is?' Shaun just stares at it. He says, 'The fuck is this?' And Velcro says, 'How old is she?' 'Fifteen,' Shaun says. 'And how old are you?' the guy goes. Shaun's getting pissed by now, and he says something like, 'C'mon, you know how old I am. Forty-six.' 'That's right,' Velcro says. 'And you know something, Shaun? The girl in the picture here, she's gonna be at *least* forty-six before you even get a shot at parole.' "

Butters snorted once, hard. He'd heard variations on this buck and wing for twenty-seven years.

Tevlin said, "A few hours later Shaun asks to see him, and you know what he says? He says he wants to make a deal, because, he says, *Apparently, it ain't a mortal sin no more.* Is that rich or what? Harris says he's the mother lode now. Yesterday they dug a small armory of handguns and rifles and explosive devices out of the wall of a garden shed belongs to Hinkle's mother."

"And what's all this, then?" Butters asked, eyebrowing the backhoe. "Tommy's dump?"

"More like Shaun's gold mine." He cocked his head in surprise. "Hey! Gold mine, mother lode. Get it?"

Butters ignored this. "Why do they have to do it in the middle of the night?"

"You know why. Word gets around fast on this. Christ, you and I got here quick enough. I guess Velcro was afraid somebody'd dig 'em up before they got here."

"Dig who up?"

"They found two bodies already. A man and a girl. Supposed to find one more, Shaun says. Talk about your cold cases." Tevlin pretended to shiver and smiled wryly at his own joke. "Shaun says the men were snitches they tumbled to. The one we found is missing his teeth. Do you think they yanked 'em out to make him talk or did it after he was dead so he'd be harder to identify?"

"Maybe both," said Butters. "A woman?"

"A *girl.* Way I hear it, she's supposed to be about fifteen, sixteen. Got involved with Hinkle, and this is how she ends up. Wrapped in plastic, buried in a trench beside a salvage yard in Bay Village. Way I hear it, Tommy strangled her himself because he didn't trust Hinkle to get the job done. Makes you sick."

"Jesus," said Butters, rapidly weighing the implications. "This'll change everything."

"Oh, yeah. And this is just the beginning. They figure Crowe gave them maybe twenty, thirty killings. I can hear Hinkle screaming all the way from Wyatt. Even if he convinces that judge he had some goofy kind of immunity for helping us, that couldn't protect him against something like this. This is *death* penalty stuff here. Way I hear it, they got Hinkle in protective custody as it is. Can't you just see him, that big side of beef in a red jumpsuit over in the pervert wing?"

Butters wouldn't lose any sleep over Hinkle. He had other concerns.

"What else do you think Crowe can give them?"

"You mean, can he give them Tommy?" Tevlin smiled at him. "Isn't that what we really want to talk about?"

Butters had a grim set to his jaw. "We have to consider any collateral damage."

Tevlin guffawed. "Oh, I like that, Ryan. *Collateral damage.* Like we been watching a bombing raid or something."

"What do you *hear*? Can he give them Tommy?"

Butters's tone dispatched Tevlin's levity. "He doesn't know where he is. If he did, they'd be knocking on his door right now instead of diggin' in the cold, cold ground. But he might be able to help find him. He was getting calls from Tommy for a while. Tommy would use a phone card to call him at public places or friends' houses. Give him instructions on running the business and setting up the next call. But Shaun claims he hasn't heard boo from him since Hinkle went public. I suspect they're out of touch."

"But you still think he could help find him?"

"Well, he's not talking to *us.* He talks to Velcro, and *he* sure isn't talking. So maybe Shaun knows a whole lot more than we've been led to believe. He certainly knows Tommy and his habits better than anybody. And he knows how he's been operating since he split. So I figure there's some risk he could lead them to him. How *much* risk I can't say, but I don't think it's too great."

They heard a shout and looked up to see someone pointing down into the ditch dug by the backhoe. Several men crowded around the hole. A man with a shovel in his hand jumped down inside it. Only his head, bare even in this weather, was visible. It bobbed up and down as he worked with the shovel.

Butters shook his head. "The press will have a field day with this. A fifteen-year-old girl?"

"Like I said, it makes you sick."

"It's all over, you know."

"The D Street Gang, you mean? It sure is. There's nobody around to pick up the pieces. Those boys will scatter to the far winds."

"No," said Butters. "I meant Tommy's hype. The reputation he had in Southie, the good guy who kept the lid on the place and drugs out of the neighborhood and steered kids onto the straight and narrow."

Tevlin guffawed again. "That's how Flukes used to sound when Tommy was his principal asset."

"*Our* principal asset," Butters corrected. "Christ, you used to hear that crap from South Boston politicians, too. How Tommy'd tip his hat to the old ladies. Deliver a pot roast to a needy pensioner. Well, it's history now, Tommy's image. Done in by a backhoe and the corpse of a little girl."

Tevlin nodded. "Nothing says forever like a hole in the ground. Even when they dig it up."

They watched in silence while cameras flashed in front of the idling backhoe. Someone handed an empty body bag to the bald man in the hole. As he grabbed hold of his end, the wind picked up sharply and the bag ballooned out between them, filled like a sail in a shouldering wind. Then the gust died away, and the bag disappeared into the hole.

CHAPTER TWENTY-SIX

SATAN'S MISTRESS

Miriam, I understand exactly what you're going through!!! When I was going through my divorce my ex-husband *kidnapped* my grey. Of course he didn't admit he was the one that took her—that might get him in trouble. He was too sly for that! But I knew it was him because of what he said. He said to me it would be better "for *everybody* involved" (I got that one!) if I started to act "reasonable" about the property settlement. And this was right in front of my lawyer, and his too, that's how brazen he was about it! I was terrified for her, but my lawyer said we couldn't prove he was the one (though I knew). He told me we shouldn't give in. And then I got a package in the mail. *It was Sophie's ear!!* It was all splochy with dry blood and sealed up in a zip lock bag and it made me so sick I threw up and everything, I really did. I didn't know what to do with it so I kept it in the freezer compartment, in a tupperware container, next to the tater tots. Then he—

Dani swiveled her head to the right and caught Arthur's eye. He threw her some eyebrow.

"Naaa," they said in unison, heads shaking.

"Too bizarre," she added.

"*Way* too," he agreed, clicking back a screen to return to the list of responses to "Miriam's" message. "That's not our Mavis. Probably a fake. As in somebody's idea of a sick joke."

From behind them Joanne spoke up. "Like J. Paw Getty, perhaps?"

The two of them looked back at her, Arthur with a grin, Dani without.

Joanne gave a sheepish shrug. "So there's *two* of us that make sick jokes." One of her eyebrows arched, tugging the corner of her mouth along with it. "Three, if you count Van Gogh."

Arthur chuckled and went back to downloading messages. There were twenty-nine of them this time. Like the responses to "Miriam's" first message, most were spare and short on detail—the kind of impersonal consolation you might jot down before signing a Hallmark sympathy card.

Dani was smiling at Joanne now. The woman towered over her, dressed in white painter's pants and a magenta T-shirt that begged you to STOP GLOBAL WHINING. She liked Joanne, had ever since that first night, when she had cuffed Leighton Taylor around for being a pompous ass. Which he was, of course, and worse. It had taken Dani weeks to realize what Joanne spotted in the time it took him to place his order. Always right in your face, she was, keeping you back on your heels.

"How," Dani wondered out loud, "did you ever end up in this business? I'm not sure the hospitality trade suits you."

Arthur gave a gentle snort of amusement as he continued to filter the sympathetic traffic of greyhound lovers.

Joanne sighed and crossed her arms over her chest. "It was a long and winding road. I was a graduate student for a while. English lit, but it didn't—well, *suit* me, as you put it. I guess the academy and I were not a good match."

"You have to understand," Arthur interjected. "Joanne was a terror even then. Her dissertation was a radical-feminist reframe of *Hamlet.*"

"Really?" Dani was intrigued.

"Alas." Joanne gave an exaggerated sigh. "*In Defense of Queen Gertrude* never got past the department's thesis committee. It could have been a paradigm shift, you know. Maybe I'll finish it someday. Publish the sucker."

Arthur's smile broadened to hear her. He watched the downloading of what looked to be a long message from someone named Hattie.

"Imagine what it must have been like for her," Joanne continued. "High visibility but powerless. Stuck with that impotent old king, realizing too late that she could only find personal fulfillment with the brother, Claudius. And then that narcissistic punster of a son, hung up on primogeniture and male honor. Acting out all over the—"

"Hey," Arthur interrupted sharply, as his eyes sped through Hattie's response. "Hey. Come look at this."

Arthur clicked on the print icon. As the printer started humming, he fished around on the desk for the *Houndbytes* newsletter. The two women leaned forward to read Hattie's message.

> Oh Miriam, I felt terrible when I read your first message, and guilty afterward that I didn't answer it right then. But when I heard you the second time, I was filled with shame and I knew I *had* to answer.
>
> I lost my dogs, two beautiful greys I loved more than life itself, and it was my fault too so I know what you are going thru. I've been there.
>
> This all happened about a year ago. I used to leave the greys in the backyard in the summer (it's fenced in) when I went to work so they wouldn't have to be cooped up all day. Maybe I shouldn't have, but I thought it was better for them, at least in the warm weather. Well, one day I got a call at work from my mother who told me my dad had just had a heart attack and could I please come home at once! She was hysterical. As you can imagine, I was quite upset by this news.
>
> Without hardly thinking I got in my car and started on the long drive—the hometown where I grew up was about 100 miles away in the country. I was worried sick for my dad and mom. Then I remembered my babies out in the backyard. I realized I wouldn't be able to get home that night so when I stopped at a spa to get a Coke, I called my friend Carolyn. She didn't answer but I left a message on her machine, telling her what happened and to please let the dogs in and look after them till I got back.
>
> But I forgot that Carolyn was away at the beach for a week, so she never got my message. I stayed with my folks for three days. My dad recovered and all, but my mom really needed the support.
>
> You can guess what happened next. When I got home my greys were gone!!!! The padlock on the gate was broken and

left hanging on the chain link fence and my babies were nowhere to be found. Needless to say I was frantic with worry. I talked to the neighbors who said they barked when night came—they could be such big babies about the dark! This went on two nights in a row, but it was quiet the third night. I called the animal control and the SPCA and Greyhound Friends, even the police (don't *bother*, believe me), everybody I could think of who might be able to help. I was just sick with worry.

I never saw them again. My friend Carolyn said maybe they just ran away, but I know better. They would have come back home if they were OK, that's just the way they were. I'm convinced an angry neighbor got mad about the barking and did something awful to them. I have my suspicions, but what can I do about it? It was the darkest time of my life—but I don't need to tell *you* that!

So Miriam, I know what you're feeling. And I also know that the pain will fade and you will be able to channel your love for another grey. I'm not suggesting you rush out to adopt another one—no way, not yet—you have grieving to do first. But remember, there are lots of dogs out there in desperate need of a loving, caring home. And time will heal.

That's what I did, finally. Today I have two of the most beautiful loving needlenoses in the world. Tho I know that Dapple and Bernadine can never replace my lost loves, they are a comfort and a joy. I hope the same for you.

—Hattie

The two women remained silent after reading Hattie's message. Dani was tilted forward, still staring at the monitor. Joanne leaned her weight on the back of Arthur's chair.

"There's no Hattie on the list," Arthur reported, his head still bent over the newsletter. "No e-mail address. So she's anonymous."

"You really think it's her?" Dani asked.

"Her story's right," Joanne said. "Forget the details. Concentrate on the shell of the thing, the narrative structure. *De*-deconstruct the text, for once. It's identical to Mavis's story. Two dogs. She's called away unexpectedly by an emergency. Tries to call a friend to take care of them. No luck. They're taken away by some faceless person—she kinda knows who but she can't do anything about it. They've been destroyed. I tell you, it's the same fucking story."

Joanne had talked herself excited.

"Plus, she didn't give an e-mail address," Arthur repeated. "When did this come in?" He clicked back to the message list.

• Re: Thanks for Hillary...BUT............ — **Hattie** 04:14:27 11/23/98

"Four fourteen this *morning*?" He was perplexed. "She's up all night?"

"Unless," Joanne suggested, "she's logging on from the West Coast somewhere. It would only be one-fourteen in Los Angeles."

Arthur nodded. "Or noon in Dublin. Don't forget, we've read stuff posted by Irish dog lovers. A lot of dog tracks there."

"No," Dani said firmly, entering the deliberations for the first time, her concentration on the screen still unbroken. "The times given are those of the sender. So it *was* four A.M. where she is. There's something else, too. She comes from Massachusetts. Our Hattie's from Boston."

She turned to her right to face Arthur. His face was screwed up with curiosity.

"You guys are from Boston, so you don't see it," she explained. "But I don't know anyplace else where convenience stores are called *spas.* Do you? They sure didn't call them that in Vermont, and that's right next door."

A grin began to suffuse Arthur's features. "And she said her friend had gone to the beach. Lots of places have beaches, but she seems to suggest that she lived not too far from the water."

"Assuming she didn't invent the details to throw people off," Joanne said.

Dani shook her head. "No, I don't think so. Not spa, anyway. It's just too, well, casual. Unplanned. And there's something else, too."

The two of them watched her carefully until she dropped the other shoe.

"Greyhound Friends is a Massachusetts rescue shelter. Remember? Out in Hopkinton? No, if this isn't Mavis, it's somebody from Boston whose story tracks hers very closely. It's too much of a coincidence. We have to assume it's her."

The three of them fell silent again. They stared at the monitor. As if to prod them, some gizmo in the computer's innards whirred at them.

"The question is," Dani said, "what do we do now?"

Arthur rolled his shoulders and waggled his fingers over the keyboard.

"For starters," he said, "we thank her."

Tommy's snore had cleared out its glottal rumble and passed on to a peaceful, whistling drone. Mavis peeked into the bedroom and eyed the fetal-curled lump under the bedclothes. The reading lamp on the nightstand was still on. A paperback copy of *Into Thin Air* had fallen to the floor on his side of the bed. One bare foot, with toenails like hard, yellowed horn, poked out from under the bunched-up chenille bedspread. She reached in and took hold of the china doorknob, twisting it gently as she pulled the door shut. Relaxing her grip in tiny, agonized increments, she let the knob slip back to its former position. At last she felt the catch slide noiselessly into place.

She tightened the terry-cloth robe about her middle and padded back across the tiny living room, her fuzzy pink slippers whispering over the linoleum. Bernadine raised her eyelids to watch her pass, but Dapple remained completely blissed out on the couch. Mavis reentered the kitchen.

She did not close the door to the living room behind her. If Tommy were to waken now, she would be able to see the bedroom door open from her chair at the kitchen table. That would give her plenty of time to toggle back to the *Presque Isle Gazette.* She pulled out the chair and sat down before the laptop.

It was scary, what she was doing, even with the precautions she was taking. It had taken some serious cajoling to convince Tommy to let her sign up with an Internet access provider. In the end he had acquiesced, but he had been immovable on one critical point: her use had to remain absolutely passive. She could surf the web, he said, download all the crap she wanted to amuse herself, but she must never, ever engage in active communication with anyone over the thing. There could be no uploading. No on-line purchases. No e-mail communications. No chat rooms. Nothing going out. Absolutely nothing. Did she understand?

She understood. Okay, she could live with that. She liked the computer for playing games mostly, anyway. Hearts. Solitaire. And the Net she used to stay caught up with stuff. The *Gazette,* of course, and she liked to check out the *Boston Herald* every once in a while to see what was going on back home. Sometimes she'd pull up the Millbank Tweed catalog. It was funny: rummaging through the changes in its fall line actually made her nostalgic for the job that seemed so humdrum when she was there.

She also loved to follow whatever was going on among houndheads all across the country. Check that: the world. She had bookmarked every greyhound website she could find, and she soaked up information from them with a lover's passion. She relished news of gatherings and jamborees, where houndheads got together for fun and entertainment and even, sometimes, coursing for the dogs. The dedication of the GUR, the underground railroad for transporting dogs from point to point on a long journey to safety. She marveled at the array of products available to dog lovers, though she didn't dare try to buy anything. The photographs of other people's dogs were wonderful. One of the sites even gave her reason to be proud of the car they drove, when it informed her that Lincolns had once borne statues of greyhounds as hood ornaments.

But most of all, she loved to lose herself in the back-and-forth of messages posted on the greyhound bulletin boards, with their delicious medley of homey advice, queries on pet care, and cute anecdotes that made her laugh out loud at the antics of the dogs. There were joyful announcements of births and adoptions, nuggets of spiritual truth, calls to political action. (She felt a surge of pride and excitement when she learned there was a referendum to abolish dog racing on the ballot back in Massachusetts!) Her heart ached to read the urgent pleas for help when some kennel was threatening to dump a litter or a shelter was gravely overcrowded. Not to mention the sad, beautiful poems posted in memory of departed loved ones. The messages made her feel less alone, like she was part of a vast but close-knit fellowship that thought and loved the way she did.

She always obeyed Tommy's strictures about making contact. It was too dangerous, he insisted, and she knew better than to argue with him. Smart as he was, he knew precious little about computers, about how even passive use left cookies on your hard drive so the site could recognize you the next time you paid a visit. Lord, he'd have a *cow* over that, if he knew. But she understood there was really no way she could be traced through the computer. The Net was anonymous; that was its chief attraction to begin with, and engaging in e-mail communication under a pseudonym was a lot safer than those calls he used to make on phone cards when he was still trying to stay on top of his business interests back in Boston. Still, she didn't want to do anything that might cause him to sever her link to the Web. So she contented herself with passive use, even when the temptation was great.

Until Miriam, that is. God, how that tore her up! It wasn't just the brimming of sympathy she felt for the woman that got to her. Miriam's whole story—especially the guilt over her failure to protect her babies—made her relive the horror and shame that had seared her soul like battery acid when she lost Cookie and Erol. What was once scabbed over was suddenly scraped open and exposed. So it was as much for her own relief as Miriam's that she felt she had to share her own grief with the woman.

Fortunately, *Houndbytes* accepted messages for posting on its board without publishing her e-mail address. She had been given one as a matter of course when she signed up with the Internet access provider. The ISP's application form had a space for a personal tag to precede its domain name, and she had chosen one that was blandly anonymous. Her resulting address, C&E@gulfnet.com, was meaningless to others, but it was built on the first initials of her slain dogs. An electronic memorial, that's what it was, even if she had intended never to use it.

All the same, it was a comfort to know that the *Houndbytes* site would never tell anyone her address. This might be a superfluous assurance of confidentiality vis-à-vis outsiders, but to her it was important for another reason. It meant she wouldn't have to worry about anybody sending e-mail messages back to *her.* The last thing she needed was to have e-mail messages popping up on her screen, right where Tommy might spot them and go ballistic on her.

She had spent hours composing her message to Miriam. It required a lot of thought and care. She couldn't give the actual details, of course, but she had to tell her enough to convey the heart of the thing. The emotional reality, that's what it was. That was what she wanted to get across. Edgy as she was about the whole business and Tommy's demands, she had meant to send something short and to the point. Once she got started, however, it poured out of her, and her message was almost embarrassingly long. As she typed and edited it, she felt a tightening of pressure in her solar plexus. Once she almost jumped out of her skin when Bernadine sat up in the semi-darkened living room.

When she had finished it, the rinsed-out light of early dawn was filtering through the cotton drapes over the kitchen window. She read over the message two more times. Her heart raced as she stared at the *Send Mail* icon. She felt horrible. Terrified. Jumpy and empty, like something was missing—as if she'd been drinking coffee for hours. Then, with savage abruptness, she hit the icon. At once the pressure lifted, the anxiety left her. The corrosive anguish that had been revived by Miriam's message streamed out of her, as if borne away into cyberspace as a contrail to her message of consolation. Something like peace descended on her. She smiled. It was true what they said about love, she decided then. It wasn't really yours till you gave it away.

It gave her a frisson even a day later. It was the thrill of a daring deed done, to see the heading of her own message for the first time. Her pulse quickened when she realized that Miriam had posted a response. To her message! A personal response! Eagerly, she clicked on the message tag and downloaded Miriam's response.

> Hattie, whoever you are, thank you thank you thank you!!! You are a doGsend and a blessing. I can never thank you enough for your heartfelt message. Its such a relief to know that somebody out there knows what I feel!
>
> Sorry about that. I just had a little bit of an interruption. You see, I'm writing this at the office and when my boss comes by, which she just did, I have to get off the site quick and pretend I'm working with the database. Not your problem, I can tell. If you're posting bulletins at four in the morning, you must be a night owl.
>
> I found your message *so* helpful. I was especially encouraged to learn you were able to adopt new babies so soon after your loss. I don't know, but right now it feels like I could never do that. It would be disloyal to Hillary somehow. Am I being too neurotic or what? How did you do it?
>
> And by the way, did you pick those adorable names yourself or did Dapple and Bernadine already have their names when you adopted them? They are *truly* adorable.
>
> Gotta go check the pipes—it's freezing here. Hope it's warmer where you are! Thank you once again, Hattie. I hope you burn the midnite oil again soon. I'd love to hear from you.
>
> With love and thanks, Miriam

Mavis cocked her ear at what she thought was a sound from the bedroom. She strained to listen, but heard only the woosh of a car passing on the road outside. Then silence again. She waited a few minutes longer, not relaxing until she was sure she could hear Tommy's rhythmic snoring. She started typing immediately.

> A night owl? No, I just like to stay up late. I'm not working right now and as a night person I naturally gravitate toward the wee hours when I don't absolutely have to be someplace in the morning. But at least I'm not freezing like you, being as you're obviously up north someplace.
>
> I don't really know what to tell you about how I "got over" losing my greys. Because, you see I don't think I ever did. And maybe I never will, at least part of me won't. But I finally realized—and it took me months and months to see it—that I didn't have to wait to get over them to adopt new ones.
>
> A very wise lady once told me the heart is a muscle and it responds to exercise. I know you'll find that if you open your home (and heart!) to a new dog, you'll have room to love the new ones while you still cherish Hilary's memory.
>
> So think about it. You don't have to actually adopt one right away—just get yourself around them, that's the important thing. The rest will follow, when you're ready.
>
> And you're half right about the names. Dapple was Dapple on the papers, but Bernadine was called Satan's Mistress when I got her. I couldn't have *that*!
>
> Hang in there, Miriam
>
> Hattie

Arthur spoke with conviction. "It's her. It's gotta be. She's got no job. And notice how she's never told us the names of her dead dogs. Everybody, and I mean *everybody* on this site, refers to their dogs by name. And so does Hattie, when she talks about her new ones. It's just the old ones she never names—out of caution, no doubt, in case somebody's heard about Erol and Cookie."

"You're probably right," said Dani, "but what do we do with it? All we really know is that she's probably in the south, where it's not freezing."

"It's a start."

"Okay. So say we've narrowed it to the South. Then what?"

He grinned slyly. "That's where you earn your end. Put on your prosecutor's hat. You know all this about a fugitive. Plus, you know she's registered with an Internet organization called *Houndbytesdotcom.* Had to, to post a message on its bulletin board. How would you get her registration data from the website? Including her e-mail address?"

Dani shrugged. "Simple. I'd hit them with a subpoena for their registration records as they relate to Hattie. But in case you've forgotten, I'm *not* a prosecutor anymore. Things are a lot easier when you've got the federal government behind you."

"But they don't know that, do they?"

She cocked her head and narrowed her eyes. He was still smiling. She wasn't. "What are you suggesting here?"

It was Arthur's turn to shrug. "How hard is it to come up with a document that will *pass* as a subpoena? You know what they look like. Christ, even *I* do, thanks to you. We could just show up with it wherever they're located—someplace in Pennsylvania, I think—and demand the records."

Dani looked furious now. "Are you crazy? Fabricate a court order? Impersonate a federal officer? My God, it's not bad enough you borrow money from Larry the Rabbit—and dine with him. Do you want to do *time* with him, too?

She was almost shouting, and Arthur felt suitably abashed. "It was just a thought."

"A thought that could get us jailed and me disbarred. And stupid, too, I might add. What do you think the first thing *Houndbytes* would do if they got hit with a subpoena? What was the first thing *you* did? Huh?"

Arthur got it. "They'd call a lawyer," he mumbled.

"Exactly. And listen to these people. They strike me as pretty suspicious of authority. I expect the *second* thing they'd do would be to warn Mavis—Hattie. She and Tommy would disappear faster than you can boot your computer."

"Okay, okay. You're right." He raised his hands as if covering his ears. "Dumb suggestion. I withdraw it."

Her glare twisted in him like a knife. "It's more than dumb. It's insulting. That you could *think* I would do such a thing."

Arthur shrank from her intensity, oddly frightened. It came to him that he was scared that she might leave—and even more frightened of how much he did not want that to happen.

"I'm sorry," he said, meeting her icy stare. "You're absolutely right. I was just thinking out loud. I'm not a lawyer. I don't think things through the way you do. If I had, I would have realized immediately that you'd never be a party to such a thing."

"Too much of a prude for something so . . . colorful? Something so impromptu and seat-of-the-pants? Is that it?"

Arthur frowned. He didn't get this. Had he swung too far the other way?

"No," he said. "I never thought of you as a prude. More—" He smiled weakly. *Straightlaced* came to mind, but he thought better of it. "*Principled* is the word I'd use. You play by the rules."

He willed his smile to stay in place, not to wilt under her blistering scrutiny. Then she looked away, to her left. When she finally wheeled back to engage him, her expression had softened.

"Maybe I overreacted a little. When you were talking, I kept seeing a replay of my dealings with Stanley Prout. He once used *prig* to describe my revulsion at *his* methods. So maybe I was overly hard on you." She swept a lock of hair out of her eyes and almost smiled at him.

He said, "A straight shooter maybe, but not a prude."

She gave him a kind of scoffing chuckle and looked away to pick through the printouts of the messages they had been discussing. Watching her in profile, he noticed a glowing spot of red over her cheekbone. Arthur felt a churning of desire.

"So," she said, her eyes on the pages she held, "what's next then?"

"Another message?"

She nodded.

It was still early evening, just past seven o'clock, when Mavis logged on again. Tommy was eating his supper across the table from her. Clicking fluidly through the *Houndbytes* website, she never lost her peripheral awareness of him there, picking at his food in his fastidious way. He permitted himself a meager collation, almost Lenten fare. A boneless chicken breast broiled in the toaster oven, undressed broccoli, dry toast made from heavy multigrain bread. All washed down with a liter of Evian springwater.

"You know what I think we should do tomorrow?" she said as she pulled up a notice for a greyhound gathering to take place next month in Huntsville, Alabama.

He did not respond. He was busy cutting the chicken into perfectly square chunks of uniform dimension.

"I thought it might be fun to drive over to Sanibel Island and see that bird sanctuary there. It's supposed to be pretty, and the dogs could have a run on the beach." She peeked over the screen to catch his reaction.

Tommy laid his knife on his plate and, switching the fork to his other hand, deftly speared a piece of chicken. He brought it to his mouth, which he opened only far enough to accommodate the chunk. His canines seized it cleanly and he extracted the fork. He chewed several times before responding.

"Let me think about it," he said. "Maybe after the library."

He unscrewed the cap to the water bottle. When he had filled his glass, he laid the cap beside the bottle. She watched him take a bite of toast and knew to a moral certainty that he would next help himself to the broccoli. After which he would repeat the cycle: chicken, water, toast, vegetable.

When they first started keeping company, she had found his eating habits mildly amusing. They seemed an amalgam of squeamishness, rigidity, and quirks—all fueled by a near paranoia about chemicals and animal fats. Amusement gave way to annoyance, then gradually to resignation. But at odd moments lately she found herself observing him closely, her attention riveted on the laconic execution of all his daily rituals. She knew exactly what he would do and she did not look or hope for variation or lapses, whether he was laying out a pair of socks on the bed in the morning or puffing through his routinized workout in the living room or, as now, eating his way clockwise around his dinner plate. It was the robotic precision that held her rapt, gripped by a species of frigid wonder at such meticulous calibration and economy of motion. He was getting old, she realized suddenly. An old man who measured out his life with calipers.

She was at the bulletin board now. It surprised her how brazen she had become. She had just started exchanging messages with Miriam, and here she was checking for new ones with Tommy sitting less than three feet away! Of course, there was little risk in it. If he bothered to look, he'd just see that she was surfing through another greyhound site. Even if he saw the list of messages on the board, they wouldn't mean anything to him. Greyhound babble, nothing more.

She felt a secret tingle of excitement when she spotted the heading for a new message from Miram. She flicked her eyes to take in Tommy, but he was carefully refilling his glass.

Why not? What the hell. She fingered the red dot until the cursor swung into position touching Miriam's name, then depressed the clicker with her thumb. She was still waiting for the message to load when she heard the scrape of Tommy's chair. He stood up abruptly.

Mavis froze. He was moving toward her side of the table. She was terrified he might see the message and put two and two together. With a scrabbling motion of her left hand, she tried to toggle back to her game of solitaire by hitting the ALT and TAB keys as quickly as possible, but her panic made her fumbling fingers miss their mark. Miriam's message materialized cleanly just as Tommy rounded the back of her chair.

As he went by, she felt his hand brush across the top of her head. An arc of static electricity between them made her hunch defensively at his touch. He gave a snort of amusement at this and kept moving. The electrical shock, she realized with a rush of gratitude as he proceeded to the counter by the sink, had masked her spasm of terror at his casual touch. Miriam's message was replaced by columns of playing cards now, and Tommy was washing his hands at the sink, the black pager clinging to his side like a deformed mussel.

Of course, he had noticed nothing. Once the relief had sluiced away the adrenaline, she felt a sour bitterness at his indifference. He didn't care enough to look. She should have expected that. The man showed so little interest in her activities, in the events of her interior life, that she enjoyed a certain latitude. With it, however, came a chilling sense of isolation. Lost, that's what she was. A long, long way from home—wherever *that* was. She had a slivery glimpse of the desperate loneliness of years ago, the little girl huddled around Uncle Army's radio in the dark.

Mavis filled her cheeks like a balloon, then blew it out soundlessly. Right now she was a wreck, wrung out like a damp washcloth. She shut down the laptop and retreated to the living room to watch television.

It wasn't until well after midnight, when Tommy's snoring sounded the all clear, that she reestablished her link to the bulletin board.

> Hattie, thank you again for all your advice. You have such a mothering way about you. I hope you're not offended if I say

that. Especially if your younger than I am! But you do, really. You're such a comfort.

I've thought a lot about what you said about surrounding myself with other greys. I'm sure you're right. I'm even thinking I should at least *start* the process of looking for a new baby to adopt. Of course, I have a couple obstacles. For one thing, we're just getting over this incredible ice storm here. Did you read about it? First the horrible freezing rain, then we got socked with frigid temperatures. Lots of power outages and tree branches are down everywhere. The orchards have been hit the hardest. And don't even ask about the roads! Hope you didn't get it, too. I hear there was bad weather all up and down the coast. Anyway, it kept me pretty much at home.

Now if you want to visit a greyhound shelter, all this bad weather just makes a bad situation worse. I should be grateful, I know, that Vermont has banned dog racing. And I am, I really am! (Can you imagine what it would be like to have to race in this weather?) Its just that this means there aren't any shelters here and I'll have to drive all the way to NY state or NH to find a grey to adopt.

But enough of my moaning. You've been such a help. I can see the light at the end of the tunnel. And I *will* take your good advice when the roads are passable and I'm emotionally able!

Please hug Bernadine and Dapple for me!!

Miriam

"Florida!" Arthur shouted, clutching the message in his fist as he bounded down the hall. "Goddamn it, she's in Florida!"

Joanne turned from her conversation with Jonathan to stare at him as he burst through the kitchen door. Dani was seated at the steel table, cradling a cup of coffee with both hands as if warming them with it.

Arthur slapped the sheet of paper down on the table. "She's in Florida!" he repeated triumphantly. "Don't you see? We know where she is!"

All three of them stared at him.

"Listen!" he begged. He read it out loud.

Good news, Miriam! I'm so happy you're starting to feel better. If I have had a part in that, no matter how small, I'm only grateful for the opportunity. This fellowship we have between all of us hound lovers is a wonderful thing. Pass it on!

I did read about your weather—and it's not even December. We got a bit of it down here. No ice storms, thank God, but we got some serious freezing. And our orchards were hit too.

I know you're moving in the right direction when you say you'll start looking for a—oh my God, I almost said *replacement*. But I know better than to think another grey could replace Hilary! Sorry! I only mean that when you make room in your heart for a new baby, there will be less room for the grief and pain you feel for Hilary.

You're very fortunate to live in a state like Vermont. Wouldn't it be wonderful if there weren't *any* shelters!! I mean, if there was no need for them. One of the "burdens" of living in a state that outlaws racing is that you have to drive farther to find a shelter. Maybe, someday, if we all stick together and work hard, there won't *be* any more shelters because there's no more abuse and greys will have the same protections as other dogs!

So thank your stars that you live where you do and have to drive so far. I only wish we had such a "problem"! Unfortunately, I read someplace that there are more racetracks here than any place in the country. But someday . . . ????

Keep the faith, Miriam.

Hattie

"You see?" he said.

They still stared at him.

"Florida! It has more dogtracks than any other state. By far. Everybody in the movement knows this. Hattie, *Mavis*, is telling us she's in Florida."

Dani was frowning. "Why would she tell us that? Isn't it too, well, revealing?"

"Who knows? The point is she *did*."

"No," Joanne interposed. "The point is she may be leading us down the primrose path."

Arthur peered at her in disbelief. "Why?" he demanded. "She has no reason in the world to distrust us—'Miriam,' rather. And it fits! The cold snap that went all the way down the east coast. It's warmer where she is. She can't be making all this shit up. I tell you, it fits too well. It's Mavis, and she's telling us she's in Florida."

Joanne said, "It's a tough call. I don't know who's being more gullible. Mavis for letting it slip or you for believing she would?"

"No," said Dani. "I think Arthur's right. You need to rephrase the question. You should ask, which is more likely: that she's gullible enough to give herself away or that she's devious enough to mislead us so cleverly. Nothing in her history, and nothing in her messages, suggests she's that devious. I agree with Arthur. She's in Florida."

Arthur bent over and hugged her hard. She held her coffee cup away from them and smiled awkwardly.

"You're beautiful!" he said, his cheek still pressed to hers. "You put it *perfectly*."

"Well, put *this*," said Joanne. Arthur pulled away from Dani. When Joanne had their joint attention, she continued. *"So what?"* She paused to let this sink in. "Florida's also the fourth-biggest state. Millions of people, hundreds of towns. Where do you go from here?"

"Yes!" Arthur said, a pedagogue's finger in the air. "Millions of people and hundreds of towns, *but how many rescue shelters*? Maybe more than in most states, I grant you, maybe more than in *any* other state, but come on, how many can there be? A dozen? Two dozen, tops."

"You're thinking you can find her through the shelters?"

"She had to get her dogs someplace."

Dani said, "What makes you so sure she got them in Florida?"

Arthur shrugged happily. "Sure? I don't got sure. I've got probabilities, that's all. Think about it. They've been on the road. The Boston press has reported Tommy sightings all over the country. Since he's not Elvis, some of them are likely to be real. So he's been on the road. It's hard to travel with dogs, *two* dogs—especially if you don't want to attract attention. That's why she left hers behind in the first place. So I figure—figure now, not *sure*—they didn't get the dogs till they found some place where they expected to settle for a while."

Joanne sat down at the table. "Why couldn't they have 'expected' to settle someplace else earlier, picked up the dogs, and *then* moved down to Florida?"

Arthur made a little nod of submission. "I suppose. But we don't know that. And we *do* know Florida."

Dani said, "There's another reason they'd have to be settled someplace before adopting the dogs." Arthur and Joanne turned to face Dani. She continued. "One thing I noticed about these shelters, you have to make some showing that you'll be able to provide an acceptable home. At a minimum, that means a stable address. I suppose you can fake some of that, but at least you have to stick around long enough to go through the process."

"You're right," Arthur added. "Just like a human adoption. And some of them say they require a home visit before they'll give you a dog." He paused and grinned. "Somehow I can't imagine Tommy warming to *that* notion."

"Which probably means," said Dani, "that we could eliminate shelters that are too tough on the application process."

"We've got something else, too," said Arthur. He rubbed his hands together like a miser before a heap of coins. "We have the names the kennels registered her dogs under. Dapple and Satan's Mistress. There's gotta be a way to trace those dogs to the shelter that rescued them.

"And placed them with Mavis," Dani finished for him. The two of them grinned at each other.

CHAPTER TWENTY-SEVEN

DESKKILL

It was Tookie Clonbraken, the court officer, who saved the day. Tookie was a pigeon-toed puffball of a man with a plump lower lip that jutted out like a ledge of greasy rock. He sat off to the left of the bench, near the side door, behind a raised enclosure with walnut-veneered sides that extended halfway up his chest. Ever since the lunch recess, you could tell he was fighting off a caloric stupor. His chin would sink to his chest, then bob up again when he caught himself. Yellow lids slid up and down in slow motion over his unfocused eyeballs.

Jimmy Morrissey was seated at a counsel table inside the rail, down in the killing fields of Judge Fanger's courtroom. Although he was dreading his turn to argue against the Commonwealth's motion to revoke his client's bail, he still maintained his vigil over Tookie's losing struggle.

A young assistant district attorney named Shad was addressing the court from Jimmy's left. Shad wore a loden corduroy suit and shoes the same color and shape as a raw kidney. His wooden gestures bore no relation to the flow of his words. Jimmy watched the man apply the heinie-lick maneuver to Judge Fanger. So far as Jimmy could tell, she was having none of it.

Which didn't mean things were going Jimmy's way. Far from it. Letticia Fanger was, by universal agreement, burned out after nine years on the superior court. The experience had tooled her soul with a rich contempt for the lawyers who appeared before her, the ones whose maunderings she had to endure when she could be clearing her docket by deciding motions on the papers. She preferred deskkill to live argument. With a mind like a cold chisel and a gavel for a hammer, she tended to kill time in the motion session by carving chunks out of the participants. At least she did it to lawyers on both sides of the *v*—an equal-opportunity bully, Jimmy had to concede. When it came time to rule, however, she displayed a pronounced bias in favor of prosecutors.

Jimmy watched her tap the eraser end of her pencil against the pad in front of her. She wore retro spectacles with sweeping fins at the temples like a '59 DeSoto. With her other hand she smoothed the bodice of her robe. Fanger was known to wear genuine silk, as if she were a Queen's counselor or something, and she now brushed the back of her knuckles over the fine black fabric. Then something Shad said seemed to annoy her, and her gaze jumped impatiently about the courtroom.

The judge's eyes stopped scanning and her expression soured—a maneuver requiring scant redeployment of the facial muscles. She scribbled something on her pad, tore off the sheet, and thrust it down toward the clerk who sat in front of her. The clerk glanced at the note and then looked up to her right. Following her gaze, Jimmy realized Judge Fanger had picked up on Tookie's plight.

For Tookie had lost the war. His head sagged off to the right, and his lower lip trembled softly in the column of air from his half-open mouth.

Shad plunged on, noticing nothing, but Jimmy watched as the clerk slipped out of her chair and made her way over to Tookie. She gently laid a hand on his shoulder and gave him a little shake. Tookie's eyes popped open. Like a predator he was instantly alert. Instinct kicked in.

"All rise!" he bellowed hoarsely, pulling himself to his feet.

And everyone rose. Except Judge Fanger, that is, who closed up her face like a fist and glared hotly at him.

Tookie soon realized the gravity of his blunder and began to sink back into his chair. Before he reached it, however, Judge Fanger stood up brusquely and moved away from the bench toward the door to her chambers. Tookie jerked himself back into a standing position. As the judge reached the door, she paused to turn toward the clerk.

"Bring him to me," she hissed with a head bob in Tookie's direction. "And I want him *alive.*"

With a rustle of episcopal silk, she disappeared behind the door.

Shad was still standing in the well and trying to comprehend what had happened, one digit of his IQ wrestling with the other. He turned to Jimmy in horror.

"Was she talking about me?"

Jimmy shook his head sadly. "I warned you not to make that argument." But the look on Shad's face made him relent. He put him out of his misery by pointing to Tookie.

Tookie Clonbracken looked miserable. He wiped his mouth with the back of his hand, then hitched up his pants and buttoned his blue blazer. The coat gaped above his belly. Head down, he trudged after the clerk into Judge Fanger's chambers. No one in the courtroom envied him.

Out in the hallway Jimmy's gaze swept along the far wall where four pay phones hung. To his surprise, one of them was not in use. He pounced on it.

"Law offices," said Taffy. He could hear the snap of her gum.

"What's happening, kiddo? Got an unexpected recess over here."

"Nothing that will make your day," she said. He could picture her flipping little pieces of paper. "Mr. Palmer wants to know where your share of the rent is. Mrs. Lewis wants you to call her—something about a chiropractor didn't get his bill paid? And Attorney Snoad called."

Jimmy had ground his teeth to hear the first two messages—bad news, both of them—but the third one was unfamiliar. "Snowed? What kind of name is that?"

"You got me. It goes S-N-O-A-D. Says he's from Bell Atlantic."

Jimmy felt a flutter of excitement. "Give me his number," he said. "And tell the others I'll get back to them."

Scribbling the number on the back of an envelope, he fished in his pocket for more change.

Kenneth Snoad sounded young and WASP. Jimmy made a quick appraisal: in-house counsel, choosing the quiet life of salaried security with a public utility. Snoad would not be looking for any extra work.

"You see," Snoad was explaining, "we usually only release call trace data to the police. I don't see that you filed a police report. Either you or your client—what's his name?"

"Mulcahey. James Mulcahey."

"Of course. It's on the caption to your subpoena. Mulcahey versus Mulcahey. Sure doesn't sound like a criminal case, does it?" A pedagogue's tone now. "More like a divorce case."

"It *is* a divorce case. Let me—"

"You see? That's just what I mean. The company certainly doesn't want to get involved in some messy divorce proceeding. Our call trace service is meant to protect people from criminal activity. You know, like stalkers. Not chase down adulterers."

"This isn't about catching somebody's new boyfriend." *Jesus.*

"If I understand the papers here, you represent the husband. *He's* the one getting annoying calls at the Barnstable number? Now you're not telling me *he's* being stalked, are you?"

"Not exactly. The situation—"

"I didn't think so. Which is why I may have to file a motion for a protective order. Maybe bring in outside counsel."

Jimmy closed his eyes. Fear flicked its tongue at him. There was no case filed under the name *Mulcahey v. Mulcahey.* It existed only on the subpoena he had served on Bell Atlantic. Even if he rushed out now and filed a bogus divorce complaint in that name, it wouldn't take them long to unearth his deception, what with the subpoena having mysteriously antedated the divorce action. Especially with outside counsel. He pictured a sable-sleek senior partner from Royce & Bell, gliding into the courtroom like a comet with a tail of bag-carrying associates.

"Ken," he said, winging it now. "Hear me out. You're right about this being a messy divorce. Why do you think we're talking about a new listing down in Barnstable? My client had to move out. His wife's waging all-out war here. A custody battle. She's deploying the kids like Panzer divisions, you know what I mean?"

"I don't see—"

"Her latest tactic is to file a 209A. Claims she's in fear of her life and asks the court to order him to stay away from her. It's bullshit, of course. Everybody knows it. Even the judge. But he's not gonna deny her motion and risk seeing his puss on the front page of the *Herald* if she should end up dead. Which she won't. So he enters a restraining order anyway. This is what we've come to, Ken. And now she claims my guy's violating the order. Which he isn't."

Jimmy shifted the handset to the other ear. A woman in a blue suit was waiting to use the phone. She looked at him questioningly, but he shook his head and turned back toward the phone.

"Ken, that's why I need the trace. We're convinced she's the one who's been making the hang-up calls. Anything to torture him—while he's restrained from contacting *her,* mind you. Is this nuts or what? But if I can prove she's been calling *him,* the judge will see right through her. You hear what I'm saying? I can blow her out of the water."

Snoad was silent on the other end. Probably weighing the paperwork he'd have to do if he brought in Royce & Bell. Have to justify the expense and all. He'll want to kill this off right here, at his desk. *Play to that,* Jimmy thought. *Save him the work.*

"Ken, all I need's the number. And a name and address. Send me that and nobody will even have to appear on the subpoena. No keeper of the records, nothing. Because when they learn what I've got, she'll cave on this, I know it."

More silence. Then a snicker.

"She live in Massachusetts?"

"Yes."

"All right, Mr. Morrissey," Snoad said, an audible smirk in his voice. "I'll give it up. But I'm afraid you're gonna be disappointed."

Jimmy braced himself. "Why's that?"

A chuckle. "Because the number's for a pay phone in Florida."

"Florida." Jimmy repeated as flatly as he could manage. He bore down hard to contain his elation.

"That's right. Someplace called Arcadia, Florida. On Hickory Street, don't you love it? I'm sorry to disappoint you."

Snoad didn't sound sorry. But, then, Jimmy wasn't disappointed either. He turned around to grin at the woman, still waiting to use the phone. *Oh, I could just die from disappointment like that.*

"Hey," he said, trying to sound down but resolute, "I took a shot. You take what comes your way, right? Still, there may be some connection I can use. She's been bopping in and out of the state the last few weeks. Just send it along and let me work with it. Okay?"

Snoad agreed, and Jimmy thanked him.

He reached back and broke the connection by lowering the cradle with his index finger. Then he gave the handset to the woman. He dropped a quarter and a dime in her other palm. He felt her bewildered eyes on his back as he walked away.

Walked, hell. He almost skipped.

PART THREE

Use every man after his desert, and who should scape whipping?

—*Hamlet* II.ii.536–37

OEDIPUS:

There's still that scruple of my mother's bed.

JOCASTA:

How can a man have scruples when it's only Chance that's king?

—Sophocles,
Oedipus the King

Death has no sense of the ridiculous.

—Gabriel Garcia Marquez,
Love in the Time of Cholera

CHAPTER TWENTY-EIGHT

LIVESTOCK

WEDNESDAY MORNING

Waiting to go through security, Arthur squatted down to stow his heavy jacket in the duffel bag. God willing, he wouldn't need it in Florida. On the drive to Logan, a snarling wind had hammered the December rain against the seaward side of the van. He was still tugging at the recalcitrant zipper when Joanne spoke up.

"There she comes. Looks like she checked her bags at the curb."

Arthur looked up and followed her gaze. Thirty yards up the terminal, Dani was striding briskly toward them. She carried a purse and a black, heavy-looking bag, both slung over the same shoulder. He wasn't surprised to see her dressed in jeans and an oxford dress shirt, starched as always and blue this time, but the cowboy boots were an almost festive break in routine. Her blond hair flounced with each confident step.

"Jesus," Joanne muttered, plucking the word right off his tongue. "I'd kill for that body."

"Me, too." He spoke without thinking and regretted it at once, for Joanne slowly twisted her head back and slid her eyes his way.

"Pull in your tongue, partner."

Arthur felt himself redden. He bent over again to finish closing the bag.

Joanne said, "I never figured she was your type anyway. I thought you went in for bigger breasts."

"Whaaat?" He scowled up at her.

"Well, the last one you brought around had bazooms out to here." She cupped her hands in front of her, in the traditional male mime. "By the way, did you know—this is really true, I swear—if you hold a silicone breast implant up to your ear, you can hear *Baywatch*?"

"What's so funny?" Dani asked when she joined them. "I hope the joke's not on me." She smiled when she said it, but Arthur sensed she wasn't just kidding. Was she less self-contained than she let on?

"It's just Joanne," he said, shaking his head and smiling to put her at ease. He pointed at her black briefcase. "What's in there? Looks like it's about to tip you over."

She peered at it and tugged down on the strap twice, as if testing its strength. "My laptop. I had a faster modem put in it." She raised her head to look at him. "You never know. We might have to resort to *Houndbytes* again to reach Mavis."

"Why didn't I think of that?" Arthur said, pursing his lips in appreciation. "Where would I be without you?"

Dani caught his eye with a quizzical look of her own, then glanced down at the folded newspaper poking out of his jacket pocket. "And what's that?" she demanded. She grinned. "The *New York Times*? You hoping they'll review your restaurant?"

"I only read it for the pictures."

"Well, I've got the *Globe*." She patted her briefcase. "Between us, we might find a couple new words for your blotter."

Joanne flapped her arms against her sides. "Well, look, guys. I gotta go before they tow the van. So pay attention: don't do anything stupid. If the spoor is still fresh and salty, fine. Go with it. Get close enough to be reasonably sure it's her. But that's it. Then get the hell out of there and call the cops. You got it?"

"Yeah," said Arthur, "we got it. And *you* see to it that Jonathan doesn't spring any of his 'creations' on you. Make him stick to the menu plan. And tell Bradley—"

"Fuhgeddaboutit," she mumbled, Brooklyn in her voice. "Bradley sleeps widda dishes. I can handle both of them."

She gave him a hug, then a more tentative one to Dani. "Keep an eye on him," she said, nodding at Arthur. "He's apt to go off on a lark of his own, you know."

Dani smiled at her. "I've noticed. And I will."

They proceeded to the Delta gate for Sarasota. They boarded

immediately. Arthur felt a cold draft where the flyway pressed imperfectly against the plane's fuselage. The outside air was raw and moist, carrying the damp New England chill that screwed into the bones. He was not sorry to leave it behind.

When they were stowed and seated, he cast about for something to say.

"I made a reservation at a Best Western that's only a couple miles from the track."

She cut her eyes sharply in his direction. "I trust you meant the plural. As in two rooms."

He winced. "Of course." *Talk about your New England chill.*

She turned to the window, staring out into the wind-driven rain, her hands clasped on her lap. He tugged his newspaper out of the seat pocket in front of him and shook it open. He pointed his eyes at the front page, but he could focus on nothing in the brittle silence. *Could be a long trip,* he thought. *We're not even off the ground.*

Then her hand was resting on his forearm. He turned toward her in surprise.

"I'm sorry," she said, when his eyes met hers. "That came across bitchy. And rejecting. I didn't mean to sound that way."

"It was, a little." He gave her a slight smile. "Rejecting, anyway. Especially since there wasn't even an offer to reject."

"I know. I jumped to conclusions. A bad habit, I confess."

"I don't mind the jumping so much. It's just that you always jump to thinking the worst about me. Right from the start, when you first put the paper on me."

She frowned, easing her hand away. "The subpoena?"

He nodded.

She said, "But that wasn't about you." She looked down into her lap. "Neither, for that matter, was that crack a few minutes ago. It wasn't personal."

"That's just my point."

She lifted her head, eyebrows knitted questioningly.

He said, "I'd *prefer* it personal. Hey, if you dislike me, okay. I can handle it. It's not pleasant, but I can deal with that. But don't blow me off for reasons that have nothing to do with me."

She said a lot of nothing for what felt like a very long time, her eyes screwed up as if examining him closely for the first time. He made a point of not looking away. It wasn't easy. He was vaguely frightened. Frightened by the force of his own feelings and the tightness he felt in his chest. It reminded him, God forbid, of the way he felt when he was trying not to cry.

"You're right," she said at last. "Every time I make assumptions about you, you prove me wrong. I'll try not to do it anymore."

She offered a soft smile. The warmth of it opened him up like a steamed oyster. He smiled bravely back at her, not trusting himself to speak.

"Because otherwise," she said more lightly, patting him on the back of the hand, "the two of us have been on a roll here. Look how far we've come on this thing of yours."

He smiled. "This thing of *ours*, you mean. *La Cosa Nostra?*"

She grimaced. "I think 'lark' was the word Joanne used. But definitely on a roll."

They were indeed. As he thought about it, he was astonished at how easy it had been, the last few days, and how close they had come.

Not that they hadn't floundered around for a time. They had rejected out of hand the notion of calling up the greyhound adoption sources in Florida. They didn't know just how to approach these people without alarming someone, and besides, it turned out there were over forty of them in the state.

They then wasted several hours at the computer trying to access track listings that might show races run by dogs named Dapple and Satan's Mistress. Dani found the website for an outfit called Rosnet Data Services, which posted the betting line for dogs scheduled to run that day, plus the results of recent races. They could find nothing in the site, however, or in any of those linked to it, that led you back to old races. There was a hyperlink to the racing histories of individual dogs scheduled to run in upcoming races—data bettors could use in handicapping the dogs. In addition to listing the dog's finish in prior races, the individual histories gave you the dog's color, sex, sire and dam, and whelping date. Most tantalizing of all, the histories told you, right there at the top of the page, the dog's owner, kennel, and trainer.

But this, too, proved to be a chimera. Only the histories of dogs currently running the courses were posted. Obviously, Dapple and Satan's Mistress had been retired—assuming they ever ran at all—and Rosnet was a dead end. It looked as if they could get no closer to Mavis and her greyhounds.

"Forget the computer," Dani suggested. "Can't we think of a human being who might know something about this?"

Arthur considered this. "You mean, like somebody in the business? A bookie, maybe? 'Cause I know a bookie, in South Boston."

The bookie couldn't help them, but he did suggest someone who might know more about the dogs. Which was how Arthur got introduced to Willy Zane, who operated a kennel up in Lynn and raced his dogs all over the Northeast. When called, Willy invited them up, so Arthur and Dani piled into his van and drove up to Lynn. After almost despairing of finding the kennel, they spotted the peeling wooden sign.

" 'Zane's *Greys*'?" Dani read incredulously.

Arthur laughed. "Do you think it was intentional?"

On meeting Willy, he doubted it very much. Willy certainly looked like a dog man, ferret-faced and built like a whippet. He dressed in expensive Nikes, a Patriots jacket, and cargo pants. The three of them sat around a tiny kitchen table in his beige mobile home, which also did duty as an office for the kennel out back. There were chain-link-fenced runs off the huts in which his dogs were housed, but the runs were dogless. Too cold, Willy advised. Greyhounds could not stand much cold. Arthur recalled the knitted doggie sweaters he'd seen on greyhounds in the South End.

Willy told them you couldn't trace the dogs without their ear numbers.

"Ear numbers?" Dani asked. A dog barked once, but otherwise the unseen animals were eerily quiet.

"Right. Every dog has his NGA registration number tattooed on his ear. That's the only way I know to trace them."

"That would be the, uh, National Greyhound Association?"

"You got it. Out of Abilene, Kansas. They're breeder folks, into pedigrees. It's like this. Greyhounds are like cars. Ear numbers are like your car's serial number, the one you register at the department of motor vehicles? You wanna sell your car, you gotta change the title, right? And register it. Same with dogs. Every time a dog changes hands, you file a registration change with the NGA. That's how you find who's got a dog."

"What if you don't have the numbers. But you have the racing name? Couldn't they, this NGA, search backwards and come up with the numbers?"

"Nope. Don't think they work that way. The race names don't mean anything to them. They just go by the numbers."

"But the tracks don't go by the numbers, do they?"

" 'Course not. You think you call out '846302!' when you want to lead one to the starting box? That's why you got race names. In fact, we usually don't even call them by their race names. Most of them are too long and too . . . what's the word?"

Arthur shrugged.

"Cumbersome?" Dani offered.

"No. Anyway, the dog's also got a nickname. That's what we call it, a nickname. So you got three names: a race name, a nickname, and a number—if you wanna call the number a name."

"All I have is a race name." Dani sounded depressed when she said it.

"That's a problem, all right. 'Cause there's a whole lotta dogs in this country. Not to mention the dogs in Ireland and Spain and—"

"What if I know the state? The state where the dog was adopted?"

Willy paused. "Adopted?" There was a glint of suspicion in his eyes now. "I don't have much time for those people. They're the ones wanna put me out of business. Got this thing on the ballot and all."

"The referendum?"

He nodded gravely. "I been in this business all my life. We got a saying: 'You can talk bad about my wife, but don't say nothin' about my dogs.' You do something bad to them and the dogs'll never trust you again. No sir, I don't mistreat my animals, like those people are tryin' to tell everybody. I don't run 'em skinny and underweight like some guys, hoping it'll make them faster. Don't work anyway, in my experience. And you don't catch me feeding them chocolate to goose 'em down the stretch. But this is a business. And those dogs out back are livestock. Some of 'em give you a return on your investment, some don't. Like I say: a business."

Arthur stepped in. "We're not looking to adopt. Just find somebody who might have adopted a dog."

Willy squinted at him, then pivoted toward Dani as if seeking assurance. She smiled warmly.

Willy pulled a crumpled pack of Marlboro's out of his jacket pocket. "Mind?" he said to her. She just turned up the wattage on the smile. He lit up.

"Well, you could try to get the lines. I don't know how far back they go, but there's some that know how to look up the lines on a computer."

Dani said, "You mean the betting lines? We tried that. It's all too current to be of help to us."

"You'd know that better than me. But maybe there's galleys still kicking around at the tracks. You could ask them for the old galleys, see how far back they keep them."

"Galleys?"

"The racing forms. Tracks publish them. They give you the line on the dogs and the match-ups." Willy seemed to take a sudden interest in the problem. "Look-it," he said, "if a guy's gonna dump a dog with these folks, these adoption people, he's likely gonna do it near home. You with me? Why haul the dog to another state to get rid of it? Unless you're off in Colorado, say, and the dog pulls up lame or something. But as a rule, you'd do it close to home. So if you think your dog's in—what state we talkin' about here?"

"Florida," Dani said.

"Okay. So the kennel that ran him was most likely in Florida. And if that's the case, the dog would run in Florida, too. Maybe—here's what you could do. You call the tracks and ask for the galleys. If your dog didn't quit too long ago, they might still have them."

Arthur looked at Dani. "It couldn't have been too long. We figure she's only had the dogs a few months. So it all depends on how long they were in the shelter."

Dani nodded. "So we just call the tracks and ask if they've got old galleys that show a dog named so-and-so?"

"Sure. Somebody might have them."

"And if they do, they could tell us the name of the owner."

"And the trainer. That's the guy you wanna talk to. The owner might be some doctor in Philadelphia who bought the dog as an investment. Same as a condo, you know? No, it's the trainer who'd be dumping them."

Dani frowned. "There must be a dozen tracks in Florida."

"Seventeen," he said cheerfully. "But that don't matter. You're not trying to find a particular track. Chances are, the dogs ran all over the state. So the more tracks there are, the better. 'Cause that means you got that many more chances to find somebody keeps his galleys long enough."

Willy followed them outside when they left. With one hand on the open door to the van, Arthur listened as Dani thanked him. Arthur nodded toward the sign in the yard, and said, "*Love* the pun in the name."

"Pun?" Willy blinked back at him in confusion.

But Willy was right that it was lucky there were so many dogtracks in Florida. After Arthur downloaded a complete list of the state's dogtracks, they started calling. Daytona, Ebro, Orlando, Bradenton, Hollywood, Seminole, Palm Beach. Flagler and Naples-Fort Myers. Three in Jacksonville alone. Some tracks couldn't be bothered. Some discarded their galleys on a weekly basis. But the eleventh track they called, a big one up in Jacksonville, had galleys in the computer going back six months. And one of them, published three months ago, showed Satan's Mistress running in the seventh race. She had come in fifth.

"The trainer?" Arthur begged. "Does it list the trainer?"

His interlocutor was a gravel-voiced woman who described herself as the executive assistant to the track's mutuel manager. She seemed bemused by his inquiries. "Indeedy," she reported. "Name's Vernon Hunnercook." She spelled the last name for him. "You gonna ask me how to find him, too?"

"Please."

"Can't help you there. Never heard of him."

But someone had. Arthur logged onto the Ultimate White Pages, an on-line assemblage of telephone directories, and ran a search for a Vernon Hunnercook living somewhere in Florida. There was one listing, in Port Charlotte, just down the coast from Sarasota on U.S. 41. He was even home when Arthur called the number. And yes, he remembered Satan's Mistress and Dapple.

"Sure do. Wasn't much to Dapple, but we brought home a few good purses with Satan's Mistress. How come you're trying to find these dogs?"

"Skip trace," Arthur said. "Lady ran off owing five figures on her credit cards. I don't know where she went, but somebody back home said he got a postcard from her. She bragged about picking up some dogs."

"Dapple and Satan's Mistress?"

"Exactly."

"Well, I put 'em out for the taking two, three months ago. Don't know what happened after that."

"Where? What's the name of the shelter?"

"Wasn't a shelter. The track over in Bradenton runs a little dating service of its own for run-out dogs. It's right there, part of the track. You could try them."

"I will," said Arthur. He thought it might be lucky the dogs hadn't gone to a shelter. The track people might be less committed to the cause of saving greyhounds—and maybe more willing to disclose information about the woman who adopted them. More comfortable with the racing people and—

"Wait a minute!" Arthur almost shouted into the phone. "Are you still there? Mr. Hunnercook!"

"Yeah, I'm still here."

"Can I use your name? When I talk to the track shelter, I mean. Can I tell them you said it was all right to talk to me? Maybe even tell them they can call you if they have questions about it?"

Vernon Hunnercook had a bit of a chuckle over this. "Sure, why not? But you gotta wonder: I know nothin' about you, so why should me vouching for you matter an owl's fart? That's what I wanna know."

But Arthur didn't care. He could tell them the man from the kennel sent him. And they could call up and verify that if they wished. He felt so good after he hung up he let Joanne and Dani drag him off to for a celebratory dinner at a Cambodian place in Waltham—his own restaurant being closed on Monday night and all. The place was called Carambola. Not bad either. But all he could think about was getting down to the dogtrack in Bradenton.

"Oh, my God." Dani sounded more sad than shocked.

Arthur turned his head toward the window seat. Dani was sitting straight up, straining at the seat belt as she snapped the *Boston Globe* between her hands. She was staring at the front page, just below the fold.

"A little girl," she said. "Fifteen when she was killed."

Arthur tried to lean over, to catch a glimpse of the picture. Was she reading about some accident? Route 6 on the Cape, maybe?

"It's Tommy," she said harshly, glaring at him as if he were somehow to blame. "Those bodies Shaun Crowe led them to? And how they wouldn't say who the female was? Well, they finally identified her. She was a fifteen-year-old girl. Named Eva Lou Starks."

"Starks? Didn't Hinkle used to have a girlfriend named Starks?"

"Yes," she said, her eye running down the page. "Dorraine Starks. Eva Lou was her daughter. They found her in that hole in Bay Village, tossed on top of two dead hoodlums."

"Jesus," he said.

When she looked up at him this time, her eyes glistened with unshed tears. “They kill *children,* Arthur. A little girl. He strangled her with his bare hands. What kind of an animal are we dealing with here?”

Arthur felt an impulse to take her hand, but something warned him off. He stuck with the subject.

“What kind of animal?” he repeated. “Did you start believing his press? You know, the tough Irishman who was ruthless with the hard guys, but took care of the neighborhood? Kept street crime down and drugs out of Southie. Ready to help you out if you were in a jam. Because it’s all bullshit. It always was, even while you feds thought he was the cat’s meow. Protecting him all those years when—”

“Not me,” she said softly, her eyes on the school photo of a smiling teenage girl. “That’s why I quit, remember?”

He hardly heard her. “They thought he was a hero because he beat up every dope dealer dumb enough to wander into South Boston. He beat them up all right—because they hadn’t paid him for the privilege, that’s why. He was too smart to get into something as risky as actually dealing drugs. It was much safer and almost as lucrative to collect rent from those who did. He sold franchises.”

He was in full lather now, and she was looking at him curiously, but he didn’t stop.

“Let me tell you a story about Mr. Helps Out People in the Neighborhood. It goes back about fifteen years. A little guy named Myron Pejewski. A Pollack who had a butcher shop on Boston Street, just down from the Polish Club where there was gambling action. Nice guy, sold the best pork around. Always with a smile and a little flirting with the women who were his customers. Polish women, Lithuanians, Italians. And Irish, of course.”

His eyes were fixed on the Airphone fitted into the back of the seat in front of him.

“Tommy and his boys needed to unload some sides of beef they had hijacked at the Conley Terminal. So Tommy thought it would be a good idea if Myron bought his beef from them. They only wanted about twenty percent more than he was already paying his supplier, so why shouldn’t he help them out? Myron doesn’t want to buy hot beef, especially when he sees what kind of shape it’s in, but Tommy doesn’t see it that way. All he sees is somebody refusing to do him a favor. But Pejewski still says no.”

Dani was watching him closely now.

"So what happens? He sends a couple hard guys to Myron's house. His house, now, not his place of business. They go into his home and reason with him. In front of his wife and kids."

"They beat him in front of his family?"

"I don't know what they did exactly. Nobody ever saw any marks on him or anything. But whatever happened, he was humiliated. Totally humiliated. With his family watching. He didn't go back to the shop for three days afterward, and when he did there was a surprise waiting for him. A rotting side of beef hanging in the window. Painted black. With his steak knife, a big one almost two feet long, stuck in its back.

"He never reopened the store. Myron Pejewski, you see, was a proud man. And he was never the same again. He couldn't face anybody. He couldn't even look at himself in the mirror. They broke him, is what they did. They took his manhood from him. Three weeks later he jumped off the Tobin Bridge."

He turned to face her, his eyes hard.

"So whenever anybody tells me how Tommy Crimmins was the prince of the neighborhood, I think of Myron Pejewski and I want to barf. It doesn't surprise me that he and Hinkle would kill a little girl. Hinkle was probably screwing her *and* her mother. Everybody said he liked them young. And if she pissed them off or stumbled onto something she wasn't supposed to know about—well, they wouldn't think twice. Either one of them."

She was quiet for a while. When she spoke she showed a grim smile.

"That just gives us one more reason to find him."

"Damn betcha," he said. He stared straight ahead.

CHAPTER TWENTY-NINE

GETTING TO ARCADIA

WEDNESDAY AFTERNOON

The Bradenton Greyhound Track was far less glamorous than it had been made to appear on its website. It played no part in the glossy theme-park necrosis that spread over so much of Florida. The track was too shabby for that. Harsh sunlight had bleached away the dividing lines painted on the parking lot. Concrete buttresses for the stadium were cracked and spalling. Someone had once planted grass in the oval bowl in the center of the track, but it had long since withered away, leaving Dixie cups and crumpled Autotote betting slips to swirl aimlessly across its parched surface. The grandstands were sparsely filled, peopled more by locals than tourists. Either this was an especially sad track or the industry itself was failing. Arthur suspected the latter. The dogtrack was where old gamblers slunk off to die, an elephant's graveyard for the luckless.

It was almost noon when they arrived, still half an hour before the start of the matinee races. A grizzled black man at the gate collected the two-dollar admission fee from both of them, plus another two bucks for the car. When they asked him their question, he directed them away from the main entrance to another gate around the left corner of the stadium.

There things got worse than shabby. They traipsed through a feebly lit concrete tunnel, a chute really, its dank cement making the air feel more close than cool. Satellite feed from other racetracks shone from CRTs mounted at staggered intervals along the wall. The tunnel descended steeply toward the center of the stadium before opening out into the grandstand area at ground level. They found themselves stepping into the blinding sunlight, the racing lanes spread out beyond the rail before them.

Shielding her eyes, Dani looked about her, then settled on a fat man seated three rows up. He wore baggy shorts and a rinsed-out orange T-shirt. He was holding a pencil in his left hand as he bent over a racing form. Binoculars were slung over his neck, but with the glasses resting stolidly on the top of his stomach, the strap was bearing no weight. She asked him where it was. He crooked a finger and made a poking motion in the direction of the tunnel. She thanked him and walked back down toward Arthur. She shrugged. They reentered the tunnel.

Sure enough, they came upon a turning off to their right that they had walked past on the way in. They took it now. Office doors had been cut into the left side of the concrete walls at regular intervals. They read the names on the doors as they walked, their footsteps echoing in the tunnel. Director of racing operations. Mutuel manager. Director of security. Chartwriter. Concession manager. At the very end, just before the fire door to the outside, they found the door they had been looking for.

Track Adoption Center.

Arthur tried the door. It opened in. He stepped inside. Dani followed.

The room was empty. There was an unmanned counter to the left, trimmed with posters showing eager dogs in the arms of rapturous children. In the center were two ratty-looking maroon chairs and a beat-up coffee table littered with brochures. On the right was a huge floor-to-ceiling picture window which, on further inspection, revealed itself to be a sliding patio door. The door gave onto a scrabbly open space penned about by chain-link fencing. It had a slash pine in the center. A dog compound, but dogless.

Arthur called out, but there was no answer. While Dani flipped through the brochures, he walked back to the nearest office, one with an open door labeled Concession Manager. He paused to peer in. It had four desks positioned tightly together in the little room. Three of the desks were occupied, and their occupants looked up as one when he entered the room. He asked if the Adoption Center was open.

A red-haired woman told him to go on back and someone would join him. He did, and the someone was the same woman, who entered through a door behind the counter as he reentered the room.

"Can I help y'all?" said the woman. She was tall and slender, in her mid-fifties, and she had a pencil stuck in her lacquered red conk. Her tone was pleasant, but there was no smile in evidence.

"We're looking for the adoption office," said Dani. "For dogs," she added lamely.

"So I hear," the woman said. "It's right on the door, hon," she added with a sideways bob of her head in its direction. "And we only *do* dogs."

"Where are they?" Arthur asked with a smile.

"Just got the one here right now, but we got associated adoption agencies all over the state. The whole country, for that matter."

"The one?" Arthur repeated, mystified as he looked back out the window at the empty run. As if on cue, he heard the click of toenails on the floor behind the counter. A dog casually walked out into the center of the room. It was a white greyhound with a black splotch thrown over it like a saddle. Dani broke into a smile and crouched down to fuss over it. The dog pricked up its ears with pleasure at the attention. Exquisitely sleek, the animal had shoulder blades that looked sharp enough to cut.

"Meet Doofus," the woman said. "Two years old, going on three. A real sweetie. Only thing is, he's run out. Early. Racing career over before his time."

"Actually," Arthur said, "we're not in the mar—I mean we're not looking for a dog right now. I mean, we *are* looking for a dog, but not to adopt. The one we're after has already *been* adopted."

The woman tipped her head to one side, examining him with owlish intensity. "You two escape from some kinda house for the slow or somethin'? Your missus can't read the sign on the door and you want a secondhand adoption. What exactly is you-all's problem, anyway?"

Arthur looked down to catch Dani's eye, and the two of them burst out laughing. The dog pulled his head back to watch them.

"I'm sorry," Arthur said, still grinning. "I guess we did come across sounding pretty lame. We're not really looking for a dog so much as the person who adopted it. Or them, in this case."

The woman said nothing.

"Here's the story," he continued. "It's my Aunt Georgia, my

mother's sister. She's in her early seventies and loves dogs. Real active in Adopt-a-Greyhound. Maybe you've heard of it?"

The woman nodded noncommittally.

"Well, Aunt Georgia struck a friendship with this woman she met in the movement. Called herself Mavis Stein. Bad news, I'm afraid. The woman was a scam artist. I won't take you through all the gory details, except to tell you that Mavis Stein took my aunt for almost thirty thousand dollars. Her *entire* nest egg."

"Thirty thousand?" the woman said, cocking her head a little. Was she showing shock or skepticism?

"Yes. Cleaned her out. This is a woman—I'm talking about Aunt Georgia now—who works as a receptionist in a dental office. So you know it was like losing everything."

Dani stayed down with the dog.

"But that's not what's torturing Aunt Georgia. The money hurts, sure, and the violation of trust—the woman was living right there in the house with her at the end. No, it was losing the dog that would like to kill her."

"The dog?"

"Millicent. A ten-year-old brindle. Georgia had her for almost eight years."

"She took the *dog*?"

"No, she didn't want the dog. Her whole dog-lover schtick was just a ruse, a way to get tight with Aunt Georgia. No, Mavis killed the dog."

The woman's eyes narrowed in anger.

"She poisoned her. Millicent. And her own dogs, too, both of them. The ones she would pant over like a hot chicken so people would think she was heavy into hounds. But once she got her hands on Aunt Georgia's money, she murdered them and left town."

"But why?" the woman demanded. "Why kill the dogs?" Her tone was dry, flat.

Arthur lifted his hands as he shrugged. "Who knows? She's a sicko, is my theory. Of course, the police are useless in something like this. That's why we took it on. Right, honey?"

He smiled bravely at Dani. She looked down.

The woman said, "That's awful. Really awful."

Arthur nodded in sympathy.

She glared at him, then shook her head. "No. I mean your *story's* awful. That's gotta be the most transparent piece of bullshit I've heard in years. You got nothing better to do, son, you gotta come in here and try to jerk me around with a cock-and-bull story like that?"

He froze, then blinked. "No, uh, I mean . . . It's not a cock-and-bull story." But he stopped. He knew he was blushing now, like a schoolboy caught in a lie. She shook her head at his feckless chicanery.

"I told you it wouldn't work, Arthur."

The voice was Dani's, and it was accompanied by a disgusted expression. He stared back at her with amazement.

"Just *tell* her, Arthur. You think these ridiculous lies make it any easier for me?" When he could think of nothing to say, she said, "Of course not. *I'll* do it, then."

Dani stood up. The woman eyed her warily. "I'm sorry," Dani said. "He knows this is painful for me, so he tries to get cute. Too cute, sometimes. Please, just let me explain."

She squared up to the counter, gently edging her bewildered companion to one side. She looked directly into the woman's eyes.

"Let me start at the beginning. I was adopted as an infant. For the last few years I've wanted to meet my birth mother. To find out what she's like and how we're alike. Or different. And why she gave me up. You know what I mean?"

The woman said nothing, but she was listening very hard.

"It's normal, I think. To want to know—if you're adopted, I mean. It can happen at different ages, but sooner or later it's natural to want to *know.* But the adoption agency—a state-run outfit—refused to give out any information. They said they'd give it out only if I had some life-threatening genetic illness, so that my health depended on it. Other than that, they wouldn't help. I thought of suing them, but eventually I had a better idea. I wrote her a letter. I asked the agency to ask her if she'd be willing to receive it. If so, she could write back through the agency. They finally agreed to do this, all the while telling me they didn't even know if they could find her after all these years."

She paused. The woman said, "Well, did they?"

"Yes. She wrote me back. A nice letter. She said she had me when she was only fifteen and had no way to care for me. She had heard nothing at all about me since then, but she wondered. She told me a little bit about herself, but she did not tell me her name or where she lived. I thought it would be the beginning of a correspondence that might blossom over time, but that was it. I heard nothing else. I know the agency's been fighting hard recently against people wanting to open their adoption records. Maybe they're just doing nothing and not telling me. Or it could be it was *her* idea to stop. That's what Arthur thinks."

She glanced over at him. He watched her wide-eyed.

"I don't know," she continued, "but it might *not* be, too. Maybe she does want to correspond with me and the agency just can't be bothered. As things stand, I've got no way of knowing. I have to find her myself."

The woman took this in. Then she raised both hands in a gesture of helplessness. "What does all this have to do with me? And this place?"

"In her letter she mentioned that she had just adopted two greyhounds. She named them. We, Arthur and I, managed to track down the trainer of those dogs. A nice man by the name of Vernon Hunnercook. He told us he sent them here to be put up for adoption. Do you know him?"

"Can't say I do," the woman said, shaking her head. "You gotta keep in mind, hon, this ain't a real adoption agency like the ones you read about. This place is set up and paid for by the track. Even my salary. All we do here is liaise between the dog owners and the public. The dogs might stay a short while, like Doofus here, he's been here almost two weeks now. But eventually we pass them on to one of the other agencies in the area. They have better luck finding homes for them."

"So you don't actually do the adoptions?"

"Oh, a few. But most of them? No, we pass them on."

Dani said, "Is it possible to run the dogs' names and tell us which agency they went to?"

"This ain't the government, honey. We aren't required to keep records, and on the short money we're paid by the track people, we don't."

Depression settled over Arthur's shoulders like a damp blanket. He had been dazzled—not just by the efficacy of Dani's story but by the fact that she was capable of such deception. Yet it was all for naught. Taking in air, he reached down to pet Doofus.

Dani said, "The dog's names were Dapple and Satan's Mistress."

The woman perked up, attentive as Doofus. "Did you say Satan's Mistress?" Her enunciation was crisp and her eyes bore into Dani's.

She nodded cautiously.

"That," she said, hauling out a spiral notebook from beneath the counter, "rings a bell. A couple months back." She was talking to herself now as her crimson-tipped forefinger ran down each page before flipping to the next. ". . . and *yes*!" Her finger rapped the page.

She looked hard at Dani, her eyes blazing with triumph. She dropped her eyes to the page of her notebook. "Satan's Mistress. And Dapple. Taken by a Hattie Collins, of Arcadia. September fourth. I remember her now. A quiet man with her."

"A man?" Arthur said, alert himself now.

The woman eyed him suspiciously. Dani stomped down on his foot. Glaring at him, she said, "I don't care about the *man*, Arthur. Just my mother." She addressed the woman again. "Did you say Arcadia? Where's that?" Arthur's could see that she was as excited as he was.

"It's a town southeast of here on Route 70. Just the other side of Myakka State Park."

"Would you," Dani asked, "trust me with the number and address?"

The woman eyed her carefully for a moment. "Maybe this woman just wants to be left alone. Why should I send you in there if she don't want you there?"

"We don't know that. Maybe she does, and it's the agency that doesn't want it. And think about it. If she doesn't want to talk to me, what could I do, anyway? Camp out in her yard? All I can do is give her the chance. If she doesn't want it, I'm on my way home. Isn't that what *you'd* do?"

The woman pursed her lips in silence for what seemed like long minutes. Then she bent over and started scribbling on a notepad, occasionally glancing over at the spiral notebook. When she finished writing, she tore off the note and handed it to Dani. Her eyes glistened a little.

"Good luck, honey," she said. "Let me know how it turns out, hear?"

The two of them managed to contain themselves as they hurried back through the tunnel, but once they hit the outdoors they whooped in triumph, running flat out to the Neon. It stood there baking in the parking lot. Arthur started the car and the air-conditioning, the latter on full blast to drive the hot air out the open windows. Dani pored over the map.

"There it is," she announced. "Arcadia. Inland. Looks to be about a forty-mile drive."

Arthur wheeled the Neon into the traffic and, on Dani's instructions, followed the signs for Oneco and the airport. After they had calmed down a bit, they agreed to pull in at a gas station, where Dani canceled their room reservations in Bradenton and made new ones in Arcadia. There was only one motel there, called the Peace River Inn. To hear the desk clerk tell it, they were lucky to get rooms at all.

Back in the car once again, they soon found themselves barreling east along Route 70 in the direction of Lake Okeechobee. Once out of the congestion around Bradenton and Sarasota, they flew through the dry prairies of central Florida. The highway was largely deserted. A few heavy trucks piled with oranges. Farm vehicles. The occasional carload of tourists heading for the alligator tour in Myakka State Park. A lot of skinny, depressed-looking cattle stood motionless in the open areas along the floodplain of the Myakka River. Oak-palm hammocks provided occasional variety, but the monotony of the pine flatlands dominated.

Once they crossed the Peace River, evidence of actual human habitation reasserted itself, accompanied by billboards for Arcadia. Soon they were rolling into its outskirts, following signs that promised to take them to the city center. Arthur left Route 70 and motored along Oak Street, the aorta of the "historic" business district. Something calling itself the Old Opera House loomed on the left, while across the street the marquee of what once had been an old movie house welcomed visitors to the Arcadia Tea Room. For no particular reason, Arthur turned right on Polk and pulled over near the end of the block in front of a restaurant called the Hot Fudge Shoppe.

Arthur said, "Can we drive by the address and see what we're looking at?"

"If we can find it, we can. It's 519 West Hickory Street. Let me go inside and ask where it is."

Arthur grinned. "Don't have to. Look." He pointed to street sign ahead of him. Hickory Street. It was also Route 70, the road they'd come in on. Arthur eased away from the curb and approached the intersection.

"Which way? Take a stab."

Dani shrugged. "Right," she suggested.

"Right it is."

They tried to catch the numbers along the busy thoroughfare, but after eliminating all the other possibilities, Arthur pulled over again, this time turning into a large municipal parking lot at the back of what appeared to be a county administration building. They peered back across the street they had just left. It was now evident that Mavis was not living at 516 West Hickory. They were staring at the only building which, through a process of elimination, could possibly bear that address.

It was not a residence at all. It was the Desoto County Library.

CHAPTER THIRTY

SOUTHERN COOKING

WEDNESDAY EVENING

Their rooms at the Peace River Inn, whose South Brevard Avenue address camouflaged its location on bustling Route 17, could not have been farther apart and still in the same building. They agreed to meet in the lobby after showering and settling in, thence to find a place for an early dinner. This was Florida, after all: there had to be early-bird specials.

Arthur finished first. He had a brief discussion with the man behind the desk, a white-haired septuagenarian with bushy eyebrows like albino caterpillars meeting in a kiss. He recommended the "fine foods and antiques" offered by the Arcadia Tea Room Restaurant, but Arthur demurred. He had just taken a seat and begun looking over the proffered list of other eating establishments when Dani walked into the lobby. He looked up and unconsciously tightened his grip on the list.

She was wearing a skirt this time, a wraparound thing made of loose cotton and stamped with a vivid floral design, bougainvillea maybe. It was short, but respectably so, its hem not quite reaching her bare knees. Tucked into the waistband was a bright blue silk blouse, open at the neck. Still damp from the shower, her blond hair fell to her shoulders, where little brushstrokes of wetness left darker streaks on the silk. She smiled to see him, like turning on a lamp, and he found himself staring at the little flecks of color that varied the bottle green of her irises.

She glanced at the piece of paper he'd been consulting, now somewhat crumpled in his hands. "Did you find anything interesting?"

"Just one," he said, swallowing. "It's not very tony, though." He looked down at the list. "Slim's Deep South BBQ. I figure it's local and—well, Southern."

"Didn't we just pass it on the way here?"

"I didn't notice."

"That's right," the man behind the desk offered. "Just three blocks up 17, there."

"Let's walk," she said brightly. She tapped his shoulder and turned toward the door.

Tony it wasn't. Slim's Deep South BBQ Restaurant had two rooms, with wooden booths in the front one and picnic tables in the other. The knotty pine wainscoting seemed real, but the fake timbers across the ceiling could never have carried any weight. Only three tables were taken, so they had the run of the place. They settled into a quiet booth beneath a window that looked out on a graveled parking lot dominated by a towering water oak.

Over cups of Brunswick stew sweetened with barbecue sauce, they discussed what to do next. Dani wanted to try the phone number the woman had given them. Arthur resisted.

"I don't think we want any strange phone calls to put anybody on edge," he cautioned.

"Even a wrong number?"

"*Especially* a wrong number. They're fugitives, remember. It's got to make them a little paranoid about things like that."

She frowned. "I suppose I could get on-line and try one of those reverse directories. You know, where you look up the number and it gives you a name and address."

"And then?" he asked. "If we've got an address?"

"Then we stake it out. See who lives there."

"And if it's not them? It probably isn't, you know. I can't see Tommy giving that woman his real number—even if she only works at a racetrack."

She turned up her hands, the spoon flashing in the right; a digital shrug. "Then we might have to talk to the people who do live there. Unless you've got a better idea."

He didn't. He changed the subject. "You were magnificent with that woman, you know. That business about being adopted. It was brilliant." He sat back in his chair, frankly admiring her. She laid her spoon in the empty bowl.

"Well, I just thought we'd have a better chance with something more emotionally direct. And woman to woman."

He grinned. "You were right. It must be those prosecutor's skills at eliciting testimony. That's what I knew you could bring to this . . . this venture of ours. You're proving me right, Dani."

"How male of you," she said dryly. "Congratulating yourself for my insight."

He laughed and lifted his arms to allow the waitress to collect the stew bowls and set out his rib plate. They were quiet until she had gone.

"Do you miss it?" he asked.

"Miss what?"

"Being a federal prosecutor. Chasing bad guys—present company excepted, of course." He waggled his eyebrows.

"I'm chasing the bad guys right now," she said. "I'm just not getting paid for it."

"The idea was, you would be. All on spec, though. But no, really: do you miss the job?"

She peered at him over the spare rib she held with both hands. "Sometimes. It's just that there aren't a lot of other jobs for lawyers that interest me all that much." She gnawed daintily at the bone.

"Careful you don't get sauce on that blouse. I don't think the fabric could stand up to it."

"Mmmnnn."

"It's different for me," he said, changing the subject. "Because I'm already doing exactly what I've wanted to do, for two years now. Having my own place, I mean. If I lost it, the only direction would be down. There aren't any 'interesting' jobs for the owners of failed restaurants. I mean, you can go back to being a line cook someplace fancy, maybe even executive chef if you're lucky." He put down his own rib and peered off into the middle distance. "Now *there's* a concept for you. *Executive chef.* Do you think they have executive painters? Or executive sculptors?"

"Those people usually aren't trying to run a business. I should think that's a major difference."

"No, that's true. You sound just like Joanne. A business. She's right, I admit it all the time, but it's not the business end that gets my motor purring. I like, I *love* the cooking, preparing meals people find satisfying and authentic. If only the business side would take care of itself, I'd be ecstatic."

"Doesn't Joanne? Take care of it, I mean?"

"She does a whole lot better job than I do. But it's such a tough business. Most fail, you know. I came *this* close."

"I know," she said dryly. "That's how we met. Remember?" She leaned forward to take a mouthful of beans without spilling. "And I, for one, think you're blessed to have a partner like Joanne."

"Jesus, yes. You'll get no argument from me on that. She always had a head for business. Started out in advertising, at one of those fancy firms in the Back Bay. Then she managed a few businesses. All kinds of things. A neighborhood newspaper. A public-relations outfit. A *sports* bar, if you can believe it. This is her first restaurant, and she put up most of the cash. She's got great business sense and plenty of experience, but the victuals trade is a bit new to her."

"I have the feeling," Dani said, "that Joanne could do pretty much anything she put her mind to."

"Ain't that the truth." He grinned. "You should get her to tell you about some of her marketing ideas. She says she's come up with the perfect wedding gift for New Age yuppies. The combination salad spinner and prayer wheel."

Dani laughed. "I'm still getting over the bumper sticker on the back of her car."

"Keep Honking, I'm Reloading?"

"That's the one."

The waitress materialized at his side. "How about some dessert over here?" she asked. "They're good here."

Arthur beamed up at her. "Kumquat pie," he said. "Tell me about kumquat pie."

"It's a local favorite. He makes it right here, his own recipe. It's kinda like key lime, ya' know? Got little bits of peel in it. You'll like it."

He ordered a piece and a cup of coffee. Dani passed.

"But seriously," she said, "why is a boy from South Boston so into Italian food?"

"Sicilian," he amended, then smiled. "But who's picky?"

"All the more so," she said. "Northern Italian food is the rage these days. People don't want red sauces. Why the push to do the Southern stuff?"

"You know *why* everybody wants food from the North? Because for at least two generations, the only Italian food available was 'Italian-American.' Bastardized stuff that Southern immigrants fobbed off as Italian during the 1950s. You know what I mean: heavy dishes with acidic red sauces and loads of factory *mozzarella.* No wonder people want complex sauces from Bologna. Or polenta from Venice. Risotto from Milan. They never experienced *real* Southern cooking."

She looked amused, as if enjoying how carried away he could get about something as trivial as food. He didn't care.

"You know about the veal line?" he asked, in full pedagogic tilt now.

She pulled her chin back and opened her eyes wide. "The veal line." Her tone was neutral. "No, I can't say that I do."

Putting the spurs to his hobbyhorse, he moved his plate aside, took a pen from his shirt pocket, and turned over his paper place mat. He sketched a rough facsimile of the Italian peninsula. "There's like this imaginary line you can draw across a map of Italy," he said, drawing one for her. "At just about the latitude of Rome. That's the veal line, the line where the veal you eat changes its sex."

"Not gender?" she added with a teasing smile, struggling to contain her mirth.

He didn't rise to the bait. "North of the veal line the soils are rich enough to support dairy cattle. So farmers keep the females and slaughter the bull calves for veal. *Vitello.* Masculine gender suffix. And with all that milk you get pasta sauces enriched by cream. The principal cooking fat is butter. The great cheeses are made from cow's milk. That's your rich, Northern kitchen. Like in Emilio-Romagna. Or Parma, where the *prosciutto* comes from hogs that are fed on the whey left over from making parmesan cheese."

"Please. I've just eaten."

He jabbed at the place mat. "But south of the line, in the *Mezzogiorno,* people are poorer. The soils aren't as rich. Water is often scarce. This is land better suited to hardy grazers, like sheep and goats. So you keep a bull calf in the hope that it will become a work animal, an ox, and you slaughter the she-calves. *Vitella.* You cook with olive oil instead of butter. The cheeses are made from goats' and sheep's milk—*pecorino, caciocavallo*—and the pasta sauces are correspondingly lighter. The cuisine is simpler, too. Because the tomato flourishes in such conditions—"

"Yeah," she interrupted. "Red sauces. Like I said."

"No, not 'red sauce,' " he said with some asperity. "In the South, and especially in Sicily, the tomato is nothing short of spectacular. Brilliant little supernovas of concentrated sunlight—so perfect all you need is good oil and fresh herbs to make you forget all about those complicated *ragus* from Bologna. There's nothing like it, Dani. Nothing!"

He paused to let the waitress put his pie and coffee in front of him.

"And Sicily," he went on. She rolled her eyes, playing the good-natured victim. "Sicily is not really Italy. I mean, they call mainland Italians *polenta-eaters.* The island has been conquered so many times—Greeks, Romans, Moors, Spaniards, the French—that its cooking is shot through with all these influences. Yet at bottom it's still poor and simple. Desperately poor, in fact, until just recently. Many pasta dishes are topped with bread crumbs instead of grated cheese. And bread is so holy there's a superstition that those who waste it will be condemned to spend the afterlife picking up crumbs with their eyelashes."

He stopped himself and grinned sheepishly. "Hey, look at me. I'm sorry. You just wanted to know why Sicilian. The short version? The food is wonderful, and I thought it presented a market niche."

"No," she said. "It's interesting. Who'd have thought you could divide up a country along gender lines—of cows?"

He chuckled and took a bite of the pie, then nodded vigorously as he pushed the plate toward her in invitation. She shook her head. He returned to his dessert, and they lapsed into silence. Outside the window the light was softening into dusk. When he looked up again to take a sip of coffee, he saw her peering intently at him. They exchanged awkward smiles.

She said, "Actually, that doesn't tell me very much about you, personally. Except that you tend to get carried away about food. But *why*? Did you always want to be a cook? That's why I asked about you being from South Boston. I mean, it's not exactly known as a training ground for the culinary arts."

"No," he conceded. "And there was no particular love of food in my house growing up. My mother cooked plain because my father liked plain. They still do. You knew the day of the week, you knew what was for supper. I had an uncle in the food business, a retail meat merchant, but otherwise it was pretty dull in that department."

"What happened? Were you struck down like Saul on the road to Damascus?"

"Something just about like that, as a matter of fact. On the road to Marseilles."

"Ooh, it sounds picaresque," she said, drumming her fingers on the table expectantly. "Tell me more."

"Well, this was just after I quit U Mass. I didn't know what I wanted to do, and I wasn't really into it anymore, so I decided to take a year off after my junior year. I worked for several months to make enough for a trip abroad. My uncle made me a gift of a couple hundred dollars, for extras he said. My plan was to hitch all over Europe. Of course, I didn't know that hitchhiking was pretty much a bygone thing; nobody picks you up anymore, even in Europe. So I find myself stuck in Paris, trying to figure out how to shorten my trip because the train fare means I'll run out of money sooner.

"Fortunately, I met this American who had a motorcycle. A big BMW. He—Steve, his name was—he was a student in England. We hit it off and agreed to share the cost of gas and head south. Down to Marseilles and Nice. He insisted on finding this place down in Marseilles where he said they'd been making bouillabaisse since forever. Me, I'd never heard of the stuff. But Steve was adamant. I had to have genuine bouillabaisse, he said, and the place he had in mind was supposed to have been adding new ingredients to a pot that had been simmering continuously for over a hundred and fifty years. Steve was intrigued by the notion that he might end up eating at least one molecule from the original batch."

"Sounds like he had it worse than you do. Did he find the place?"

"Who knows? He found *some* place anyway, a grubby joint down by the waterfront that I can promise you was not in any guidebook. So I had my first bouillabaisse. With that spicy rouille to stir in. And that was it. Kapow! I was totally hooked. There was nothing like *this* in Perkins Square. This was a whole new world, a universe no one ever told me about. I've been chasing it ever since."

"You became a cook."

"Not right away, but I did get right into the food business. Knocked around all over Boston, working in restaurants. Prep cook, line cook. Sous-chef. I was working at Olives over in Charlestown when I finally decided to try and open my own place.

"With Joanne."

"With Joanne."

They were quiet again. The Spanish moss on the water oak stirred listlessly like fur boas in the gentle breeze. The waitress brought the check and left it on the table.

Dani said, "You're a funny man, Arthur Patch. You start out seeming—what? Self-contained and a little conniving, I guess. Enough to trash my investigation of Larry Coniglio anyway. But a straight shooter. I like that about you. You're basically honest. And then, sometimes, your feelings come so close to the surface they're like a ripple under the skin. Your passion for cooking. For your precious words. And there's your—what's the right word? Defensiveness, maybe?"

This was new territory. He gave her an uneasy grin. "You mean like when I get a chip on my shoulder 'cause you act like I'm some kind of wiseguy wanna-be? An Irish mope? I'm not even Irish, you know."

"Well, that, too. But I—what are you, if you're not Irish?"

The waitress reappeared, and Dani paid the check. When she looked up at him again, she seemed to have lost the thread of their conversation. Then, finding her place, she said, "No. I didn't mean the 'chip,' as you put it. That I can understand. I was thinking about on the flight yesterday. How plain it was that your feelings were hurt."

He felt his neck flush. "That business about the room reservations? Your preemptive rejection of the offer I never made."

"Yes. It was insulting. To presume you would be so presumptuous."

"Well, it's a pretty effective way to deter offers."

She took a beat. She said, "I hope not *too* effective."

She held his eye without blinking, then smiled—shyly, he thought. His heart raced and he felt frightened again. All he trusted himself to do was to shake his head no and smile back at her. Idiotically.

Neither one of them said a thing. Neither made a move. It was, Arthur thought, as if he were playing easy to get and she were considering whether to take him.

"You're not wearing a wire, are you?'

She laughed, giggled almost. Chinks of ivory light from the streetlamp on Route 17 shone through the vents in the Venetian blinds. They gave her bare skin a spectral sheen in the semidarkness.

"That's right, Arthur," she whispered as she rounded the foot of the bed and headed up its right side in his direction. "This whole adventure, the trip to Arcadia, everything—it's all part of an elaborate scheme to get you to talk on tape."

The silk blouse was still on the pillow next to him, pressing softly against his left cheek. Leaning over, she reached across his body for it. Her breasts swayed above him as she scooped up the blouse. She bunched it up and tossed it to the floor on the other side.

"Talk about what?" he asked hoarsely. "I cave so quickly under pressure."

She sat beside him and laid the palm of her hand on his chest, then slid it softly upward until it lay on his cheek. "Your secrets, Arthur. Your recipes. I've promised to sell them to Hamersley's Bistro."

"They'd just botch them. They require the right touch."

"Give us one," she said. Still sitting, she bent over to kiss him. "That Southern touch. That is, if you're up to it again."

"South of the veal line?" He laid his hand on her far knee.

"Mmmnn." She lay across him.

Arthur felt his hand glide up the outside of her bare leg until he reached the crease where it met the droop of her buttock. The touch galvanized him, and he pulled her close. The scant light made the skin on her hip gleam like porcelain. The last thing he saw before he closed his eyes was the oxford dress shirt she had worn earlier. It hung across the back of a chair near the window. Still crisp and unwrinkled, too, at least all the way to the tails, where they had been tucked into her jeans.

CHAPTER THIRTY-ONE

GRRRR

WEDNESDAY EVENING

She was two, maybe three years old, in her short cotton dress with the spray of violets across the bodice. Beneath her feet were railroad ties. Their spacing made for pleasant walking, requiring a small hop from one to the other, and she had to keep her eyes down to maintain her rhythm. The creosote smeared on the ties smelled like the oily floor of Mr. Cormier's garage. Rusted spikes clung magically to the gleaming rails. Looming high above her on both sides, cattails and other tall grasses she couldn't name turned the roadbed into a fringed trench, an open-air tunnel to eternity.

She came to a trestle and stopped. She knew she had to turn back. The trestle wasn't that high, really, just a serviceable archway across a two-lane country road, but it was high enough to scare a little girl—a guilty little girl who was supposed to have kept to the backyard. Reluctantly, she turned around and began to retrace her steps.

With the turn came an odd change in the light, as if the sun's rays suddenly found it difficult to see over the tall grasses on either side of her. The ties were farther apart now, and the spaces widened farther as she walked. Soon she could no longer leap from one to the other in a single bound. She tried to pick up the pace, but her steps fell on ties and crushed stone at irregular intervals, breaking what passes for a stride when you're three years old. The broken rhythm made her tire rapidly. She yearned to reach the sloping path that led up through the reeds and toward the weed-choked backyard of the tiny house she shared with her parents.

The path never showed itself. Dusk was gathering, and she began to feel anxious, uneasy. A call of a nighthawk made her jump. She froze and glanced wildly about her. She must have missed the cut to the path, but she didn't know for sure. If she missed it she might wander up the roadbed into inevitable darkness. That was too terrifying.

With a decisiveness born of fear, she plunged headlong up the bank and into the reeds. She believed she knew the rough direction, and the going wasn't too bad while she was in the cattails, near the roadbed. There was mud, though, and she slipped and slid as she crashed through the cattails. Their brown cotton felt fuzzy against her cheek when she brushed against them.

Once out of the roadbed she found herself in an upland field of tall grasses. She couldn't see over them. She realized she was completely lost. Plunging forward blindly, she felt stinging pain swipe at her arms and legs. She looked down to see fine lines of blood like paper cuts lashed across them.

Cut weed! She had heard older children talk about cut weed. It could flay you like the sharpest of knives, leaving you to bleed out your lifeblood in the field. She was in terror now and, riveted to the spot where she stood, she began to sob uncontrollably—racking sobs, on and on, for forever.

A voice wriggled through the sound of her wailing.

"Mavis! Mavis, honey! Where are you?"

It was her mother. She tried to cry out but only sobbed louder. She could not call or even scream. She could only sob.

And then her mother was there, sweeping her up into her arms and hurrying back to the house with soothing words.

Once lifted out of the grass, she could see that she had only been a short distance from the yard. She laid her cheek against her mother's warm neck on the way back. Her crying subsided, except for a convulsive gasp every now and then.

They reached the little house with its peeling trim and weathered cedar shakes. Her grandfather sat on a kitchen chair next to the stoop, with a view of the railroad tracks spread out before him. He was whittling again. He worked on the lopped-off crotch of an alder branch that was wedged between his knees.

"Look, Grampa," her mother said, hiking Mavis higher up on her hip. "Mavis got lost and cut herself. Poor baby."

Her grandfather lifted his head from his work and idly turned the bruised blue of his eyes on her. Mocking, malevolent eyes.

Mavis started to shriek, a keening sound that streamed out of her and didn't know how to stop itself. It rose in pitch and volume, taking on corporeal dimensions, as if another person were present in the tiny yard.

Her grandfather twisted his mouth into a sleepy smile and casually bent to his work again. He drew the buckknife slowly toward him, peeling a long yellow curl of rage off the wood in his lap. It tumbled to the ground beneath his legs where a pile of shavings glistened like spun gold. She screamed and screamed.

Her mother was shaking her, to quiet her, but she realized it was Tommy reaching over to wake her.

"Hey!" he barked. "Wake up. You sound like a goddamn banshee."

She jerked up straight, her eyes darting every which way in confusion. There was sweat on the sides of her neck and her heart fluttered like a wounded bird. Gradually, the interior appointments of the Lincoln took shape and floated into perspective.

She was still riding through the Florida flatwoods with Tommy.

She had fallen asleep, obviously, on the drive back from Sanibel Island. She remembered now how she had struggled to keep her eyes open. She had been tired to begin with from her late-night peregrinations over the Internet. Mix in sun and sand, the long walk on the beach, and the grilled red snapper she'd eaten for supper, and no wonder. At first she only sagged against the car window. There was something oddly soothing in the gentle bumping of her head against the cool glass and in the thrum of tires on pavement. Then she was gone completely, slipping into a twisted replay of an old, old memory.

The trip to Sanibel had been pretty much a disaster. It had started badly, with Tommy missing the exit off the interstate and stubbornly plowing all the way to Bonita Springs before turning back up toward Sanibel. They soon found themselves caught in the clotted traffic on Route 865, inching their way back up through the Times Square section of Fort Myers Beach. Tommy smoldered beside her and Bernadine whimpered pitifully in the backseat. Uncharacteristic, that whimpering, and it worried her. Was she getting sick?

Things didn't improve much once they got to Sanibel. Dogs weren't permitted in the bird sanctuary, so that was out. They were relegated to walking the shoreline, where she scoured the beach for shells. Dapple reveled in it, bounding along in and out of the water and doing her best to engage Bernadine, but Bernadine had clung gloomily to Mavis's side. Bernadine would have done better to hang with Tommy, whose sullen manner was more in keeping with the dog's. Mavis loved hunting for shells, though, and she had added a purple janthina and a glittering bleeding tooth to her beginner's collection.

It was dark now, the sky starless as the Lincoln sped north on the country road. The dogs slept in the back, no more whimpering from Bernadine to fret about, thank God. Tommy stared straight ahead as the car was sucked into the tunnel its headlights dug into the darkness.

She thought about the dream again. It was odd the way they worked, the logic of them. The cut weed incident down by the tracks was her earliest childhood memory, preceding by almost a decade the onset of her grandfather's midnight visitations. Yet there he was, in the dream, freighting the memory with anachronistic menace. Of course, time and sequence were meaningless. Dreams ran by their own rules, and she stoutly believed they were the medium by which her soul sought to communicate with her corporeal self. There was a teaching in it somewhere, she was certain.

Signs of habitation began to show themselves. Yard lights in the near distance appeared like lighted peepholes punched in the blackness. Then they became more numerous, eventually giving way to a creamy dome of diffused light over the sleepy little town. Soon Tommy was wheeling the big sedan into the bungalow's driveway. He shut off the engine. The two of them sat in silence for a moment. She could hear the ticking of the cooling engine. Then Tommy shouldered open his door and climbed out. He walked straight up the driveway, glided even, in that precise way of his. He entered the building by the side door, the one into the shed-roofed addition that housed the kitchen.

Dapple was awake now, panting over her shoulder, but Bernadine was not moving. Mavis got out of the car. The air was warm and very humid. If this was December, she was not looking forward to summer. She opened the rear door, stepping aside to let Dapple bound into the vacant lot to the right of the property. While the dog squatted to relieve herself, Mavis peered into the backseat. Bernadine slowly lifted her head from the upholstery to look back at her. The dog was not well, she knew it.

"Come on, Bernadine," she called softly, patting her hip with the flat of her hand. "Inside, baby. You'll feel better soon."

The dog complied, sliding off the seat in slow motion and gingerly stepping out of the car. Obediently, she trailed after Mavis and, a few strides later, Dapple. The three of them traced Tommy's steps into the kitchen.

He was standing in front of the refrigerator, the open door in his hand as he chugged bottled water with the other. While she filled the dogs' water dishes, he moved into the living room, switching on the floor lamp on his way to the bedroom. The bedroom light came on, too.

Dapple lapped the water noisily, but Bernadine just sat listlessly in front of hers. Mavis led them into the living room, where Dapple circled the oval throw rug before curling up on it. Bernadine just stood there. Mavis helped her up onto the couch. Stroking her head, Mavis noticed how dry the dog's nose was.

It's the vet for you, she said to herself. *First thing in the morning.*

While standing over the dog, she heard the creak of bedsprings as Tommy extinguished the bedroom light. She let out a worried sigh, for Bernadine's sake, and plodded back into the kitchen. She knew she wouldn't be falling asleep for a while.

With a cool can of Diet Pepsi open beside her at the kitchen table, she booted up the laptop and listened to the modem's subdued dialing noises. She brought up *Houndbytes* first, but there was nothing new from Miriam. This left her disappointed, even a little down. Funny, she thought, how she had come to look forward to hearing from her. With a little start, she was caught by the thought that Miriam was her only connection outside of Tommy and the small circle of Arcadians with whom the two of them had casual, circumspect dealings. The two librarians. The Bells, neighbors just to the south. Waitresses at a few restaurants. Her hairdresser. A couple of the men who worked out with Tommy at the exercise club. Pretty vacant, all in all. Nothing like it was back home in Southie. No wonder she felt lonely.

Southie. She typed *Bostonherald.com* in the address panel and waited for news from home to congeal in tardy pixels on the screen before her. The mayor was feuding with a waterfront developer. The weather apparently sucked. The petition to ban greyhound racing was gathering signatures and momentum (great news!—she read *that* one avidly). The Big Dig—the project to bury the central artery beneath the surface of the city—was galloping past previous cost estimates and projected completion dates. The body of the victim of a gangland killing had been identified as—

Mavis jerked her hand away from the mouse as if from an electrical shock. She stared at the monitor.

Eva Lou Starks.

She *knew* that girl. She knew her mother, too. She had seen them both with Phil Hinkle. She had even met one of the men the article said had been found lying next to Eva Lou when they dug up her body.

With mounting dread she forced herself to read through the article, wincing sharply each time Tommy's name was mentioned. But when she had finished, it was Hinkle, not Tommy, who occupied her thoughts. She remembered how the big man had brought around Dorraine Starks, a loud, dark-haired woman with a husky laugh, who had clung to him like a limpet. Tommy had never cared for her—she got sloppy when she drank—but Hinkle went out with her for the better part of a year. She was fun, he said.

And Eva Lou was Dorraine's daughter. Dark like her mother. Very slim. *Very* quiet. She would sometimes accompany them on daytime excursions, a sullen teenager who obviously wished she were somewhere else. Mavis recalled how Tommy had once offered to buy her something to eat from that greasy concession stand at the entrance to Castle Island. She had responded wordlessly, just shaking her head—until Hinkle talked to her. Then she lit right up. She seemed always to brighten around him, as if animation were only possible in the warmth of his attention, in the sway of the big man's charm.

She remembered a comment Tommy had once let slip about Hinkle, how he had a taste for much younger women, and she knew with sickening certainty what had happened to Eva Lou. Hinkle was a pig, a personable pig, but a pig nonetheless. He had taken advantage of her. Used her as he had used her mother to get at her. And when he finished with her, for whatever reason, he didn't just discard her, as he had with other young women. No, she was underage, substantially so, and therefore posed something of a danger to him. So he killed her. Dumped her body in a trench with some lowlife who had crossed him and Tommy in business.

Mavis shook her head, but she could not dispel the image of that doomed, slight little girl. Or of Hinkle, with the sweet talk and that amiable smirk of his. She visualized his huge hands moving greedily over Eva Lou's fragile body, manhandling it into some position or other so she could do his bidding. His eyes mocking the childlike sincerity of her sacrifice.

She heard a ringing in her ears. Looking off into the living room, she noticed how the open door to the bedroom where Tommy slept seemed framed in the center of the kitchen doorway, while inside the darkened bedroom itself she could see the outline of the window, the streetlamp glowing bone white through the scrim of the window shade. The openings gave her a weird sensation of cavities opening up like the segments of a telescope, and she lost all sense of her periphery, as if she were staring into an endless tunnel. Then her mind's eye traded Hinkle's visage for that of her grandfather, all those many short years ago, and she shuddered.

Of course, there were differences. No doubt Eva Lou was a more willing participant than Mavis had been; she had never hunkered in the dark dreading the arrival of the light and the old man, as Mavis had. Eva Lou had at least been spared that horror. But when you thought about it, what does *willing* mean if you're a fifteen-year-old girl? Was it so different, really?

And he *killed* her.

A chilly deadness suddenly settled over her. *He* didn't kill Eva Lou. *They* killed her. With an unshakable conviction, she knew that Tommy had been involved, too. What was it he always said about him and Hinkle? How one of them couldn't even feel an itch on his ass without the other starting to scratch it? (And she didn't even want to *think* about that). No, Tommy was in on it. She could see him directing the disposal of her body.

She lived with a man who killed little girls.

Mavis lurched to her feet, loudly knocking over the chair in her haste, and ran through the living room and into the toilet. Without even pausing to turn on the bathroom light, she fell into a kneeling heap and threw up violently into the black hollow of the toilet bowl. The heaving went on and on, lasting long after there was anything left to bring up but the sour reek. When the spasms finally did stop, her stomach muscles ached from her exertions. Still sitting on the floor in the dark, she gripped the cool rim of the bowl with one hand and wiped her watering eyes with the other. Dapple appeared beside her, the dog's sharp face nudging her shoulder out of concern and sympathy.

Suddenly the darkness disintegrated in the living room and Tommy's image loomed in the doorway. Flicking the bathroom light switch, he brought the harsh light with him. She spun her head toward him, briefly immobilized by terror. But she made a midair correction and managed to smile weakly at him. He was standing there in his white undershorts.

"You gonna be sick, too?" he demanded.

She didn't follow him at first, then realized he was referring to Bernadine. She shook her head. "I don't think so. I think it must have been that fish for supper. I been queasy for the last hour."

He looked down at her as she pulled herself to her feet. "You need anything?" he asked.

Mavis felt unsteady on her feet, but she smiled back. "No, nothing. You're sweet to ask."

Sweet? You murdering asshole!

Looking into the untroubled blue of his eyes, she thought she must be seeing him for the first time as he really was. She had thrown away everything in her life for him. Somehow she had remained blind to his nature—a blindness it had cost her strenuous effort to maintain—in the face of all the evidence there for the gathering. When she had let herself think about it, of course she knew he had had a hand in killing people. But they were gangsters—murderous rivals or treacherous associates—and it just came with the business. It was in the nature of things, in the nature of his business, off in another world cleanly separated from the one she and Tommy inhabited together.

But Eva Lou obliterated that separation. It filled her with self-loathing to discover the two worlds had been one all along. She looked at him now with a mixture of terror and revulsion, alternately torn between wanting to scream invectives at him and to shrink from his gaze.

As if channeling her feelings, Dapple uttered a low growl at Tommy. Tommy cocked his head and peered down at the dog in amusement. "Grrrr," he echoed, smiling. "Come to bed," he said to her. Then he left. As he padded back to the bedroom, she heard him say, "Grrrr" again, followed by a half chuckle. The living-room light went out and silence reigned again.

Mavis looked into the bathroom mirror at her drawn face and

red-rimmed eyes. She had to find a way to leave. *Had* to. She remembered the lawyer from the Cape, the one handling Uncle Army's estate. With all that money. *Her* money. What was his name? Maybe he could help her. There must be something she could do, some way she could escape from Tommy and Arcadia. Yes, she would call him in the morning.

She bent her head to scratch Dapple behind the ear. She felt a hot rush of love for her. She had never known Dapple to growl at anyone. Not ever. And now, just when Mavis finally saw Tommy for the monster he was, Dapple had picked it up.

And they call them dumb animals.

"Grrr," she whispered lovingly as she stooped to rub her nose on Dapple's cheek. "Grrrrrrrrrr."

And with a little jolt of recognition, she straightened up. *GUR,* she said to herself, her mind turning over the possibilities.

G.U.R.

If they rescued dogs . . .

CHAPTER THIRTY-TWO

THE OTHER GUY'S YARD

THURSDAY

Arthur Patch was in love. What had started as a tentative, impossible crush was in full heat now, after their night together, and the force of his feelings came off him in waves as he stared at her from across the booth in the motel's breakfast room.

Dani found it tempting to bask in that glow, but it frightened her, too. She felt a little in love herself—but only a little, she reminded herself, and her own feelings shrank from his intensity. So she just smiled back at him and sipped her coffee and agreed that, yes, she might as well hear what it was Jimmy Morrissey called her.

"The Snow Queen," he said with a grin, shaking his head as if at his lawyer's myopia.

She winced, then set down her cup. "Somehow I doubt that's because I grew up in all that ice and snow in northern Vermont."

He seemed to savor the dryness of her response. "No, I don't think so. I think he was referring to the icy princess of the fairy tale and certain . . . *traits* he thought you had in common with her. You know, beautiful but cold. Unfeeling. Straightlaced."

"*You* try being a woman prosecutor in the U.S. Attorney's Office," she said. It came out harsher than she meant. She softened her tone. "It's a macho world, Arthur. Your 'colleagues' are anything but collegial—young studs glowing white-hot with ambition, climbing over one another for juicy assignments. And the defense lawyers are just as bad. They're constantly probing for an exploitable weakness, and they trip into professional road rage at the slightest provocation just to see if you'll wilt. No, if you want to survive in that environment, you don't let them see you warm. Or soft. Or, God forbid, vulnerable. They'd *savage* you. Trust me, icy is the only way."

He laced his fingers before him on the table as his smile narrowed into something of a conspiratorial leer. "Well, I'm pleased to report it's *not* your only way."

She felt her neck flush to hear this, but she covered with a facetious glower. "Don't be smug. And keep it to yourself. I don't like this talk of 'reporting.' "

"Your secret's safe with me."

"Me, too," said a voice to their right.

They turned to behold a mocking grin above a mustard yellow polo shirt and madras Bermuda shorts, maroon and white. The ensemble was finished off with black socks and matching wing tips.

They gaped in unison at Jimmy Morrissey, who spread his arms before them in welcome, as if his arrival had been expected and overdue.

"Hey, kids. Did you miss me?"

Arthur looked him up and down. "I almost didn't recognize you in mufti," he said, clearing his throat.

His head moving from side to side, Jimmy peeked down to check himself out.

Dani said, "What are *you* doing here?" She wondered how much of their conversation he had overheard. She hoped he wasn't there for that Snow Queen stuff and Arthur's gloating allusion to the night before.

"Isn't that *my* line?" he rejoined, scratching his soft belly absently. "After all, Counselor, you're not supposed to be talking to my client without me present. At least, not about that subpoena business. But then, it looks like this is a personal conversation. Am I right or what?"

She felt herself blush now. There was no innocent way to explain why the two of them were breakfasting together in a motel at least a thousand miles from home. Then her anger kicked in.

"What *are* you doing here," she repeated.

"I suspect," said Arthur, "he's here for the same reason we are."

She got it then, and was annoyed that her embarrassment had kept her from seeing it at once.

Morrissey, however, chose to play dumb. "Alas," he said mournfully, "I'm not so lucky." His eyes slid back and forth between the two of them as he waggled his eyebrows in salacious innuendo. "I'm just a lonely tourist, I'm afraid."

"Come on, Jimmy," Arthur said. "Arcadia is no resort town, and it's not a coincidence we should meet *here.*"

"Here? But it's the only decent motel in town."

"Jimmy." She said it peremptorily.

With a good-humored snort, Jimmy gave up the clowning. His smile turned genuine.

"Guilty," he acknowledged, lifting his hands as he shrugged. "So, I'm not here for the waters. It's gotta be the same reason as you. Got in late last night. So now what? We're not going to end up in some unseemly contest here, are we? A race? Unless you've already found him."

Dani and Arthur exchanged glances. He gave his own shrug, with the eyebrows and an upward tug at the corner of his mouth. She nodded. There was no other way. It was just too small a town, and they'd be falling all over each other if they went into open competition. They were going to have to make a deal.

"No, Jimmy," she admitted. "We haven't found him yet."

Jimmy reached behind him and pulled a chair over from a table in the center of the room. He scuffled it up next to the booth and sat down, pressing his meaty arms on the surface of the table.

"So how we gonna work this?" he asked. "You show me yours, I show you mine?"

"The terms first," she said. "We determine the split, commit it to writing, *then* we share."

"Fair enough," he said. "Should be two teams, two shares. I got my own expenses, you know."

Arthur shook his head brusquely. "No way. It's not just me and Dani. I have Joanne in this, too. Half the reward, then split three ways again? No, it's not enough."

Jimmy molded his mouth into an upside-down horseshoe as he thought. "Well, I'm not settling for a quarter, if that's what you're saying. You got other people to take care of—I mean, besides who's in this room—fine. That's your problem. Just like it's mine."

"Three shares, then," said Arthur. "You get one. We get the other two."

There was a pause as Jimmy considered this. His lips moved a little as he thought. Dani smiled to herself; she could almost hear him do the arithmetic.

"It's not that hard, Jimmy," she said, still smiling. "A third of three hundred thousand is one hundred thousand, no matter how many places you carry it out to."

He looked at her in amusement, admiring her little poke. "*That's* not the calculation that troubles me. It's my creditors I have to figure. And yes, I think I can get by on a third. Better than risking you guys scooping the whole thing, right?"

"Precisely my thinking," said Dani. Arthur nodded his agreement.

"So, whatcha got?" he asked.

"Not yet," she said, reaching for her purse on the seat to her left. She pulled it up onto the table. "First, we commit this deal to writing. So nobody has an incentive to go off on their own." She fished in her bag and produced a leather-bound notebook. Looking up at Jimmy, she said, "This way, there should be no unpleasant surprises." She tore off a sheet and started writing.

In a matter of minutes they had a mutually satisfactory draft, and all three of them signed it. She handwrote another copy, which they also signed. Now that both sides were armed with a written contract, she felt ready to do business. Jimmy recounted first how he had inveigled Mavis into phoning the number in Barnstable in hopes of inheriting her uncle's ersatz estate; they told him about the dogs and "Miriam's" on-line communications with her.

"Jesus," Jimmy said, his eyes wide. "Was *she* a loose cannon. We *both* got to her. I tell you, Tommy's gonna be some pissed at his lady friend when they pick him up. She's a walking disaster waiting to happen to him."

"I wouldn't want to be in her shoes when he finds out," Arthur agreed.

Dani considered this for a moment, then made up her mind. "No," she said firmly. "We don't tell them how we found out. We just found him, that's all we tell the FBI. We leave her out of it. She doesn't deserve that."

Jimmy stared at her in disbelief. "Are you kidding? The guy's been on *America's Most Wanted*—twice, in fact. The FBI must get fifty calls a week from people who think they saw him on the monorail at Disney World. Or her coming out of her hairdresser's in Santa Monica. *How* we know is what makes us credible. Because it's critical that they believe us. Otherwise, they just send some dipshit to check out the next story on his list and Tommy flies the coop again. Dani, we gotta use what we got."

"No." She let him feel the weight of her eyes. Arthur, she noticed, was just watching the interplay between the two of them. "She's a human being, not somebody you trample on to get what you want. It's bad enough we tricked her into trusting us. And that we now plan to betray her trust. Okay, I can accept that. We have to do it. But I won't endanger her physical safety, put her at risk for the rest of her life. I just won't."

Jimmy paused, his eyes narrowed to slits. "You been in the public sector too long, Dani. You never had to scramble around in the nitty-gritty of private practice. You just don't get it, do you? You know what a lawyer's job *really* is? It's putting the turd in the other guy's yard. And to do that you sometimes get your fingers dirty. Well, this time the turd's gotta go in *her* yard."

She said, "Oh, I 'get' it, Jimmy. Even prosecutors have to put people in unpleasant situations to do their job. Ask Arthur; he's been there."

She glanced at Arthur. He dipped his head in acknowledgment.

"It's a little different," Jimmy pressed. "She's a fugitive from justice, you know. She's gonna go to jail as it is."

"Not different enough," she said. "We don't do this."

"Can you at least give me a *reason* why you wanna jeopardize everything?" Jimmy was pleading now.

"A reason?" she repeated. "Because it wouldn't be right."

He looked saddened. "You got anything better?"

Dani smiled, and Arthur laughed.

"Okay, we'll do it your way," said Jimmy with an air of resignation. "I just hope to hell we don't blow this because of your squeamishness. Your *sudden* squeamishness." He shifted in his seat and turned to Arthur. "So what have you got?"

"We got an address and a phone number in Arcadia. We already know the address is no good."

Jimmy reached in his hip pocket and removed a sheet of paper. It had been folded twice, into a wallet-sized quarto. He opened it and handed it to Arthur. "I got a number, too. It's for a pay phone, but I know where it is at least. She's used it at least three times."

Arthur read what was written there and smiled. He slid it across the table to Dani. Looking up at Jimmy, he said, "It's a good thing we did agree to join forces. Otherwise, we'd be bumping into each other every step of the way."

"Huh?"

"You've got the same number and address we have."

"Five-one-nine West Hickory?" Jimmy looked astonished.

"Yup. It's the library. And the number must be for a pay phone in the library. Or right near it."

"That's good news," Dani offered. "It means she's used that phone pretty consistently. You got three calls in a span of how many days? Two, three?"

"More like twenty-four hours."

"And she gave out the same number back in October, when she got the dogs. That was two months ago. Maybe she uses it a lot."

Arthur straightened up. "Of course. The library. That would make sense. Tommy's supposed to be a heavy reader—as gangsters go, anyway. And he'd want to follow the local papers to keep up with what's going on back home. Maybe she uses the phone when he's in the library."

"So," Jimmy said with enthusiasm, picking up where Arthur left off, "we just keep an eye on the library and hope he shows up? Let's do it!"

"Hold it," Arthur said. "Not so fast. Three people on a stakeout? Three's too many. Too conspicuous."

"Arthur's right," Dani said. "We should do it in shifts."

"And whoever's off duty can check other things," Arthur said. "I can't believe he wouldn't be working out at a health club. We can also take all his old aliases, the ones listed on the FBI Most Wanted page, and run them through the new phone listings. Maybe he got sloppy when he had a phone installed."

"Assuming he's got one," Dani said.

"He *must* have. You'd attract more attention *without* one. There's no risk there as long as he doesn't make dumb calls. And it looks like they know enough, even Mavis, to use a pay phone for anything that could be used to trace them. Well, almost, in her case."

Jimmy raised both hands. "Hey," he said. "We can at least go check it out now. Get the lay of the land, you know?"

Arthur looked over to Dani for confirmation. "Why not?" he said.

She couldn't think of a good reason why not. All she said was, "Not till I finish my complimentary Continental breakfast."

The three of them sat in Jimmy's rented Cavalier in the municipal parking lot across Hickory from the library. By common assent the Chevy looked less obviously like a rental than the aquarium blue Neon. Tilting forward from her position in the backseat, Dani rested a forearm on the top of each bucket seat and brought her head into rough alignment with those of the two men. They beheld the building across the street.

The Desoto County Library was set back about fifty yards from the traffic on Hickory Street (which doubled as Route 70), the intervening space serving as a parking lot dominated by a great umbrella of an oak. The building itself consisted of a single story of recent construction. With walls of light brown brick, it had a metal roof surmounted by a square, gabled structure like a postmodern chicken coop. Black wrought-iron grillwork was latticed over its windows. The cornice of its no-nonsense portico, painted a flat white and supported by simple pillars, blandly identified the building as "LIBRARY." Someone, a litigation-phobic alderman perhaps, had arranged to have alternating stripes of maroon and yellow painted on the portico's cement riser. They were just able to read the sign on the front doors; it forbade in-line skating and roller-skating.

"Do you think," Jimmy asked, his face screwed up in the scorn, "these crackers are so dim they have to be told you can't roller-skate in a fucking *library*?"

Dani said, "I think they mean on the portico—and that long handicap ramp going off to the left there. It's probably irresistible to a ten-year-old."

"There!" Arthur declared sharply. He pointed toward the portico. "You see? On the right-hand pillar? Right next to that curlicue bench."

"What?" said Dani, turtling her head down to sight along his finger.

"It's a pay phone," said Jimmy. "Bolted right on the pillar."

"The fateful telephone," said Arthur, portentously. "That's where she did the deed. I'd lay odds on it."

The three of them were quiet for a moment.

"Let's take a look around inside," said Jimmy as he opened his door.

Dani gripped his shoulder suddenly. "Wait," she commanded. "Check out the bike rack."

"What bike rack?" Jimmy asked, one foot on the ground now. Then he saw it and froze. "Sweet Jesus," he whispered. "You think . . . ?"

"Why not?" said Arthur, whispering, too.

Tethered to the bicycle rack to left of the library, just past the entry to the handicapped ramp, was a dog.

"It's a greyhound," Jimmy pointed out needlessly.

"But just one," Dani added. "It might not be hers. Mavis has two. Why, if the dog is hers, wouldn't she have both of them with her?"

Jimmy considered this, but not for long. He rolled his shoulder to shake off her clutching fingers and moved toward the open door.

"Where are you going?" she asked. "Are you nuts?"

On his feet outside the car now, Jimmy laid both hands flat on the roof and leaned in to talk to his new partners. "Look," he said. "We may have hit pay dirt here. Somebody's gotta go in there and see if she's there. If *they're* there. Now, Arthur here, he's too much of a man about town in Tommy's old neighborhood. You tell me, fella: are you confident he wouldn't recognize you if you bumped into him in there?"

Arthur maintained eye contact for a moment, then looked away.

"That's what I figured. And you, Miss Heavy-Duty Prosecutor that gets her mug in the paper every chance she gets? Will he make you? Maybe, maybe not. But it's a chance we can't take. So that leaves me, the court lizard from Charlestown. Who Tommy's never heard of and who doesn't even have a photo on file at the *Herald*, is how nobody *I* am. I should be able to saunter in there and have a bit of a look-see without blowing everything. Unless, of course, you've got a better idea."

He let it hang there, as if to see if either of them would pick it up. When they didn't he stepped back and made to close the car door.

"Just a look," she warned. "Then get out of there."

He tipped his head slightly to one side to give her a look of disappointment, his eyes half-hooded by scowling brows. "You think I'm stupid or something? No, don't answer that. I can stand not knowing; the ignorance won't kill me."

He turned and walked away, weaving through parked cars on his way to Hickory. There he waited for a break in the traffic before scuttling comically across the street and stepping into the library parking lot. He made steady, rolling progress, running his fingers across the coarse bole of the wolf oak as he passed it. With exaggerated care (for their benefit, she was sure), he lifted his leg to step over the colorfully streaked riser and sprang up onto the portico. When he got to the pillar he leaned over theatrically to inspect the phone. He stood up straight and shot a grin back at them.

"It *is* the phone," Arthur interpreted, a slight note of triumph in his voice. "He checked the number."

As if to confirm this, a still-grinning Jimmy Morrissey held both thumbs up in front of his chest as he backed toward the library doors. He had not yet completed his clockwise revolution back to face the doors when one of them opened out and struck him on the side of head. They watched him stagger backward two steps before losing his footing entirely and landing butt first on the cement floor of the portico, his body twisted to face the sloping chute of the handicapped ramp. A white-haired man in sunglasses and a baseball cap stepped briskly through the open door and extended a hand to him. Jimmy didn't respond at first. He shook his head hard once, then again, as if trying to clear it.

Dani moved quickly to open her door, an impulse to help him, but Arthur stopped her with a sharp, "Don't!" Puzzled, she looked back at him, but he was staring fixedly out the windshield. Then he pointed in Jimmy's direction.

"Look," he said. "It's *him*!"

She looked. Jimmy had now grasped the extended hand and was being hauled effortlessly to his feet by the elderly man. They watched as Jimmy and the man exchanged a few words, Jimmy brushing off the seat of his shorts with his left hand and massaging his right temple with the other. Then the man began to walk away down the ramp, looking back once to take in a becalmed Jimmy. *Yes,* she thought, *it is him.* It was a good thing Jimmy had insisted he be the one to check out the library.

Jimmy seemed at a loss for a moment, as if wondering whether to approach the man.

"Go inside!" Arthur hissed. "Go into the library, Jimmy. For Christ's sake!"

And miraculously, he did. He opened the library door and disappeared inside.

"Yes!" Arthur shouted, pumping his fist.

"Shhh." Dani nodded in the direction of the white-haired man. At Tommy Crimmins. Emerging from the ramp, he walked up to the greyhound. He squatted briefly to untie the leash, freeing it from the bicycle stand. He stood up. He coiled the end of the leash around the palm of his right hand. The dog immediately took up the slack, straining to be off. The leash quivered from the stress, a length of rope in red, white, and blue bands.

"Quick!" Dani whispered. "Slide over and start the car. We'll follow them."

Arthur did as she suggested, while she scrambled into the front passenger seat. But he just sat there.

"Come on," she urged. "What are you waiting for?"

"I can't," he explained. "Jimmy's got the keys."

She slapped her brow with the meat of her hand and groaned.

"Wait," he said. "It's all right. He's walking, not driving. We can follow on foot. With that dog to make him stand out, we can stay a block or more behind him and still not lose him. Just wait."

They waited. Man and dog walked back across the front of the library, then cut diagonally through the parking lot before picking up the sidewalk along Hickory. They watched him make his way up the block, at a fluid pace marked by economy of movement. The dog strode lithely two steps ahead of him.

He was half a block up the road when Arthur saw Jimmy push open one of the library doors and peek cautiously outside. Arthur leapt out of the car and, after checking to see that man and dog were still facing the other way, frantically waved Jimmy back into the building. Jimmy nodded and complied.

Arthur leaned in to face Dani. "Leave him a note on the dash to wait here for us. And let's take a stroll."

He peered avidly over the roof of the car at the retreating figures while she scribbled hurriedly. When she got out of the car, he moved quickly around to her side and took her hand, pulling her to the sidewalk on their side of the street. Tommy and the dog were just visible a block ahead, still on the other side of the street. They started to follow.

Progress was straight ahead for the first five blocks. The man did not look back. Then, as he reached Route 17, where he had to wait for the light before crossing, he turned around and seemed to be staring right at them. Arthur slowed instinctively, but Dani pulled him sharply to the right—dragging him, he realized, into a retail store.

It was a print shop, Kwik-Press it said over the counter. Once inside, Dani went straight to the counter and asked the clerk, a red-haired boy in his late teens, the directions to their motel. Arthur hung back, near the plate-glass window, where he tried to catch a glimpse of Tommy. The angle was too sharp. To his dismay, Dani seemed unhurried as she repeated back the directions the kid was giving her. At last, she turned and walked over to him.

"I had to do *something,*" she whispered. "As soon as he looked back, I knew we'd made a mistake. Look out there, Arthur." She dipped her head toward the view out the window. "There's nobody walking. No one. No foot traffic whatsoever, except for him. We stuck out like sore thumbs."

"Let's go look," he said. "If he's still standing there, we'll just walk back the way we came and start all over."

She nodded. Thanking the kid, she led the way out the door. They looked up the street. He was gone. No, there he was, a block past Route 17, taking the next left. Man and dog disappeared.

"Let's go!" he said, pulling her after him.

Hand in hand, they half jogged up to 17, sprinted kitty-corner across it, and hurried up the other side of Hickory. When they approached the intersection where he had turned—North Volusia Street, the sign said—Dani tugged hard and made him stop.

"Don't show yourself around the corner," she insisted.

"I won't. I'll just sneak a look here. Take a discreet peek around the corner."

He did as he described, stepping up to the very wall of the corner house and sidling forward until he could crane his head around the corner of the building.

Tommy and the greyhound were still visible, a full block up Volusia. He crossed the next street and kept going, straight ahead. Arthur pulled his head back.

"Let's give it a couple minutes," Arthur said. "Then we'll walk north up Volusia on the opposite side of the street. This is much more residential than Hickory. There's no reason to think he'll get excited by the sight of a couple of strolling lovers."

"Unless he got a good look at us back there, before we ducked into that shop. No, Arthur. I don't like it."

He sighed, but he knew she was right. They didn't want to get overeager and blow everything. He peeked around the corner again.

"He's gone!"

"What?"

"Disappeared completely. Take a look."

She was already looking.

"He's gone to ground," Arthur said. "He's home, I *know* it. And he lives in one of those houses on the next block. Let's go take a peek."

She said nothing, still straining to see up Volusia as he hauled her with him. They crossed to the other side of the street and headed north, the way he had gone.

Viewed from this end, Volusia seemed entirely residential, palmettos and moss-draped live oak lining the quiet street. They walked along, still holding hands, until they came to the street he had crossed when Arthur last saw him. It was East Cypress. As they began to cross it themselves, Arthur glanced to his right to take in a stolid municipal structure, the building that occupied the near corner of Cypress and Volusia. When he realized what it was, he started grinning.

"It's him, all right," he said to Dani. "Who else would have the stones to hide out half a block from the sheriff's office?"

"Stones?" she said, looking at him blankly. Then she seemed to figure it out. She said, "Or hubris."

"Maybe they're the same thing." He took a deep breath as they neared the spot where Tommy had abandoned the sidewalk. "Come here, sweetness. We're lovers on a stroll, remember?"

She resisted at first, then went along. He reached his right hand across her back and around her waist. They slowed their pace to a lovers' amble and looked casually about them. There were no people visible anywhere. As they progressed, Arthur's eyes swept over the façades of the houses on the other side of the street, the side Tommy had been walking on.

He made a sharp intake of breath, and his stride broke for a second.

"There!" he whispered hoarsely. "Look at the door at the end of that driveway."

She did. And she smiled, first at the sight, then looking up at him.

Draped over the knob of the side door was a dog's leash. One with bands of color, like a coral snake. Like the one that ran from Tommy's arm to the eager greyhound.

"Did you get the number?" she asked.

"Two-one-five."

He gave the house a good hard look as they ambled by. Number 215 was a long, low bungalow. It had a gabled front porch, three steps up, with double windows on either side of it. The windows to the right of the porch were shaded by a tattered awning with orange-and-white stripes. The building's siding, wide clapboards, off-white and peeling, was dimly set off by faded blue trim around the doors and windows. An addition with a shed roof had been attached on the far right, at the end of the driveway. A big, late-model Lincoln filled the driveway.

Arthur looked back at Dani. He squeezed her against his side.

"It's like Jimmy said," he whispered. "Pay dirt."

CHAPTER THIRTY-THREE

THE CALL

"Who makes the call?" Jimmy asked.

Arthur just stared back at him. He didn't know. He'd been wondering the same thing himself. He couldn't figure how to play it.

The three of them were back in Jimmy's Cavalier, still parked in its spot across from the library, the engine running. The morning was beginning to get hot now, and the air-conditioning was a welcome amenity.

Sitting in the driver's seat, Jimmy sported a purple bruise above his right cheekbone, a bulbous memento of Tommy and the library door. ("A rematch," he'd said as Dani inspected the lump. "I demand a rematch.") He clutched the steering wheel as he talked, wringing his hands like a man revving a motorcycle engine. The resulting squeaks were just a hair this side of really, really irritating.

"Well, it can't be me," said Dani, staring straight ahead through the windshield from the shotgun seat. "If Prout finds out I'm in this, he'll think I used confidential information from office files to find him. And even if he doesn't think that, he'll *pretend* he does—just to screw me out of the reward. I know him. We could lose everything if I make the call."

"That raises another interesting question," Arthur said. "*Who* do we call? Or whom, rather. The reward notice on the website says to call your regional FBI office. Why would we call Prout?"

Dani said, "I wasn't suggesting we call him. My point was that if I make the call, to *whom*ever, he'd find out and raise a stink. We don't need a stink."

"Arthur's put his finger on another problem, though," Jimmy added. "If we follow the suggested protocol, we end up with some cracker from the what? The Tampa office? Somebody who doesn't know Tommy from Adam. And since we've been *forbidden*"—he glared meaningfully at Dani—"to explain why we're so sure we've got the right man, the local SAC is not gonna put us very high up on his to-do list. Probably send some rookie to knock at two-fifteen Volusia and flash Tommy's photograph. You guys following me here?"

She signed in exasperation. "I thought that subject was closed."

"No, no," he said with a shake of his head. "I'm not suggesting we reopen it. All's I'm saying is, we got us an opportunity here to get *around* that problem. *If* we call Prout. Or somebody in the Boston office, anyway—Butters, maybe. We're not exactly strangers to them, so if we tell *them* where he is, they're more likely to believe us. Plus they've got an incentive to bring him in themselves, after all the shit they've taken recently."

"Incentive?" Dani said, her voice rising a little as she turned to face him. "They've been protecting the asshole for twenty years."

"Ah, but that was then," he said, bobbing a finger at her. "When he was *their* asshole. And this is now. They'll want him bad now. To rebuild their credibility after living through that shitstorm of publicity—that career-burying shitstorm. And all started, I'm proud to say, by our own Arthur Patch, through his Herculean efforts to wiggle away from your subpoena. No, they'd love to be the ones to bring him in."

They were silent for a moment, Jimmy looking pleased with himself. Arthur was pleased, too, but for different reasons. Involving the Boston office would give him cover—and time. They, too, would have to fly down here. It wouldn't be just a short drive from Tampa.

Dani finally broke the silence. "I still can't be the one to call. We don't want to have to sue the FBI to recover the award. If Prout raises a stink—and he would—we might have to."

"It should be you, Jimmy," Arthur announced, his mind made up at last. "Dani's right; she can't do it. And I can't, either. My relations with Larry are in a . . . *delicate* state, I guess you could say. If you owe money to a mobster, it's not a good idea to go public with how you've just helped the FBI catch another one. It doesn't make me sound like a guy who can keep his mouth shut—which is what he's been worried about all along."

Dani said, "Larry wouldn't have to know, Arthur. The Bureau's promising to preserve the anonymity of anyone who comes forward to claim the reward."

Arthur stared at her in disbelief, but Jimmy voiced his. "Are you *nuts,* girl? This is the Commonwealth of Massachusetts were talking here. Nobody keeps secrets. And the FBI—Christ, they're in a state of civil war over this guy. Those agents will spill everything just to fuck one another up. Have you been out of it *that* long?"

She looked chastened by this. Silence washed over them again, broken only by the rushing noise of the air conditioner. A truck rolled past them on Hickory. Hauling Peace River citrus products, according to the lettering on the box. Arthur heard the squeak of Jimmy's fingers as they torqued around the steering wheel.

"Okay," Jimmy said at last. "I make the call. I never got all that much business out of South Boston anyway."

Mavis was still waiting edgily for a call of her own when Tommy and Dapple returned from the library.

She was sitting on the couch in the living room with Bernadine's head in her lap, poor thing. She'd been in the same position so long her bare arm bore, where it rested on the arm of the couch, the patterned imprint of the coarse upholstery fabric. Bernadine couldn't even walk anymore. She had to get Tommy to carry her everywhere, even to the vet.

The vet. God, she wished the vet would call.

She had taken the dog in first thing in the morning. A tall, horsy woman with wild curls, a flattened nose, and not the slightest trace of a Southern accent, the vet had examined Bernadine brusquely and without comment. After several minutes she announced she would need to draw blood for lab tests, but she gave no hint of her reasons or suspicions. Mavis had been swamped with dread. The woman had no bedside manner at all—a predictable shortcoming, she supposed, in a veterinarian who serviced more farm animals than pets. But it was agony, all this waiting.

And not just for the test results alone. Twice she had called Mr. Mulcahey, the lawyer back in Barnstable, but each time she had succeeded only in reaching his answering machine. She would keep trying, of course, but opportunities to call Cape Cod without Tommy knowing were scant and precious. So she had to wait.

She was waiting, too, for word on the GUR. At least these communications were made over the web, not the phone. She had been checking *Houndbytes* with neurotic frequency. Still nothing. And still no word from Miriam, either. After all their intimate exchanges, the sharing of mutual grief, why had the woman disappeared from the board like that? Miriam had mentioned she was driving over to a dog shelter in upstate New York, but that was three days ago. She should be back by now. Why the silence?

Dapple burst in through the kitchen door, her toenails clacking on the linoleum before she wriggled happily over to the couch to be petted. Mavis heard the fridge open as Tommy stopped for his hit of Evian. He would head her way next, she knew. Breathing deeply, she steeled herself to be sweet. And brave.

Arthur had pleaded fatigue after lunch and excused himself to take a short nap back in his room. This seemed to annoy Dani, but Jimmy figured it wasn't because Arthur wouldn't be around when they made the call. Arthur was getting the evil eye, he surmised, because he had failed to anticipate Jimmy's all-too-foreseeable reaction to the news that Arthur was in need of rest. She was right, too. He couldn't help but launch into an innuendo-laden arching of eyebrows. Stoically doing her best to ignore him, she led the way to her room to make the call.

Once inside, Jimmy moved directly to the bed and sat down, his wide bottom sinking deep into the groaning mattress. He resisted the impulse to bounce up and down and grin at her. Better to be all business now. He peered over at the telephone on the nightstand, then looked up at her. She was across from the foot of the bed, leaning back against a long, waist-high dresser with a mirror mounted on the back.

"Well, it's your office," he said. "Is it Prout or Butters?"

She considered this. "I think Prout. Butters would probably just route you to Prout anyway. Call Prout."

"How do I get the number?"

She gave him a number. He scribbled it on the notepad next to the phone. "It's Prout's direct line," she said. "There's no secretary to go through. If he's there, he'll pick up."

He lifted the receiver and punched in the number on the base. Waiting for the connection, he winked at her, and said, "Be sure to deduct half the cost of the call from my share."

She ignored this. He cleared his throat.

"Stanley Prout," said the familiar, peremptory voice.

Jimmy straightened up and squared his shoulders. "Stan," he said. "Jim Morrissey. Long time, no hear. How you been?"

If Prout was surprised to hear from him, he didn't give it away. He took the offensive immediately.

"How did you get this number?"

Jimmy blinked. The Snow Queen hadn't thought of everything after all.

"Hey," he said blandly. "I'm not without resources, you know. You may be a big shot and all that, but your direct line isn't exactly a state secret." Dani squeezed her eyes shut in self-reproach, grasping at once what Prout had asked him. "Plus I think you'll forgive me when you hear what I have to say."

"I doubt it," Prout said dismissively. "In fact, I've been wondering if I shouldn't have a new subpoena served on your client."

Jimmy smiled. "Oh, you don't want to do that, Stan. I've got something much more to your liking. And mine, too. It's going to bring me a nice piece of change."

"Oh? Have you found something better than scamming little old ladies in nursing homes?"

Jimmy winced. So the guy had heard about the reprimand. *Thank you, Sieglinda.*

"Very droll," was all he said. "No, Stan. I've got something much better."

"Indeed?" He didn't sound convinced. "And what would that be?"

"The present whereabouts of one Thomas Crimmins. You've heard of him?"

There was a brief silence on the other end. Jimmy winked at Dani again. Her arms crossed, she had one haunch perched on the edge of the dresser.

"Is this your idea of a joke?" Prout asked, but there was less hauteur in his voice now.

"No, sir," Jimmy responded. "I found him. And I want my reward."

"*You* found him? How?"

"I did indeed. Just *how* I'm not at liberty to divulge. Confidential sources, you know. Needing protection. *You,* of all people, should appreciate that. All I can tell you is Tommy got a little careless with the Internet."

Dani stood up abruptly, her arms dropping to her sides. Her eyes seemed to crackle with shock and fury. Jimmy waved her off with his left hand, twice, and focused on Prout.

"All right," said Prout. "I'll take care of it. Where is he?"

There was an edge to the man's voice, a sliver of excitement glinting through his bureaucrat's fog of suave indifference.

"And the reward?"

"It's right there on the poster. If we apprehend him based on your information, you get the reward. Where is he?"

Jimmy swallowed some air. "In Florida. A tiny dump called Arcadia. The best little small town in Florida, according to the chamber of commerce. It's sixty, seventy miles east of Fort Myers. He and a couple of dogs and his lady friend are holed up at two-one-five North Volusia Street. Am I giving you too much detail here, Stan?"

He couldn't resist that last one.

"I've got it," said Prout, sounding preoccupied.

"Okay. You got any questions—like how to make out the check or whatever—just call my office. Taffy will know how to reach me. So long, Stan. A pleasure, as always."

He hung up. Feeling satisfied with himself, he looked up at the woman who still glowered down at him.

"What?" he almost shouted. Innocently, he hoped.

"You told him." She almost spat the words.

"No, I didn't. I didn't so much as *mention* Mavis."

"You mentioned the Internet."

"So what? Look, it's okay. I told him just enough to get him off my back on how we, I mean *I,* located the guy. That's all. And I've set it up so I won't have to answer any more questions about it. If they press, I'll tell 'em I'm acting on behalf of a client who wants his anonymity preserved. Emphasis on the 'his.' The attorney-client privilege will protect her. As well as your precious secret."

She stared at him, hard.

"Okay?" he pressed. "It's done, Dani. And it's gonna be all right."

She didn't look entirely convinced, but she was letting go, he could tell.

Everything was going to be all right.

Nothing was right in Arthur's stomach. Seated on the bed and staring at the cream-colored telephone crouched on the nightstand, he felt the sulfurous burn of acute indigestion. With a harsh back-taste of nausea, too. This was not some tardy reaction to the grease-laden barbecue of the night before. No, he knew the source of his discomfort. It was a dyspeptic blend of queasy guilt and consuming dread.

He knew that Jimmy's sudden appearance presented a neat solution to the conundrum that had perplexed him since the day he launched this venture: How could he collect the reward from the FBI while simultaneously keeping his bargain with Larry? He did not want to be explaining to Larry why the FBI just happened to be showing up in Arcadia at the same time. Or explaining to the FBI how Larry got here.

Jimmy might solve all that. If the reward was claimed in his name alone, Morrissey would be, as far as the Bureau was concerned, the one who found Tommy. If the Bureau asked him how Larry happened to show up on the scene, Jimmy wouldn't have a clue. He'd be a firewall between the feds and Arthur.

And Larry? As far as he knew, Arthur and Morrissey were strangers to one another. Morrissey's involvement in the grand jury proceedings had been kept secret, thanks to the judge. In fact, Grutman still thought *he* was representing Arthur. So Arthur could just shrug innocently and point to Jimmy as the reason the FBI was horning in on Larry's little party. The wild card nobody anticipated.

It imposed a tidy symmetry. The FBI would have Jimmy to thank, Larry would have Arthur, and neither the agency nor the Rabbit would know that Arthur was playing both ends. The result, if it worked? Larry off his back. A hundred thousand for the restaurant, his share of the reward. And one way or another, Tommy goes down—either to Larry's people or the feds. It was perfect. An ideal solution. Except for one drawback.

Arthur didn't want to make the call.

He hadn't explained that to Joanne, whom he *had* called as soon as he reached his room. As the only person who knew of Arthur's deal with Larry, she had lost no time in grasping the serendipity in Jimmy's appearance. And she was ecstatic at the news that they had found Tommy. She was still singing Arthur's praises as he eased his way off the line. Because he didn't want to make the call.

To some extent his reluctance had been there all along. He'd had no need to face it until the venture succeeded and he actually had to make the call. For one thing, he couldn't get past the distasteful business that he would become a snitch himself. It went against everything he'd learned growing up in Southie—on the playground, in the schools, the code on the streets. Knowing he had no real choice in the matter (how else could he ever get out from under Larry's meaty thumb?) helped a lot, for even paying the debt with the reward money was no guarantee that Larry would leave him alone. No, he needed a very grateful Larry. But the sour self-knowledge was still there. And it rankled.

It also scared the shit out of him. Right now he was just one of Larry's debtors. That was an unfortunate and very dangerous position to be in, even if the U.S. Attorney had never tumbled to their relationship. But if he made the call, the stakes went up. It would make him more than a snitch. He'd become a fingerman for Larry. And despite all of Larry's promises, it would signal an inevitable shift in their relations. If Larry used the information to take out Tommy, how comfortable would he be, knowing Arthur possessed information that could tie him to the killing? Arthur had no idea. Maybe Larry's gratitude for the tip would beget loyalty. But gratitude had a short half-life with wiseguys, and loyalty, though intoned like a mantra among them, corroded quickly when exposed to the caustic atmosphere of a murder investigation.

And then there was Tommy. Tommy (may his soul rot in hell) probably didn't deserve to live, but it was one thing to wish him dead all these years and another thing altogether to collude in his execution. He had no idea how that would sit on his soul when, as an old man, he looked back on his life and took stock.

There was nothing new in these ruminations. He had put them off as best he could, knowing—as he had when he first made his pitch to Larry—that he had no real choice. There was simply no other way out. Otherwise, Larry would likely keep him on as a sort of culinary retainer until he tired of him (and then what? Would he call the loan? Dump him?), and how else could he keep Joanne from suffering the consequences of his bad judgment in borrowing the money in the first place. All of which explained why, when the time came to make the call, he had believed he would swallow hard and do what he had to do.

Until Dani.

She complicated everything. She had started out as little more than the object of (yes, admit it) an adolescent fantasy—the beautiful, icily unapproachable creature from another world whose very inaccessibility fired his attraction. But that seemed a lifetime ago, now. During the time they'd spent together, nominally as partners in this curious financial venture, his infatuation had blossomed into something much richer. And when, last night, fantasy yielded to overpowering reality, he was lost. Never had he known such a sense of wholeness as in her arms. He shivered again to recall her touch, and he basked anew in the light of those open, urgent eyes that had held his own. Her look of earnest, of easy welcome, of connection. Perhaps love?

Whatever it was, he knew it would never survive his making the call. It was the big secret between them, his deal with Larry, and he did not know how she would respond if she learned of it. Oh, she wouldn't like it, he knew that. It wasn't aboveboard, concealing this wrinkle the whole time. And she wouldn't like the idea of it anyway. She'd view the deal as immoral (rightly so, he had to admit), and he could hardly blame her if she saw him—as she had when they first met at the courthouse—as just another snitch, a wanna-be sucking up to the underboss.

So it wouldn't be good. But if he made the call? And brought down the kind of carnage Larry lusted for?

He had no illusions. It would destroy everything. She'd never speak to him again. A straight shooter, she had called him. It was what she said set him off for her, made him different. The quality that overcame her doubts about him. If he made the call, he would be trading that quality away—forever, in her eyes.

And when he put it that way, the answer was clear. He couldn't do it. *Wouldn't* do it. No, he would just have to take his chances. Maybe he could buy off Larry with a piece of the reward money. Because he couldn't pick up the phone.

Until it rang, that is.

A volley of gunfire could not have scared him more, given how lost he was in his thoughts. It passed quickly, however, when he recalled that Jimmy would have news to report. He bent over and lifted the receiver.

"Hello."

"You know who this is?"

The spasm of terror was staggering. Swift and violent. He closed his eyes and clenched the phone as accumulating saliva signaled an urge to vomit. He struggled against it, waiting until the feeling subsided before responding.

"Yes," he said to Nick Tramontana. "I know."

"I'm in the pay phone outside your restaurant," Nick said. "Right on the corner. Larry's still inside finishing his lunch. Chatting with your partner. And wondering what the fuck you're doing in Florida. When you should be back here in Boston lookin' after the shop, you know what I mean?"

"I'm not sure," Arthur said, listening intensely and trying desperately to follow the man's drift.

"Well, this is a hell of time to take a vacation. With your joint barely getting by and all. Now Larry, he might buy that shit. Vacation. 'Cause let's face it: he ain't the sharpest tool in the shed. I understand that. I deal with it all the time. But that don't mean I have to buy the same shit he buys. So me, I figure maybe Artie's onto something. And maybe he gets the drizzlin' shits when it comes time to do what he's gotta do. Like, maybe it's easier to call the feds, collect that reward. You with me here, Mister There-Ain't-No-Chicken-in-Cous cous?"

"I think so, but—"

"Don't *but* me, Artie. It makes me feel like you think I don't know my business. 'Cause I do. I know what I'm doin' here. Which is why I convinced the broad to give me your number. So listen to me, Artie: You know where he is?"

There it was—and Arthur froze. He was silent for only a few seconds, but it was enough for Nick.

"Ain't that a kick in the nuts," he said, barking out a half laugh. "I gotta admit, I thought Larry was fulla shit, thinking there was a chance you could find him. So okay. Live and learn. Where is he, Artie?"

Arthur closed his eyes again and squeezed the bridge of his nose with his left thumb and forefinger.

Nick gave him no slack. "You're gonna tell me, you know. Do I gotta spell out for you what happens if you don't? Things got consequences, Artie. You never seen Larry get a real hair across. It's not a pretty sight. And it's not just *your* ass, you know. The broad—what's her name? Joanne? She's in it, too. And she don't deserve this, Artie. *Now give me the fucking address.*"

Arthur breathed deeply and did as he was told.

Tommy stood over her in his white T-shirt, khaki Dockers, and Devil Rays baseball cap. He looked down at Bernadine's head in her lap.

"Did you hear anything?" he asked.

She pressed her lips together and shook her head. Reaching out, she petted Dapple, who leaned into her hand. Dapple was eager for her attention after accompanying Tommy to the library.

He was still standing in the same spot. Puzzled, she said, "Did Dapple give you trouble on the walk or something? She's usually very obedient. And restrained."

"No," he said. "I thought maybe you'd like to do something, take your mind off the dog for a while."

She wrinkled her brow in confusion. This wasn't like him.

"You know," he explained. "We could mess around."

Oh, sex. So that's it. Her heart sank at the thought, but just before it showed she willed her facial muscles into a smile. She hoped it came off shy; for all she knew it might be a crazed grimace. It would be easy to beg off, to plead preoccupation, but not now. She needed him complacent, unsuspicious.

She gave him her hand and smiled again. He took it and, as she eased out from under Bernadine's head, he pulled her gently to her feet. He let her hand drop and stepped briskly into the bedroom.

She tried to make Bernadine comfortable on the couch, then kissed her on the top of the head. Leading Dapple into the kitchen, she filled the dog's water bowl. When she turned to retrace her steps, she stopped and cocked her head at a noise from the bedroom. No, it was not the squeak of bedsprings. It was a wheezy exhalation from the musty armchair in the corner of the bedroom. She smiled grimly. His mating call.

What the hell, she thought as she trudged back through the living room. *Thank God for the ten-minute blowjob.*

CHAPTER THIRTY-FOUR

ALL THE AMATEURS

FRIDAY

A sleep-soaked voice in St. Petersburg.

"Hullo."

"Stevie?"

"Yeah. Who—"

"Stevie, shut the fuck up."

"Whaat? Hey, it's two o'clock in the morn—?"

"I said shut the fuck up and listen. You hear me?"

"Uh?" Then a sharp intake of breath, a snort of recognition. "Is that you, B—?"

"SHUT THE FUCK UP, STEVIE! Don't use no goddamn names! Your phone is tapped."

Total silence. Thought breaks out.

"Jesus." Chastened now. "That's friggin' spooky, man. Whatcha think I should do?"

"Do? You don't do nuthin'. There's somebody on the 'muffs listening to everything you say. So you let *me* do the talkin'."

"Ohhh. I get it. They can hear *me* but they can't—"

"Right. Now listen. Listen good."

"Yo."

"You go to the airport in the morning and you meet a plane."

"Okay."

"You go straight to the—"

"Wait a minute! Wait. What airport?"

"Whatta you mean, what airport? How many airports we got in this town? You think I'm sending you to fuckin' O'Hare or something? Newark, maybe?"

"No, but there's one up in Clearwater, too, ya know."

"Stevie." Like a man with a headache. "That's for puddle-jumpers. Biplanes and shit like that. Gliders. Not for 747s coming in from Boston."

"Oh, well. Boston. Of course. You didn't *say* Boston. That narrows it down."

"To one airport?"

"Right."

"It's thinking like that, Stevie, explains why you empty candy machines for a living."

A beat.

"I do other things." Hurt in the voice.

"Well, this here is one of them 'other things.' You go to the airport tomorrow. You meet some people on the ten-seventeen flight from Boston. That's MetroJet two-six-oh-two. You writing this down, Stevie?"

"Yeah. It's just this . . . goddamn pencil. It's dull."

"Flight two-six-oh-two. You go to the gate and hold up a sign for Mr. Greco. You got that?"

"Greco. Two-six-oh-two.

"You take 'em straight to the car and you give 'em the keys. Then you walk away."

"What car?"

"The one you're gonna bring to the airport. You pick it up tonight. You make sure it's clean, no prints. Switch the plates so no cop will have it on his hot sheet."

"Okay. Snatch a car, wipe it down, change the plates. And I deliver it."

"With the ordnance in the trunk. In a briefcase."

"Ordnance?"

"That's right. Ordnance. That means *weaponry*, Stevie. Two pieces. Nine millimeter. Both clips fully loaded. You got that, Stevie?"

"Jeez. You ain't givin' me a lot of time here. Nine millimeters, I mean."

"Stevie. These people, they're heavy. They throw a lot of weight up in Boston."

"This Mr. Greco."

"I don't think it's their real name, Stevie. Listen, willya? It's important we show 'em respect. That we can be counted on to do a thing. This is too much for you, you tell me. I can get somebody else."

"No, no. It's just it's kinda short notice, is all. I'm gonna have to rearrange my schedule here. Cancel some shit I hadda do."

"You mean like get outa *bed*? Stevie, for fuck's sake. I don't call, you don't get up till one in the afternoon."

"Not always." Hurt again. "Hey, wait a minute! I just thought of something. If I give Mr. Greco the car, how do I get home?"

"You think I give a shit? Take a cab. Walk. Jesus, Stevie. Sometimes I think they shoulda left you in Jersey."

Special Agents Ryan Butters and Bryan Tevlin strode through Terminal C toward the gate for MetroJet 2602, the first flight out for Tampa-St. Pete. A casual observer might have mistaken them for brothers. Both had thick builds, charcoal suits with double-vented coattails, and identical travel bags on casters, dragged along by their retractable handles. Butters was the older—bulkier, his hair thinner—while Tevlin played the kid brother: his belly was still mostly flat, and his thick chestnut hair, piled high on his head, was as glossy as the fur on a wet otter. Though they marched in unison, there was no harmony of clicking footfalls, just the squeak of the Vibram soles of their black Rockport Sports.

"There he is," said Tevlin sourly. "The ferret."

He indicated the direction with a slight lift of the jaw. Butters spotted the gleaming bald dome of Gower Velcovitch, who was waiting in line at the check-in for their flight. Oblivious to his surroundings, Velcovitch stood rigidly erect with a garment bag slung over his shoulder and an open paperback in his right hand.

"Hey, Velcro," Tevlin said, as the two agents approached. Velcovitch looked up from his reading. Tom Clancy's *Red Storm Rising.* "Guess who was asking for you at the office yesterday?"

"Who?"

"Not a friggin' soul."

Velcovitch eyed him blandly, then shifted his gaze over to Butters.

Butters said, "I should give you both a swift kick." He looked from one to the other, shaking his head in disgust. "What a pair. Velcro and Teflon, they ought to call you. Surf and Turf. Except you'd have to swap scalps for the names to fit. Look, we got a long flight and a longer day ahead of us. So let's just keep focused on the task at hand. The sooner we bring him in, the sooner Gower can shuffle back to D.C. That should make both of you happy."

Tevlin glanced over at Velcovitch, then down at the ticket extruding from the paperback. "You already got a boarding pass," he said, his head bobbing toward the ticket. "You don't need to stand in line."

"I like to make sure."

Tevlin looked back at Butters and shrugged. *See what I mean?*

Butters said, "Be good. I gotta leave a message for Stan."

Turning on a squeaky heel, he made his way to the line of pay phones across the corridor from the gate. He walked by two that seemed designed only for long-distance before finding a conventional pay phone. He fished for pocket change as he pulled a small card from his shirt pocket. Dropping coins in the machine, he punched in the number, twice glancing down at the card for assurance.

"Mike Nolan here."

Of course. The number would be for Nolan. Jackie's pantryman. His undershirt. He should have anticipated that. The governor wouldn't have arranged to take the call himself.

Butters twisted his head around. He was satisfied he couldn't be overheard. "Mike," he said. "It's Ryan Butters."

"Ryan, boyo. You caught me at my morning rashers. Hey, you're not in the office already, are you?"

Always careful, Michael Nolan. Wants to know if the line is clean.

"No, Mike. I'm calling from a pay phone at Logan."

"So early?"

"It's the reason for my call, Mike." He paused for emphasis. "It looks like that rainy day we've all been dreading. Could start pouring real soon."

It was Nolan's turn to pause. Then he said, "How soon?"

"Could be as early as this afternoon. I tried you last night, but there was no answer."

"Yes, well, we had us a little do at Amrhein's last night. Didn't get in till after one."

"I'm sorry for the short notice."

"I'm sure it couldn't be helped. We all have to make do with what's before us. Which is what?"

Butters filled him in on what he knew.

"I'll see that it gets passed on," Nolan said when he had finished. "And Ryan?"

"Yes?"

"It's appreciated. I want you to understand that."

"I'm glad I could be of help, Mike. Pass that on, too."

Walking back to the two agents, now seated next to each other in the gate area, Butters felt tired all of a sudden. Heavy. It wasn't that he harbored any regrets. He had a family to look after, three boys at Boston College, and the trajectory of his career with the Bureau was flat at best, after all this business about Tommy. With help from Jackie Crimmins, he could become the new director of security at Gillette. So, no, he didn't regret making the call. He just felt a little older. That was all.

MetroJet 2602 began to board. He pulled his boarding pass. Seat 29D.

Larry Coniglio was headed for the same plane. He hopped along, doing his best to keep pace with Nick's long-legged stride, but it was hard on him. His legs were weary from the run up the escalator and his breath came in ragged gasps.

He could kill Peetie, he really could. Showing up late this morning, of all days. He'd wanted to crack his head against the steering wheel. They had made up a lot of the time because there was so little traffic this time of day, but it pissed him off all the same. Even when they pulled up to the terminal, it was clear they'd have to hurry to make the plane.

The plane. Jesus. How Larry hated flying! It scared the shit out of him, to tell the truth. The last time he'd flown was returning from Palermo what, six, seven years ago. He'd spent the whole time listening. For the popping of rivets. The buckling of struts. What was all that shit he learned in school about metal fatigue? No, sir. He'd tell anybody who asked: flying was for the birds. And if it was so fucking safe, how come they called them *terminals*?

The gate. Sure enough, they were starting to close the door.

"Hold it!" Larry hollered. "I'm on that plane!"

The stew (or whatever they called them now) smiled indulgently as she held out her hand to take Nick's boarding pass, then his own.

"We're a little late," Nick said.

"First-class boards anytime, sir," she said, her smile brightening. "Seats three-A and-B. Have a nice flight."

Larry stopped and glared at her with suspicion. "Wait. How come you're not going?"

She frowned at him.

"Why aren't you getting on the plane?" Larry demanded. He could feel the sweat running down his jawline, behind the ear. From the hurrying.

"I just work the gate," she explained. "I don't work the flight."

Nick said, "Come on, Larry. Relax, for crying out loud."

Larry eyed her suspiciously for a moment, then let Nick pull him into the chute.

That's what it was, too. A fucking chute. Loading people into the thing like hogs in a slaughterhouse line. He trod morosely after Nick.

Nick settled into 3A, the window seat. Larry sat down next to him and began to fasten his seat belt. When he looked over at Nick, the son of a bitch was smiling at him.

"Look at it this way, Larry. You get used to this, you'll be able to visit Sicily again."

"Sicily," he said harshly. "Sicily needs paint."

Nick barked once, a laugh.

Larry said, "What about the other end? Who'd you get to set us up?"

"Bennie Karkas," Nick answered. "He can do a thing. He says he'll have somebody meet us. Set us up."

Larry grunted. It wasn't that there weren't competent guys in Florida. He had no reason to think there weren't. He just didn't know any. The ones he'd met couldn't organize a two-car funeral. It stood to reason, too. Why would a self-respecting man go down there in the first place? Where everybody's either a senile Jew or a dumb-ass cracker, living with the snakes and alligators?

Maybe this was a dumb idea. Maybe he should just get the fuck off the plane and go back home. Eat a decent *pranza*, for a change. Screw the wife. Wife? Hell, screw the girlfriend. Let Nick and some local talent take care of Tommy. Who needed this?

But he knew he couldn't do that, not this time. For one thing, nobody in Florida would jump at the opportunity to do a clip for him anyway—not now, after all that shit about Tommy and Hink hit the streets. They didn't come right out and say it, but everybody was leery of the Boston operation, guys thinking the FBI knew more about what he was up to than he did.

Besides, he had a duty here. A responsibility to Francesco. Poor Chicco. Doing push-ups in a cell. Eating slop even Nona, his *contadina* of a grandmother, would never have touched, for Christ's sake. And Tommy put him there, all the time smiling and coiling and pretending to show respect. No. He had to do it himself. It was a matter of honor. It wouldn't hurt with the guys, either, him doing a little wet work. To show he had a belly.

The plane lurched backward as it pulled away from the flyway. Larry clutched the arms of his seat and ground his teeth.

"Take a look out there," Nick said, jerking his thumb toward the window. "It's nice out. At least we got good weather for flying."

Larry ignored the porthole, his gaze concentrated on the seat back in front of him.

"Yeah," he said, in no mood for solace. "All the amateurs will be out."

Behind them in coach Velcro read his thriller. Teflon nodded off. And Ryan Butters worried. What if Tommy didn't get the heads-up in time? What would he do then?

But he was just kidding himself. He knew what he'd do.

CHAPTER THIRTY-FIVE

THE SORROWFUL MYSTERIES

FRIDAY

Despite the air-conditioning, she felt hot, overheated, even though she was lying on top of a bed shorn, she vaguely noticed for the first time, of all coverings save the fitted bottom sheet. Her skin was flushed and moist, while every spot that counted was exquisitely hypersensitive. Skinless in a sandstorm. Which was why she stopped him, clutching his hand spasmodically as his index finger began to slide up the wet slit toward her overstimulated clitoris.

"No," she whispered, her eyes squeezed shut.

"No?" A playful voice.

"No." She opened her eyes and saw the smile in his as he brought his face up to hers. "No more hands. No more tongue. No more coming."

He bent to kiss the side of her neck, just above the collarbone.

Her voice was thick when she spoke again. "I want you inside me. Finish inside me."

He raised himself over her to comply. Teasing, he rubbed his cock in the damp, scratchy hair on her mons, as if fumbling for entry. The pressure on her clitoris made her gasp, recoil even. She reached down to guide him, breathlessly luxuriating in the silky slide until he was home. When he started to move, his face was inches from her own, smiling and staring into her eyes. *I could love this man,* she thought. She reached out with both hands to hold his ass as his stroking picked up speed. His eyes narrowed and lost focus, dimming as if the current were being drawn off for the surge. He arched his back and pulled his face away from her. She lifted her head to follow him, her tongue bathing his nipple as he started to come. And then, impossibly, she felt another orgasm of her own begin its spiraling climb, higher and higher, until she plunged over the rim and lay shivering in his arms.

After several minutes she felt him slide off to the side, but she kept her eyes shut, not wanting to break the spell just yet. She was no longer putting out the heat, however, and her bare shoulders soon felt chilled from the air-conditioning. Still lying on her back, she rolled her head toward him and opened her eyes.

He was right there, his face only inches away again, with the same half smile as he watched her. She gave him back a carbon copy.

"Hi there," he said.

"Hi there." She folded her arms across her breasts and hugged her shoulders. "I'm a little cold."

"Here." He reached over the side of the bed and lifted the duvet, tugging hard to free it from the tangle of bedclothes. He spread it over them, then snuggled up to her, his left arm around her, their noses almost touching.

He said, "That was . . ." He gave an almost imperceptible shake of the head.

"Me, too."

They grinned at one another.

"What do we do now?" he asked.

"Have our Continental breakfast?" It was like a reflex. Keep it light.

"I feel like I just had it." His expression took on intensity. A corrugation of the brow. "No, I meant afterward."

She widened her eyes. "Go back to Boston?"

"No, not yet. And that's not what I meant anyway. I mean, what about us. What do we do now?"

She gave it up. Serious now, she said, "I'm not sure, Arthur. It's happening so fast."

"Fast? It feels like I've been waiting *years* to be with you. Since the first day I showed up for the subpoena."

"No," she said. "I mean . . . *this.* This alteration in our relationship. Arthur, we've only spent two nights together. It's going to take a little time."

"Two *great* nights." His smile was back. A lightness, for which she was grateful. But something else, too. Sadness? Trepidation, maybe?

"Yes, great nights."

"You blow me away," he went on. "I don't know what I expected, but *this* . . ."

"You expected the Snow Queen, is that it?" She said it with a smile, but with a bit of an edge, too.

"No, no," he said, heading for cover.

"You know, Arthur, just because somebody thinks you should play by the rules doesn't mean they don't play hard. I play hard at my job—my former job, I should say. No doubt you noticed. But I played by the rules. It's the same with sex. If I decide it's okay to have sex with somebody . . . well, I play hard."

"And the rules?"

"Well, if it's okay to have sex, then there aren't really any rules when you do it. Almost."

"I noticed," he said, with an exaggerated shiver. She pretended to push him away from her.

"Anyway, I need to get used to this," she said. "I've got no complaints, no regrets. But it's a little scary, Arthur."

"What? What's scary?" He looked scared himself.

"My feelings. For you." There. It was out there. "How strong they are. It's absolutely petrifying."

"I know," he said. There was something dead earnest in the way he looked at her now. "I've been feeling that way for . . . weeks."

She was silent for a moment, taking this in. Then she said, "In that case you've had a head start. More time to get used to it. So please, a little patience. A little space, okay?"

"Okay." But he tugged the duvet tighter around them.

She frowned. There was something he had just said. On another subject. Oh, yes.

"What did you mean about not going back to Boston yet? I thought you had a restaurant to run."

"Joanne can make do for another day or two. I want to be here when this thing plays out."

"Why? They sure don't need us to be here. Jimmy's gone home—or should be on his way by now." She glanced at the clock radio. "Why can't you?"

He broke eye contact, staring off toward the wall over her shoulder. "If I can," he said, "I want to watch it go down. I have to." There was a sudden grimness to his tone.

She sat up now. The duvet fell away from her breasts. "Watch it?"

"Yeah. I got a lot at stake here. A lot of money. My financial independence. The survival of my business. They told Jimmy they'd take him today. I want to be here when it happens. Is that so strange?"

She eyed him carefully. His eyes, she noticed, kept dipping toward her breasts.

"No," she confessed. "I guess it isn't so strange. I used to go with the Strike Force on a raid sometimes. I even went along the first night Special Ops planted the mikes in Francesco's club. I watched from the back door of a van for an hour and a half."

"See, I'm not so odd," he said. "I just like to watch."

"Breasts, too, I see." She smiled in spite of herself.

"Mmnn. I guess so."

"Well, at least you're not hung up on big ones."

"Good thing, too, huh?" He grinned at her.

"Bastard!" she said. She grabbed a pillow and ground it into his face to smother his laughter.

"What a fuckin' moron!"

"You still goin' on about that guy?" Nick said, his eyes never leaving the road. "What was his name? Stevie Something."

From the passenger seat Larry lifted both hands in mute wonder. "Who cares what his goddamn name is? A *lift*, he asks! The asshole wants us to give him a lift to St. Pete. I tell you, Nick: we're dealin' with a moron here. What's he think, we're tourists? We got nuthin' better to do than drive his ass around town?"

Nick made his sleepy smile now. "Maybe Orlando, Larry. You coulda took him to Epcot. Buy a T-shirt for Cristina or something."

"Nick. Listen to me. This ain't no laughing matter, this. This ain't like up north here. We're betting our ass on a moron. The setup guy—and he's a fuckin' moron. You understand American?"

Nick eased the Buick into the left lane of I-75, accelerating smoothly to overtake a semi. Tampa was far behind them now, signs for Palmetto and Bradenton popping up beside the road.

"Well," said Nick, as he wheeled right again in front of the truck. "The moron did all right with the car. Runs good. Even changed the plates."

"He says."

"And the guns look okay. Loaded. Seem to be in good shape."

"*Seems,* Nick. Seems. But we're dealing with a moron here. You gotta trust your instincts."

Nick lifted his thumbs off the steering wheel as a kind of shrug. "So what you wanna do? Give it up? Go home?"

"No, no. I just don't like it, is all. That guy. The hair in the egg, that's what my *nona* used to say. Guys that can fuck up anything. We just gotta be careful, is all. You trust your instincts, like I say."

"Or use your fuckin' head."

"Whaa?" Larry looked over at Nick. Was he giving him shit?

But Nick wasn't looking. He was getting off the Interstate, pulling into a rest area. It was nothing more than a long, curving road leading to a parking lot cut into a scrub wood, with outdoor toilets and slumbering truckers.

"You gotta take a whiz?" Larry asked.

"No. A *quiz.*" He smiled. "For the artillery."

He parked the Buick as far from the other vehicles as possible. Leaving the engine running, he popped the trunk and got out.

"Come on, Larry. Let's check 'em out."

Larry got it. He climbed out and followed Nick, who had taken the attaché case out of the trunk. They walked off into the scrub a ways, where Nick opened the case and handed one of the guns to Larry. Big automatics, he knew that much.

"Watch," Nick said. He fired the other weapon, once, at a runty pine. A little puff of dust from the trunk told of a direct hit. Then he turned back to Larry.

Larry's ears were ringing from the report. He looked down at the gun in his hand. Turned it over to examine it. Felt its heft. Felt the coolness of it, the satisfying fit of the trigger against his finger.

The gun went off, so unexpectedly he dropped it.

He looked up at Nick, whose eyes were narrow slits now.

"Jesus!" Larry gasped. "What happened?"

Nick recovered his sleepy smile. He said, "You got a hair trigger there, Larry. Make sure you keep the safety on."

Nick looked down between his legs and lifted his right shoe. The bullet had made a half-moon notch in the inner edge of the sole.

"On the right here," Arthur said. "Take a look when we drive by."

"Where?" She peered out at the palmettos and oaks on the soft rise to the right of Volusia, directly across from number 215.

"Up there, at the top of the rise. There's enough cover in the trees and brush there to hide while we watch what happens across the road. We can bring a blanket."

They were past Tommy's place, with the big Lincoln still in the driveway, nose in.

"You're crazy," she said. "What if somebody spots us?"

"We're lovers, remember. The weather's gorgeous. We'll take a picnic. What could be more natural?"

Arthur took a left at the first intersection, starting the loop back to the hotel.

"And just how long do you think we can hang out as 'lovers' and remain inconspicuous? All day?"

"No. Just this morning. It'll happen early. They won't waste any time going after him."

"You don't know that, Arthur. The FBI does nothing spontaneously. They plan. For every contingency. They schedule *bathroom* breaks."

"They'll come early. I know it."

But Arthur's mind wasn't really on the FBI. He didn't know if they'd come on time, and he hoped to God they came before Larry's people. If only he'd had the presence of mind to give Nick some story to delay their arrival—how Tommy'd gone away for a few days, something like that. Then Larry's crew would just show up too late, and how could Arthur be blamed for that?

But he'd frozen like a stunned ox. And if they beat the feds to Tommy's door . . . ?

Jesus, it was some sight. There she was, bawling at the kitchen table with that goddamn computer up and running in front of her. Pictures of skinny racing dogs loping across the screen. The cordless phone lying in her hand right there on her lap, emitting that irritating noise that's supposed to make you hang it up. The dog, the well one, trying to nose in under the phone, whimpering to see her crying like that.

His finger marking his place in the book he wouldn't get a chance to finish, Tommy stepped through the doorway and into the kitchen.

"What's going on?" he asked.

She twisted around toward him. She must have been rubbing her eyes, because the smudged mascara had formed little blurry rings around her eyes. Like a raccoon. She sobbed.

"Who called?" he asked. "I thought I heard the phone."

"The vet called," she said.

Or that's what he thought she said, anyway; it was hard to tell over all that blubbering. So he just said, "Yeah?"

She had a pleading expression as she looked up at him. "She says it's bone cancer. The vet. There's nothing to do for her. A couple weeks—that's all she's got."

She broke down again. Oh, great. He had to go through this crap all over again. These fucking dogs.

"Well, look," he said. "If it's—"

And the pager went off.

The pager. Just like that. And only one guy in the world knew the number.

She stared at the pager. Which was understandable, since this was the first time it had gone off, with him wearing it every day for more than a year. He had explained that it was his lifeline, an early-warning system if there was serious trouble. He plucked it off his belt, found the off button, and shut it down.

He looked down at the phone in her hand. Tempting to use it right here, just make the call on the cordless. No. Stick to the plan. Stay disciplined. There was a pay phone just outside the library, he remembered.

"Uh, look," he said to her. "This thing is important. Like a fire alarm going off, remember? I gotta make a call."

He started for the door. She said, "You look like you've seen a ghost."

"I don't believe in ghosts," he said without looking back. But when he got to the door he stopped, his head cocked to one side for a second. Thinking. Then he turned around and strode quickly past her, on through the living room and into the bedroom. He opened the little drawer in the nightstand on his side and reached in. The first one that came to hand was the .22. *No. This isn't a whack. Think self-defense.* He reached in again and pulled out the .44 Special, nestled in its little holster. The belly-gun. With a ballistic cavity to make a god-awful mess of a man at close range. He clipped the holster onto the back of his belt. Fished through his closet for something to cover it. Rejected a nylon shell. Too hot. He slipped on a lightweight linen sport jacket, then checked himself in the mirror. Good enough.

Mavis had her head in her hands when he passed through the kitchen again.

"Hang in there, kid," he said. "I'll be back in a few minutes."

The Lincoln roared to life and he was off. No time for the leisurely walk to the library today.

The agent who met their plane, a black-haired hard guy from Brooklyn named Sikora, promised there would be three vans of SWAT teams waiting for them at the sheriff's office in Arcadia, and they were. Sikora seemed to know Velcro, so Butters and Tevlin ignored them both. Everybody hung out around the vans in the big garage, fitting up and waiting. Butters did his best to pretend he was still running the operation, but it was becoming increasingly obvious that the teams were responding to Sikora, not him. As a consequence, even Velcro had a bigger piece of the command than either of the Bostonians. Butters didn't like feeling the loss of control.

They already had the house under surveillance by the time Butters and Tevlin reached Arcadia. The subject, as Sikora kept calling him, had left the house by car a few minutes ago. From there he had driven at a stately pace to the county library, where he placed a call from an outdoor pay phone. The subject was, even as they spoke, still talking on the phone.

This being Friday noon hour, there were too many people coming in and out of the library to take him there. Unless he appeared to be taking flight, they would just have to keep him under surveillance until he went to ground someplace workable—back to 215 Volusia, they were hoping. No, they were not able to monitor the call, either on the line or with a directional mike. And yes, they'd made arrangements to track the number he had called.

So Tommy wasn't on the move yet. Had Jackie decided to let him swing in the wind? Butters did not relish the prospect of an unhappy Tommy Crimmins behind bars. He was a crafty son of a bitch, always had been, and Butters didn't doubt for a minute that the guy had evidence (tapes, something) to lay bare all the compromises he and

Prout had had to make along the way, just to keep him as a productive asset. Tips on action contemplated by the local gendarmes, on imminent raids by the DEA. A phone call eleven years ago to suggest he take a short vacation while certain legal unpleasantries unfolded in his absence. No, it wouldn't do to have an angry Tommy in custody. Alive. With scores to settle.

They didn't have a Kevlar vest big enough for Butters—younger men, all these SWAT guys—but he paid it no mind. He'd started doing heavy work like this when these fuzzy-cheeked crackers were still hoping to get a sweaty hand inside a brassiere. So he just watched Tevlin strap his on. Tevlin also accepted a shotgun, to go with the Glocks they'd been issued once they got in the car at the airport. Butters was pleased to observe, however, that Tevlin had declined the helmet. Like Butters, he would go bareheaded.

Butters took a seat on a folding chair and waited. He felt dead calm. Ready.

"Filibuster." There was a lot of noise in the background, and the man who answered was almost shouting into the phone. Tommy could picture the Beacon Hill bar where his brother sometimes lunched with cronies. It made sense that this was the number he gave him: untraceable to Jackie, because whoever answered the phone during the busy lunch hour would not remember the call. All he'd have to do if his need to speak to Tommy was dire (and they had agreed it would have to be dire indeed), was to cancel any other lunch plans and book his usual room at the Filibuster.

"This is a call for the governor," Tommy said. "He'll want to take it."

"He's in a private room. Who should I tell him it is?"

Tommy said, "You just tell him it's the call he's expecting. He'll take it."

The man's only response was to put him on hold. He expected cybersilence. What he got was "Raindrops Keep Falling on My Head," arranged for strings. He gritted his teeth and waited.

"Hello," said the Great American Altar Boy.

"Jackie."

A pause. "Well," Jackie said. "And would it be the lamster himself? You're a long way from the neighborhood, Thomas. Shouldn't you be playing cards at the Morgue Club in Gallivan's Funeral Home?"

Tommy closed his eyes and tasted the sourness in his mouth. Always with the words, Jackie, laying them down in neat courses between the two of them like bricks for an emotional spite fence.

"You paged me, Jackie."

"So I did. As we agreed. Sometimes I wonder why, though. As Porky Pig once said, you buttered your bread, now lie in it." He sighed audibly. "But. I'm afraid they're onto you, my brother. Wherever you are, they know where. I got a tip from a very highly placed source this morning. In the Strike Force. They're flying down to get you."

"The Strike Force?" Why would *they* come after him?

"That office has been rudderless since your . . . *participation* was disclosed. All spokes and no hub. I hear Stanley Prout is whipping his liver like a slavered horse these days. And some of them don't love you anymore, Thomas."

"*That* cocksucker."

"Curse is the work of the drinking class, Thomas. If your muse is unbiddable, it's best to remain silent."

"Can't you fucking speak English for a change?"

"I try, Thomas, I try. It's one of the sorrowful mysteries why the two of us had to share a family, but there you are. You know, even growing up it got tiresome when people asked *How's Tommy?* and my knee-jerk response was always a wary *Why?*"

Fucking Jackie. Always turning everything around on him. With his words and his politics and that medieval crap with the Church and all. Tommy's resentment was buried deep, a piece of dark marble best worked in seclusion—but heavy, too, something he had to lug around with him.

"How'd they find me?"

"Beats me. Something about leaving tracks on the Internet. You should master Gutenberg, Thomas, before trying to join Bill Gates and the barbarians."

"I don't use the fucking Internet."

"More's the pity. But that's what I hear."

Tommy was puzzled, but only for a moment. Then all his distilled rage found sudden vent. "That stupid bitch!" he hissed.

"Remember, Thom—"

He drove the receiver into the cradle like a man driving a nail.

CHAPTER THIRTY-SIX

COPSUCKER

FRIDAY AFTERNOON

Whatever coolness had been there in the morning was burned off by now, and it was hot even under the palmettos. Hot, but bearable. Arthur had found a fairly level spot near the top of the rise, shielded from view by some kind of tropical vegetation he could never have named. Dani had spread the blanket, folded in half lengthwise, and the two of them lay on their stomachs watching the house.

Arthur checked his watch. One-seventeen. So much for a morning raid. Dani had been right about the FBI. It had been almost twenty minutes since Tommy had driven away in the Lincoln, alone. Would they show up while he was gone? And give themselves away? Or wait in the house for his return?

Dani poked his shoulder. He twisted his head to the right and gave her a questioning glance.

"Lighten up, okay?" She said, looking amused. "It's not going to happen any faster just because you keep glaring at the place."

He smiled. "You're right," he admitted. "I was just thinking. About Tommy."

"What about him?"

He turned back to face number 215. The orange stripes on its awning, hanging motionless across its frame, weren't really orange at all. They were red, he realized, bleached out by a merciless sun to something resembling orange.

"In Sicily they say you can see Cain in a man's shadow."

"Cain."

"Yeah. You know, like the mark of Cain. That the evil in all of us dogs us like our shadows."

She paused, thinking. "Okay. But what's that got to do with Tommy?"

"Well, I was thinking: if you're as purely evil as he is, what does that leave for the shadow?"

"Abel?"

He smiled at this. "Or maybe he doesn't have a shadow. Don't they say the Devil has no shadow?"

"I thought that was Dracula. And anyway, *we're* his shadow. For the last few weeks, anyway. Shadowed him right here. So the FBI can put the mark on him."

"I guess that's true. Superficially, anyway."

"Superficially? You call *this* deep?"

He chuckled. "The stuff about Cain in the shadow? No, it's not deep. It's Tommy who's deep. Way, way down, deep inside of him. That's where he keeps the vileness."

He could feel her staring at him, wondering. She said, "Cain again? Actually, I don't think so. Psychopaths like Tommy and Larry? My experience with these guys is there's no depth there at all. There's no there there, as somebody once said. Automatons. Just a set of meshing gears, working and turning. And all on the surface. Superficial, to use your word."

He took this in, quiet for a moment, aware that her eyes were still studying him.

"Why," she asked, "do I get the sense that this is personal? This business with Tommy, I mean. It is, isn't it? Personal?"

He watched the dappled sunlight play on her face, the green eyes boring into his.

"If you grow up in the Boston neighborhoods, everything is personal. You know how they say that in New York it's *what* you know and in D.C. it's *who* you know? Well, in Boston it's who you *hate.* A net of interlocking grudges, tribal and personal. Old hates. Scores to settle."

She twisted her mouth, an almost scornful expression taking shape. "Is this that Irish thing?"

He shook his head. "I told you. I'm not Irish."

She was at a loss for a second. "That's right. You did. It never registered. What are you, then?"

"Polish. Lots of us in South Boston."

"Patch is *Polish*?"

"Pejewski. My father compressed it. He would never admit it, but I think he was afraid people would get the impression he was Jewish. Like I said, everybody hates somebody."

"Pejewski . . ." He could tell she was struggling to place the name.

"My uncle. Myron. You remember? The butcher who didn't want to take Tommy's stolen beef?"

She stared at him.

"Myron was good to me. When my old man was not—too much vodka and cheap wine. Myron was always there. Taught me how to grade meat. How to cut it. It was thanks to him, really, that I got into the food business in the first place."

"It's not the money," she said quietly, seeing it for the first time. "It's about payback."

He nodded. "There's that. And the money, too. So you see, I had to watch. For Myron. For *all* those guys he killed, one way or another. Somebody has to be their witness."

"Their witness," she repeated doubtfully.

"Why not? *You* made me a witness, with your subpoena. Well, that's what I'm gonna be. A witness. For the dead."

"Guy thinks he farts fresh air," Larry said as he climbed back into the Buick. "What's this?"

He bent down and grabbed his right foot by the instep and turned the sole of his shoe upward. There was a putty-gray disk in the center of the sole.

"Shit. Fucking hillbillies with their gum." He looked about him helplessly, in search of something to use to scrape it off. With an irritated sigh, he pulled himself out of the car again, then started rubbing his sole along the ridge of metal above the rocker panel.

"We should get moving," Nick said from the driver's side. "Did you find out where it is?"

"Yeah. I think so." He lifted his foot and leaned over his back to inspect the sole. "It don't help they gotta print these maps in the goddamn acrylic alphabet or something."

He was back in the car now.

"And?"

"Guy says the street we want should be the next left. Up there, where that blue Lincoln's pulling across."

Nick put the car in gear.

Dani clutched Arthur's wrist when she saw the Lincoln come to a halt just past the driveway, then back into it. When the car came to a stop, they watched the trunk lid rise behind it. The man got out of the car.

"It's him!" she whispered. He knew.

Still wearing the beige sport coat despite the heat, Tommy Crimmins looked up and down the street once, twice. Apparently satisfied, he turned and moved swiftly toward the rear of the car.

He walked past the car and went directly into the house by the kitchen door. A man in a hurry.

They were rolling now. Butters was on his knees, between but just behind the lead van's two front seats, leaning forward to see out the windshield. Velcro drove. Sikora rode shotgun. There were four guys in SWAT gear behind him. Butters heard the guy through the crackle on the radio.

"Green Giant, this is Birdseye. Subject has returned to the dwelling. Car's in the driveway. Backed in, this time. He's gone inside."

Sikora grabbed the mike. "Okay," he barked. "Del Monte, what is your position?"

Frozen vegetables?

"Desoto and East Cypress."

"Go up to Maple, then approach going south on Volusia. About three minutes now. Then we—"

"Hold it! Hold everything!" It was Birdseye. "This car just pulled up and stopped, almost directly across the street from the place. A gray Buick. I see two guys in it."

"What the hell . . . ?" said Sikora, the mike in his hand on his lap. Then he raised it to his mouth and pressed the talk button. "Everybody hang back a second till we can get a handle on the situation. What's happening, Birdseye."

"Nothing yet, Green Giant."

Fucking vegetables, Butters thought. *I'm dealing with a bunch of niblets.*

Larry rolled down the window and looked out at the house. His heart was pounding so fast and so loud he was amazed Nick couldn't hear it. When he clenched his hands, they felt cold and clammy, despite the heat streaming in the window.

A lesser man would have realized he was scared, but Larry didn't deal in such things. He could only hear the roaring of blood in his ears. And if he was scared, he knew he couldn't show it around Nick.

"How you wanna work it?" Nick asked. Larry looked over at him in wonder. The guy's voice just as goddamn calm and slow as it always was. No sign whatsoever of the turbulence inside of Larry.

So this was wet work.

"I'll tell you how we're gonna work it," Larry said as he popped the glove box. "I get out and walk to the front door." He reached inside. "You follow me, as backup." He took out the big automatic, flicking the trigger safety on and off. "I ring the doorbell. He comes to the door, I give him two in the face. Make sure he's finished off, then we get the fuck outa here."

"Only two?" Nick said.

"Two shots." He nodded knowingly.

From the house came the sound of two shots. Three seconds apart. Muffled, from indoors.

Larry almost peed in his pants.

"No!" Dani gasped, starting to rise before Arthur pulled her back down. Because she understood it all at once, in a shiver of intuition. "Oh, no. No. He didn't!"

"What's the matter with you?" Arthur whispered urgently.

"Can't you see? He *knows.* He's backed in to load up quickly so he can run. Somebody tipped him. And he knows it was because of her. Because of Mavis."

"Mavis?"

"Jimmy told Prout. About the Internet. He didn't think it gave them anything, but it was enough for Tommy."

She looked at him through the blur of her tears now. "Oh, Arthur. He killed her. Because of us, he killed her."

Arthur just stared at her. Whether in horror or simple incomprehension, she couldn't tell. Then something drew his attention back to the house.

"Shots!" shouted Birdseye. "I hear shots! And there he is! The subject just exited the dwelling."

"Okay," said Sikora into the mike. "Go! Everybody, go, go!"

Butters eased the safety off on the Glock. He slipped the fingers of his other hand into the well in the console, the hole where you put a cup of coffee so it wouldn't spill, and held on tight as the van lurched forward.

He was coming out the door! With a bag, headed for the open trunk of the Lincoln.

Larry hustled out of the car, leaving the door open. He moved quickly toward the driveway, staying low to keep the Lincoln's trunk lid between him and Tommy. The only sound he heard was the snap of gum that still clung to his shoe. When he reached the car, he took the driver's-side route around it, in case the guy headed that way. He was level with the back door when Tommy lowered the trunk lid.

Trembling, Larry lifted the big revolver, heavier than ever now, and put it right in the guy's face.

"Hey, copsucker," he said harshly, relishing the look of total surprise on the guy's face. It was speckled red, like the guy had the chicken pox or something. Then Larry figured out it was dotted with blood. He vaguely heard the squealing of tires behind him, but he was too focused to process tangential information. He pulled the trigger.

And nothing. No boom. No click. Nothing.

He tried again. Same thing.

Fuck you, Stevie. You moron. And you, too, Bennie Karkas.

It was as if he were underwater, watching it all unfold in silence and slow motion, Tommy reaching inside his jacket and pulling the gun from behind his back. He brought it up and pointed it right at Larry.

The hair in the egg, he thought. Then he thought nothing at all.

Three vans had pulled up, screeching, and Arthur watched a small army come rushing out of more doors than he could count.

He heard Tommy fire the gun once and saw Larry's head explode, a pink haze materializing briefly above his shoulders. Then there was gunfire everywhere, a din so cacophonous it swallowed everything, drowning all the senses for a moment. He was aware only of Dani, clinging to him with all her might, her face burrowed into his shoulder.

It was quick, though. In a matter of seconds the sound had cleared, except for the ringing in his ears. A reek of cordite reached them. He pulled himself up to his knees to look. Dani did the same.

Larry was now a disheveled heap beside the Lincoln. Nick was on his side between the Lincoln and the street, both knees pulled up against his stomach, his long frame shriveled like a salted grub. And Tommy lay flat on his back on the asphalt driveway, head toward the house, his arms outstretched like a crucified Jesus. Black-clad soldiers in helmets wandered about the yard, weapons before them, poking and prodding the dead with muzzles and toes.

"Hattie!" Dani cried out—shouted, really, though there wasn't much volume to it. She scrambled to her feet and began to run toward the street.

"Dani, don't!" he called, leaping up to follow her.

When she crossed the street, she paused before Nick's body, obviously recognizing him. She turned back to look at Arthur now. Right through him.

"Larry?" There was accusation in her voice, and both her question and her indictment were complete with that single word.

All he could do was nod. A confession.

Her face registered nothing, told him nothing. Fury, maybe. She just turned and ran again, toward Ryan Butters. "Hey!" Butters said as she burst past him. He, too, turned to watch her as she shoved in the kitchen door and disappeared inside. Butters turned back then, to Arthur, and stared at him in astonishment.

"I'm with Jimmy on this," Arthur explained.

Butters took a beat, then jerked his head back in the direction of the house. "And her?"

"She's with me," he said. He hoped.

"And Larry," Butters said, glancing at the crumpled body, "looks like he's on his own."

Arthur followed his gaze. On the dead man's shoe he could make out what looked like a wad of gum.

The smell of the cordite was even stronger inside the kitchen, but it wasn't what made her pull up short. Dani halted when she saw the bloody footprints on the yellow linoleum. Some were clean, distinct prints; others were streaks smeared in haste. For a minute she thought she was going to be sick, but it passed. Sucking the acrid air into her lungs, she moved slowly toward the darkened living room, stepping carefully to avoid the footprints.

Girding herself, she entered the gloom of the living room itself and forced herself to look. There was an open laptop on the coffee table. A small, deep red puddle had formed in front of the backless couch. The wall above it was spattered with a fine spray of blood and tissue.

Shaking uncontrollably now, Dani tiptoed farther into the room, painstakingly picking her way on a floor that was slick with slaughter.

CHAPTER THIRTY-SEVEN

GUR

WEDNESDAY, FIVE DAYS LATER

All the way through Connecticut the skies were leaden and heavy. Somewhere east of New Haven the early-morning clouds, worn out from carrying all that water, dumped their load all at once. Visibility on the interstate dwindled to almost nothing, and the traffic slowed to a tense, spasmodic crawl. She, too, found herself gripping the armrest and peering over the front seat to stare at the sheets of running water that mocked the puny efforts of the windshield wipers and blurred the brake lights of the cars ahead of them.

Then, as they crossed into Rhode Island, the rain stopped almost as suddenly as it had started. Clouds rapidly disintegrated into scattered wisps trapped in all that superseding blue. New England. She felt her spirits lift for the first time in a week.

As if reading her mind, the woman in the front seat turned around to smile at her. "Now *that's* an improvement, don't you think?"

Mavis returned the smile, feeling Dapple's nose burrow into a warm nook between her left hip and the seat back. She reached out to massage Dapple's pelt at the back of her neck, where the sleeping dog's raised chin made the hide gather in folds. She felt a tiny tingle of pleasure, so welcome now. *The privilege of touching living fur.* Jacques Cousteau said that on television once.

"You know," the woman said, "I think that's the first time I've seen you smile."

Mavis couldn't argue with her. Her name was Sylvia. In her early fifties, she wore a mottled gray sweatshirt that protested sneakers manufactured in Asian sweatshops—with the Nike swoosh and the words "Just Don't Do It." Her husband, the driver, was called Gerry. They were good people, warm and supportive, as were the six or seven others before them. Oh, there was that spacey woman in Maryland, the one with dirty hair and an odor of cardamom, who kept "picking up negative auras" from the cabs of passing eighteen-wheelers. For the most part, however, she had felt nothing but love and intelligent concern from those who had taken turns transporting her north. Like fresh horses for a stagecoach, she thought. Links in the human chain of love that made up the GUR.

Yes, it had been horrible—hell, even—leaving Bernadine behind when she got word that the Greyhound Underground Railroad would send someone to pick her up. She knew she couldn't take Bernadine, who wasn't able to stand up, let alone walk. She'd have had to carry the poor thing, which she couldn't do, physically. And every nerve cell in her body told her she had to hurry, to lunge at the offer like a Mae West.

Because she had seen Tommy's face when that pager went off. Seen a ghost, she had said. Worse. The man looked rattled. She had *never* seen him that way before. Not when he picked her up after learning of the indictment. Not when he watched the news clip about the big reward. Not even when they saw his face on *America's Most Wanted.* But this time he was shaken. He had told her the pager, the one that never once went off before, would only go off if there was very, very bad news.

Like they were coming for him.

For her, too, she had quickly realized. Distraught as she was by the vet's call about Bernadine, she knew in a single flash that she had to get out immediately. Otherwise, she'd be arrested with Tommy. Or at best (or was it worst?), she'd be back on the road with the baby killer.

No. Not this time. She'd had the courage once to strike out on her own, when she left Aroostook County and headed for Boston. She could do it again—this time without help from the likes of Ernie Riley and Tommy Crimmins. No, she would take the step.

He hadn't driven off to answer the page before she was logged on to *Houndbytes* and pressing with new urgency her plea for help from the GUR. Help me get away. Save us. Save Dapple.

She had hauled the laptop into the living room so she could hold Bernadine while she waited for a response, something, to pop up on the bulletin board. She'd scribbled a note to Tommy, telling him only that she couldn't live on the run anymore. Begging him, too, to call the lady at the racetrack shelter and ask her to pick up Bernadine and care for her.

When she got the message—that Glennis, driving an apple green Beetle, would swing by in five minutes to pick her up—she had pecked out a frantic response. *Don't come to the house!* He could be back any second. She and Dapple would slip out the back door, cut through the neighbor's yard, and meet Glennis on the next street over. The busy one that ran parallel to Volusia. Desoto, that was it.

And she had. A heart-wrenching farewell hug and kiss for Bernadine, then scooting out the back. Crying the whole way. Bringing nothing but a change of underwear and seventy-four dollars. And Tommy's special shaving kit. When she reached Desoto, she scanned the street for several anxious minutes before she spotted the VW approaching from the south. Dapple leapt in the backseat and they were off.

All the way to Orlando. Where they were passed on to two young men in a van in the parking lot beside a Winn Dixie supermarket. They drove her all the way to Charleston. And so on, always bearing north, like a runaway slave. No one sought to pry beneath the surface of her tale of the physically abusive boyfriend who had threatened her and Dapple. They just bore her northward. Put her up in their homes. Cooked for her. Pressed clothing on her for the trip, especially after they had covered enough distance for December to mean something again.

She was leaving a Denny's near Durham when she learned what had happened to Tommy—and Bernadine. It was right there, on the front page of *USA Today*. The old photograph of him in the navy watch cap stared out at her from the coinbox, the blue one that had always struck her as a replica of a television set.

That he had killed Bernadine did not add to the grief she was already experiencing. It set the episode apart from those months of horrible uncertainty after the abandonment of Cookie and Erol. If anything, Bernadine's sudden death was oddly merciful. He had put down a sick dog. Not that she deluded herself into believing *he* had seen it that way. No, she was sure the shooting was a rageful response to the discovery that she had left. He probably wished it was her.

Tommy. Dead. She turned it over in her mind. Trying it on. To see what power it had for her now. Not much. It was funny, really. Once she saw him for the monster he was, saw that he was no different from Grandpa Tremblay, from the Creep—worse, even—there was nothing left of him. Nothing inside her. He was just another sick dog. And they put *him* down, too.

Mavis fell asleep shortly after the rain stopped. An untroubled, dreamless sleep. When she awoke, she felt rested for the first time since the visit to the vet with Bernadine. They were crossing the Sagamore Bridge, she noticed with a start. Passing over the old canal, laid out beneath them like a sheet of molten lead. Once off the bridge, they would be on Cape Cod.

She was transported to earlier trips to the Cape, in her early thirties, when she and Ernie were newly married. Dunes and hot sun. The tang of low tide and salt in the air. Crisp colors to knock your eyes out at suppertime along the harbor in Provincetown. Dreamsicle sunsets. Saffron moons leaching into Cape Cod Bay off Corn Hill.

Another coincidence: Uncle Army had been living in P'town all those years. They had probably walked past his bed-and-breakfast at one time or another. And she'd never even known he was there. A coincidence freighted with possibility, signifying the spiritual connection between all events. Promising a new beginning.

Could it happen? Was there a way the lawyer could help her get Uncle Army's money, money that was rightfully hers?

It was the only hope going, and she clung to it.

Excitement mounted as the car sped along Route 6. Signs for Barnstable. She dug in her purse for the address from the lawyer's ad: 210 Main Street. P.O. Box 447. She still had the phone number, too.

They got off Route 6 at the Hyannis-Barnstable exit, then headed north past a Burger King with a gigantic parking lot. They rumbled into downtown Barnstable. Main Street, as its name implied, was easy to spot. They turned right. Mavis began scanning the buildings for 210.

They had gone past it, the numbers declining now, when she realized that the store had to be 210. Mail Boxes Etc. She asked Gerry to pull over, and when he was able, he backed into a parking spot right in front. Mavis stared at the storefront in confusion.

"You sure you got the right address?" Sylvia asked.

Mavis just nodded. There was no mistake. Unless the *Presque Isle Gazette* had misprinted the ad itself.

"Let me ask," she said, opening her door and stepping out. "Stay," she said to Dapple. She shut the door and squared around to face the store. It was cold here, shockingly cold after months in the South. She hurried to the door and entered.

Inside, she looked around her. There was a counter directly across from the doorway. Post office boxes studded the walls on both sides of her. She peered at a small desk stand next to a display rack of mailing and wrapping materials. Her eyes sweeping along the numbers on the wall boxes, she walked slowly toward the counterman.

"Can I help you?" he said.

"Um . . . I'm looking for . . ." She spotted box 447, but there was no name on the face of it. She spun her head slowly back toward the counterman. He eyed her with mild curiosity.

"I'm, ah, looking for a Mr. Mulcahey. James Mulcahey. He's an attorney. I was given this address."

"There's no Mulcahey here. And as you can see, this isn't a law office. This is a mail drop. Anybody can rent a box."

She frowned. This made no sense. "Does he rent one of these? I mean, I even know the number. It's four-forty-seven."

The man shook his head. "I'm not allowed to give out the names of our customers, I'm sorry."

She twisted her head around to look at 447 again. The glass panel in the door revealed an empty box. She still didn't get it.

She heard the door open behind her. Sylvia, anxious to be getting back to Stamford. Or a customer, maybe.

"Ms. Riley?" said a man's voice behind her.

She froze. Had they tracked her here somehow? She tried to pull herself together. Turning around, she saw a chubby man looking at her. Smiling.

"Are you talking to me?" she asked, pretending to look around for the person he must think he was addressing.

"Yes," he said.

"Well, my name's not—"

"Please," he said, taking her arm and gently pulling her aside, away from the counterman. "It's all right. I'm Mulcahey."

She stared at him, hope fluttering back to life.

"I've been watching for you," he said. "From the coffee shop across the street. Since yesterday morning, in fact."

She continued to look, more confused than ever.

He opened the door for her. "Why don't we get your dog and your things. Send your friends on their way. Then we can walk up the block and maybe have a drink at that little pub there. Then I will explain everything. Okay?"

She looked from him to the opened door, then back at him. She nodded.

"Good," he said.

The bar didn't even squawk about bringing the dog in. Dapple sat on her haunches while she and Mulcahey faced one another across a booth at the back. A waitress came. Mavis ordered a glass of white wine. Mulcahey asked for a vodka martini. She asked if he wanted it with a twist.

"If I wanted a lemonade," he said, "I'd have ordered one." Then he turned his attention to Mavis.

"First off," Mulcahey said, "there is no James Mulcahey, and there's no money coming from Uncle Armand. I'm sorry. My real name is Morrissey. Call me Jimmy. Like Mulcahey, I'm a lawyer. I invented him and the inheritance to get you to contact me. So I could find you."

She was stung. He had hunted her down? The fear came galloping back. Apparently, he sensed this, for he smiled, and said, "I'm here to help. Dani sent me—Miriam, to you."

"Miriam!"

"Yes. Your friend on *Houndbytes.* After she learned that you'd run away from Tommy, she got back on the Web and followed your tracks through that underground-railroad thing. The messages just stay there on the bulletin board, for anybody to read, she said. People posting answers to queries and such. In one of them, someone mentioned that you were coming here. To Barnstable. Since Miriam knew about my little . . . charade, as Attorney Mulcahey, she figured that had to be the reason you were headed here. And she called me."

Mavis gave her head a quick little shake, as if to clear it. "But how do you know Miriam?"

"Ah," he said, as the waitress brought the drinks, "*that* is a very long story. Which I will recount, I promise, on the drive to Boston." He raised his glass, a toast. "Dominus Nabisco." He took a healthy swig.

Boston. She didn't say anything this time. She just downed half her glass of wine.

"Miriam, alas, was too preoccupied to join me. She's trying to figure out what to do about this new boyfriend of hers. She's so furious with him she's not even *speaking* to the poor guy right now. Call me a hopeless romantic, but I think it'll work out. Miriam's not her real name, by the way, and she's a lawyer, too. But that's not the issue of immediate concern to you. The first thing on your plate is the FBI."

Mavis put her arms around her shoulders, hugging herself to keep from shaking.

"Now you could walk out of here. Try to run someplace. Hole up for a while. Get some nothing job making nickels and dimes under the table so you won't attract attention. Doing—what? Hawking Bebe Rebozo memorabilia? Something like that."

"Who?"

"It doesn't matter. Trust me, you don't wanna go back on the lam. Put a lot of yesterday between that thought and tomorrow. Because things have changed, Mavis. Now that your boyfriend has . . . suffered an industrial accident? Well, I gotta figure the official interest in you has taken a bit of a nosedive."

"You think they're not looking for me anymore?"

"Oh, maybe, but not very hard. More to the point, they're probably open to a deal. Think about it. It just takes a bit of a reframe. You're no criminal. You just loved the guy. Plus, I hear there's all this stuff on that doggie bulletin board about what an abusive asshole he was. You couldn't have gotten away from him if you wanted to. Wait. Check that: you *did* get away from him—and because you *had* to. Had to be saved by an organization of dog lovers—what do you call it?"

"The GUR."

"Right. The GUR. Living in terror the whole time. And so on, ad mausoleum. Now. If you were represented by the right guy—say some smash-mouth lawyer like me . . ." He batted his eyelids like a coquette. "Well, I figure the odds are pretty good you could make a deal. For short time, at worst. Maybe even straight probation."

She eyed him warily, still confused. "I don't know what you think, but I have no money. None at all."

He smiled. "That's all right. I'm about to come into some myself. Which will make me and a lot of my clients very happy. So this one'll be on me."

The man was full of surprises. Then she remembered. Digging into her shoulder bag, she pulled out Tommy's brown shaving kit. "I do have this," she said. "His insurance, he called it. Tapes of meetings with FBI people. He said they would make heads roll."

He reached out. After a brief hesitation, she handed it over. He shook it lightly, held it up to his ear. He grinned at her.

"Were you serious, though?" she asked. "About what you said? Do you really think you could make a deal?"

Jimmy Morrissey beamed at her, smile lines radiating out from bright blue eyes.

"Mavis, honey, there's always a deal."

DATE			